A
GLIMMER
OF
HOPE

ALSO BY STEVE McHUGH

The Hellequin Chronicles

Crimes Against Magic

With Silent Screams

Born of Hatred

Prison of Hope

Lies Ripped Open

Promise of Wrath

Scorched Shadows

Infamous Reign

A GLIMMER OF HOPE

STEVE McHUGH

47NORTH

Published by 47North, Seattle

www.apub.com

Amazon, the Amazon logo, and 47North are trademarks of Amazon.com, Inc., or its affiliates.

ISBN-13: 9781503951808 (hardcover)
ISBN-10: 1503951804 (hardcover)
ISBN-13: 9781477817964 (paperback)
ISBN-10: 1477817964 (paperback)

Cover design by @blacksheep-uk.com

Cover illustration by Larry Rostant

Printed in the United States of America

To the Fleet Performance team.
Never have I had the pleasure of knowing such a hive
of scum and villainy.

1

Wisconsin, USA. One Week Ago.

Elias Wells had to admit to being genuinely impressed with the escaped experiment that sprinted through the snowy forest in search of her freedom. She had fled the prison she'd been in, along with two others, an hour earlier. They'd not only made it to the edge of the forest—a rare act that deserved respect—but the last of them, Liz Barnsley, managed to outpace the monsters that chased her.

Elias didn't bother running. He didn't see the point. Not only because he considered it a waste of his energy, but also because the snow beneath his leather-booted feet had begun to turn to slush. He didn't want to slip on an unseen spot of ice and make himself look like an idiot. Elias jogged at an easy pace, making sure to keep the creatures he worked with in his view, but allowing them the freedom to do their jobs. Besides, it wasn't like Liz had a lot of choices when it came to an escape route.

Liz had escaped a half hour ago, and upon hearing the news Elias had been genuinely shocked. The fact that, during the years of the prison being active, she was the only one of four escapees to have lived long enough to reach the forest surprised him even more. He'd always taken her as the sort of person for whom the idea of running came a distant second to the idea of sitting. He guessed that adrenaline and the need to be free drove people to perform better than they'd ever be able to otherwise. He made a mental note of it; it was something to try on the rest of the subjects. Maybe they'd get better results.

A scream from up ahead signified that Liz wasn't as far away as she'd probably like to be. Elias didn't need to concern himself with anyone hearing it who wasn't meant to. Civilians were not an issue in the middle of nowhere. The only things likely to hear the screams and pleas for help would be the animals who lived in the forest, and he doubted that Liz was able to call the animals to her aid like Sleeping Beauty.

As he got closer to the noise of fighting, he heard the laughter of the creatures that served in the prison, and the cursing from Liz. Elias began to wonder if there was a way to take her back without damaging her. He shook his head as he pushed aside a branch, letting it fly back to its position after getting past it.

Liz stood in a clearing, blood seeping down her left arm where an arrow had struck it. A second arrow protruded from just above her left ankle. She couldn't put weight on it.

"Hello, Liz," Elias said, his tone conversational and light. His English accent was still evident, even after all these years away. "Feel like coming back to the compound with me?"

"Go to hell," she snapped.

Elias glanced over at the three creatures that had accompanied him on the hunt. They were all baying for blood, but would do nothing until he commanded it. "Go deal with the other corpses," he told them.

They did as they were ordered without comment, and were soon lost from view in the darkness of the forest.

"I really would rather you live," Elias said. "But if you're going to fight me, you might as well get it started now."

A spine, three inches in length, flew toward Elias, who easily avoided it. The next four were even faster as they left Liz's palms, and Elias had to catch one mid-flight to stop it in time.

"Nicely done," he commended. "Your bone mass must regenerate at an extraordinary speed." He turned the bone spines over in his hands.

"I was taught by the best," Liz said.

"Sarcasm, my dear? We've been trying to teach you to accept your new abilities."

"Abilities I never wanted! I just want to go home."

"To where, that park bench we found you on? We've given you shelter, food, and warmth. We haven't beaten you, or tortured you. I think personally that we've been quite pleasant."

"You forced this onto me. You murder those who can't cope."

"Well, sometimes things don't go according to plan, but you have exceeded my expectations." He wagged his finger at her and smiled. "No one has ever made it this far. But what were you going to do next?"

Liz looked behind her at the cliff.

"You were going to jump? That's a two-hundred-foot fall into water. I'm pretty sure that even if the water was deep enough, you'd still die."

"I'd rather die than be one of your pawns."

"Fine, I'll tell you what. You try to kill me and manage it, you can enjoy your brief life as a cliff diver. You don't kill me? You'll be dead. Either way, you win."

Liz fired a half dozen spines at Elias, who moved smoothly as he dodged them, sliding under the last one and drawing out a nine-inch stiletto dagger, then plunging it up and into Liz's stomach. He twisted it and pulled the knife out, pushing Liz onto the ground. He watched her writhe for a few moments as soft cries escaped her lips. He felt nothing except relief that the job was completed. Her pain would last longer than he liked. A quick kill was important. Professional. Kills should only last a long time if you needed something from the person, and he needed Liz to suffer a little—she had escaped after all. He'd end it soon, and then she'd be at peace.

Elias held the stiletto up to the light of the moon. A stunning piece of craftsmanship; a black handle, with silver pommel and matching cross guard. The blade itself had a percentage of silver in it, and had been polished to a high sheen. As he turned the dagger over in his grasp, a drop of blood fell from the tip onto the snow below.

He looked at Liz; her already pale face appeared ashen. She didn't have long left. The silver in the blade had made sure of it. Even so, he needed to ensure that the fight to survive was extinguished. "I realize if we take you back, you'll either escape again, or kill someone. So you really do get your wish."

"You should not play with your prey," a male said from behind Elias.

Elias turned to the newcomer and dropped to one knee, bowing his head. "My Lord Nergal."

Nergal was a head taller than Elias's own five feet nine inches, with broader shoulders and dark skin. A smooth bald head and deep brown eyes that looked almost black gave him the appearance of someone who was not to be crossed. Several thousand years earlier, Nergal had been considered a god by the Mesopotamian people, and it was easy to see why—just being near him made people nervous. To Elias's knowledge, there were few people who possessed Nergal's level of power; it practically came off him in waves.

"Get up. It's cold and wet and you've already gotten yourself filthy fighting this one." Nergal walked over to Liz and bent down, slapping her across the face to get her attention. "She's almost done. End it. We need to talk."

Elias wanted to tell him that was exactly what he'd intended to do, but there was no point in angering the man. Instead, he nodded, and used his foot to push Liz over onto her front. He placed a knee on her back and pressed the tip of the dagger up against her throat. He pushed it in without comment, removed it, and stepped off her to avoid the arterial spray.

He removed the black trilby from his head and dropped it into Liz's blood, wiping the knife on his expensive suit trousers before replacing it in the sheath at his back.

"Are you quite done?" his lord asked.

"I did not know you were coming," Elias said, turning around. "We had some issues with escapees. First in a few years. She was good too. Shame about how it ended up. Not to change the subject, but I'll have to recharge soon."

"Well, that will have to wait. We found her, Elias. I need you to go to England. To Southampton. I'll have all of the details e-mailed to you."

Elias didn't want to question his lord, but he'd been here before. "Are we sure she's there?" He made sure to say *we* too.

Nergal smiled. "We've been searching for so long, Elias. Yes, I'm *sure* she's there."

Elias picked up his hat from the ground; it had absorbed all of the blood that had once been inside Liz. Despite the amount of liquid it had taken, it was completely dry. To all outward appearances, the hat remained black and nothing had changed. In the few minutes since he'd killed her, Liz's corpse had turned into a mummified husk.

Elias placed the hat on his head and a slight trickle of blood slid down his pale skin. He caught it with a finger, leaving a smear, and licked the digit clean.

"Picked it up too early," Elias said, by way of explanation. "You want me to go now?"

"Yes, Elias. Take whoever you need. Just find the woman, and bring her back here. Alive. And do it quickly."

"Not a problem, my lord."

Nergal turned and walked away as the three creatures arrived once more, looking hungrily at Liz's corpse.

"Make it quick, leave no trace." Elias knew he didn't have to say that to them—they were always quick and clean—but sometimes he liked to tell them anyway. Just in case they ever forgot who was in charge.

He walked back to the compound, his mind ablaze with possibilities. He had a lot to think on, and a lot to achieve in a short time. Going back to his ancestral home would have to wait until the job was done. Find a human girl and bring her back to Nergal. Easy.

2

Southampton, England.

Layla Cassidy landed back first on the padded mat in the gym. She looked up at her friend, Chloe Range, who stood above her with a grin fixed to her face. "Ouch," Layla said.

"Don't be a baby. Just get up so I can do it again," Chloe said with a barely concealed chuckle.

Layla got back to her feet and removed the hairband that had been holding her shoulder-length, dark blue hair in a ponytail. She retied it and got back into a fighting stance.

"You know, attackers don't wait for you to do your hair," Chloe pointed out.

Layla mouthed Chloe's words in a mocking fashion.

"You're not as funny as you think you are," Chloe responded, a stern look on her face, but Layla could see the twinkle of laughter in her friend's eyes.

Layla winked, causing Chloe to break her expression and smile. An instant later, the smile vanished, and she lunged forward, lurching for Layla, who avoided her grasp and managed to get hold of Chloe's t-shirt under her bicep. She snapped forward, using her free hand to grab Chloe's lapel, and planting her knee on Chloe's hip, she launched herself up, wrapping her legs around Chloe's neck and putting her in a flying arm lock.

Layla dragged Chloe to the floor in an instant, locking the arm in place. The entire move took a fraction of a second, and although it had taken a lot of practice to master effectively, the look of surprise in Chloe's eyes was worth the work.

"That's it, people. It was a good practice." The instructor, a South African woman by the name of Mosa, clapped her hands twice, signaling the end of the session. She was a giant of a woman, and looked like she could crush people between her hands if she so wished. Layla liked going to her classes because of the endless patience and good spirits she exuded. She hoped that she'd learned more than her fair share of patience and control while under her tutelage.

"No way," Layla shouted. "Chloe needs to tap."

"I will not surrender," Chloe yelled.

Mosa walked over to them, a smile on her face. "Layla, are you willing to break your friend's arm?"

For a split second Layla's mind screamed yes. It would be easy to win this round, just apply a little more pressure, and . . . she forced herself to quickly release the hold. "No," she said, more to herself than anyone else. She pushed herself away from Chloe, afraid that the thoughts might come back. She never wanted to think about hurting Chloe again.

Chloe did a small victory dance.

"You didn't win," Layla pointed out, hiding her concern at the violent thoughts that had yet again entered her mind. She'd hoped that time would stop them, would allow her to control her emotions better. Despite all these years of training, those thoughts still occasionally leaked out, wanting her to lose that control she'd worked so hard to maintain. It was her father's fault. Most awful things in her life could be traced to him in one way or another.

"Didn't lose either," Chloe shot back.

Mosa laughed. It was a deep, rich sound. "Go home, both of you. What you do outside this building is not my concern."

Once her mind was calm again, Layla called after Mosa, "I had her."

Mosa gave her the thumbs up.

Layla turned back to her friend. "I had you, Chloe."

"Yep. And if we had been in class, I'd have tapped. But I wasn't going to give in that close to the end, and then it was just a matter of principle."

"I could have hurt you." *I wanted to win. I wanted to beat you.* All joking had vanished, and Layla's expression had turned to one of concern.

"No, you couldn't. You're not that person. You have technique, speed, and a lot of power, but you're not the person who would break an arm to win a point."

Sometimes I'm not so sure, Layla thought as she picked up her gym bag. "And you are?"

"I'm like a ninja."

"Tell me, do ninjas commonly have blonde pixie hair and colorful tattoos? Just asking."

Chloe raised her arms as if inspecting them for the first time. They were both covered in a variety of styles and pop-culture characters. "Probably. I'd like to think it's a progressive job."

Layla stretched out in the corner of the gym while she waited for her friend to pack her bag. Both five foot four, neither Chloe nor Layla could be considered the tallest people in Mosa's class. However, they were probably the most enthusiastic, and Chloe was certainly one of the most formidable. Mosa had sparred with Chloe once, and had been visibly surprised at the strength and speed she possessed. Layla was athletic, and in good shape, but she wasn't sure, in a straight fight between herself and Chloe, who would win. It would be a close thing.

"Are we going out tonight?" Chloe asked after taking a swig of water.

"I have no idea, are we?"

Chloe pushed open the gym door, letting in the cold March evening air. "Oh, come on. You've got a few months until you're twenty-one, and only a few more until you're officially finished with university. You haven't been out with me for a month at least, and frankly I miss my wing-woman. Besides, I got these light brown lowlights put in my hair, and they look awesome, and now everyone else must see the awesome."

Layla wondered just how much anyone would be able to see of anyone's hair color in a dark nightclub, but she let it slide. "Wing-woman?"

"I'm not entirely sure if there's a version of wing-man for women, so I took a shot."

Layla chuckled. She'd known Chloe for the last two and a half years, and Chloe had quickly gone from the girl who served her coffee and went to the same self-defense classes to her closest friend.

Layla glanced at her watch. "It's after nine."

"I think by the time we get home, get ready to go out, and leave, it'll be ten at the latest. I don't think that's too late for you, is it? Or do you need to drink your last cup of warm milk by then?"

Layla laughed, which was unfortunate timing as she'd just taken a mouthful of water, spraying it all over the concrete paving slabs as they walked back toward Chloe's car.

"Fine. A few drinks," Layla conceded.

"I knew you'd come around."

"Shall we just go straight to yours? It means me stealing some of your clothes."

"I'll manage. I've got some electric pink hot pants?"

Layla stopped. "I'm not wearing anything where the color is described as electric. And not hot pants. I'd rather wear a burlap sack."

Chloe paused as they reached her car, a black BMW M4 coupe. "I don't think I have any burlap sacks. I could probably find one for you for next time."

Layla opened the passenger door and got in, pulling on the seatbelt as her friend got into the driver's seat. "You're a witty woman," Layla said when Chloe started the engine.

"Did you just wait ten seconds to come up with that as a comeback? Because that's really bad, Layla. We need to work on that."

The car's engine roared through the early evening, turning more than one head as they drove past.

"So, it's almost that time of year," Chloe said.

Layla smiled. "Is that why you want me to come out? I'm fine."

"You say that, but I really do think you hide yourself away in books a little too often. You did it at this time last year, and the year before, so I'm sensing a pattern. I worry about you."

"Thank you." Layla meant it too. "But I'm okay. My mom dying four years ago was an awful thing, one in a long line of awful things that have happened. I miss my mom every single day, but I've learned to cope with her not being here."

Layla's mom and her new husband had been driving on a country lane when their car had skidded off the road and hit a tree. Some people had told Layla at the time that the fact they'd both died instantly on impact was a good thing. Layla wasn't really sure how any kind of dying was a good thing, and distanced herself from everyone who'd tried to pay her their respects. She'd wanted time to herself to grieve, not to have to deal with how everyone else was feeling. In hindsight, she felt sorry for being so selfish, as if the grief was hers and hers alone, but at the time she'd been sixteen, and the constant pity everyone had shown her had been overwhelming.

"You sure?" Chloe didn't sound as convinced as Layla had.

"I really am. I just like to spend time alone because I can throw myself into my work and not sit and feel sorry for myself."

"So, going out drinking would achieve that too, yes?"

Layla smiled. "Yes, I guess so."

"Excellent. I have a bottle of vodka at home with our names on it."

As it turned out, Chloe wasn't exaggerating. Once they'd both returned to her two-bedroom apartment overlooking the Itchen Village marina—only a few minutes' walk from the coffee shop Chloe owned—Chloe had gone into her freezer and produced a bottle of Russian vodka. She'd proceeded to write her and Layla's names on it in big letters with a black Sharpie pen, before passing it, and two shot glasses, to Layla.

Layla poured out two shots, passing one to Chloe, and both women raised them in a toast. "Let's have some fun," Chloe said, and knocked back the vodka in one go.

"Let's try to remember how to get home," Layla countered, before drinking her own shot, as Chloe laughed.

Chloe had chosen her outfit of black jeans and white top that showed off her midriff almost the second she'd walked into her room. By the time Chloe had finished in the shower, Layla had picked out a pair of dark blue jeans and a black off-the-shoulder top. Both wore black, strappy high heels and, just like Chloe had said, both of them were ready and out of the door by ten o'clock.

Layla was surprised to discover that even though Chloe hadn't called for a taxi, one was waiting for them outside of Chloe's apartment.

"You planned this all along?" Layla asked as they both climbed into the back of the car.

"I was planning on going out anyway," Chloe pointed out. "You give me too much credit."

The taxi took them through the city of Southampton to the Green Rooms nightclub, a sizeable venue that on Friday nights played a mixture of seventies and eighties classic rock. Layla had been with Chloe several times in the past—mostly because it played music that was even slightly tolerable.

Layla paid the taxi driver and the pair entered the club to the sounds of Van Halen's "Jump," which was exactly what the dozens of people on the large dance floor in front of them were doing. They weaved around the enthusiastic crowd and walked over to the bar, where Chloe ordered two bottles of beer and two shots of vodka.

Chloe passed one of the vodka shots to Layla. "To fun and frivolity."

"To not having a hangover tomorrow."

They downed the shots in unison and picked up their beer. "What is this stuff?" Layla asked after having a swig and reading the bottle. "Lurcher. This beer is called Lurcher. Why would someone name their beer after a dog?"

Chloe shrugged. "All I know is, it doesn't taste like watered-down cat urine."

Layla paused, the top of the bottle touching her open lips. "Thanks for that image."

Chloe raised her bottle.

"Hey, you two, good to see you here."

Layla turned around and smiled as Harry Gao, a smile on his face, stood beside them. Layla hugged her friend tightly; she hadn't seen him for a few weeks. Harry was just as prone to throwing himself into his work as Layla. "You were told to meet me here, weren't you?" she whispered.

Harry looked slightly confused. "Chloe said she'd already arranged for you to come out tonight." Knowledge dawned on him. "You had no idea."

"Not even slightly, but I'm glad I came. How are you?"

Harry did a sort of half shrug, half nod that Layla knew meant he could be better. "Turns out having a degree in marine biology doesn't really do a lot for the job market. I know, shocking, isn't it? So, since I last saw you two weeks ago, I've decided to train to become a teacher."

"You mean, at school level?"

He looked aghast. "Oh, heavens no. I do not want to deal with a bunch of hormone-crazed teenagers. I'm going to get my PhD and become a lecturer. Essentially, I'm going to stay in education for as long as possible. It's like a security blanket."

Layla laughed. "Sounds like a plan to me."

"How about you?"

"I'm good, thanks. University is almost done, and I might actually get a good grade from it. After I've finished . . . I have no idea. I'm doing a degree in metallurgy because I like it; it's interesting and fun. But I honestly don't know what I want to actually do with my life once the degree is over. Aren't we meant to know by now?"

"I think some people never know."

"How is that helpful?"

"Oh, you want helpful? I'm sorry, you'll need to go speak to someone else about that."

Layla smiled as Chloe joined them. "Glad to see you found us, Harry."

"Well, you said be here at this time. I might not be good at understanding signals from women, but I do understand directions."

"You set me up," Layla said, leaning toward Chloe and whispering in her ear.

"Yep," Chloe said with a grin. "We all need to let our hair down once in a while. And you needed a break. You mad?"

Layla held Chloe's stare for a few seconds, before smiling. "No, it's fine. You're right, I needed this."

The three of them spent the next few hours drinking, dancing, and enjoying themselves, forgetting whatever stresses of daily life might be getting to them. The merriment ended just after 1 a.m., when Harry caught a glimpse of someone walking into the club and cursed under his breath just loud enough for Chloe to hear.

"What's wrong?" Chloe asked.

Before Harry could answer, Layla appeared next to them. "How are you not drunker?" she asked Chloe. "Drunker, is that a word?"

"Metabolism," Chloe told her. "Mine is just better than yours."

"But you've had more than me, more than Harry too. And you're just . . ." She waved her hands around Chloe. "There."

"That's exceptionally eloquent," Chloe replied with a smile, before turning to Harry. "What's wrong, Harry?"

"A certain ex-boyfriend has just arrived."

Chloe followed Harry's gaze as it settled on the man in question.

"Oh, bollocks," Layla said from beside the pair, having seen who her friends were looking at.

"We can go," Chloe assured her.

"No. I don't want to go. I'm having fun." She took a deep breath. "Maybe we could go for a walk, get sobered up a bit."

Chloe agreed and went to get their jackets, while Harry followed Layla outside.

"Layla," her ex-boyfriend, Blake Davis, called after her.

Layla sighed when she realized that Blake was walking toward her with two of his idiot friends in tow. "Oh, this will be fun," she muttered to herself.

She turned around. "Piss off, Blake."

Blake's expression darkened. "That how you want to talk to me after nearly a year together?"

"We haven't been together in three months," Layla said, the fresh air making her wish she could be anywhere else but where she currently was. "And you remember why we broke up, right? Because you were shagging Bianca? For six months of our relationship, you were cheating on me. You're lucky I didn't set fire to your car. Now go away."

Blake took a step forward instead.

Layla's eyes narrowed in anger. "You remember what happened when I tried to leave you, Blake? You want to try again? I think things will end differently this time."

15

Anger flashed in Blake's eyes.

"Hey, don't," Harry said, trying to calm things down.

"You need to keep your nose out of it," Blake said.

"Yeah, go back to your own country, you little nothing," one of the two men standing with Blake said. His name was Robert Mitchell, although everyone knew him as Rob. Layla thought of him as being one of those people who took a few classes in fighting and immediately thought themselves to be the next UFC champ. He was about five and a half feet tall, and while muscular, Layla wondered how much of that muscle was natural and how much came from a needle. He was also a massive misogynistic dick, and as she'd just discovered, a racist. Exactly the kind of person she wanted to avoid.

It had taken Layla a year to find out who Blake Davis really was, and three months to forget he existed. She really didn't want to have to deal with him or his "me man, you listen" crap.

Layla didn't know who the third man was; she'd never seen him before. But judging from his muscular physique, he was someone who liked to spend time in the gym.

"My own country?" Harry asked, quizzically. "Well, let's see. My father is American, my mother English, and I was born here, in Southampton, so England *is* my own country. Or do you mean because I'm half Chinese? Because if that's what you meant, then you meant for me to go back to my father's parents' country—my grandparents—who left China to move to America. So, whose country am I meant to go back to, you racist little troglodyte?"

Rob stared at Harry for several seconds, before shoving him back a step. "Blake said this is none of your business. Now, if you stay here, I'll make it your business, and none of your little kung fu is going to help you."

"My word, you really are an unpleasant little dick, aren't you?" Chloe said as she walked toward the group.

Rob looked Chloe up and down. "I could show that to you if you wish."

Chloe's expression was one of disgust. "Not for all the surgical gloves and antibiotics in the world." She turned to her friend. "You okay, Layla?"

"I'm good," Layla told her. "Blake. Go. Now. I don't want to talk to you, or be near you, I just want you to leave."

"I thought we could be friends," he said.

"And I thought you could keep your penis out of other women, but apparently we're both wrong. Good-bye."

She turned to walk away, and Rob leaned over, grabbing her arm. "He said . . ."

He never got to finish that sentence, as Layla spun toward him, smashing her elbow into his nose, which exploded with blood. Rob staggered back and she punched him in the gut, doubling him over, then she drove her knee into his face, doing even more damage. Rob collapsed to the ground, his face streaming blood, as several bystanders began to scream, or cheer, depending on which side they'd chosen to support.

"Don't you ever touch me again," Layla said.

Chloe removed a tissue from her bag and dropped it on Rob, as Blake and his friend stared in shock. "You need to clean yourself up, you've got a little something where your nose used to be."

That was seemingly too much for the new friend, who swung a punch at Chloe. She moved quicker than Layla had ever seen, driving her fist into his stomach and immediately catching him in the temple with a punch that knocked the big man out cold.

"Is this really the kind of person you call a friend?" Blake screamed at Layla. "What the hell happened to you? You used to be sweet and . . ."

"Meek," Layla finished for him. "You remember what happened when we split up and I went to leave the apartment? You remember?"

"I said sorry."

"You barred the way to the door, and when I tried to get past, you raised your hand to me."

Layla had never seen Blake angrier than she had at that exact moment, and the same expression was on his face now.

"Raise your hand to me again, Blake," Layla said. "Go on, see what happens."

Blake took a step toward her.

"I think we should go," Harry said.

"It's okay. Blake's a coward, he'd never do anything if he thought I'd fight back."

"This . . . dyke has you all confused," Blake snapped. "She's changed you. Probably trying to change everything about you."

"*Moi?*" Chloe said. "That's it? Calling me a dyke, that's the best you've got?"

Blake stared at Chloe, and Layla shoved him hard in the chest, forcing him to step back and regaining his attention. "Rob got what he deserved because he placed a hand on me. The next time someone raises their hand to me, I'm going to break their arm. You ever come near me again, Blake, and you won't find that meek woman who froze in fear. You'll find the person who'll kick the shit out of you and not think twice about it."

Layla wanted to hurt him, wanted to make him feel how he'd made her feel. She knew she could. She'd played down how good at fighting she was around him because she hadn't wanted to show him up while he trained. But that was done now.

Layla fought the feeling of anger as the three friends walked away into the night.

"You've been holding back," Harry said to Layla when they were far enough away from the club. "I didn't know you were such a badass."

"What about me?" Chloe asked.

"I've always known you were a badass."

Chloe laughed. "You've certainly never shown that level of ruthlessness at class," she said to Layla.

"Lost my temper. I don't like being grabbed."

"What was that about Blake raising his hand to you?" Chloe asked, her voice hard.

"I'll explain later. Let's just enjoy the rest of the night."

"Did that man really tell you not to use your kung fu on him?" Chloe asked Harry after several minutes of silence.

Harry nodded. "Racists never change."

"Don't you know several forms of martial arts?" Layla asked.

"And none of them are kung fu."

The three of them laughed for the remainder of the walk to the closest taxis, where they split up to go back to their respective homes. But as Layla sat alone in the back of the taxi, she felt euphoric, buzzing from the excitement of her fight. She'd wanted to hurt him more, and Blake. She'd hoped Blake would raise his hand to her again. Last time she froze because she was terrified she'd hurt him if she allowed herself to. She looked at the blood on the knuckles of one hand; she hadn't felt like this for a long time. She'd almost forgotten how good it felt to fight. Properly fight, not just spar.

Layla pushed all thoughts of the fight aside and went back to the other problem at hand. She'd seen Chloe move faster than she'd ever seen anyone move before. She shook her head; maybe she'd imagined it. By the time she got home, she was convinced it was the alcohol that had made her see the impossible.

3

Layla woke up without a hangover. Whether it was because of the amount of water she'd drunk when she got home, her age, or just the fact she'd sobered up after the whole Blake incident, she didn't know; she just knew she didn't feel like she'd been hit by a truck. And that was all that mattered.

She sighed when Blake's name popped into her head. When they'd first met, he'd been this six-foot-three blond man who looked like a Viking and treated her with respect. He'd liked to go hiking and surfing, and he'd been fun. Being with him had been fun. And for a while, she'd thought that maybe she'd found someone who made her so happy that she no longer felt the urge to fight. No need for the little voice in her head to make its presence known. She got out more, she met new people, and she grew closer to Chloe and Harry.

And that was the problem: as soon as anyone else was involved, Blake didn't like it. He didn't like her having male friends and would ask her who she was going to meet on a constant basis. He was allowed to have friends, he was allowed to go out and not have to explain where he was going, or who would be there, or when he would get back. But Layla wasn't allowed such freedoms; he'd go nuts if she was ten minutes late in returning a text. When he'd asked her to move in after four months of dating and she'd said it was too early, he'd gone out and started seeing someone else behind her back.

It had taken her a while to realize he was a controlling, manipulative jackass, and by then she'd also realized he'd been cheating on her for several months of their ten-month relationship. She'd told him she never wanted to see him again, and Blake had spent the next three weeks bombarding her with phone calls and e-mails, telling her he loved her and that if she'd only give him another chance, he'd change. But she didn't believe it. Seeing him again had just proved how much she'd ignored, or rationalized, when she should have been running to the hills.

Blake had turned out to be exactly like all those people who had lied to her over the years. She didn't need liars in her life; she hated the idea of someone professing to care for her but lying to her face. It was something she'd never been able to get over since her father had managed to ruin her life in such spectacular fashion.

She climbed out of bed and took a shower, washing away the memories of past lovers, and the smell of cigarettes. She didn't smoke herself, but it didn't seem to matter. It also didn't seem to make any difference that smoking was banned inside the clubs themselves. If you went to a club, you always ended up smelling of the stuff just because of the number of people smoking outside, and there were few things she liked less. It reminded her of her father. And those were not memories she wished to pick at.

She'd just got dressed in an old pair of faded blue jeans and a cream t-shirt with a picture of a black spirit wearing a white mask on it, when the doorbell went. She ran from her bedroom at one end of her apartment to the front door, opening it to a grinning Chloe.

"How are you feeling?" Chloe asked, passing Layla a bottle of energy drink and some paracetamol. "Just in case."

"I'm covered, but actually I feel good." Layla stepped aside to let Chloe in.

"Nice t-shirt. What is it?"

"No Face from *Spirited Away*. It's an anime."

Chloe's face lit up. "Ah, I didn't know you were into your anime. You should speak to a friend of mine, Kase. She's obsessed with them all."

"I just like the Ghibli films. They're pretty much the perfect films to watch on any occasion."

"Kase once got me to watch every episode of *One Piece*. And there were about five hundred of them at the time. I was pretty much done with needing to watch anime again after that."

"You didn't like it?"

"Quite enjoyed it. It was just a bit of an overload. Maybe I should get some Ghibli and start again."

"The Blu-Rays are in that cupboard under the TV. I need to eat something. You hungry?"

"Coffee, please."

"That's not food."

Chloe smiled. "Yet it's all I need."

Layla walked away to the kitchen and put the kettle on. Her apartment was a nice two-bedroom abode with decent-sized rooms, although the second bedroom was only big enough for a spare bed or, as she used it for, all the junk that she still hadn't sorted since moving in three weeks earlier. She'd taken the apartment because of the massive front room, which was great for entertaining. The beautiful, high ceilings were due to the fact that the whole building had once been a large hotel that had been divided into six smaller accommodations. Even though she lived on the ground floor, she'd never once heard any of her neighbors while they were in their own apartments. Layla's apartment was close enough to the main city center without actually being *in* it.

Normally a student wouldn't be able to afford such luxury, but Layla had inherited a considerable sum of money after her mother's death. Money she was only allowed to take an allowance from on a monthly basis until she turned twenty-one, when the whole thing would be unlocked. She had no idea what she was going to do with it once it was available, but it was nice having enough money to be able to afford such a pleasant place to live.

"Are you working tonight?" Chloe asked when Layla brought the coffee. Layla had grabbed a cereal bar and made some tea for herself.

"Yes, unfortunately." One of the conditions of her inheritance was that she had to have at least part-time employment. Her mother had been big on ensuring that Layla always knew the value of money. She only worked three evenings a week, and it wasn't exactly the most exciting or stimulating job, but it was still a job, and, frankly, most of the time it was nice to get out and do something different a few times a week.

"I guess I'll have to find other entertainment then."

Layla smirked. "Maybe you could punch out some more people? Thanks for that, by the way. Not for the beating him senseless, just the having my back."

Chloe raised her coffee. "Always. What about you? You were pretty badass yourself."

Layla paused, ready to tell Chloe about how she really felt and how much she'd always had the voice in her head, telling her to commit acts of violence, but something stopped her. She wasn't sure that Chloe would understand. Or how anyone would understand. Would she think she was a psycho? When Layla had been twelve years old, she'd stopped a bully—a fifteen-year-old girl—from beating up one of her friends. Layla had beaten the bully so badly—going so far as to break her wrist—that the name *psycho* had stuck with her for the rest of her time in school. Right up until the day she'd left.

"My father taught me how to fight from the day I could walk," Layla explained. "I don't like to show people what I'm capable of, so I drop it down a notch or two when sparring."

"Well, you don't need to do that with me," Chloe said with a warm smile.

"You heard from Harry?" Layla asked before Chloe could ask about her father.

"He's chilling out. He mentioned something about having a date."

"He never said anything."

"Yeah, well, he kinda likes you, so maybe that's why. Can I assume you still find that whole conversation to be really awkward and weird?"

Layla nodded. It hadn't been the finest hour for either her or Harry, primarily because he'd decided to come clean and tell her how he felt about a week after she'd broken up with Blake. It had ended when she'd told Harry that he'd picked a bad time, she wasn't interested in anyone, which had been true because of the break-up. But now she wondered whether or not things might have progressed between the two of them if the timing had been better.

"You know, Blake was a really big douche. And I told you that after, like, four months of him behaving like a normal person."

"Really?" Layla asked. "An *I told you so*, coming from you?"

"Hey, none of my exes were quite as bad as Blake."

"I've got two words for you." She counted them off on her fingers as she spoke. "Maggie Zayn."

"Maggie was a *little* intense."

"She was nuts. A great big bag of crazy. She asked you to drink her blood."

"She did. But on the plus side, she was *really* attractive."

"And nuts."

Chloe sighed. "Yeah, she was really something, that's for sure."

"She stalked you for a month after you broke up with her. She once came to my old place and asked if you were around."

"She did do those things, yes. It was a fun time for everyone. Luckily, she eventually got the hint and left."

"Hint?"

"Okay, I threatened to break her fingers if she didn't leave my friends alone. Which in itself is a sort of hint. I'd tried asking nicely, telling her I'd contact the police, and anything else I could think of. Apparently threats of physical violence were my last resort. And it was a good thing it worked, because I didn't want to have to break her fingers. She had lovely, elegant fingers, and she played piano. It would have been a shame."

"Yes, also I'm pretty sure it's not legal to do that."

Chloe waved the sentence away as if it were a mere formality. "I would have managed it. And, worst-case scenario, I'd have been awesome in jail. I'd have come out like a mafia don."

Layla laughed. "Don Chloe Range. I don't think that works."

Chloe joined in the laughter. "I'd have made it work."

The pair chatted for a few hours until the post dropped through the letterbox to the carpet below. Layla picked up the envelopes and flicked through each one, throwing the junk mail into the bin beside the door. She was down to the last two when she paused and felt a cold shiver run up her spine.

"You all right?" Chloe asked from the sofa.

"It's from my dad." Layla's voice shook as she spoke. "Since Mom died, he sends me a card every year around this date. It's to say he's thinking of me at this difficult time. I don't think I've mentioned it before. It's not something I like to bring up."

Chloe was up from the sofa in an instant and by her friend's side. "You okay?"

Layla nodded slowly, walking over to the sofa and sitting down.

"How does he know where you live?"

"I'm the only one on the list of approved contacts. I have to update my address and phone number if I move."

Chloe sat beside her. "He's in jail somewhere. Why don't you get your name removed from the contacts list?"

"I need to be on it. I need the prison staff to let me know when he's dead. That's my closure for everything he's done over the years. Everything he's in jail for."

"Do you get anything else from him?"

Layla shook her head. "The agent in charge occasionally sends me an e-mail asking how I am. She's really nice. Her name is Tabitha. But not from my dad—he's not allowed access to the Internet." She glanced down at the small envelope; it weighed heavily in her hand.

"Do you want to read it?" Chloe asked.

Layla tore it in half and placed it on the table. "I want nothing from him," she said. "I don't care how he's doing, or what he feels about me. He's the closest thing to evil I've ever met. He's in a jail cell, in solitary for ninety percent of the day, only allowed out when there are no other prisoners around. That's where he deserves to be. I get another letter from him at Christmas. And one on my birthday. Three letters a year, all with that stamp."

Chloe looked at the stamp. "At least this proves he's still where he's meant to be."

Layla nodded. "That stamp right there is something Tabitha from the FBI promised would be on every letter he sends. If that's there, I know he's still in his cell, far away from me and anyone I care about. All of his letters go to her first, so I know I can breathe a little easier."

"The FBI are the ones dealing with this? I didn't realize they dealt with prisoners."

Layla sighed. "Yeah, I have no idea why either. Tabitha told me it's because my dad used to work for them. I don't really care who keeps an eye on him, but the FBI seems to be good at keeping him where he's meant to be."

"Is he in the UK?"

She shook her head. "He's somewhere in the USA. My mom was British, and I have dual citizenship—it's why we moved to the UK after it all kicked off over there. Besides, there's an ocean between me and my father. Which makes me feel better."

"You think he'd come after you?"

"No, I was never his target. He was nothing but a perfect father to me, a perfect facade of a father. I think that's why it hurts so much; he was able to lie to my face about the kind of person he is. I was living in a blissful ignorance until one morning at 3 a.m., when a task force smashed the front door to our house down." She thought back to that night, as a nearly fourteen-year-old girl cowered under her bed because she thought bad men had come to hurt her family. One more thing she hated about her father. What he'd done had *caused* that. Another thing to never forgive him for.

"Sorry," Layla said, picking up their cups. "I'm being all down. You want another drink?"

"Tea, please." Chloe followed her to the kitchen, leaning up against the doorframe as Layla boiled the kettle. "Did I ever tell you about my mum?"

Layla spooned coffee into her mug and dropped a green tea bag in Chloe's. "I know she's in jail."

"My mother spent most of my life putting me in harm's way to ingratiate herself with people she desperately wanted to impress. She put me in dangerous situations three times from the age of thirteen to seventeen, and was personally responsible for me almost dying on one of those occasions. Once, she also made it look like I'd been kidnapped, and is directly responsible for the murder of my father. My mother is frankly the most awful human being I've ever met, so if you ever need to talk about your dad, you never need to tell me you're being down. Just talk. We could compare notes on crazy parents if you like."

Layla chuckled. "It sounds like we'd be here for a long time."

"Don't ever think like you can't talk to me, or that I might judge you. Last night I beat the shit out of a bloke for trying to hurt you. I think it's safe to say I'm nonjudgmental."

After they'd finished their drinks, Chloe had to go home to see how the coffee shop was doing, and Layla needed to get ready for work. She felt better after talking to Chloe. She hadn't shared everything, and had no intention of ever doing so, but knowing that she could if she ever wanted to made her feel more relieved than she'd ever imagined it would.

4

Elias Wells had been in England for five days, and had done nothing with the information he'd been given. He didn't want to hurry anything, and liked to get used to his new surroundings before starting a job. He didn't want to have to rush out, or try to evade anyone, without knowing the area where he'd be working. That just made sense to him.

So, for the last five days he'd scouted the area, taking photographs of the house he needed to get into. He'd made sure it was empty before breaking in the first time, quickly opening a downstairs window before climbing inside. It was nice to do a dry run, and he soon familiarized himself with the layout of the two-story, three-bedroom house.

There weren't any photos of the target, which he did find slightly strange, but then it was strange enough that she'd been completely off the grid since her father had been arrested, only now deciding to apply for a credit card. Elias guessed it was because she'd assumed she was safe. He tried to remember that saying about assuming things but couldn't, and decided it probably wasn't worth remembering anyway.

He stayed in the house for an hour, before leaving it in exactly the same shape as when he'd arrived. He walked into the woods behind the house, keeping an eye out for anyone who might be about and wonder what he was doing. About fifty feet from the house, and after being satisfied he was alone, he climbed a huge conifer tree and sat on one of the large branches to wait.

The needles were annoying and he had to flick off more than his fair share of bugs, but his position let him watch the rear of the house with a good assurance that those inside, and those living nearby, couldn't see him. Unfortunately, Elias had no way of really knowing *who* had arrived home. If it was a large group, he'd rather not have to kill a bunch of people to get to just one. He thought about it for a while and decided that if that was the case, he'd have to come back tomorrow, but he was hopeful that he'd be able to get the job done quickly and go back to America in the private jet waiting for him.

The rest of his group had wanted to come and take part in the extraction, but he'd left them behind. Some of them were less than subtle, and while there was a time for hitting hard and fast, it wasn't usually in a built-up neighborhood when you're trying to be quiet.

Eventually, lights came on in the house, but Elias remained where he was until the darkness had settled, and even then he sat motionless for several more hours. When he finally climbed down from the tree it was 1 a.m., and the neighborhood was silent. He'd purposely selected a weekday for that exact reason: less chance of revelers coming home drunk and catching him, or the occupants bringing home a group of friends who would be passed out on the sofa by now. That was the thing about his job: if he didn't think of an outcome as possible it was almost guaranteed that it would happen.

He scaled the wooden fence and dropped into the garden. There were lights still on in the house, and the one in the kitchen bathed the back garden in patchy light. Elias easily avoided it as he crept up the garden, unconcerned about the motion sensor for the security lights, which he'd disabled earlier in the day.

He reached the side door to the house and quickly picked the lock, opening the door slightly. He took a moment before he pushed the door fully open and stepped into the kitchen-diner, closing it behind him.

Elias had put on leather gloves before descending from the tree. His prints wouldn't show up in any database, but he didn't want to link whatever he was doing here with anything he'd done in the past. Or, indeed, might do in the future. In his mind, it was always better to be safe than sorry.

There were voices somewhere upstairs, and more coming from the living room, and for a second Elias was convinced that his target had brought guests home. He cursed inwardly and ignored the voices upstairs, deciding to deal with whoever was in the living room.

Elias was grateful for the carpeted floor of the hallway softening his footsteps as he made his way toward the front room. He moved silently until the hall turned ninety degrees, putting the stairs out of his view. He paused; if anyone went to the top of the steps, he'd be spotted the second he stepped away from the wall, but there was little choice. He took a breath and moved quickly, hoping none of the floorboards would creak as he moved. He'd checked earlier, and while he hadn't found any creaky ones, that didn't mean one couldn't be discovered at an inappropriate moment. Sod's law existed for a reason.

Fortunately, the walk remained creak-free and Elias soon found himself outside the living room. He glanced inside, keeping back just in case someone spotted him, but saw no one. The sound had been coming from the TV. Elias cursed himself. It had been necessary but dangerous to check the room out, but even so he was unhappy with the need. He walked back along the hallway and was about to go up the stairs when he heard something in the kitchen. He flattened himself against the wall, moving back away from the stairs and peering through the open kitchen door, where he could see a young woman with long, black hair. She wore a dark blue t-shirt that was clearly two or three sizes too big.

She was just over five foot in height and probably weighed no more than half of Elias, and while she wasn't the target, she was a complication.

The woman stood at the sink, her back toward Elias as she got a drink of water from the tap. Elias moved smoothly into the kitchen-diner, reaching the woman before she even had time to turn around. He clamped a hand over her mouth and brought the knife up to her throat, puncturing the artery and going up through her jaw into her brain, killing her. He caught the glass before it fell from her hand and pushed her head over the sink to ensure the blood remained in one place. He considered going on, but instead tossed his hat into the sink to collect the blood. It was a pity there hadn't been the time to ask her any questions, not with more people in the house; she might have had useful information.

He stayed there for several seconds, making sure she wasn't going to fall. When he was satisfied, and with his hat remaining in the sink, he wiped the knife on a tea towel. He took it with him—he might need it again—and made his way back to the stairs, ascending them as slowly as he would allow himself.

"Are you coming back?" a male called out from above, and for a second Elias wondered if he had the wrong house. He thought back to the information he'd been given. No, this was the correct address; he'd been given a map of the area confirming it. Maybe the target had moved? He considered that unlikely, as the information was fresh and people don't usually apply for a credit card and then move a week later. Something was amiss, though, and he wanted to know what and why.

He reached the landing above as the man began chuckling. "Come on, baby. I'm ready for you."

Elias walked to the door and stepped inside, enjoying the look of shock on the man's face.

"Well, now, this *is* unexpected," Elias said and took several steps toward the man, whose arms and legs were tied to the bed with colorful silk scarfs. He was naked and had obviously been expecting some sort of sexual liaison.

He opened his mouth to scream, but Elias placed the tip of the stiletto dagger against his penis. "Don't."

The man closed his mouth.

Elias removed the dagger and used the tea towel as a gag on the incapacitated man. "I'll be back in a minute. Just stay there."

The man's eyes showed his terror, and Elias left him there, going back downstairs to find the body of the woman he'd killed. After checking that she'd been drained of her blood, he picked her up, threw her over his shoulder, and walked with her to the living room, dropping her onto one of the two small gray sofas that were in there.

He went back to the kitchen and retrieved his hat, finding it dry. He tested the rim before putting it on his head. He'd been embarrassed that it hadn't been dry when he'd put it on in front of Nergal, and didn't want to make such a rookie mistake again.

Once he was sure he'd cleaned up, he made his way back upstairs and looked around the bedroom. Apart from the king-size bed with the naked man tied to it, there were two chests of drawers, both in a wood so dark it almost looked black, a large TV, and a small table and chairs. Elias found himself wondering where they got the chests of drawers from as he rather liked them. He considered taking them, but he wasn't there for thievery. The dark blue curtains had been pulled shut. Elias moved them aside slightly and checked that the windows were all closed. When he was satisfied, he closed the bedroom door, took a chair, and placed it next to the bed beside the man's feet.

"Here's how this works. I'm going to remove the gag and you're going to answer my questions. If you don't, I'm going to hurt you. Badly. I don't want to do that. Mostly because I don't like doing it. But not liking doing something doesn't mean you're not *really* good at it. Do you understand me?"

The man nodded.

Elias removed the gag and returned to his seat. He felt the dead woman's memories fluttering into his mind. "Your girlfriend Bianca is dead. Your name is Blake, yes?"

Tears fell down Blake's cheeks. Elias couldn't decide if they were tears for Blake's current predicament or the loss of Bianca.

"Who are you? Why are you doing this?"

"My name is Elias, and I'm a redcap."

"A what?"

"A monster, or mythological creature, or whatever tag you wish to put on it." Elias tapped the rim on his fedora. "You see, I use my knife to kill people, and the blood spilled is collected in this hat. It's a little more complicated than that, as clearly this hat can't hold several pints of blood, but those are the basics. The important bit that you need to know is that once I've absorbed someone's blood into my hat and put it back on, I know their memories. Only the last week or so, but it's quite handy. Unfortunately, your deceased loved one didn't know anything useful about my need to be here, and I can't take two people's blood in a twenty-four-hour period, so we'll have to do this the old-fashioned way. Me ask. You answer."

"You murdered her," Blake snapped. "You bastard. You didn't need to do that."

"Oh dear, it seems you're upset. Well, yes, I did kill her, and no, I didn't have a choice. Would it make you feel better if I searched her memories for something about you?" Elias was silent for a few seconds, his eyes fixed on the floor. "She liked you. Never more than that. Who is Rob?"

"My best friend."

"You sure? Because he's been riding your girlfriend like a pony. She *really* enjoyed it too. I don't think she was all that nice. But then you don't come off too well in her memories either. You're hung up on . . ." He paused. "Layla Starsmore. That's really the surname she chose?" Elias chuckled to himself.

34

Blake's eyes opened in shock.

In an instant the humor was gone from Elias's face, his expression replaced with one of cold determination. "Tell me about Layla. Where is she?"

"I don't know," Blake said.

Elias removed a second blade from its sheath, this one only a few inches long, but with a serrated edge. "I've used this blade to skin animals. Would you like to see what it does to you?"

Blake shook his head. "I don't know where she is, we're not together anymore."

"Where does she live?"

"I don't know. She never lived with me here. She moved out of her old place about six months ago. But she moved again a few weeks ago. No one she knows will tell me where she is."

"I get the feeling that the problem in these relationships isn't the woman. Bianca thought you a controlling bully. You said some awful things to her, and you hit her once too. Although it's weird that you like to be so controlling in every part of your companion's life, but you also like to lose that control when having sex. You like to be tied up, hurt. She found it weird, uncomfortable . . . unpleasant. It's no wonder she wanted something extra from someone else, although Rob comes across as a total asshole too. Maybe that was her type." He placed the edge of the blade on Blake's shin. "Where does Layla live?"

"If I knew, I'd tell you. I'd tell you everything."

"I know." Elias counted to three in his head and then cut through Blake's leg in one motion. The wound was deep and bled severely. Elias waited for Blake to stop crying and begging before speaking again. "You done?" He understood that people didn't deal with physical pain exceptionally well, but that was no reason to beg. Crying he could understand, he had no problem with that, but begging was something he couldn't stand in a person. It was just so unnecessary.

"I know where Layla works," Blake almost shouted.

"Excellent. And where would that be?"

"Train depot. She has some evening job there three nights a week. Wednesday to Friday. It's the only depot in the city, near the football stadium."

"That's excellent news, and should make finding both it and her easier. Thank you for your help."

"You'll let me live?"

Elias shook his head. "No. You die today, and there's nothing I can do about it. But I can make your death quick and painless, or lengthy and drawn out. I do have a few more questions, though, so maybe you'll be able to convince me to let you go."

Blake nodded in agreement.

"She applied for a credit card using this address. So tell me, why doesn't she live here?"

"Bianca and me, we used her old address details to try to blag a credit card."

"Ah, that makes sense. How'd that work out for you? It wasn't exactly smart, was it?"

Blake shook his head. "I didn't know she'd moved house, and when they called the phone number we put on the application to confirm her address, I gave this one. I panicked."

"Doesn't explain why you used the name Layla Cassidy instead of the one she was using. Cassidy is her real surname."

Blake appeared confused. "She used a fake name? I used to go through her things when I had the chance, to make sure she wasn't doing anything she shouldn't have been. One time, I found some old letters that Layla had hidden in a drawer. They were addressed to her mother, but used the last name Cassidy. I assumed that was her mother's maiden name, that's why we used it."

"Her mother's maiden name?" Elias chuckled. "This is quite an impressive level of screw-up on your part. You thought you were being clever, but in reality you gave us the information we needed to find her. And you got yourself and your lady killed too. Not anyone's finest hour." Elias stood, preparing to finish the job and leave.

"So, you're not human?" Blake stammered out, clearly looking for more time.

"A redcap. I wear neither a red hat nor a cap. Although the latter was true once. The name is meant to be more symbolic than anything else, I think. And that's all I plan on telling you. I'd like to say it was a pleasure, but according to these memories, you're a nasty little toad of a human being, and frankly the world is better off without you in it."

"You're going to kill Layla?"

"That's not the plan."

"She needs taking down a peg or two. Thinks she's better than me."

Elias placed the tip of the stiletto against his jugular. "From everything I've seen, she probably is." He pushed the blade up with incredible force, killing Blake instantly. He stepped aside, removing the blade as he walked, avoiding the inevitable blood that left the wound.

Elias would need to spend a few hours cleaning up after himself. He wanted to leave as few clues at the scene as possible. The police wouldn't have a chance of finding him, but he did consider leaving evidence to frame the friend, Rob. Bianca's memories showed him to be even worse than Blake, a man with few morals. Maybe a man like that would be better off punished too. Elias smiled at the thought and pushed it aside. Maybe later.

He removed the phone from his pocket and dialed the rest of the team.

"Yes?" a woman asked.

"Dara, it's done here. I'll be back soon. I need details on a train depot near a football stadium."

"There's an American football stadium in the city?" She sounded confused.

"No, a normal football stadium. Soccer, as you like to call it, much to my chagrin."

"I'll get on it."

He ended the call. Dara Kanevsky was a valuable member of his team. Born in America in the mid-1950s, she'd lived with her family in San Francisco. That was where, at the age of seven, she'd discovered a talent for hurting people. Something she had seemingly inherited from her parents. Her father was quite the celebrity at the time, having killed several people in and around Northern California. That had stopped when Dara killed them both in 1975, after deciding that her parents were getting too sloppy. Taunting the press and police was a pointless action. Grandstanding for the sake of it.

Elias remembered meeting Dara for the first time, and realizing whose daughter she was. He'd been genuinely starstruck. People like her father had spread terror all over, and it was something that Elias had always been impressed with. He hadn't liked her father's taunting, though, which was just a step too close to idiocy for him. Like all members of Elias's team, Dara wasn't human, but she was the one he felt the most akin to. He knew she'd do what he asked.

Elias glanced down at Blake's body and sighed. Tomorrow night they'd go after Layla. But tonight, well, tonight he had less fun things to deal with. It couldn't all be about getting his own way.

5

It had been nearly two days since Layla had talked with Chloe about her father and she'd felt as if a weight had been lifted from her. That night, the entire evening shift had flown by. But now that she was driving back out of the electric gates of the train depot for the second time in two days, she began to wonder how much longer she really had to work in this place.

It wasn't that the job was hard, or that the people were bad; it was just a combination of boredom and a complete and total apathy from those in management. It was as if they didn't care what happened to the majority of people who worked for them, and it created a "them and us" scenario that made work feel like she was constantly trying to do a good job for no reason whatsoever.

The night had been long, and when she'd finished at midnight, she'd been looking forward to getting home and crashing into her bed. She pulled into the private parking area at the rear of her property and parked her ten-year-old Volkswagen Golf in her designated space.

"Hey, you," a woman shouted at Layla as she got out of her car.

Layla sighed. "Hello, Sharon. It's a bit late."

Sharon Weaver was one of Layla's neighbors. She lived on the top floor of the building with her boyfriend, and was about as pleasant as leprosy. Layla had heard from several other tenants who hated the pair of them. They had a tendency to have lots of loud, drunken parties, to which they would invite their loud, obnoxiously drunk friends, and they would always get out of control and often spill out of the building. If the police ever came to the block, it was pretty much always because of them.

"Late for what?" Sharon asked, slightly slurring her words. Sharon was a bully. She intimidated, or got her boyfriend to intimidate, anyone who spoke out against her, usually by threatening to attack them or their property. Layla had crossed paths with her on a few occasions, but usually just ignored the pair of them. They were more trouble than it was worth.

"I'm tired, Sharon. It's been a long day. What's up?" Layla kept her voice calm, not wanting to cause an argument.

Sharon stepped toward Layla until only a few feet separated them. She was a few inches taller than Layla, her long blonde hair tied back in a ponytail. She told everyone she did kickboxing, and from her build, Layla imagined that to be true.

"There a problem here?" Sharon's boyfriend asked as he left the rear entrance to the building.

Sharon's boyfriend, Nigel Johnson, was six-four and weighed at least eighteen stone. Layla had often seen him wearing football kit, surrounded by similar-looking men who appeared to be under the impression that their size gave them the right to intimidate.

"You're always looking down your nose at me," Sharon said.

"I'm really not," Layla assured her.

"You tell her, Shaz," Nigel shouted. He cackled to himself and took a swig from a bottle of beer.

"You are not all that, bitch," Shaz said, seemingly bolstered by support from Nigel. She wagged a finger in Layla's direction.

Layla wanted to grab the digit and snap it. Snap all of them one at a time until Sharon apologized and promised to stop being an asshole to everyone in the building. Layla forced her mind to calm down.

"Sharon, I think you should go back home."

Sharon took another step forward and jabbed Layla in the chest with her finger. "You *think*?" She turned back to Nigel. "This bitch *thinks*."

Nigel laughed once again.

"So, you think I should go back home. Well, let me tell you something, you stuck-up cow. I'm going to knock you out, and then maybe you won't be able to look like you're better than me. I want to see you watching the floor every single time I walk past. You understand me?"

Layla forced herself to not make eye contact as the smell of alcohol and cigarettes permeated her immediate surroundings. "You're drunk, Sharon. I . . . thi—" She paused for a heartbeat before continuing. "I would go home and sleep it off, if I were you, before I call the police."

Layla immediately knew it was the wrong thing to say. Sharon's eyes narrowed and she shoved Layla back up against her car.

"Knock her out," Nigel called from somewhere behind Sharon. Layla didn't want to risk even the slightest glance.

"Don't do this," Layla said, as part of her screamed to hurt the larger woman.

Sharon pushed Layla again. "Make." Push. "Me." Push.

"Do you need your boyfriend to feel big? Is that why he's there? You scared what might happen if you're all alone with me?"

Sharon laughed and turned to Nigel. "Go back in, baby. You can watch from our bedroom window."

Layla watched Nigel finish his beer, throwing the bottle at a nearby bin, missing, and smashing it. He shrugged and entered the building.

"Just you and me now, *bitch*," Sharon said smugly. She turned back toward Layla, who punched her in the side of the head.

Sharon staggered away to one side, closer to her red Ford Fiesta ST. She placed one hand on top of the car, trying to steady herself. Layla came up to her side, swiped the arm away, and smashed Sharon's forehead onto the car roof.

Sharon dropped to her knees, and Layla noticed the dent in the Fiesta's roof, stepping back to allow Sharon to get to her feet.

"Sucker-punched me," Sharon said, spitting blood onto the floor. "Little bitch."

"I really don't like that word."

Sharon rushed forward. All of the hours and hours of training that Layla had gone through as a child, constantly being told the need to win at any cost was the most important thing, fought for supremacy over her need to not take it too far.

Layla blocked a punch and grabbed hold of Sharon's wrist, stepping around her and forcing the larger woman off her feet and onto the ground. A voice told her to break Sharon's wrist, to hurt her more, to make a point, but she ignored it. A knee to the side of Sharon's face ended whatever fight she still had left.

Layla stood in the car park. Her breathing remained heavy, her hands shaking, as excitement coursed through her body. A voice told her to keep going, to make a point that she wasn't to be messed around with.

"What the hell?" Nigel shouted from upstairs after opening the window and seeing a triumphant Layla standing over his unconscious girlfriend.

The window slammed shut and Layla knew it wasn't over. Nigel would try to hurt her, that was just the way people like him were. The constant need to dominate. To hurt anyone who made people question his toughness. In another era he might have been a gangster thug, roughing people up for nonpayment of loans.

Nigel burst through the door, making a huge racket in the process, and charged toward her without a second thought.

Break him, she thought to herself, but instead she calmed her mind and let her years of training take over.

Layla stepped toward Nigel at the last second, grabbing hold of his jacket and launching him over her shoulder. He slammed into the rear of the Fiesta, smashing the back window. He slumped to the ground and tried to get back to his feet, but the second he put his arms in front of him to steady himself, Layla kicked them out, sending him back to the concrete.

She grabbed his arm and locked it at the elbow, causing him to cry out. *Break it*, the voice said.

"I'm gonna kill you for this," Nigel screamed.

"Take your time," Layla said, and broke his arm at the elbow.

Break more.

She placed a foot on the back of Nigel's head and was about to stomp his face into the concrete when she stopped herself and darted away. She'd come too close to seriously injuring him, but that wasn't who she was. She wasn't a psycho. Sharon began to stir, forcing Layla to take immediate action.

Layla used Sharon's phone to call the ambulance, before running into the building, hoping that none of the other tenants had seen what had transpired. She reached her front door and almost broke the key in the lock in her haste to open it.

She slammed it shut behind her, locking it and using the chain and bolt to make her feel more secure. She expected the police would come for her at some point during the evening. She'd badly beaten two people, leaving them breathing, but hurt.

She had a shower, and watched the water turn pink as she washed away all traces of blood from her hands. She wasn't a psycho. She wasn't her father. She remembered how good it had felt to hurt Sharon and Nigel, how much tension had been released after doing it, and she knew she'd enjoyed it. She knew she'd felt good about it. She refused to become her father's daughter. She refused to allow that enjoyment of violence to turn her into a new version of him.

Once she was washed and dressed, she sat on her sofa and waited for a knock at the door that never came. The ambulance turned up—she could see the flashing lights through her second bedroom window—but no police knocked, no one came to arrest or even question her. How was that possible?

Eventually she fell into a fitful sleep, full of dreams where she hurt people and enjoyed it. Where she went out to hunt random people, reveling in their pain and torment. Where she'd become the very thing she feared most.

6

Layla spent the following day in a sort of semi-daze. Half expecting the police to come by at any moment, she stayed in rather than have them track her down while she was out. By the time she had to go to work, her concern about the police had disappeared. She'd seen both Sharon and Nigel return home; neither of them looked good, and Nigel's arm was in a sling. She wanted to feel guilty, but it didn't last for long. Her neighbors were bullies, threatening people they thought they could get away with intimidating. Hopefully that had now come to an end, at least for a while.

Just as she was about to leave for work, she discovered a card put under the door. She opened it, feeling nervous that it was a death threat or something, but it merely said:

Hopefully we'll get some peace for a few weeks.

Thank you.

Your friendly neighbors.

It had made her feel better, although she had no idea how they'd come to figure out that she was the one who had done something.

By the time she got in her car and set off for work, she was beginning to feel better about what had happened. She was still concerned that she'd come home to a broken window, and there was always the fear of what she would become if she continued to fight, but she had been forced to defend herself. Just as she had been against Rob. What were the chances it would happen three times in the span of a few days? Hopefully zero. With any luck, she could go back to ignoring the joy she got from fighting. From hurting someone who deserved it.

She pulled up next to the card reader at the train depot and wound down the window, swiping her card and waiting for the large gate to move slowly open. Her car now had so many miles on it that it was probably due for retirement. It had developed the ability to start only when it felt like it, and reliability had been replaced by a game of chance as to whether or not the car would make it to its destination, no matter the distance. On the plus side, it hadn't been damaged in the fight. Small mercies and all that.

Eventually the gate opened enough to allow her entrance. She drove inside, the gate closing behind her. She had never really thought about it before, but one electric gate was hardly going to stop anyone determined to get in. A child could probably climb it in a few seconds; it wasn't as if it had a barbed-wire top or anything.

She parked the car and got out. The evening was cold and drizzly, as it usually was at this time of year. Several people waved or said hello as they ended their shift for the day. She returned the courtesy automatically, wishing she were joining them as she entered the depot. It wasn't that she disliked the people; the majority were both pleasant and friendly. And in fact, she considered a few of them to actually be her friends, but there was a minority who thought that because she wasn't a technician, she wasn't worth their time. And the majority of management were dicks, but she imagined that was the same in every company on the planet.

From the outside, the main building looked like a large aircraft hangar, but inside it was divided into two parts. There was a walkway along the left-hand side where those not working on the trains could walk in safety, although they had to wear a bright orange high-vis vest at all times. It was a rule that once broken was quickly punished with a trip to some random human resources person, who'd probably been employed a week earlier, and would be replaced a week later.

"Hey, Layla," a man called from behind her.

She turned and smiled as Marcus Dawson walked toward her. He was nearly six feet tall and a little chubby, although he'd recently started going to the gym to get rid of it. He was in his mid-thirties and had grown a beard since Layla had last seen him a few weeks earlier. Unfortunately for him, it was growing in patches and didn't look as cool as he'd probably hoped. "Hey, Marcus, how's you?"

"Late," he said, as he caught her up and they began walking together. Layla checked her watch. She was thirty seconds late. *Damn it.*

Before anyone was allowed to work in the depot, they had to go to the shift manager's office and sign in to the big book on the desk next to the supervisor. Being late was punishable on a random basis, depending on who was sitting at the supervisor's desk.

Marcus worked in the main office downstairs, while Layla worked upstairs, where the majority of the management sat during the day. She knew him well enough to say hi and keep a conversation going, but that was how she would describe her acquaintance with most people in the depot. She kept mostly to herself at work, preferring to come in, do the job, and leave.

Marcus opened the door to be greeted with the smiling face of Jack Simmons. "You're late, Marcus. Do you want to tell me why?" Jack Simmons was the kind of man who, after being given a small measure of power, thought he was a king amongst men. His inflated opinion of himself was only matched by how much of a kiss-ass he was to those above him.

Layla hoped she could just sign in and leave, but Marcus was in front of the signing-in book, blocking her and forcing her to wait.

"I didn't realize you were my supervisor, Jack," Marcus said, his ability to open his mouth and put his foot in it more than evident.

"I'm *a* supervisor, Marcus. If you like, I can have a word with your manager about your attitude."

"You go right ahead," Marcus said and left the office.

Layla signed in to the book.

"Late, Layla?" Jack asked.

"Little bit."

She looked over at him and he winked. She fought down her gag reflex and managed a weak smile before leaving the office. Jack was well known in the depot for hitting on every attractive woman almost as soon as they arrived. And to him, "attractive woman" meant anyone who wasn't male.

Everyone on site knew about this tendency, although only a tiny number of people actually complained about it. Some women even seemed to find it charming or funny, but Layla just thought he was a creepy jerk. A man with a huge ego who liked the sound of his own voice so much that he couldn't imagine a world where a woman wouldn't find him irresistible. Layla wondered how his wife felt about that.

Layla left the office as quickly as possible and walked a short distance to a gray door. She opened it and stepped into the corridor beyond, walking the few steps to a second identical door, which she pushed open to reveal the staircase to the floor above.

"He's such a dick," Marcus said as he left the nearby kitchen area, a cup of something hot in his hand.

"Yes, but you antagonized him."

"Because of his earlier mentioned dickish personality."

"You know he's going to talk to your manager, right?"

Marcus nodded but didn't seem overly bothered, and walked off humming something to himself. Layla shook her head; sometimes people just couldn't help themselves.

She ascended the stairs and used her swipe card to get into the managerial section. The reception area was unmanned, the receptionist having gone home some time earlier, along with most of the managers. Layla imagined work here during the day was something akin to having to sit next to a hornets' nest for eight hours; working from four o'clock to midnight might not be many people's idea of a good shift, but it was quiet, peaceful, and it was a lot easier to ignore e-mails than it was to ignore someone standing beside you.

She entered the office and found her desk at the far end, next to a large window overlooking the rails that sat outside of the main building. A bridge ran over them, connecting the main office to the outside world, and a quick count told Layla that four blue-and-white trains were waiting for work to be done on them. She had no idea what work, and she didn't much care.

Each train coming into the depot would be given an examination, and the work completed was written down to be inputted onto the database. Layla's job was to input that data.

She'd recently started going out onto the depot floor to help with simple tasks, but she wasn't safety-critical competent, so wasn't allowed to do anything that involved the electrical or safety systems. Even so, she was looking forward to a two-week block where she was going to shadow one of the teams of technicians. She'd spent a lot of time as a young teenager learning how to fix her mom's old motorbike, which was probably where she'd gotten her love of metallurgy. Maybe working on trains would bring back that same sense of enjoyment.

Until that time, though, Layla was, to all intents and purposes, left alone to work without outside interference. She didn't mind that. The work was repetitive and easy, with little in the way of taxing mental stimulation.

Layla logged on, and after waiting for the system to come to life, opened her e-mail, before leaving the office to go to the small kitchen to make a cup of tea. It would be a while before the computer was capable of doing anything much, thanks to the background security stuff opening and running checks. She wasn't really sure what people might want to steal, but upper management sure liked telling everyone that they should be on the lookout for such people.

She returned to her desk a few minutes later, mug in hand, to read one such e-mail: apparently attackers were out there ready to steal sensitive information. She clicked on the little green tick, acknowledging she'd read it, and promptly removed it from her mind.

She'd been working for two hours when she stretched back in her chair and realized she needed another drink. Keeping track of over a hundred trains was hard work, and the fact that she was the only one in the depot doing the job meant a lot of people were waiting for the information. Even so, everyone needed a break.

She walked down the stairs to the kitchen, where she found several technicians just leaving, about to start the night shift.

"You still here?" Andrew Green said as Layla entered the kitchen. The depot was ninety percent male, and that percentage went up during the evening shifts. There were nights when she was the only woman in the entire building. Andrew had once been a technician, and was one of the old guard, someone who'd been here since the depot had opened fifteen years earlier, and would likely retire here.

He worked with Marcus, doing something that Layla had never quite figured out. Most people seemed to think that the downstairs office was where they put the people no one else wanted to work with, but Layla didn't agree. She liked the people in there; they were fun and chatty, and actually had a sense of humor. Trains are all very well for work, but at the end of the day they're just trains. Layla thought that sometimes people in management needed to be reminded of that.

"I could say the same about you," Layla said as she flicked the switch on the kettle.

"Overtime. I'm here for a few more hours yet. We've got to get the figures out by Monday, so it's all hands on deck. Even Star and Aoki are here."

Star was the third member of the team, a twenty-two-year-old woman, fresh out of university, who was not only excellent at her job, but also well known for saying exactly what she thought to anyone who annoyed her. Aoki was the final member of the team, and the youngest at just over twenty. Layla didn't know much about him, except that he'd moved over from Japan to work for the company only a few months ago.

"Say hi for me," Layla said, pouring the hot water once the kettle had boiled.

"We're having a team-building thing next weekend, if you want to come?"

"What are you doing?"

"Paintballing. The whole office is going, twenty-two of us. Marcus suggested it. Personally I just think it's an excuse for him to shoot the boss and get away with it."

Layla paused for a second. "Sure, e-mail me the details and I'll see if I can make it." She returned back upstairs to her office and, after a few minutes, received an e-mail from Star.

You coming next weekend then?

Layla replied straightaway.

I don't know.

You have to come; otherwise it's just going to be me and twenty blokes. Most of whom will try really hard not to shoot me because I'm a fragile flower of a girl.

Layla laughed, her voice echoing around the large room.

I guess I'll have to join you then. We can gang up on the others.

That's the plan.

I assume there will be drinking afterwards.

It wouldn't be a team event if drinking wasn't part of it. We're not allowed to charge the company for the alcohol, though, so if anyone asks, we had Coke or orange juice all night.

The boss is okay with that?

What the boss doesn't know won't kill him. So, you're coming?

Layla nodded and then reminded herself no one could see her.

Looks that way, yes.

Star sent back a smiley, and Layla went back to work, barely looking up until it was completely dark outside. The entire shift had, as usual, lacked anything one might call eventful. By the time she'd finished inputting all of the data from the work done by the technicians earlier in the day, it was just before midnight. She had about an hour's worth of work left to do before she could go, and considering she wasn't going to be in for a few days and didn't like leaving work for the day shift, she decided to complete an overtime form and work the extra hour.

It was half past twelve when she looked up from her computer screen and glanced out of the nearby window. Lights were on below her, showing the safe walkways between the tracks, and she considered getting one last hot drink. But when she looked at the bridge, she thought she saw movement on it. She got up from her chair and stared at the top of the bridge, but there was glare from the office lights and she couldn't make anything out. Switching off the lights was impossible—they were triggers to motion sensors—so she cupped her hands around her eyes to try to see better.

"Probably just a bird," she said to herself, although she knew she didn't believe it. Whatever she'd seen had only been there for a moment, but it had been big.

She got up from her desk and walked to the opposite end of the office, pushing open the only working window—the rest remained locked at all times. The second she put her head out, allowing the noise of the depot into the office, there was more movement on the bridge. Something was on top of it. For a second, Layla couldn't quite work out what it was. It was too bathed in darkness for her to make out. Then it stood up.

Layla's mouth dropped in shock as a near-eight-foot-tall figure stood up on top of the bridge. She stepped back from the window, tripping over the cable that ran behind her. She fell to the floor just as the window and surrounding wall in front of her exploded, raining down bits of glass and brick all around her. She rolled under the nearest table, covering her head with her hands.

After a few seconds, Layla scrambled to her feet, ran for the door, and almost launched herself through it in one motion. Coughing as the cloud of brick dust surrounded her, she caught a glimpse of a huge twin-headed battle-ax imbedded in the wall further down the corridor. Whatever had thrown it had been strong enough to send it not only through the outer wall and window, but also through the internal wall. Layla knew she didn't want to meet its owner, and sprinted in the opposite direction.

The door at the far end of the corridor burst open and a monster stepped through. He had dark green skin with brown splotches across his bare arms and wore some kind of leather armor with two spikes across each shoulder that reminded Layla of something out of a fantasy film; all black and foreboding. The creature's long black hair was tied in plaits, as was his long beard, and two horns jutted out from either side of his head, nearly touching the ceiling. He smiled at her, showing fearsome, razor-sharp teeth. He looked like he could crush steel in his frying-pan-sized hands.

Layla backed up toward the door behind her as the beast grabbed hold of the ax's haft and ripped it free, dragging a portion of the wall with it. Layla turned and bolted through the door, sprinting down the stairs and out into the main shed, straight into Marcus, almost knocking him over.

"You okay?" he asked, concerned.

Layla was about to tell him to run when one of the shed windows shattered as the creature leaped through, landing on the path next to one of the trains. He roared, and for a moment after he finished there was no other sound. The beast turned toward Andrew, who had left the ground-floor office to check out what was happening, and then to the technician, who had unfortunately opened one of the train doors right next to the creature.

He whipped the ax up with ferocious speed, catching the man just below the ribcage, cutting him in half. Someone somewhere screamed, as Layla stood transfixed with shock. She forced herself to run, turning and sprinting away, feeling the reverberations of the creature's massive feet on the ground as he gave chase.

Marcus cried out in pain, and Layla stopped running and turned to find the beast with one hand around Marcus's head, holding him several feet off the ground. He looked between Layla and his prey, before flinging Marcus head first into the nearest train, sending him right through the body of the train, leaving only a bloody smear in his wake.

Another technician left the office at a run, but the creature grabbed him, threw him up against the train, and flung the ax at him. It cut through him as if he were made of paper, the ax lodging itself in the train's body. Layla ran toward the train, dropping down into the pit beneath it, hoping to find some form of sanctuary. She landed awkwardly and shock went up her leg, but she pushed the pain aside and ran on under the train, ducking beneath any parts that jutted out.

Layla's instinct was to find a way to fight back, but that was against people who weren't capable of crushing steel in their hands. She knew she had no way to fight this monster, and her hatred of him grew. People were dying, and she couldn't do a damn thing to stop it. She was angry at her lack of options, and the position she'd been put in. She knew her only choice was to get as far away from the depot as possible and hope that the creature followed. She'd figure the rest out later.

The monster retrieved the ax and tore one of the trains apart, throwing huge pieces of metal around as if they were nothing, until he'd created a hole big enough to drop down into the pit. The pit wasn't wide enough, so he launched himself into a carriage, sprinting through it, tearing it apart from the inside out. Nothing could stop him: gangways were destroyed and doors were smashed as if they were hardly there.

Beneath the train, Layla continued running, while people scrambled to get out and find shelter. Eventually she made it to the steps at the end of the pit and charged up them, as the creature burst through the fly doors at the front of the train, destroying the driver's console in the process. He landed beside another technician, who was frozen with terror, and kicked him in the chest so hard that Layla could hear the bones shattering from the impact as she resumed running toward the shed exit.

She burst through the doors and found herself standing in front of a young woman. She had a shaved head, a pleasant, almost friendly, face, and several tattoos on her bare arms. She wore similar leather armor to the monster, although it was considerably smaller. She looked at Layla and smiled.

Four men lay dead at her feet and a fifth, whose back was toward her, was impaled on the sword that seemed to be a part of her arm. The sword vanished, showing no sign it was ever there, and it was only then that Layla noticed the dead man was Aoki.

"He was smoking," the woman said. "Terrible habit. It makes you stink for the rest of the day."

The woman glanced to the side, and Layla followed her gaze, spotting Star crouched on the floor, her eyes wide with terror. Behind her a man seemed to be hanging from the wall. When Layla looked closer, she realized that one of the metal office panels had punctured through the man's body, leaving him hanging several feet in the air, like a horrific piece of art. Layla wanted to be sick, she wanted to cry, she wanted to do something, anything that would take her out of this nightmare.

"My name is Dara," the woman said, bringing Layla's attention back to her. "That in there is Brako. He's an ogre."

As if on cue Brako tore through the side of the depot shed, the large ax dripping with fresh blood. "That was fun," he said.

"You're not done yet," Dara said. "What was with the ax-throwing? We wanted her alive, remember?"

"Ax wouldn't have hit her," Brako said, sounding somewhat offended that Dara might have thought otherwise.

"What do you want?" Layla asked.

"You're going to come with us. Quietly, or more of your friends will die, and we'll just knock you out. Pick. Now." She reached over and grabbed Star, dragging her toward her and placing a glistening blade at her throat.

Layla wondered how many had been killed by these two evil creatures since they'd arrived. She wanted to fight. She wanted to wipe the smug grin off this woman's face. She took a step forward, then stopped herself; she couldn't risk having more people killed on her account. "I'll come with you. Just don't hurt anyone else, please. What do you want me for?"

"Our boss wants to talk to you. That's it. Then you can go."

Layla didn't believe a word of it, but going with them willingly would allow her time to try to escape, and hopefully save the lives of more people.

"Okay," Layla said, wanting to be away from Brako as quickly as possible. The smell of blood mixed with his own natural musk hung over him and the resulting combination was repugnant.

Dara removed a pair of handcuffs and tossed them over to Layla. "Put them on and come with me."

Layla did as she was told, following Dara to a white Range Rover in the car park. Dara opened the door and motioned for Layla to get inside.

A young man sat in the driver's seat and he turned to Layla. "Nice to meet you." He had several days' worth of stubble, bright blue eyes, and long dark hair tied back in a ponytail. From his accent, Layla thought he might be from the southern states of America, but she couldn't be more exact.

"The name is Shane. Nice to meet you."

"You're kidnapping me," Layla pointed out. "And you've murdered innocent people. I'm not feeling all that happy right now."

Shane nodded. "That's understandable. Unfortunately, Brako gets a little overenthusiastic on missions." He turned to Dara. "You coming with us?"

She shook her head. "Just got one last thing to do. We'll take the van. Brako!"

"What?" the large ogre asked.

"No witnesses."

The ogre smiled and ran off toward the depot shed.

"No," Layla said. "You said they'd be okay."

"You're right, I did." Dara closed the door, a smirk on her face.

Layla reached for the door handle, but it was locked. She threw herself onto her back and began kicking at the window in an effort to break it. Shane placed his hand on her leg and her entire body calmed. It was as if nothing in her life mattered.

"There, isn't that better?" he asked.

Layla nodded enthusiastically.

Shane switched on the radio.

"They should have taken me with them," Shane said as he pulled away. "I could have gone in, done my thing, and left with you. No death, no blood. Well, maybe a little. I'd have wanted to have some fun, after all."

7

Layla didn't lose consciousness throughout the entire journey, but if anyone had asked her where she'd been, or if she could have named a single thing she'd seen, she wouldn't have been able to answer accurately. Everything was a swirl of fog and happy thoughts. She'd never been so relaxed. She wasn't sleepy and didn't feel like she'd been drugged either; it was just a complete and utter lack of caring about anything outside of the backseat of the car. She would have lived there forever if they'd let her.

Instead, the car eventually stopped and Shane climbed out. He'd spent the journey in silence, occasionally changing the radio station or muttering how much he wanted to kill one singer or another. Somewhere deep inside her, Layla knew she was in serious danger. She just didn't care.

"Hey there," Shane said after opening the rear passenger door and looking at Layla. "You ready to leave?"

Layla shook her head. "I really want to eat some chocolate, though. Do you have any chocolate?"

"I'll see what I can do," he told her, and helped her out of the Range Rover, offering her a steady arm to hold onto while they walked into a large man-made hole in the side of a cliff.

"The stars sure are pretty," Layla said wistfully, before they vanished from view completely as she was led to a lift and then taken several hundred feet below, into the heart of the land around her. She tried to focus on where they were going, but the tunnels and caverns that she was led through were a maze, and she soon stopped trying.

"What is this place?" she asked Shane, as he took her into a cell and placed her on a chair.

He clicked his fingers, and the fog in Layla's head and all the contented feelings vanished as if they had never been there. Every horrific memory rushed back into her head at once: the smell of blood, the death, the fact that she hadn't fought back, and that others had died because these people had come for her. An overwhelming feeling of nausea crashed down onto her.

"It takes a few minutes," Shane told her.

"She doesn't look so special," a woman with a Spanish accent said, entering the room.

Layla's vision cleared and she managed to get a better image of the newcomer. She was Layla's height, but curvier, and was wearing jeans, a deep red strappy top, and black boots. Her long, light brown hair was left loose and reached the bottom of her spine. She had several colorful tattoos over her bare arms. They seemed to be Asian in influence, and a large dragon curled around one arm, starting at her wrist and moving up to her shoulder. Layla might have thought it beautiful if it wasn't on someone who was clearly working with a group of psychopaths.

"She doesn't have to look special, Reyes," Shane told her. "She just has to be who Elias needs."

"Do you think he'd mind if I bled her a little?" Reyes asked. She watched Layla like a cat might watch a mouse it's going to eat.

"Try it," Layla snapped.

Reyes burst out laughing and walked over to Layla, bending down so close that only an inch separated their heads. "Try it."

Layla's head snapped forward with incredible speed, right on the bridge of Reyes's nose. Reyes cried out and dropped to a seated position on the floor, holding her face in her hands and periodically looking at them to check for blood.

"I'm going to tear your hair out for that," Reyes screamed, murderous intent in her eyes.

"Enough." The voice boomed around the small room. A man had entered, taken one look at Reyes, and stepped between her and Layla. "Go."

Reyes, her eyes cast to the floor, was led out of the room by Shane, who looked at Layla, clearly impressed.

"My name is Elias Wells, and you're not here to injure my people."

Layla choked down the fear she felt. "You murdered people I cared about."

"Yes." He said it as if that were just what needed to be done. There was no emotion in his voice; nothing to suggest the murders even bothered him.

"Why am I here?"

Elias picked up a chair and placed it in front of Layla. He removed his fedora and placed it on the table beside him, revealing short, almost military-style brown hair. "If you try to head-butt me, I'll break both of your arms and allow them to set badly. You are not here to be a pain in my ass, you're here because we need something from you."

"You could have just asked."

"No. We couldn't. You see, you have a certain knowledge that we require, and just asking nicely wasn't going to cut it. We had to show you the kind of people we are, and we were running out of time. Unfortunately, you were not at the property occupied by your ex-lover,

Blake. We had to take you at work, and Dara asked me so nicely if she could do a full extradition, and I'd already said no so often that it felt unfair to deny her this one pleasure."

"Blake is dead?"

Elias nodded and adjusted the cuff on his immaculate black suit. "Yes. You weren't there. I needed information. He died giving it. He was not a good man. I also killed his current lover, Bianca. You'll probably hear about it on the news tomorrow. That's if we let you watch any TV. They'll also say that one Robert Mitchell was having an affair with Bianca, which he was, and that he was so overcome with jealousy that he went there, murdered them both, and then killed himself. Sometimes you need to leave someone to take the fall or the police will never stop looking. This way it's in the press for a few days, then over and done with, and I'm free to continue working without having to wonder if the police might turn up. I don't like killing police; they care too much about finding the culprit when the victim is one of their own. Same reason I don't kill children."

After seeing the ogre in action, she thought there would be nothing that could frighten her more. She was wrong. Elias terrified her. His calmness when discussing murder was like her father all over again. "You're insane."

"Probably, although I don't really have the backstory for a good crazy murderer. I had a pleasant upbringing. My parents died when I was only twenty-one, but that's probably not enough to turn me into a killer. They were murdered in their own home by a crazed madman. The fact that I *was* said crazed madman doesn't really factor into it, I don't think."

Layla just wanted Elias to shut up and get on with why she was there. "What do you want me to do?"

"It's not a matter of want. It's what you *will* do. You see, if you don't, we're going to kill ten people a day until you agree. No, make it twelve. One every two hours is a bit nicer. They'll be random people, might be anyone, and I assure you not all of my comrades have the same dislike for killing police and children that I do.

"We'll grab them, bring them here, and make you watch while they die. A never-ending conveyor belt of death and pain. That's going to be your life for the next . . . well, however long it is until you agree to our demands. And to make things a little more interesting, we're bringing those who managed to survive tonight's attack here. They're going to be our extra-special insurance. You mess about, and they die first."

"What do you want?" Layla shouted.

Elias smiled. "Your father. You're going to contact him, and you're going to get him to help us."

"I don't know where my father is."

"Liar," Elias screamed in Layla's face, slamming his hand on a metal table beside her, causing her to jump. "You are one of only three people who knows where he is. Your mother made it four, but sadly she died before we could get to her. The other two are the director of the LOA for the east coast of the USA and the agent who put him there. We can't get to either of those without having some pretty serious trouble heading our way before we're prepared. So, it's down to you.

"You see, Layla, we've been searching for you since the day your mother died. We were searching for her, but she was smart: changed her last name, got fake IDs, the whole thing. And she taught her daughter to do the same."

He walked over to the door, and someone beyond Layla's vision passed him a small purse, which Elias showed to her. "This is yours, yes?"

Layla nodded.

Elias opened it. "Layla Starsmore. That's what everyone knows you as, yes?"

Layla nodded.

"Fake name, fake credit cards, and fake bank account. I'm sure if we traced this, we'd find a fake rental agreement for your apartment . . . sorry, flat. I've been in America too long. Everyone knows you as Layla Starsmore. But your real name is Layla Cassidy. Your mother was Elizabeth Cassidy. Your father is Caleb Cassidy. Otherwise known as the All-American Ripper."

Layla nodded.

"Caleb is a hero of mine."

Layla looked up. "What?"

"Your father. He murdered three hundred and eighteen people in a twenty-year period. Do you know why they call him the All-American Ripper?"

"Because he killed people in every state."

"Yes, but it's not true. Although I guess the media would never let facts get in the way of a good name. He never killed in Hawaii or Montana. Not once. And he didn't rip people apart either. He used different methods depending on the situation."

"He murdered over three hundred people. I'm not sure why anyone would be so happy about that."

"Three hundred on the outside. Some idiot put him in with the general population when he first arrived in jail. Do you know the number for the eight hours he was there?"

"Nine," Layla said. She didn't want to tell the story again, to go into how her father had killed six inmates in three minutes in the prison showers. She'd heard it all before. A guard had been bribed by another prisoner to let him and some of his friends into the shower room while her father was in it. It turned out that the prisoner had been related to one of her father's victims, and wanted revenge. After killing the six men, her father had left the shower room and killed the guard who'd brought the attackers. Once the killing was over, her father had cleaned himself up and waited for the guards to come and take him back, but two more prisoners turned up first, so he killed them both.

Layla had been given a briefing about it. And another one, six months later, when he'd managed to escape and get into the cells of eight more inmates, killing them all in the space of one hour while the guards assumed he was in his cell. She knew that even mentioning this to Elias would bring him joy. And while she couldn't physically fight back, she could stop him from feeding off the pain of those memories.

"And you don't think that's impressive?" Elias asked when it became apparent that Layla would not respond. "The LOA think he had inside help. Nothing was ever proven. Since then he's been moved to a secure location, and no one outside of the LOA knows where he is. No one except you, that is."

Elias clapped his hands together with glee. "I love talking about him. He's just so inspirational. So many murders, so many ways of killing, he was just so professional for all of those kills. He never let his emotions override his desire to do what needed to be done."

"The LOA? What are you talking about?"

Elias raised an inquisitive eyebrow. "You've never heard of the Law of Avalon? They were the ones who arrested your father."

"The FBI did that."

Elias laughed. "The FBI? Is that what they told you? Oh, my child, the FBI doesn't deal with people like your father. That's the LOA's role. It's just like them to keep something secret, especially when dealing with someone as proficient as your father."

"You sound like a fanboy. He murdered people."

"Yes, I guess I am a bit. Dara's parents were the Zodiac Killers. Everyone always assumed it was one, but he had help."

"You're a team of serial killers? That must be horrific in every single way imaginable."

"Well, we can't take every serial killer, or even every psychopath; most aren't exactly team-friendly. But we find the best and work with them."

"You want my father to help you find new serial-killer friends?" Layla guessed.

"Almost, yes. Do you know what your father is?"

"Broken."

Elias backhanded her across the face. "I don't like that word. We're not broken because we see the world differently."

After the initial shock of the blow, rage exploded inside of Layla. She wanted to hurt Elias for hitting her, to make him regret everything he'd done. She controlled her breathing and pushed the rage back down. "You murder people. For fun. What would you call it?"

"I don't murder for fun. I murder for lots of reasons, but not fun. As for why some of us kill, well, that's simple. It's predatory. Just like wolves, or lions. We're fulfilling a need to be the predators we were born to be. We're better than you, than *humans*. Your kind deserves to be beneath us, watching in awe as we decide whether you live or die."

"You *look* human."

"I am a redcap. I haven't been human for a few centuries now. No, like the rest of my group, I'm something better. You've already seen what the ogre and Dara can do, and felt Shane's power. We're going to find more people who think like we do, who know that we should be at the peak of power on this planet. And when we have our army, we'll burn those who dare oppose us."

Layla wanted to say that Elias was deluded, insane, a madman. But she didn't want to antagonize him further, and her face still stung from where he'd struck her. She wanted to hurt him for that, though. "Why do you want my father to help you?"

"What do you know of spirit scrolls? Did your father ever mention them to you?"

Layla was confused. "I don't know what you're talking about."

Elias sat back in his chair and smiled. "I see there's a lot he's been keeping from you. Your mother kept it from you too. She knew. She knew all about it. You think you ran and hid because of your dad? Your dad is in a maximum-security prison, in a part especially designed for people like him. Unless he's literally the A-Team and he makes a nuclear weapon, he's staying put. You were never running from your father."

"The media. We ran because my mother was terrified they'd hound us."

"The media didn't do anything. Everything about you and your mother was kept out of it, people in positions of power within the LOA made sure of that. No, you didn't run because of your father or his crimes; you ran because of us. You ran because the last thing your father told your mother before he was taken was to hide you. He knew we'd come for him through his family. He'd tried to prepare for it.

"For twenty years he killed criminals while working for the FBI in a serial criminal task force, and for twenty years we had no idea he existed. And then he got caught, and the people I work for got wind of it, and now there's a man right there who can help us. It's taken seven years to find you, Layla. And you're going to do what we want. You're going to help us make your father work with us."

"I'm not interested in his crimes. He's in prison, and he deserves to be there. And you getting him out isn't going to help."

"Oh, we're not going to get him out. No, he wouldn't be a team player. We just need his help. So, here's what's going to happen. You're going to contact him and tell him we have you. We're going to ask him really nicely to help us find some people who are outside of our area of influence, and if he refuses, we're going to start cutting pieces off you."

Layla knew she should be scared, and deep down she was, but a righteous fury took over, and all she wanted to do was reach over and beat Elias until he could no longer speak, until his face was a mash of pulp. It was more than just a need to fight; it was a need to hurt. Not in self-defense like with Rob or her neighbors, but for the pure *need* to hurt the person in front of her. She'd felt such anger before in her life, although it had been long ago, but it was terrifying and liberating to feel it course through her again. She wondered for a brief second if that was how her father felt when he killed someone, and then just as quickly as it had come, she forced herself to be calm, and the anger vanished.

Elias got up and walked around Layla, making the anger flicker back inside of her.

He removed her handcuffs and picked up the chair he'd been sitting on, placing it against the far wall, retrieving his hat as he walked past. "We'll be back in a few hours with food, and there's water in the tap over there." He pointed toward a sink that Layla hadn't even realized was there, she'd been so focused on what was in front of her.

Elias stopped at the doorway. "When I come back, I'm going to ask you to help us. If you say no, I'm going to hurt someone badly. You might be thinking we won't kill you, and you're right. But, my dear, there are many, many worse things than death, and if you mess me around, I'll show you a few of them."

"My father doesn't care about me," Layla almost screamed. "He pretends to be this person with emotions, with feelings, but none of it is real. He's a monster hiding inside a human body. You could kill me and he'd barely notice. He won't listen to me; he certainly won't do anything to help me. I don't even know where exactly he is."

Elias smiled. "You underestimate the power of a daughter in her father's affections. We know he loves you. We would not be doing this if we were not certain of his devotion to his daughter. You say he doesn't care? Well, I think he cares a great deal." He tipped his fedora toward her and left the room, locking the steel door behind him.

Layla sat on the chair, not knowing what to think, and for the first time since the death of her mother, she cried. Not for herself, not for her situation, but for all of those who had died to get her here. She cried for those who had died for what appeared to be a madman's insanity. She cried for not fighting back, for wanting to fight back, for the inevitable drift toward her father if she allowed her control to waver. And when she finished crying, when there was no more to give, she was left with a hollow feeling inside of her. A feeling of regret and sorrow. But alongside it was an ember of rage. And that was what would sustain her, and help her get free.

8

"Can I assume that could have gone better?" Dara asked as Elias entered the main room of the underground compound they currently called home. It was furnished with several large sofas, a table with an open laptop on it, and a big TV. Elias's employers had built the compound as a last-resort retreat for when things got bad and they needed somewhere to hide. So far, it hadn't been necessary.

"Where is everyone else?" he asked her, ignoring her mocking tone.

"Shane is playing cards with our helpers, and Reyes is in the gym beating the crap out of a punch bag. She's lucky she heals fast."

"And Brako?"

"Sleeping further down in the compound. We don't need him now; it's better to let him have his rest. A grumpy ogre is a bad ogre."

Elias had to admit she had a point. Maintaining control over an ogre was a delicate balance between allowing them to kill and keeping them fed. They didn't eat human flesh, so it meant bringing in a steady supply of sheep and cows.

"How have *our helpers* been?"

"You like that phrase?" Dara said with a smile. "Creepy, as usual. I don't honestly know why you brought them."

"Nergal told me to bring them, so bring them I did. Doesn't mean I have to use them for anything but the most menial of tasks. They're just as bad as Brako in terms of enjoying the death and blood a bit too much."

"Well, it's right there in their name. Blood elves."

Elias was about to reply when the laptop beeped. He walked over and opened Skype, seeing a picture of Nergal.

"Is it done?" Nergal asked, getting straight to business.

"Yes, we have her. She's been given some time to consider her options. I imagine she'll refuse at first, and we'll have to follow through with the threat to kill people in front of her."

"You're using her friends?"

Elias shook his head. "We took some of her work colleagues. We'll use them first. I didn't want to go straight to anyone she's close to in case we have no leverage to go anywhere after. Honestly, she's not the type to let innocent people die. She'll help."

"Excellent. I expect you on a plane this afternoon."

"You don't want me to stay and oversee this? I really do need to visit my old home. It's almost time to recharge."

"The recharging will have to wait. Someone else can oversee Layla, that's why you took your team. The compound misses you, Elias. I think you being there brings a calming influence to those living within its walls. Without you, a few of them thought they had a chance of escaping. Examples were made."

Elias sighed. Nergal had executed more of the subjects at the compound. "I usually let them escape, kill them outside of the compound."

"You suggest I did the wrong thing?"

Elias quickly shook his head. He was always happy to give his opinion, but telling his boss he was wrong was a good way to get hurt. He'd seen it more than once and he didn't want to be the person receiving that kind of treatment. "I just like to give them a little hope that the escapees made it. It means you can crush it later if they get out of hand.

It's why I haven't put Layla on a jet back to you yet. I want her to think she has a chance to leave this place if she helps us. Flying her across an ocean removes that hope, makes her less likely to help outright."

Nergal appeared to think on this, then nodded. "I will try your way if it comes to it. Hopefully the leak has been plugged. I believe those you stopped before you left had given instructions for others to use a second escape route. I didn't realize your job here was so involved."

In other words, Nergal had assumed that Elias's job as head of the compound was easy. That sounded about right. "I'll be on the jet as soon as possible and back tonight. I'll debrief you then, and we'll arrange the extradition of Layla once we have her confirmation of assistance."

"This is the start of something glorious, Elias. Soon, we'll start our army. We can rule this world."

"I look forward to it." Elias ended the call as Dara chuckled.

"Got something you want to say?" he asked her.

"Nergal has no idea, does he?"

"He knows exactly what he's doing. He's making sure that those left in the compound are happy when I return. Eighty percent of the people there are there because they *want* to be. We have no trouble. It's the twenty percent who want to flee, who came to us and then decided to back out. They're the problem. And twenty percent is a big deal when it's a hundred people. By the time I get back, Nergal will already have found willing replacements for those he killed."

"Why not just kill those who don't want to be there?" Shane asked as he entered the room. "I was listening in."

"Because some of them are there to show us what happens when it all goes wrong. We need people loyal to us, who have the mental fortitude to deal with taking the power we're giving them. Those who aren't, those who refuse, are kept there to see just how long they can refuse, and what happens when they do. And now I have to go back and sort that out, instead of getting Layla to join us. Dara, you're not to talk to her."

"Excuse me?" Dara asked.

"You murdered people she worked with. She hates you, and if she doesn't, she'll at least resent you. Besides, I have another job for you. Shane, this is for you to deal with."

Shane smiled.

Elias stared intently at the younger man. "You screw this up, and I'll skin you alive and feed you to the blood elves. Not an exaggeration."

The smile faltered. "She's not my type."

"Keep it that way."

"So, what do I do?" Dara asked.

"You're coming with me. Shane and Reyes can cope for a few hours, and we can talk about compound security while we're on the plane. After that, I want you to fly straight back here, and then, if she's being helpful, you can bring her and everyone else back to the compound."

Dara sighed. "Twenty hours of flying is not my idea of a fun time."

"Don't care, it's your job. We need to talk about security; we can't have any more breakouts. Eventually, I want Layla's father out of that prison and in our custody. We can't do that without making sure he's no danger to us or anyone else."

"You really like this guy, don't you?" Shane asked.

"Caleb Cassidy is a genius, and one of the most dangerous people on the planet. He worked with the FBI for over two decades while maintaining his hobby as a murderer. He kept meticulous diaries of every single kill. Their names, location, reason for killing, method of killing. Everything. He has an incredible amount of power at his disposal. No one should underestimate him. Ever."

"Did you know that we found loads of scrolls in this compound?" Shane asked with a smirk. "Any chance some of those are spirit scrolls?"

Elias shrugged. "Be my guest and go through them. I know allies of Nergal used this place to study the spirit scrolls before they were shipped all over the world. A few of them might have remained. I assumed Nergal and his allies would have taken all of the scrolls, but it's not like we're short of them, so maybe they were left here for safekeeping."

"Gives me something to do between talking to Layla."

"Leave her for twenty-four hours. Give her food every six. Normal food, nothing weird, nothing pissed on. We want her help. It's one thing to threaten, it's another to begin torturing her before we've even given her a chance to say yes. We're not monsters."

"Speak for yourself," Dara said with a smile.

"And keep Reyes away from her," Elias continued, ignoring Dara. "I don't need to hear about deaths or injuries. Clear?" He didn't actually think that Reyes would do anything—she was a professional after all—but he had to say it nonetheless. Even if it was just to make himself happier.

Shane nodded. "Anything else?"

Elias shook his head, and Shane walked off.

"He'll do fine," Dara said when they were alone.

"I know. I just like to be in control, and this is important. Nergal has been after a way to track down those who already have scrolls, and Caleb Cassidy is our best chance of doing that. We need to be able to find those who escaped our grasp, or who are working against us. Caleb can help us find them all and remove them or force them to help. This is a game changer. I won't be the one to make a mistake here. I won't be the one who has to go to Nergal and tell him it's not happening. He'll kill us all for that."

Dara shivered slightly. "Let's get going. You think Layla will agree to help before I get back here?"

Elias glanced over at the door leading to the cells. "That woman is going to help us, or she's going to bathe in the blood of innocents until she does. And either way is fine with me."

9

It didn't take Layla long to get her emotions under control and prioritize what she was going to do about her current circumstances.

She wasn't going to stay there and wait for Elias and his band of crazies to come and kill her, that was for certain. She had to get out. Had to figure out how to do that too. Her father might have spent years training her how to fight, but he hadn't trained her to fight an ogre. That was something even his sick, warped mind hadn't foreseen.

Being alone in the cell allowed Layla to get her first real look at her surroundings. The room was large: twenty feet square, according to the rough measurements in Layla's head. The floor was a mixture of old stone and concrete, with the walls and ceiling constructed entirely of cold, gray concrete. It had been created in haste, and the concrete had set with bumps and jagged parts jutting out from it.

A sink, once white enamel and now a speckled gray color, sat against one wall. Layla ran her finger over it and found that it was covered in concrete powder and dust. She took a good look at the door. It was thick and well made, and appeared to have been created almost entirely of steel. That made it about as impossible to get through as a door could be.

She sighed. She wasn't in the best situation of her life, but refused to give in to the fear that bubbled up inside of her. She looked up at the single light in the center of the room, the dim glow doing little to help her spot any loose bits of wall that might be a sign of a structural weakness. It was a long shot, but at that exact moment in time, long shots were all she had left.

She turned back to the door and kneeled down in front of it, staring at the lock and remembering the hours and days of lessons with her father. Continuously practicing unlocking locks of all different shapes and sizes. By the time she was nine, she could open pretty much anything. The lock in front of her was something normally seen on cell doors. Picking it would require something a bit more robust than anything she had on her, and even then she wasn't sure she *could* actually pick it. She needed a key. And she doubted that she was going to be able to get her hands on one anytime soon.

Layla rested her forehead against the cool metal door and wished she could think of a way out. She walked over to the rear wall, searching for any way to escape. Considering they were a considerable distance underground, she wasn't exactly surprised at the lack of windows, but at least they would have given her some hope.

There was a stone slab just in front of the wall that was slightly raised in comparison to the rest of the cell. She stood on the slab and it wobbled, as if not quite set.

At this point, she would be happy to take anything useful, and she tried to dig her fingers into the side of the stone, but there wasn't a big enough gap, and the stone was far too heavy for her to lift alone. She looked around the room, desperate to find a solution, something to use as a lever, but there was nothing. She wasn't really sure what she'd expected; just because the stone was loose, it wasn't like she was going to dig herself to freedom. She got up from the floor and walked over to the sink, ran the tap, and washed her hands free of the dirt and mud.

She watched as the water disappeared down the plughole, which was really just one big hole with no grate.

In her haste to clean her hands, she'd forgotten to remove the silver ring her mother had given her on her sixteenth birthday, and she watched it drop down the plug into the darkness beyond.

Layla screamed as the frustration of what had happened to her threatened to overpower her senses. She took a deep breath, stepped to the side of the sink, and kicked the white plastic waste pipe that ran into the wall. She kicked it over and over, dislodging the pipe from the sink, spilling water all over the floor. She grabbed hold of the pipe and moved it from side to side, until she heard something crunch and she ripped it free, along with part of the wall it was attached to, causing her to fall back on her butt.

She stared in the pipe and found a mass of gunk at the end furthest from the plughole, where the pipe was attached to a wooden board that had been painted to look like concrete. Presumably it was the idea of whoever had done the plumbing, so that if anything did block it, the people here didn't have to smash open concrete to get to the problem. Layla pulled the mess of stuff she didn't want to think about out of the hole, and the ring fell onto the floor with a satisfying noise. It was a small thing, but it had been her happiest moment in days.

It was immediately followed by a glimmer of hope as she saw the hole where the pipe and wooden board used to be, on the wall. She dropped the pipe and moved over to the hole she'd created, gagging at the smell of stale water. There were no plumbing pipes, just a big hole that went down into the darkness beyond. It was big enough for her to climb into, although it would be a tight squeeze. Even so, it was go down there into who knows what, or stay in a cell where she would be forced to help murderers and monsters. There was barely any decision to be made at all.

She grabbed hold of the piece of pipe she'd just broken and dropped it down the opening, listening to it bounce around like a pinball on its way down. She was about to try to squeeze into the hole when the door opened and a creature walked in.

Layla glanced back and paused, watching the thing enter the room, its red eyes staring at her with anger.

"What are you doing?" it demanded, dropping the tray of food onto the floor with a clang, spilling some sort of mashed potato or vegetable onto the concrete.

"There's no water," Layla said quickly. "There's part of the pipe missing."

"Move." The creature walked over to the sink and began to look into the hole.

The creature wasn't human, Layla was certain of that, but it was humanoid. It had mauve skin with blotches of darker or lighter purple across its bare arms. Long brown hair flowed from the top of its bumpy skull and across its shoulders. It wore deep red, leather armor, and carried a vicious sword at its hip the likes of which Layla hadn't ever seen outside of a fantasy film. The sword was black, curved, and had the appearance of something used solely to cause pain. From the look it had given her upon entering the cell, Layla got the impression that causing pain was something the creature enjoyed.

The creature's black eyes looked up at Layla, checking that she'd moved far enough back. It smiled, showing a row of razor-sharp teeth, each one a small red triangle.

"Move and die," it snapped, and went back to looking in the hole.

Layla darted forward, and as the creature looked away from her, drove her knee into the side of its head. The skull bounced off the enamel sink, and she drove her knee in once again, crushing its nose. When it moved she took hold of its forehead and repeatedly smashed the back of its head against the sink, causing black blood to spill out from the wound. She let the creature fall to the floor, before stomping on its face several times in an effort to knock it out.

Layla grabbed the sword, pulling it free from the creature's side, and was about to drive the blade through its chest when she paused. She couldn't kill, she just couldn't. She wouldn't be like her father. She spun the blade and smashed the hilt into the side of the creature's head. It finally stopped moving.

Layla found the cell keys on the floor and ran out of the room, closing and locking the door behind her as she went. She stopped. Elias had told her that those people who had survived the attack on the train depot were going to be brought here. She needed to figure out if she could save them. But she didn't even know where to start looking.

She kicked the door with the toe of her shoe. What if he'd been lying? What if she found them and they were already dead, or couldn't make it out of here? Right there and then she knew that she couldn't spend time looking for anyone else that might be trapped here. Elias and his people would just capture her again. She needed to get to the police, to tell them what had happened so that they could come and deal with it. Somehow.

Layla kept hold of the sword and searched around the cavern she found herself in, looking for any incoming threats. Instead, all she found were several stalagmites and a small stream.

It wouldn't be long before her captors realized she was missing and went looking for her, and Layla wanted to be as far from here as possible when that happened. Where *here* was, she had no idea, but there had to be a way to get back up the stairs toward the lift and her freedom.

She walked down the stream, following several lights that had been set up around the area, until it took her into a gigantic cavern. Stalagmites and stalactites fought for numeric supremacy, leaving little space for her to get around without walking through the middle of the stream. Occasionally, she saw movement out of the corner of her eye, and wondered just how big the insects got this far under the earth. She increased her pace.

After walking through several more chambers, Layla eventually came to a set of brick stairs leading up toward a tunnel. She walked up the stairs and into the tunnel, following its incline for several minutes until she arrived at a steel door. There was no lock, or even a keyhole, and she pushed it open with a squeal loud enough to wake the dead. She stepped through into a corridor, although this one reminded her of the cell where she'd been kept, all concrete slabs and gray brick.

She followed the tunnel until it opened out, showing her three new paths to take, but with no clue as to which one was actually the escape she desperately needed.

"He's been gone too long," a voice shouted from one tunnel. She counted that tunnel as a bad idea, and ran down another. It snaked for a few minutes, and then she smelled blood. She stopped walking, flattening herself up against the wall, moving slowly along it. Lights hung from the ceiling every few dozen feet, but about halfway between each one was a patch of darkness. Metal boxes and stacks of building supplies were left all over the tunnel, and Layla used them to cover herself as best she could.

As she moved further down the tunnel, the sounds of crunching and slurping echoed around her. She began to see thick metal bars on one side, with a huge space behind them. The bars stretched along as far as she could see, each bar twelve feet high and a foot in diameter. She continued on, until she could no longer use old boxes for cover, and looked into the darkness of the cavern behind the metal bars.

What had once been a sheep was lying on its side in the center of the floor. The sheep's head and legs were missing, as was most of the flesh around the section of the ribcage that Layla could see. She ducked back and took a few deep breaths, before turning back to the sight before her.

Behind the remains of the sheep was the ogre. He had part of a sheep leg in one hand and was ripping lumps of flesh off with the other and putting them into his waiting mouth. Occasionally he made a noise of contentment.

There was no chance the ogre wouldn't see Layla coming out from behind the large crate she was crouching behind, and there was fifty feet of open tunnel before she could make it past the creature's cage. She studied the bars, hoping they would hold if he tried to do something. The door to the cage had a huge lock on it, and Layla wondered whether it would work. She took a deep breath and stepped out into the open, walking steadily toward the end of the cage.

"Hello, little one," Brako the ogre called out. "I could smell you."

Layla froze as the ogre tossed the sheep's leg aside. "Be on your way."

Fear gave way to confusion. "Why aren't you going to chase me?"

"I'm locked in here. I couldn't even if I wanted to. Besides, you're not going to get far, and I've just eaten. I didn't eat your friends, by the way. I killed them, but I don't eat people. Don't like the taste."

Anger bubbled up inside of Layla.

"Want to kill me, little one?" Brako asked. "Bet you do. You can't, though. You're just a little human, barely capable of doing much aside from breeding and dying. Run along, little one, they'll find you soon enough, so you might as well give them some sport before they do."

Layla turned and sprinted away from Brako and the stench that surrounded him. She eventually came to a flight of metal stairs, which she ascended slowly, hoping she wasn't making too much noise, wincing with every step that brought unwanted sound.

When she reached the top, she found herself in an identical tunnel to the one she'd just left. A moment of despair hit her. She had no idea where she was going, or where this new tunnel would lead; she was just running, and sooner or later she'd come across those hunting her.

She forced the thought aside; she could be upset later, when she wasn't in danger. Now was the time for keeping it together and forging on. A few minutes later she came to another fork in the tunnel; she picked the turning closest to her, running down it until she passed a door that was standing ajar. Hearing noises up ahead, she ran into the room in a panic, closing the door behind her.

The room was easily the size of the cavern the ogre lived in, but instead of monsters and death, it contained scrolls. There were thousands upon thousands of them, each tied with string and stacked on the shelves. Two sets of stairs led to a walkway above. It reminded her of a library. She picked up the closest scroll and unfurled it. In the top left-hand corner there was a yellow sticker with the number 936 written on it. But the rest of the scroll was written in a language she'd never seen before that appeared to use runes or glyphs of some kind. She couldn't begin to think where it had come from.

She put it down and looked at a few others. Each one had a different number and different writing; she couldn't read any of them. She quickly gave up and walked between two of the huge shelving units. It didn't take long to reach the end, but she'd counted a dozen separate rows, each with four different shelves. A huge amount of information. Part of her wanted to start going through them, to discover what they were, but she needed to leave, needed to put more distance between herself and those pursuing her.

Layla walked back toward the door, hoping to figure out if whoever she'd heard had gone. But before she was halfway there, the door began to slowly creak open. She darted back behind the nearest set of shelves, peering through the scrolls, hoping the darkness that surrounded her concealed her from whoever was entering.

"Are you in here?" The voice was deep, guttural. "Come out and play."

The words sent a shiver down Layla's spine, but she dared not move, dared not draw any attention to herself. She gripped the hilt of the sword tightly, her knuckles turning white from the pressure. She wanted to show them she was not afraid, to show them exactly what happened to those who cornered her, but she knew it would only get her captured, or worse.

Layla watched the creature walk over to the stack of shelves on the far side and sniff the air, before repeating the same behavior on the side of the room closest to her. Even though Layla was four rows back, she still held her breath.

"Did you find anything?" a second creature said as it entered the room, this one shorter than the first, with a bald head.

"Smells of musty paper in here. We should check the shelves on each side, upstairs too."

"You're welcome to," the bald one said, and left the room.

The first creature took another look around and sniffed again. "If you're here, we'll come back for you. You can't hide forever." It left the room and she heard the familiar and awful sound of a key engaging the lock.

Layla ran to the door and placed her ear against it, but heard nothing. She looked through the keyhole, but there was no sign of whatever those creatures were. She tried the key she'd taken from her jailer, but it didn't fit. She sank to her knees. She was trapped once more, and this time she doubted she'd be able to find a way out before someone found her. All of her hard work for nothing. Well, if she was going to be caught, she was going to make it hard for them to get to her. She'd take every single scroll she could find and stack them up in front of the door; maybe that would buy her some time.

Layla reached up to the shelf above, intending to use it to pull herself up, but she grabbed a sharp piece of metal, slicing through the palm of her hand. She cried out, then quickly forced herself to be silent. Her hand was bleeding and she grabbed several sheets of paper, pressing them hard onto the wound.

The paper soon turned red, so Layla grabbed several more sheets, all of which had notes about the scrolls on them. She started to read them, but they, too, soon turned red. All out of paper, she picked a scroll from the nearby shelf and used that. When the bleeding finally slowed, she saw that the cut wasn't long, but it was deep enough that it would need stitches.

Layla kept a tight grip on the scroll, just in case, and got to her feet. She searched through another pile of scrolls until she found a piece of string long enough to enable her to wrap the paper round her hand and tie it tightly in place.

She took a step forward and the world began to spin, causing her to crash to her knees between two shelves.

Do you accept the gifts we can give you?

The voice appeared to come from all around the room. Layla shook her head, forcing herself back to her feet. The door swung open and the creature who'd been in the room earlier, the one who had sent a shiver up Layla's spine, walked in. It turned its head toward Layla and smiled. Layla was directly in its line of sight.

"I knew you were in here," it said.

Do you accept the gifts we can give you?

"Who keeps asking that?" Layla shouted. "Why are you doing this?"

"Asking what?" the creature said.

This is a blood elf. It will kill you. Do you accept the gifts we can give you?

"What gifts?" Layla shouted.

"Who are you talking to?" the creature asked, looking around to ensure it wasn't about to be attacked.

"Blood elf," Layla stammered.

The shock in the elf's eyes was easy to see. "How do you know of my kind?" It drew its sword and took a step forward. "You will answer my question."

Layla noticed that she'd left the sword she'd taken from the blood-elf jailer by the door. She had no way of defending herself against an armed opponent.

Do you accept the gifts we can give you?

Layla stared at the creature walking toward her. She wanted to fight, and she wanted to win. "Will you help me fight?" she asked the voices.

The blood elf stopped. "I'll help you scream."

Yes.

"Yes, then. Please help me. I accept."

And Layla's whole world vanished into darkness.

10

The second Layla accepted the offer she found herself looking down on her body, which was no longer under her control. She hated it.

She watched from afar as the metal shelves closest to her exploded toward the blood elf, impaling it with a dozen foot-long spikes. The elf dropped to its knees, blood pouring from multiple wounds. Layla's body picked up the blade the blood elf had relinquished and examined it. The metal in the sword liquefied and traveled over her hand and forearm before solidifying into a gauntlet.

Her body retrieved the scroll at her feet, sliding it down the inside of her jeans against her outer thigh, and kicked the blood elf onto the ground. She stepped over its body and walked toward the door.

"The first time you accept the spirits in the scroll is always like this." The female voice was all around Layla, and she couldn't figure out who'd spoken. She could see no one other than her own body, which appeared to be moving of its own accord.

Layla's body and the scroll room vanished, and she found herself in an old-fashioned carriage, like something out of a period movie. Blinds covered the windows and the seats were comfortable and soft. The sound of a horse galloping could be heard outside.

"Surreal, isn't it?" a young woman asked. She was dressed in dark gray trousers, a green blouse, sturdy boots, and a long dark green coat.

"Who are you?" Layla asked. "And where am I?"

"You're in your mind. Well, my memories, which are in your mind. It's a bit strange."

"Where am I?"

The woman smiled. She had long, dark, braided hair. A scar ran from one eye and across her nose, stopping just above her lip. Her skin was pale, and she wore little or no makeup. An emerald pendant sat around her slender neck, the chain made of silver. Rings adorned several of her fingers, except the wedding finger, and her fingernails were painted black.

"A knife," she said with another smile, touching the scar. She had a nice smile; it was disarming, but it was at odds with the feeling of danger that emanated from her. "The woman who did it is no longer with us."

"Please don't make me ask a third time." Layla was getting impatient, and her tone suggested that she did not appreciate what was happening. She wanted to lash out, but fought to remain calm.

"Well, right now, one of the other spirits is in control of your body. A woman. There are three of us in total, but it was decided that I was better suited to talking to you. I'm sure you'll meet the other two later. The spirit in charge of your body at the moment is called Gyda. She's going to get you out of the situation you're in, and when you're safe, put you back in your body. It's all part of the service we provide. At least it is the first time; after that, none of us can take control. As for where we are, we're in my time, 1873, London. My name is Rosalie Kendall. You may call me Rosa."

"I'm Layla Cassidy. And I don't understand any of this."

"You will. You'll come to understand a lot about your world and your life. A world you never knew existed, but has existed since the dawn of civilization, maybe even longer. But for now, you're safe. Gyda won't allow your body to be hurt. We are capable of using your new powers right now. Eventually, you too will be able to access them, but it will take time. Time we don't have."

Layla shook her head. "Scrolls, spirits, power. What power?"

"You bled on a spirit scroll, a scroll that contains the spirits of those who wielded it before you. Bleeding on it is the start of a binding contract between you and the inhabitants of the scrolls. In this case, us. You then accepted the offer of our gifts."

"The power, is that what they did with the metal?"

Rosa nodded. "The spirits in the scroll grant a unique ability to whoever accepts our offering. We have no way of knowing what the ability will be until it's bestowed. In your case, it appears that you have the power to manipulate metal."

Layla's first thought was that everything she was being told was insane. There was no way it could be anything else. It was quickly replaced by the realization that Rosa was telling the truth. "I could use my power to break free. I could use it to escape." She felt elated that she finally had a means with which to fight back, and a means with which to stop more innocents from dying because of her.

Rosa shook her head. "As I mentioned before, you don't have control over your powers yet. You'd get yourself killed."

Layla rubbed her eyes as frustration began to set in. "But I *can* fight."

"I know. But right now, you can't fight these enemies. Your time will come, but you need to have patience. I promise you, you'll get your turn to deliver any and all the retribution you can muster."

Layla knew that Rosa was making sense, but that didn't mean she had to be happy about it. After several seconds of silence, she decided to change the subject. "So, what was yours? Your power, I mean."

"We'll get to that. You'll have more time to meet us all, to see how we lived and what we bring to the table. And then you have to pick one of us."

"Why?"

"Because one of us will become your teacher. Someone has to train you how to use your new abilities. We can't have you running around without knowledge."

Layla reached for the curtain on the nearest window, and Rosa leaned over to stop her. "Don't. The barrier between my memories and . . . the . . . demon is weak. You don't want to look out there right now."

Layla removed her hand. "Demon?"

Rosa sighed. "This is all information for much later. For now, just sit back and enjoy the show." The carriage roof vanished, replaced with a picture of what Layla's body was doing, as if she were watching it on a giant drive-in movie screen. "These people kept you prisoner. Some turnabout is fair play."

"You killed that blood elf."

Rosa nodded. "This isn't your old world. This isn't a world where you get to leave your enemies alive. And it wasn't human."

"I'm not sure that matters. You used my body to murder someone. I'm not that person. I'm not like my father." The anger that she felt at having her body used to commit murder was all-consuming. She couldn't believe that the one thing she'd fought against for so long had happened without her even being in control.

"Your morals will have to wait until you're in a more secure place."

"Stop the carriage," Layla snapped, her voice hard and cold.

Rosa shook her head.

Layla darted forward, grabbed hold of the curtain across one window, and shoved it aside just enough to see what was outside. She clamped one hand over her mouth and moved back to the far side of the carriage, still holding the curtain, pulling it free.

The carriage was in the middle of some woods, circling around a glade. In the center of the glade was a large cage, shrouded in darkness except for two eyes that burned red inside it. The occupant grabbed hold of the bars and screamed, as terrifying power tore across the clearing.

Layla opened her mouth to speak, but Rosa tapped her on her forehead and she fell into a deep sleep.

She will be mine, the creature in the cage said.

"No, she won't," Rosa told him without taking her eyes off Layla. "I'm sorry for this, but things will be easier when your emotions aren't so high."

She will never accept me. Never accept the darkness in her heart. I'll take her, just like I took Gyda. Poor Gyda. She lost so much. Maybe she can sit around and cry about it with Layla once I'm finished with her.

Rosa shook her head. "Be gone, demon. Your power is limited here, your reach small."

It won't stay that way.

"No, eventually you'll vanish into nothing, only coming when summoned to obey her commands for your power. You'll become a small memory that will plague no one."

The creature laughed, causing the carriage to reverberate as its power swept out across the glade. Rosa stared down at the sleeping Layla. "Please make me right. I would hate for you to become the monster we all have to fight against."

◆ ◆ ◆

Gyda had never taken control of a host before, but the link between spirits and host was weak when first established, and better her taking control than Layla getting killed. Or the demon freeing itself and slaughtering all before it. That would be much, much worse.

The blood elf that died in the scroll room was quickly forgotten. Gyda had been told about the blood elves' destruction of her ancestral home. Even though it had happened hundreds of years after she'd died, she still felt a rage at being unable to protect her people's way of life.

She'd hated the blood elves for their part in that. Hated them then, and hated them now. Killing them was never going to be an issue for her.

She ignored the remnants of her past and left the scroll room, moving into the corridor outside. She found the next blood elf several minutes later. It was leaning against a wall, its back toward her. She used the metal on her arm to create a spear and threw it toward the blood elf. The spear impaled the elf through the heart, pinning it to the concrete wall beside it. She tapped the metal spear as she walked past, and the metal became liquid once more, returning to her forearm. She watched the creature crumple to the ground, and felt nothing but happiness that there was one less of them alive.

Gyda continued on through the tunnel system, but found no more blood elves to fight. By the time she'd reached the lift and pressed the button to bring it down, she'd seen no one else. She was beginning to feel like she'd gotten away with her escape. The noise of the lift as it slowly moved down the shaft echoed around the large tunnel.

The lift had just finished its journey when Gyda spotted a young man walking toward her. She searched Layla's memories and found that his name was Shane.

"Now what do we have here?" he asked with a large smile.

"I'm leaving," Gyda told him.

"Not on my watch you're not. Reyes and the rest of those elves will be up here soon enough, so you should just give in, come back to your cell, and keep quiet. Just like a lady such as yourself is supposed to."

"I'm not going anywhere with you."

The smile faltered, just a little bit, but Gyda saw the darkness in Shane's eyes. She knew the type of man he was. She'd seen more than enough of them during her lifetime—killed more than enough of them too. One more wasn't going to make much of a difference.

He darted forward faster than Gyda had been expecting and grabbed hold of her arm, his grin widening. "I think you'll be a lot calmer now."

Gyda looked down at his hand, and then back up at his face. She smiled. "You're expecting something to happen, aren't you?"

She could see the crushing realization that something was terribly wrong as it hit Shane, but he didn't move fast enough to get away. Gyda drove her elbow into his jaw. Shane staggered back and Gyda kicked him in the chest, causing him to fall to the ground.

"That should have worked," Shane said, his nose and lip both bloody.

Gyda didn't reply as she went on the offensive, kicking out Shane's knee as he got back to his feet. He staggered slightly, but Gyda was faster and more aggressive, driving her knee into his chest. She grabbed the back of his head and brought it down onto her knee, before kicking him in the stomach, sending him up against the far wall.

Shane spat blood onto the ground and blocked a left-hand punch, ducking under it and striking Gyda in the stomach. Gyda moved back, showing no outward indication that she was injured. She hadn't felt pain for a long time and the physical sensation after so many centuries was almost too much for her senses to take, but she fought to ignore it. As she wasn't the host of the body, it would be a while before the pain wracking Layla's body would have any effect on Gyda's ability to use it. And, hopefully, by the time the body got used to her presence, she'd be able to let Layla back in control. She kept a distance from Shane as he drew a dagger from behind his back. It was seven inches long and slightly serrated on one side, with a wooden handle.

"I've used this a lot over the years," Shane told her, holding the knife down by his leg.

The metal covering Layla's hand and forearm began to shimmer, but Gyda didn't want to give away what she could do.

"Want to come back now?" Shane asked. "I really will get into trouble if I cut you, but I'm thinking a little off the ears won't cause too many problems for me. Maybe a finger. Something you can live without."

"How many have you killed?" Gyda asked.

Shane smirked. "Humans? Fourteen back in Texas, before these fine people found me and gave me a better purpose. That was ten years ago. Another dozen since then. Nonhumans? I stopped counting some time ago."

"People like you never stop counting." Gyda ran forward, dodging the swipe of the dagger, and drove her fist into Shane's stomach, igniting the power inside her at the same time. The metal around her hand and forearm tore into Shane as if he were made of paper, cutting through his body as a dozen thin blades punctured his stomach.

Shane gasped and dropped the dagger, before falling to one knee. "I always thought you were a sweet girl, Layla."

"Sorry, Layla is sleeping."

Shane's eyes widened in recognition and surprise. "She found a spirit scroll." It wasn't a question.

Gyda retracted the metal and wrapped it around her hand. She walked behind the kneeling Shane and placed her hand on the top of his head. "Final words?"

"They're going to . . ."

Shane never got to finish his sentence, as a scream from behind her caused Gyda to knock him out with a punch to the back of the head. She spun around to face the blood elf that had charged her, its wicked sword drawn. She transformed the metal into a sword and parried the blade the elf swung toward her. It didn't care how she died, it just wanted to kill.

It swung the sword with power rather than accuracy, and Gyda easily dashed back out of the blade's reach. She waited until the sword had moved far enough through another swing that it was no longer a threat and sprinted forward, driving her own blade up into the face of the blood elf, cracking through the skull, and killing the creature instantly.

She left the metal sticking out of the blood elf's skull, and went back to Shane, searching his pockets. She found a set of car keys and pocketed them. After using Layla's power to tear all the metal out of the controls so that no one could bring the lift back down, Gyda boarded and pressed the green button to take her to the outside.

It was a long journey, and she spotted Shane's allies arrive a minute after it had started. They screamed at her, but Gyda ignored them, the words all mixing into a torrent of abuse she barely gave any thought to. It wasn't until she heard the sound of a gun firing and felt a gut-wrenching pain tear through her arm that she used Layla's power to move most of the nonessential metal beneath the lift to create a shield against more shots. Blood ran freely from the bullet hole in her shoulder and every movement was an agony she'd forgotten could even exist, but she wasn't about to let it stop her escape.

As soon as she was outside in the darkness of the night, she spent a few seconds getting her bearings. The exit to the underground complex had taken Gyda up into a large wooded area. A hill sat behind her, and a dirt road ran just in front. She couldn't see much, except what moonlight managed to break through the leaves, but it did illuminate a white Range Rover parked just in front of a large tree. She removed the keys from her pocket and pressed the button to unlock the car, which it did with a click and flash of the head- and brake lights, illuminating the otherwise dark woods.

Gyda had no idea where she was, or how to get to safety, but after searching Layla's memories, she knew that she was several miles from a town. She hoped Layla's memories of driving would be enough, and took the vehicle out of the woods at a slow but steady pace. It was faster than running. Eventually she came to a main road and stopped, using the built-in sat nav to find the nearest hospital.

Gyda parked the car around the corner from the hospital and walked toward the entrance of their Accident and Emergency department. The automatic doors opened and Gyda allowed Layla to take back control of her body. Layla crumpled to the floor, the pain that crashed down on her almost too much for her to bear, as doctors and nurses rushed over to her.

11

Layla woke up early in the morning, the sun streaming through the window of the private room she'd been placed in. The heart monitor beside her bed beeped, and she sat up, her body aching. She wasn't sure whether or not she'd dreamed the previous day: being kidnapped, talking to a spirit, and the murder of the people she worked with. People she liked. She found a remote on a small table beside her, and used it to switch on the TV that was attached to the wall facing her bed. She was horrified to learn that everything had been real. The news was covering the attack, and she turned it up to be able to hear the reporter standing in a car park across the road from the depot. The electric gates that had opened for Layla only a short time ago could be seen behind her.

"Thirty-nine people died here last night in what police are calling 'an act of unparalleled brutality.' Details are few and far between, but what we do know is that those working in the depot were attacked by an unknown number of assailants; at the moment we know of thirty-nine victims of this attack. It happened not long after midnight, and police are urging anyone who heard or saw anything to come forward."

The remote fell from Layla's hand onto the bed, as the sound of the reporter's voice became a distant memory. Thirty-nine people were murdered because of her. Because Elias needed to get to her. Layla felt sick. She couldn't understand why anyone would do such a thing, why anyone would think that was their best option. She remembered Elias and those he worked with, and realized that they simply didn't care about anything but their insane goal. They would kill and maim and destroy with impunity until they were stopped.

She rubbed her eyes and switched off the TV, placing the remote on the table beside her. The door opened and Chloe stepped inside. She carried a blue carrier bag, which she dropped into a nearby chair once she'd seen that Layla was awake, then ran over and embraced her friend.

"Are you okay?" she asked, finally releasing Layla and taking her hand.

Layla tried to find the words to tell her what had happened, but instead rested her head against Chloe, while her friend wrapped her arms around her once again.

They stayed that way for several seconds, neither of them speaking. Layla was so glad to see her friend, a friend Elias had threatened to kill. Layla's escape had put people she cared about in danger; maybe she should have just stayed and contacted her father, told him to do whatever they wanted. At least that way, Chloe, Harry, and those she loved would be safe. She thought about survivors at the train depot. Was Elias telling the truth? Had he really spared people just to use them against her? After what Elias's people had done at the train depot, no one was safe. It wouldn't have mattered whether Layla had helped or not, if they'd wanted to go after her friends, there would have been nothing she could have done to stop it.

Eventually, Layla let go and lay back on the bed.

"They had to take a bullet out of your arm," Chloe told her. "Who did this to you?"

Layla was in the middle of telling Chloe everything—although she omitted the blood elves, and the fact that an ogre had killed everyone in the depot—when the door opened again and a man and woman walked in. The man was just under six foot in height, well built, and gave off an imposing presence. He had pale skin and wore a dark, well-tailored suit. Clearly he hadn't shaved for several days, giving him a rugged look. He glanced over at Chloe and a small smile creased his mouth. Layla wondered if the two had met before, presumably while she was asleep.

The woman was taller than the man by a few inches, her skin more olive in color. She wore a pair of black trousers and a red hoodie. While the man appeared to be from some sort of law enforcement agency, the woman looked like she was security or a bodyguard. She rolled up her hoodie sleeves, showing muscular forearms, and Layla had the impression that she could probably bench-press her if she so wished.

"Hi," the woman said, offering Layla her hand. "My name is Diana, and this is Thomas Carpenter."

Thomas waved a little, and Layla noticed Chloe smile and look away.

"You're police?"

They both shook their heads. "We're from an independent security firm," Diana told her. "Thomas here is the managing director of the company."

"Thomas, what's the company called?" Layla asked, wanting to remember to Google it later. She didn't know these people, and wasn't sure if she was meant to trust them.

"Enhanced Security, and you can call me Tommy." He smiled again, and Layla thought he had a nice smile, warm and inviting. She noticed the wedding ring on his finger, a simple band of white gold or silver, she wasn't sure which.

"I don't understand," Layla said. "I don't understand why you're here."

"They're here to help you," Chloe told her. "They spoke to me last night and asked if they could discuss the people who took you."

"Elias Wells is the person who kidnapped you, yes?" Tommy asked.

Layla nodded.

"He's a dangerous man," Diana said.

"He had thirty-nine people murdered to get to me, so I assume so. He told me that he took some of those working at the depot hostage. Elias said they were kept in the same place where they'd taken me. They're in danger."

"We found the car you used to escape. We checked the sat nav system and retraced the route you took last night," Tommy said. "Several armed agents are currently en route to find where you were kept and deal with any threats found there. Anyone who is there will be freed, you have my word."

Layla felt like a great weight had been lifted from her shoulders. She looked between Tommy and Chloe. "I don't understand why the police aren't dealing with this."

Tommy picked up a chair from a small table and placed it next to the bed. "Layla, we know that you went through a terrible ordeal last night. Several hours in their captivity, having to escape, being shot. It's a lot, but we deal with things the police can't. And Elias Wells is one of those things. You've seen what these people are capable of; the police just aren't equipped to deal with them like we are. We're here to make sure Elias is taken down. One way or another. I don't want to have to sit beside anyone else's bed telling them what I'm telling you. I don't want Elias free to hurt anyone else."

Layla told them all that had happened, but once again left out the blood elves, ogre, and she didn't mention the spirit scrolls at all. She wasn't sure exactly how much she could trust Tommy and Diana. Both of them listened intently without ever interrupting. Chloe held Layla's hand the whole time, which Layla greatly appreciated.

When Layla was finished, Tommy nodded. "Thank you. Is that everything?"

Layla nodded, although she was certain that Tommy wasn't convinced, but he said nothing about it.

"Thank you for your time," he said and got to his feet. "You're going to be staying in hospital for a few days, the gunshot needs to heal, and I've made sure to keep security on the door at all times. Diana here is your security."

Diana winked. "I've brought some books to read if you want any, and I'll be in the hall."

"What if I just want to go home?" Layla asked.

Tommy paused at the door. "Right now, this is the best place for you. The only people who will come to question you are me and Diana. No one else will come here that you don't know. The police are not involved in this side of the case, they're more interested in finding out who killed thirty-nine people last night, and even then that's only for the public. We're the ones looking into it, we're the ones trying to find Elias and anyone he kidnapped."

"Will you find him?"

Tommy nodded. "Finding him isn't the trick, it's getting him without him hurting innocent people. With you here, hopefully he'll think twice about coming for you, and if he doesn't, then Diana will be able to persuade him and his people."

Layla shook her head, no matter how in shape Diana appeared, there was little chance she could go up against the ogre and live. "One of his people is a monster. If it comes here people will get hurt."

"A monster?" Diana asked with a smile. "We'll be fine. We're on the seventh floor of Southampton General Hospital. You're the only person in a private ward. I will be outside your door for the next two days, and we've placed two more guards outside of this room who will check everyone coming and going. Tommy has been doing this an extraordinarily long time, he knows what he's up against."

"I doubt that," Layla said, but both of them were already through the door.

"They seem like they're good at their jobs," Chloe said.

"They're going to get hurt. The thing that came after me . . . it wasn't . . ." She paused, unsure how to continue.

"Wasn't what?"

This was it, the part where her friend either believed her or thought she was crazy. "It was an ogre. An actual, ogre."

For just a split second, Layla was certain she saw fear in her friend's expression. "I'm sure Tommy and Diana can handle an ogre," Chloe eventually said.

Layla was certain that Chloe was mocking her. "You don't believe me."

"If you say you saw an ogre, then you saw an ogre. Tommy and Diana seem like tough people, I'm certain they can handle anything thrown their way. Why wouldn't I believe you, Layla? There's enough weirdness in the world that occasionally you have to take a leap of faith. Besides, something had to attack those people, and I find it more comfortable to think it's a large monster than just some random nut job human with a gun and knife. Why didn't you mention this earlier?"

"Because they'd think I'm crazy. Ogres and the like, it's not exactly believable. It makes me sound like I've hit my head a bit too hard. Besides, I don't know them. I don't know anything about them."

Chloe took hold of Layla's hand and held her gaze. "Never think you're crazy. If you say there are ogres, there are ogres. That's all there is to it. I'll go tell Tommy and Diana what you just told me, and I'll be right back."

Chloe left Layla alone for a half hour, until she returned with a smile on her face. "Well, they said thanks for the info."

"So, they *didn't* believe me after all? They think I'm crazy?"

"Not at all. They said it'd mean they'd take extra precautions. Tommy said he's seen an ogre before."

Layla wasn't sure she'd heard her friend right. "You serious?"

Chloe nodded. "From talking to both of them, I'd say they've seen their fair share of weird shit. I get the impression they're trustworthy. I know you've been through a lot, but these people want to help."

Chloe stayed with Layla for several hours, until Harry arrived and wanted to know what had happened, and how he could help. It took several minutes to get him to accept that Layla was actually okay and that her shoulder was more sore than actually painful. The latter of which was something she found a little odd as she hadn't been given any painkillers apart from the odd paracetamol from a young nurse who'd stopped by a few hours before.

Eventually her friends had to leave, and Layla switched the TV back on, settling in for a long night alone. Chloe's bag had contained grapes, several bottles of water, and two massive bars of chocolate that got eaten by the three friends long before they'd left. There was also a pair of jeans, some underwear, and a few t-shirts, all of which Layla was exceedingly thankful for.

She wasn't sure exactly how much she believed Tommy and Diana's story. They were clearly security of some kind, but who had hired them, and why? How did they know where she was? Were they another part of Elias's plan? The answer was a resounding no. If they had been, Layla doubted they'd have allowed her to have Chloe and Harry in the room. As for the other answers, maybe the police had brought them in. She assumed that the hospital had contacted the police, who had contacted Tommy. Maybe Tommy and Diana did this sort of thing all the time, traveling the country and defeating monsters, like a UK version of *Supernatural*.

She'd mentioned the ogre, but why keep the blood elves and spirit scrolls to herself? To be honest, she wasn't even certain what the scrolls really were. Spirits inside a scroll giving her power? Maybe she'd had some kind of psychotic breakdown and used that as a way to justify what she'd done to escape. As for the blood elves, she had been going to mention it, until she saw Chloe's fearful reaction to the ogre. Layla wasn't so sure it was a good idea to add to that fear.

After a few minutes, Layla climbed out of bed and walked over to the mirror in the en suite bathroom. Although the bathroom was more functional than anything she'd seen in a hotel or house, she didn't have to share, and she was grateful for that. She unfastened the hospital gown and pulled it aside, revealing a white dressing on her shoulder. It was three inches square and secured in place with tape. She knew she should leave it, but she wanted to see how bad the injury looked, so she picked at the tape and slowly pulled one section of it free, causing a lot less pain than she'd been expecting. She removed the adjacent piece of tape and took a deep breath before pulling the dressing aside so she could see the wound.

A second later she tore the whole dressing off, dropping it into the sink as she stared at the complete lack of a bullet wound.

She'd been shot. She remembered being shot. Although she hadn't been in her body at the time, the memory of it was still there. As was the memory of her killing the second blood elf. She paused. She'd killed two people on her way out of the compound. She pushed the thought aside for the moment to deal with the fact that her bullet hole no longer existed. In its place was some tender scar tissue, but even that didn't look too bad.

"What the hell is going on here?" she asked herself in the mirror. For a second she half expected a monster to appear in the mirror beside her, but that didn't happen. More memories from the night before flashed into her head: her in a Victorian carriage, the cage in the center of the glade. The creature inside it.

"I need answers. I need to know what's happening to me."

You're becoming something more than human, a voice that she recognized as belonging to Rosa said inside her head. *Please don't do the "You're not real, this is all a dream" thing. I did it, and it was annoying.*

Layla knew it wasn't a dream; no one could have dreams where they actually got shot, not unless they were in *A Nightmare on Elm Street*.

We need to talk. Face to face. You need to learn who you are, and what has happened to you.

"And how do I go about doing that?"

For now, sleeping will lower the barriers between us. It takes a few days before we can appear easily to you when you're awake.

"You knocked me out."

I promise I will explain everything when you see me. I swear to you, I did what I needed to do to keep you alive.

She didn't know why, but she somehow knew that Rosa was telling the truth. She walked back into her hospital room and checked the time. It was only eight, but she wanted to know what was happening, what *had* happened. There really were spirits in her mind. It wasn't a psychotic breakdown, it wasn't some dream; it was real. She had power that she hadn't had before she'd accepted the scroll. She needed to learn how to use it, and talking to the spirits seemed like the best way.

Layla climbed into bed, and after initially tossing and turning, fell into a deep sleep.

12

Elias was over halfway to America by the time the call came in telling him of Layla's escape. He'd wanted the pilots to turn the private jet around immediately, but had been told doing so would make them crash in the middle of the ocean. Instead of continuing with any threats, he admitted that stopping in New York and refueling was the better option. But he hadn't been happy about it.

By the time they'd reached the private runway in New York, filled up, and set off again, several hours had passed, and Elias's mood hadn't improved.

"So, are you planning on telling me what our employer said?" Dara asked after several hours of silence. The jet was just about to begin its descent to the airfield in England.

"It wasn't the best conversation I've ever had with him. He seemed to be happier that the blood elf in charge of Layla is now dead. I had Reyes kill the elf, and told her to ensure that the rest of the blood elves know what happens to those who fail us. I don't think a second screw-up is going to be tolerated. On top of that, Shane was bested by Layla, a mistake I'm sure he'll want payback for."

"Ah, Shane. He was never quite the professional. Always looking for his next hunt, and having to rein himself in. I assume he survived the confrontation."

"It seems that way, yes, although I doubt he feels too good. We'll get more details when we get back to the compound."

"So, with Layla killing two blood elves in her escape, and Reyes killing the one who failed us, do we need more people?"

Elias shrugged. "There's five of us, and including the blood elves, ten. The boss said if we need it, he'll send extra staff, but I'm hoping this can be done with the numbers we have. We got caught out and royally spanked for it. I don't plan on making the same mistake with Layla again."

"How did she get out of the compound? How did she manage to kill two blood elves *and* disable Shane?"

"She took a spirit scroll. My guess is a spirit was in the driving seat. If it had been Layla, I doubt she'd have killed so quickly, and if it had been the demon, we'd have seen a smoldering crater where the compound had been. It would have stayed there and killed everything, or at least tried to."

"Her having a spirit scroll complicates things."

Elias rubbed his temples. He didn't really need Dara telling him something he already knew. "She won't be strong with her new abilities yet. We still have a few days before the bonds are complete. And I doubt she'll be in any hurry to accept the demon into her psyche, so she won't have anywhere near the power she could have. This is still a job we can complete without trouble. We just need to find her, get her, and get out of the country. No more hanging around there to get her to talk, no threatening her friends; just get her unconscious and on this jet. Nothing else matters. We've tried the easy way, now we make it hard on her."

Dara's expression of glee was all that Elias needed to see to know that she was looking forward to whatever came next. Elias had worked with Dara for several decades, and the pair had grown close. To him she was the most trusted, and in many ways, most valuable member of the team, and on more than one occasion that closeness had grown physical. "Even monsters need to love," she'd told him after their first night together, and Elias had to agree. They were both killers: murderers of the innocent, and not so innocent, in equal measure. He cared a great deal for Dara, and while he was sure she felt the same way, there was no indication that their relationship would ever be anything more. Settling down and growing old together is hard to do when those people might never grow old in the first place, when both of them enjoyed their work a bit too much to ever live peacefully in some suburban idea of paradise.

The plane landed at the same private airfield they'd taken off from the day before. Once the jet was stationary, the pilot opened the door to let everyone out. Ordinarily there would have been a steward to do that, but one hadn't been supplied on this occasion, and Elias wondered if that was a small measure of punishment by Nergal. He was certainly petty enough.

Elias found that the red Audi RS5 coupe was still parked in the spot he'd left it in, something he was grateful for. He didn't want to go looking for a car, and he'd taken a liking to the Audi.

"I'm hungry," Dara said as they both got into the vehicle.

"We'll grab some food after we've spoken to the rest of the team. I want to talk to them immediately," Elias said as he started the engine. The rest of the drive was completed in silence.

They reached the dirt road, stopping the car outside the entrance to the compound, and then rode the lift all the way to the bottom, where Shane met them.

"Evening, boss," he said, with a lot less cheer than usual.

"What happened to that?" Dara asked, pointing toward the lift-activation system.

"Our house guest removed all of the metal from it, frying it completely. I've had to completely rebuild the mechanism and circuitry.

Hopefully it works now, because otherwise getting out of here is going to be impossible."

"You haven't been out since she escaped?"

He shook his head. "Couldn't get the lift back down. I figured this was a better use of my time than what Reyes was doing."

"And *what exactly* was she doing?" Elias asked, putting just enough irritation into his words.

"She's been in the gym for the last twenty-four hours, pretty much. She hasn't exactly been a barrel of laughs. She took a shot at Layla when she was leaving too, put a round through her arm."

Elias wanted to hit something. "Reyes shot at Layla?"

"Lost her cool after Layla killed two of the blood elves. The rest had to stop her from taking a second shot."

"While you were unconscious," Dara said, irritated.

"Yes, Dara, while the spirit that had taken over Layla's body beat me like a drum. I don't know who it is she's got in there, but she fights like a demon . . . no pun intended."

"Just be grateful it wasn't the actual demon, or you'd be dead right now. Why didn't you use your own demon to fight her? Your power is right there." Elias tapped Shane on the chest.

"Didn't have time. Besides, when I activate the demon's power, I enjoy it a bit too much, if you catch my meaning."

Elias understood perfectly. If Shane had used the demon's power, he would have killed Layla. For a spirit-scroll user, tapping into their demon's massive well of power could be incredibly addictive, and some people found it difficult to put that cork back in the bottle.

Dara scoffed. "You're lucky she didn't kill you. Have you gone through the records and found out who her spirits are? That would have been a good way for you to spend your time."

"Well, I would have tried to figure out exactly *what* scroll she took, but I've been busy here. Besides, there are several thousand of the things, and while I know they are all numbered, it's not exactly easy to find out which one is missing."

"Enough," Elias snapped. "I'll go fetch Reyes. I want to see you all together in the mess room."

He walked into the makeshift gym and found Reyes hitting the punch bag like she was trying to tear it in half.

"We need to talk," Elias said.

"Later," Reyes snapped. "You can leave now."

Elias's eyes narrowed in anger. He darted toward Reyes, who turned at the last second as he grabbed her by the throat and slammed her into the wall.

"Not *later*," he seethed. "Now." He squeezed tightly. She tried to get loose, but couldn't. Elias knew that she could use her power and fight back, but if she did, he'd be forced to put her down. Hard.

"Don't you ever dismiss me again. Do I make myself clear?"

Reyes nodded, and Elias released his grip, letting her fall to the ground. She sat and coughed for several seconds, rubbing her neck.

"Sorry, boss," she said.

"Get to the mess room. *Now*." Elias's eyes still blazed with the anger he felt. Ordinarily he might have given Reyes more punishment, but the fear he saw in her eyes when she looked at him was enough. She wouldn't be speaking back to him again anytime soon.

Elias waited until he was alone and then tore the punch bag in half, spilling the sand all over the floor. He was calm after that. It wouldn't do for him to lose his temper again. It was unprofessional. Even if Reyes had deserved it.

Reyes was the newest member of the team, and the one Elias trusted the least. She was combative, argumentative, and vicious. All of which were great when fighting an enemy, but not so great for fighting amongst the group. She'd been with them two years, and Elias had considered replacing her for at least half of that time. The only problem was that Nergal was unlikely to approve it. He was unlikely to even listen to the request. Nergal had been the one to place Reyes in the team, and he wasn't the kind of man to be told that his decision had been wrong. She might have to meet with an *accident* if she continued on her current trajectory.

Elias noticed that his fedora had fallen off when he'd grabbed hold of Reyes. He picked it up and dusted it free of any sand, before replacing it on his head and walking off to find the rest of his people in the mess room.

The mess room was essentially a large space with half a dozen yellow tables and lots of beige chairs. As he entered, Elias could tell that the blood elves inside were angry that two of their own had been killed. They weren't known for being overly sentimental about their own kind, but they did like revenge. It was almost a species trait.

"So, we find her and drag her back here?" Reyes said with a fire in her eyes, which quickly extinguished when Elias matched her stare. "Slight problem: we don't know where she is."

Elias waved away the concern. "We'll find her. You shot her, yes? She went to a hospital then. If what Shane says is accurate, the spirit controlling her body wouldn't have been able to do so for long, and for now the bond will be too weak for any of the spirits to take control again. So that problem is no longer something we need be concerned with. I want us ready to move out in an hour. We take nothing we don't need."

"What about the prisoners?" Dara asked.

"Any of them that can walk, we take with us. We might need them. Anyone who can't, just kill them and get it over with."

"Do we have a back-up location?" Shane enquired.

"An abandoned farm. It's not as nice as this compound, but it will suffice. Layla probably told someone about us, and we won't have long before this place is completely compromised."

"Anything else?" Dara asked.

"I want an address for Layla within the next six hours," Elias told everyone. "And I want to know *exactly* which scroll she took. She might have a dozen spirits in her mind right now, and I want to know a) how screwed up she's going to be; the more spirits the better. And b) who those spirits are. We need to come up with a way to neutralize them."

Reyes and Shane both walked off, the blood elves in tow. They all knew what their jobs would entail over the next six hours.

"And for me?" Dara asked.

"I need to know where Layla's friends live and work. If we can't get to, or find, Layla, I want to make sure she knows what happens to those who continue to cross us. Get me a name and an address, and we can go twist a few screws."

Dara smiled. "It'll be my pleasure. Maybe one of the prisoners can tell you where Layla lives? They might try to go there."

"It's worth looking into, but we'll do it once we're secure."

He waited until he was alone in the room before allowing himself a smile. A few things had surprised Elias about Layla's escape. Firstly, that she'd either ignored or disbelieved the fact that he had some of her colleagues still alive. He'd expected her to try to rescue them. It would have been futile, and she would have been easily captured, but even so, it was something he hadn't expected.

And then there was the spirit scroll. That really was a turn up for the books—a piece of good luck—for Layla at least. And more than a little interesting from Elias's point of view. Those he hunted were rarely interesting, barely more than a mediocre distraction from his day-to-day duties. But Layla was proving to be something he relished: a challenge. Everything back at the compound in America was so regulated, so . . . dull.

The reason he'd *allowed* people like Liz Barnsley to escape the compound was so that he could hunt them. It was something new, something . . . interesting. And that was what Layla had become. Yes, he'd have to break her. That went without saying. The line between fun and irritation was a fine one, but until he reached that point, he was going to enjoy himself.

That's not to say that Elias would show anything other than complete irritation and anger at what had happened, but inside he was almost . . . yes, glad for her escape. And glad for her having taken a scroll. It would be amusing to see her try to fight the demon, to see if she was strong enough to fight it. And maybe she too could join Nergal's army. Stranger things had happened. And if she turned them down, well, he could always let her escape from the compound. And then the hunt would be on again.

13

In Layla's dream she found herself on a bench in a park. The sun shone high above her, but it didn't feel overly warm. Children ran around close to a large pond that was nearby, splashing and laughing as they went. There were trees behind her, casting a shade that didn't quite reach her, and for a few seconds nothing seemed out of the ordinary. And then she realized what everyone was wearing.

Every man, woman, and child there was in Victorian clothing. Most of the men wore smart suits in blacks and grays, with lighter colored waistcoats. Many of them also carried walking canes and wore top hats. There were several men who wore scruffier clothes, but they didn't appear to be the norm.

The women wore bright dresses in greens, reds, or purples, many with matching hats. Layla saw no hint of flesh below the neckline; even their hands were covered by gloves. Several women had congregated over to one side and were in deep conversation. One of them, a lady in a deep green dress, used a white umbrella to keep the sun at bay.

"This is my time again," Rosa said as she sat beside Layla. She wore trousers, boots, and a red blouse. A long, dark gray coat completed the outfit, and her hair was pulled up into a bun. "This is 1876, Oxford, or just outside of it. I was here to do a job, not one I relished, but one that needed doing."

"Why am I here?" Layla demanded, barely holding in her temper.

"You're angry about last night, about my knocking you out. Understandable. I guess I need to explain what you now are."

"I'm human."

Rosa shook her head. "Not anymore. You bled on a spirit scroll and accepted the spirits inside—that makes you an umbra."

Layla thought for a moment. "An apparition? I'm a ghost?"

"No, not even slightly. Back when the spirit scrolls were made, an umbra meant a vessel of a spirit. I guess over time that's changed. A lot of things have changed in the time since I was last alive. I died in 1915."

"Over a century then."

"An *exceptionally* long time."

"Why don't you sound old-timey?"

Rosa raised a questioning eyebrow.

"I stand by my use of the word," Layla said defensively. "I could have said ancient. Would that have been better?"

Rosa's eyes narrowed. "The spirits take on the speech pattern of the era the umbra is from. We don't even know we're doing it. One of many weird things about your new powers."

"What are the other things?"

"You want the guided tour? That's fine with me, but then you have a problem."

"What problem is that?"

"You will need to sit through what happened here, in this corner of my past, and then you'll need to go meet the other two spirits and see their lives too. You'll be learning a lot about us over the next few days. And after that you need to see the demon. That's not negotiable." She held out her hand. "Deal?"

Layla shook it. "Let's see what craziness is now in my head. So, exactly what is an umbra?"

"It's a human who has accepted the spirits from a spirit scroll. They're always human, and no one is born into this power. It's something we're given, or in your case, something you fall into. As an umbra you're not immortal, bulletproof, or able to heal yourself indefinitely. Silver will kill you—don't wear it, and don't get cut by it, although it's not as toxic to you as it is to some species. While you're not immortal, you won't age normally either. Some umbras are a few hundred years old. They're rarely much older, though. You won't age much, but you will still age.

"The languages of the spirits in the scroll will become second nature to you. Gyda knows a few of the old Viking languages, and a couple of others too, and Servius knows more than I can possibly remember. Whatever we know, you know. It'll take a while to sink in, but don't be surprised if you start speaking a language you've never studied. I know when I first did, it was a little bit of a surprise."

"Anything else?"

"You're much stronger than a human. I don't know how strong. That depends on how strong you were beforehand, but you'll soon figure it out. Your senses are improved, although don't go thinking you can hear like a dog or anything, and you'll heal a lot quicker than you could have before."

"The gunshot wound is almost gone."

"Get used to that. Also, get used to not going to the hospital when you get hurt—they find it odd when a patient who was bleeding to death on a table an hour ago gets up and walks off. Trust me on that." Rosa thought for a moment. "Oh, yes, you'll know all of our muscle memories too, so if one of us was good at fighting, you will be too. Sword, ax and shield, knives . . . you'll start to realize you can do things you never thought possible, and you'll just *know* you can do it. Takes a while to get used to."

"I already know how to fight," Layla said, keeping her voice neutral. "I don't need to learn more about how to fight."

"The spirit scrolls were created for one reason: to make weapons out of humans, to try to ensure that they wouldn't die as easily as they usually do. The only problem was they worked too well and made some people into monsters. I'm hoping that's not you. But we're some way off from finding out."

"I'm assuming you're going to get to the really bad side of my new life soon."

"Still on the good for the moment. You'll need less sleep but more food. You'll also be able to use your ability. It's unique to you, and based on what Gyda did the other day, it's the manipulation of metal. You won't be too powerful until you accept the spirits and demon, but you'll have us to help you learn control. How the power actually works, and what it's actually capable of, is something you'll have to discover for yourself."

"Accepting a demon? Power to manipulate metal?" Layla rubbed her eyes. "It's a lot to take in."

"Yes, it is. But you need to understand everything that's happened to you, and quickly. It won't be long before you get used to it all."

"So, what could you do?"

"I could become invisible as needed. You'll have to ask the others about what they could do. The scroll looks inside a person and assigns a power based on their personality, along with their wants and needs at that moment. You needed to escape, and you study metallurgy, according to your memories, so you get metal manipulation. We can see all of your memories—it's a two-way street."

"What if I don't want this power? What if I don't want you to see my memories?"

"Tough. It comes with the scroll. There's nothing you, or I, or anyone else can ever do about it."

"So I no longer have secrets?"

"We're part of you. You don't have secrets from yourself, so you can't keep them from us. It's to ensure that we are always honest with one another. So, yes, I can see that fire in you. Your need to fight and hurt people who could hurt you. And I understand it."

"I don't want understanding. I want it gone."

"That's a part of you, Layla. The best you can do is learn how to control it, just like you'll learn how to control your new powers. On the plus side, I can't lie to you, not ever. No spirit can."

"What about the demon?"

"In theory he can't lie to you either, but I don't know whether or not to trust that."

"And I have to accept him."

"If it is a him, yes."

"*If?*"

"I'm not sure demons have a sex; it just never came up. I referred to the demon as a *him* simply because he appeared in a male form the majority of the time. I think they change gender according to who they're talking to and how they feel on that occasion."

"Are they asexual?"

"Able to change as needed to suit their audience. I think that's part of what they are. To my knowledge, no one has ever gotten close enough emotionally to one of them to learn about their species.

"Physically, demons aren't anything like humans. They're something entirely different, and they're full of incredible power. Accepting the demon will be the hardest part of bonding with the scroll and the spirits in it. It will tell you awful things, it will show you things you'll never forget, because it wants to break you, it wants to weaken you so badly that it gets to take control."

"And how do I accept the demon, or any of you for that matter?"

"You just have to tell us. But you have to mean it with every fiber of your being. Otherwise it won't work."

"And once I've done that, I'll be more powerful?"

"Considerably, yes, and you'll be able to tap into the power of the demon, drawing it out to use. Although that in turn lets the demon closer to the surface, where your emotions, or overuse of power, can allow it to take control."

"Is that permanent?"

Rosa shook her head. "No, he'll let you back in when he's done. But while he's out—" She glanced away across the park and took a deep breath. "Let's just say you don't want that to happen."

Layla wanted to ask more about what Rosa had experienced, but she got the impression that while a spirit couldn't lie, that didn't mean they would want to tell her. Besides, if what Rosa said was true, she would soon know anyway. The thought worried her. "Anything else I should know?"

"The next few days are going to see changes happen to you, to what you know, to what you can do. It might feel overwhelming. It might feel like everything in your life is crashing down around you. I promise you, it gets better." Rosa stood and stretched. "You probably have time to go see one of the other two. You need to pick one of us to be your main contact as quickly as possible. The one you have a stronger affinity with than the others."

"So, once I pick one of you, I can't speak to the others?"

"No, you can talk to any of us at any time, especially once you're bonded, but while you're learning, it's helpful to just have one point of contact. Makes life easier on you. It was easier for me—I only had two people to choose from."

"Who did you choose?"

"Servius. I just felt like he was the right choice for me, just like whoever you pick will be the right one for you."

Layla nodded. "So, what happens now?"

"Now, you get to see a pivotal moment in my life. It's the one where I decided that I needed to change what I was becoming. Stay here and don't move."

"What were you becoming?"

Rosa didn't bother answering. Instead she set off across the perfectly mown grass toward the group of women. She stood beside them, looking as if she was waiting for someone, while Layla wondered exactly what she was doing. Eventually, a middle-aged man walked over to the group, ignoring Rosa, and began talking to one of the women. Another of the group laughed at something the man said, but Layla was too far away to know if it was genuinely funny, or if they were just being polite.

Rosa moved smoothly and with incredible speed. Stepping up behind the man, she reached around his neck with one arm, her hand holding a blade. Another blade appeared in Rosa's free hand and she repeatedly stabbed the man in the back. Layla tried to shout out, but found she wasn't able to. Rosa released the man and stepped away as screams filled the air.

The man turned as he collapsed to his knees, and Layla saw the cut across his throat. People ran over to him, trying to help him, shouting for help, and in the commotion Rosa just walked over to Layla.

"In reality, I was running at this point," she said to Layla.

"You murdered him."

"Him and people like him, yes." Her hands were red and she dropped two daggers onto the grass beside Layla.

"You're a killer."

"An assassin. I worked for Queen Victoria. I removed people who needed removing."

"And what was that man's crime?"

"He was a wealthy man with a lot of influence, and someone who met a young woman by the name of Elizabeth. A woman he and his equally rich friends forced into prostitution. This group were hurting a lot of people in London at the time, and I was tasked with the removal of each of them. Eighteen in all. He was the first. He had no idea what was about to befall the rest of his comrades. He thought the group untouchable. He was wrong."

"You murdered all of these people for the queen?"

"It was my job, yes. I didn't enjoy it, but they certainly deserved it. They needed to be removed from this planet. They were too rich, powerful, and influential to be simply exposed as the vermin they were, so a more permanent solution was required. Prostitution, drugs, the murder of anyone who investigated them—they were responsible for a lot of awful things happening. I believe one of the people they hurt was the sister of one of Victoria's maids, and that was what started this whole thing, but I have no proof of that.

"You think because your father murdered all of those people that it's either black or white, you either kill or you don't. That's not how things work. Some people need to be threatened, some need to have their crimes exposed, and some need to be expunged from the face of the earth in such a way that it sends a message to anyone who might cross you. I understand your need to see things so distinctly, but they're not that easy to tell apart. Your father's crimes, crimes I only know because you're thinking about them, were committed because he wanted to satisfy his own need to administer punishment. I killed for queen and country. I killed because leaving them alive meant more lives ruined.

"This was a pivotal moment in my life. Before this, I killed bad people, I ruined bad people, but this group stretched out across London, across the entire world. This group needed to be stopped. This was a turning point for me. It was the time I decided I wanted to do some good, to care about more than just me."

"I get that. I get that sometimes killing is necessary. Self-defense for one. I just don't know if I can do that. My father did it so often that . . . what if I'm the same? What if I kill someone in self-defense, and then I'm on the road to becoming him?"

"I was a soldier in a war. It might have been a hidden war, but it was a war nonetheless. It wasn't just me; there were several of us. Most died before the task was completed. I was one of the few who lived through it. I even outlived my queen. A month after what happened here, I discovered the spirit scroll you now possess. It changed everything about my world. About my life. I found it in the safe of one of my victims; he had no idea what it really was. Probably best for everyone."

"If I accept you, does that mean I'll accept your ability to murder without pause?"

"You think I didn't pause? You think I didn't see the faces of those lives I've taken? You're unbelievably wrong. I killed because I had no choice, but I never took pleasure in it. I just did what was needed. If you accept me, then yes, maybe you'll be able to kill without crying yourself to sleep that first night, or scrubbing your skin for so long it bleeds. Maybe you'll be able to rest knowing you did some good. Or maybe you won't. I don't know. But know this: the world you now reside in will destroy you and spit you out if you're not willing to do what you need to do."

14

The world around Layla changed to white and she found herself atop a large hill. A gradual curve down one side ended at the flatness of the beach a few hundred feet in front of her. Several dozen longboats sat on the dark sands, their sails blowing in the strong wind.

She saw no one inside the wooden boats, nor anyone close by. She took a few steps forward.

The grass was several inches high and caressed the backs of her calves. She wore a dark blue dress that stopped just above the knee, and black Adidas trainers. An outfit she'd worn the previous summer at a party Chloe had dragged her along to. It had been a fun time. She had no idea why she was wearing it now, though.

"It's a comforting thing, that dress," a woman said, as she appeared further down the hill. The woman paused and glanced back at the ships, before walking toward Layla. She was taller than Layla by several inches and had many scars across one of her bare arms. They crisscrossed over one another. Her long blonde hair was tied behind her head, although strands of it had broken loose and were batting around in the wind.

The woman's skin was pale, and she wore an ankle-length red dress with a burgundy apron-like dress over the top, which was clasped on her shoulders. Layla instantly knew it was called a hangerock. A rope, golden in color, was tied around her waist. She wore no jewelry that Layla could see, and thick leather boots adorned her feet. She drew a long sword from the sheath on her hip and stopped in front of Layla.

"My name is Gyda," she said. "I'm the spirit that took control of you in the compound."

"Thank you for getting me out alive."

Gyda shrugged. "That was nothing. Couldn't let Rosa do it, she only likes to kill from the shadows."

"You don't like Rosa?"

Gyda shrugged again. "She's not bad, at least as far as assassins go. Fighting shouldn't be done with a blade to the back. It should be done face to face. Anything else is just . . . well, it feels wrong to me."

Layla wasn't sure she agreed with Gyda. If you're forced to fight, win. It was another of her father's many lessons, but one that she actually found herself agreeing with. "So, I guess you'll tell me about yourself."

"My name is Gyda. I was born in the city of Darim in the dwarven realm of Nidavellir."

"Dwarven realm?"

"You would call them the Norse dwarves. Dwarves from mythology."

"Wait, like Odin and Thor? That kind of mythology? So these dwarves are the ones from the stories of gods and goddesses?"

Gyda stared at her. "What other dwarves from mythology are there?"

"But they're just stories."

"You have three spirits living in your head, as well as a demon. You can control metal to your whim. Why is it so hard to believe that the characters from mythology are in fact real? The stories aren't necessarily accurate—I knew that even before I took a spirit scroll—but the people in them are."

"So, you lived in a different realm?"

"Earth realm is the center, and all around it are hundreds of other realms, all linked to earth. Each realm is a separate world. This world, my home, is here. Nidavellir."

"And humans live here?"

"Lived. Humans haven't lived here in centuries. At least not to my knowledge. I was the first person given the scrolls. I had only the demon to deal with, and it drove me insane. It broke me and I refused to accept it. Obviously it's easier now, because there are three of us to help, but back then, there was nothing and no one who could help me. I volunteered to help the dwarves create the spirit scrolls. In hindsight, it was a mistake."

"What did you do?"

Gyda pointed to the tree line, which began to glow a fiery orange, until part of it exploded. Wood rained down over the landscape as trees collapsed into one another, causing a domino effect as several more succumbed to the force exerted on them.

Screams were carried by the wind as Gyda, covered head to toe in incandescent flame, burst through the remains of the trees, sprinting toward Layla. Gyda ran past and continued until she reached the water. She dove in, screaming as the flames refused to die, crying out for help every time she resurfaced.

"I couldn't get the flames to stop," the spirit of Gyda said from beside Layla. "They didn't hurt, I just panicked. The demon kept telling me that I would kill everyone I loved. That I would burn them to a cinder. It showed me visions of a future I was sure would come to pass."

"Did they come true?"

She nodded and took a deep breath. "Whether those visions came to pass because it said so, or because I was destined to do it, I don't know. My husband tried to help me, but the fire that didn't hurt me incinerated him in an instant. Twelve people died in seconds for the crime of being good people who tried to help me.

"I died soon after. I killed myself with a silver dagger. And sometime after my death, the scroll was taken into the earth realm. I tried to do the right thing by my people and was driven mad for it. The only thing I could do to stop the demon before it took total control was kill myself."

Layla didn't know what to say. She placed a hand on Gyda's shoulder. "I'm sorry."

"The demon is a monster. It should not be trusted. It should not be given into. You should kill yourself before it has the chance to do so."

"What kind of help is that?" Rosa said, as she appeared beside Gyda and Layla.

"This is my time with the umbra, assassin," Gyda spat. "I am to offer her aid and advice. And my advice is that she should kill herself and ensure that no one can ever find the scroll afterward."

"I'm not going to commit suicide," Layla said, utterly flabbergasted that anyone would suggest such a thing.

"Then the demon *will* take control of you and will destroy your life. Just like it destroyed mine."

"That's nonsense," Rosa snapped. "You allowed the demon to take control because you had no one else to help. You were scared and alone, and I get that. Layla isn't alone, and she's not afraid to face this thing."

"She's afraid she'll become a murderer like her father," Gyda snapped back. "And if she lets the demon in, it'll make sure of it. She'll either be driven insane and the demon will take control, or she'll somehow accept it and then the second it takes control, it'll gut everyone she loves, and laugh while it does it."

"You keep calling the demon an 'it,'" Layla said. "Not he or she. Rosa said it can change its outward appearance."

"No matter how the demon looks, it will always be an *it* to me."

Layla sensed so much anger and fear still in Gyda, and wasn't sure whether, even as a spirit, she would ever be able to let go of what the demon had done to her and those she loved.

"I won't become a murderer," Layla said. "I won't kill for the sake of killing, and I certainly won't allow something to take control of me."

Rosa sighed. "You're not helping, Gyda, you're feeding your own fears."

"Perfect little Rosa," Gyda snapped. "Always capable of keeping the demon at bay, always able to have friends and loved ones. You just enjoyed murdering people a bit too much for even a demon to stomach, I think."

For a second Layla thought that Rosa was going to punch Gyda, but instead she took a step away.

"Do you remember when I first took the scroll and came to see you?" Rosa asked. "You were all *kill yourself and save the demon the trouble* back then too." She turned to Layla. "Killing a monster or doing it for self-defense doesn't make you your father. You've decided that fighting leads to killing, which leads to your father. And that's not how it works."

"But I always want it to go a step further. I think, *What if I just hurt them more?* They'll stop then."

"You have an instinct your father cultivated, an instinct to win at any cost. He taught you from a young age that to win, you might have to hurt someone. He taught you this to survive in his world. I know that you didn't choose to be a part of his world, but now that you're here, you'd better figure out how to fight back and survive, or else you'll die. Someone new will pick up your scroll, and we'll just have to do this all over again."

15

Layla woke up feeling tired and with a headache behind her eyes. She felt as if she'd been sleeping in a room where all of the air had been sucked out. She climbed out of bed and padded over to the window, but the pain behind her eyes wouldn't budge. The metal frame surrounding the window glass had long since been sealed closed. Parts of the runners had a block of metal soldered to them, one on either side of the window, to give extra protection against being able to open it. Layla placed her head against the cold glass and sighed as the headache began to dissipate.

She held her hand against the frame and wondered whether or not she'd be able to use her newly discovered powers. There was no point in denying what had happened to her; it wasn't as if she could just pass it all off as a dream. She was no longer human. She paused. "I'm not human anymore." Saying it out loud stung more than she'd expected it to.

She knew that not being human and not acting human were two exceptionally different things. She was determined that whatever power she'd managed to acquire wouldn't change who she was.

She stared at the metal and wondered how she was meant to get her power to work.

Just think what you want to happen, and if you're powerful enough, it'll happen, Rosa said in her head.

"I thought we couldn't talk when I'm awake."

We're closer now. You've seen part of my life, you've seen part of the person I am. I see no reason to go on as if we can't communicate during the day.

Layla looked around the room. "I can't see you. I expected I'd be able to."

Rosa appeared in the doorway to the en suite bathroom. "Is this more what you had in mind?" Unlike the clothing she'd worn in Layla's memory, Rosa wore faded blue jeans and a black t-shirt.

"That's not especially Victorian."

Rosa glanced down at herself. "Ah, modern clothing. Looks like a lot really has changed. The spirits can wear the clothing of the current period, same as our speech patterns. I think it's meant to make it easier for the umbra to adjust to what's happening to them."

Layla turned back to the window. "So, I just think about moving the metal around this window and it should move?"

"Picture it in your mind. Picture what you want to do, and then do it. It'll become easier over time."

Layla pictured moving the metal frame and immediately felt a connection to the metal. It was as if they were two magnets attracted to one another. She turned her hand and found a connection to the metal blocks that had been soldered onto the runners years earlier. Another slight movement of her fingers and the solder in the runners melted, and the metal blocks fell out of the runners, allowing the window the freedom to slide. The window slid open at high speed, slamming into the stop that had been placed at the top and bottom of the frame. A remnant from days gone past when opening windows wasn't forbidden.

Layla turned back to Rosa as the door burst open and Diana stormed in. "What happened?"

Layla pointed to the open window. "I had a headache."

Diana walked over to the window and stared at the metal runners. "I didn't think these were meant to open."

"Must have been defective. Once it started, I couldn't stop it from slamming into the stops. Sorry."

Diana's serious expression softened. "That's okay. Did you sleep well?"

Layla sat down in the pink leather chair next to the window, and immediately decided that sitting in it was better than having to look at it. "As well as can be expected, I guess. How long do I have to stay here?"

"A few days. The doctors want to make sure you're okay."

Layla looked out of the window. "Do you think Elias will come for me, then?"

Diana was silent for several seconds before answering. "In hospital? I honestly don't know. I know it's easier to defend you from here than from your home. Once the doctors give you an all-clear, we can always move you to a more secure location."

"I just want to go home."

"I know."

"I'm not hurt. I feel fine."

"You were kidnapped and held by a group of psychopaths. They murdered your friends, and managed to hurt you. You arrived here covered in blood and had a bullet wound. The doctors want to know how you're doing, but they'll also want to know how it managed to heal so quickly."

Layla opened her mouth to speak, but said nothing.

"It's okay, weird shit is sort of my job specification. Healing a bullet wound isn't anything I haven't seen before."

"How?"

"It's probably best you just concentrate on you for now. Don't worry too much about the world around you. But just know this: what you can do now is incredible. It's nothing to be afraid of."

Layla maintained eye contact with Diana. "What do you know about it?"

Diana smiled. "There are more things in heaven and earth, Layla, than are dreamed of in your philosophy."

"You're quoting *Hamlet* to me? That doesn't exactly have the happiest ending."

"It was the first thing that popped into mind. I always liked the play, saw it not long after Shakespeare first put it on."

"That's over four hundred years ago."

Diana shrugged. "I like to moisturize." She winked and walked over to the door. "Like I said, you shouldn't be afraid of your new powers. Just accept them. It'll make life easier, I promise."

Layla took a shot. "Did you accept yours?"

"I'm not an umbra, Layla. Not even close. When the doctor comes, tell him the truth about the wound. He'll know more about your circumstances than you could possibly imagine." Diana opened the door. "And, yes, I accepted them. I love everything about what I can do. Except the shedding. I'm not such a fan of that. Call if you need anything."

Diana walked out of the room, closing the door behind her, leaving Layla staring after her. She wondered what Diana was, and exactly how many others were like her. It was odd discovering that something you thought was unique, wasn't. She sat for a few minutes before going to the door and opening it, catching Diana mid-bite of a bacon sandwich.

"Can I have one of those?"

Diana swallowed the mouthful and nodded. "Sure. Anything else?"

"Something to drink that isn't lukewarm water?"

"Coffee?"

Layla nodded. "That would be amazing, thank you. And some fruit. Apples or oranges, just something to snack on."

Diana smiled. "Anything else on my shopping trip?"

"I have university work to do. It needs to be handed in next week, and I can't do it sitting here."

"We'll talk to your university and get you an extension. These are exceptional circumstances, and I think a few of our people turning up at the university will be able to convince them to grant you an extension. You're in your last year anyway, yes?"

"Yes, my dissertation is on the application of different compounds in nanotechnology."

"Sounds like hard work."

"I find it interesting. I'm not sure anyone else would be able to say the same thing. Looking at the manipulation of tiny particles of metal isn't everyone's idea of a fun time."

"That explains the window then. You moved the metal in the frame to move the window?"

Layla paused, and then tentatively shook her head. "I moved the metal solder in the runners."

Diana nodded as if impressed. "If you want to keep that window open, can you put bars across it?"

Layla looked behind her at the open window. "I don't know."

"Try. I'll feel better knowing it's not an entry point. I'll get you your stuff too."

Layla thanked her and walked back over to the window. She placed her hands on the runners and tried to think about moving the metal inside them.

You don't need to touch the metal to use it, Rosa said from behind her.

Layla bit back a reply, and moved her hands a few inches from the runners. She imagined the metal coming out of them and forming a cage around the open window. She imagined taking metal from the two blocks and the runners, making sure that parts of the metal gripped the window in place first. She didn't want the glass falling out.

She opened her eyes and the metal slowly moved out from the runners, as if it was made of nothing more than modeling clay, until the various strands of metal linked up, forming several bars across the window.

Layla stepped back and admired her work. "Wow."

It's an impressive talent.

Layla turned around and saw Rosa in the same spot she'd been in earlier. "And I'll get more powerful?" she asked.

Rosa nodded. "That's the plan."

Diana arrived shortly after with a stack of books and some food. "We found these at your house. I thought you'd like some reading material."

Layla picked up each book; most of them were about metal usage and technology.

"Thought you might get some ideas."

"Thank you."

"Just take it slowly, Layla. Don't push yourself too hard; I've seen what those scrolls do to people who allow their emotions to take control. That demon inside of you can't ever be let out. Trust me."

Layla was shocked. She hadn't really thought about how many others were like her, but she imagined there weren't all that many. Her mind raced with excitement. She wasn't alone. "You've seen it happen? How many umbra are there? Are they like me? Did they accept their demon? Can I meet one?"

Diana smiled. "You have questions then."

"Sorry, but yes, lots."

"Okay. I've seen it happen a few times. I've met a half dozen umbra in the last few years. We only discovered they existed as a species a few years ago, but they've been living in this realm for hundreds, if not thousands, of years. Most are just like you: a human who found a scroll and bonded with some spirits through no fault of their own.

"We're trying to get an umbra to come meet you once you're done here. Right now, they're busy with a few other things, but I promise they'll come see you when they can. They did accept their demon. I spoke to them about it after, and they told me it was the hardest thing they'd ever done. From what they told me, trust the spirits, and trust yourself. That's the only advice my friend ever said mattered. I'm sure they'd tell you that if they were here."

"I wish it was that simple."

"Nothing worth doing is ever simple, Layla. If accepting the demon and spirits was simple, we'd have a lot more umbra running around." Diana stood and stretched. "I'll leave you be for now."

"Aren't you worried about me losing control? About the demon breaking free?"

Diana paused. "Yes. It is a concern. But after talking to you and spending time with you, I don't think I have anything to worry about. The demon can't just take control like that." She clicked her fingers. "It takes time. Time enough for us to make sure you're safe and get you any help you need."

"I feel like I should be more surprised about all of this."

"Surprised?"

"About the world I never knew existed. I think the spirits are somehow making me accept things without question. It's like they already knew all of this, so I'm okay with it. It's a bit weird."

"That's probably for the best then. It's a lot to accept. And there's a lot more to come. Magic, monsters, and more species than I can even remember."

"And you kept all of this secret?"

"It was decided long ago that humans would have no knowledge of our world. It was too dangerous, and humans were too easily influenced by people who want to do us harm for their own benefit. Besides, humans make up about ninety-nine percent of the population of the planet. Having them know we exist wouldn't have ended well, not with all the different governments and religions. People vying for their own agendas, control, riches, or anything else that drives them to deal very badly with the idea that they were no longer the top of the food chain, so to speak. It was better to stay hidden."

Diana left the room, and Layla spent the rest of the day reading the books and watching TV, occasionally practicing her new power on the metal legs of the table. The doctor arrived just as the night was beginning to settle in. He was a middle-aged man who appeared to know Diana, and came across as a pleasant and easy-going individual.

He checked Layla over, asking her a few questions about herself and how she was feeling. He appeared to be happy with the answers.

"Doctor?" Layla asked, as he was writing in a notebook.

He glanced up. "Yes?"

"What are you writing?"

The doctor smiled. "Your bullet wound is healed. The power inside of you will increase over the coming weeks and months. Less than two days after being shot and the scarring is all but gone. It's impressive."

"Thank you for being honest, Doctor . . ."

"Grayson. You can call me Doc, everyone else does." Grayson had a trim white beard and bald head. He was a short man with pale skin and a wooden bracelet on one wrist, which had several marks carved into it. He wore a dark blue suit and carried himself with the kind of confidence you get when you know exactly who you are as a person.

"You work with Diana?"

"I work for Tommy, and with Diana when she manages to injure herself, which isn't often."

"Are you human?"

Grayson shook his head. "I'm something entirely different to you and Diana. Can't tell you what, though . . . It's complicated."

Layla nodded an understanding, although in reality she had none. "Can I go home?"

Grayson placed the pen and paper on the table beside him. "Short answer: no. Not for a few more days. Long answer: no, because while you're here we can monitor you and the spirits inside of you. We can monitor your power and how you cope. And we can monitor that demon and how well it tries to screw around in your head too. I know it doesn't feel like it, but this is the safest place for you right now."

"Why don't I just accept the spirit and demon and be done with it?"

"From what I understand, it's not that simple. I wish it was, for your sake." He stood and picked up the notebook and put the pen inside his jacket pocket. "I'll be back to see you tomorrow. In the meantime, sleep. You need as much rest as possible."

Layla watched the doctor leave, before settling in to watch TV for a few hours. Eventually she drifted off to sleep, ready to face whatever came next.

16

Layla stared at the opulent palace in front of her: the tan painted bricks, the white columns, and perfectly manicured lawn. Birds chirped somewhere nearby, and there were several trees that sat alongside a twenty-foot gray stone wall behind her.

"This is where I worked," a man said as he walked down the steps of the palace toward her. "My name is Servius Tullius." Servius was a giant of a man. Over six feet tall, and as solid as an oak tree, he gave the impression that he was not to be trifled with. He had dark skin, short black hair, and was clean-shaven. His eyes were a mixture of brown and green, and a scar stretched from the right side of his top lip, curving under his nose and finishing just under his left eye.

"Spear deflected from my shield," he said, touching the scar. "It's the first thing people asked back then."

"You're a Roman?"

He nodded. "A *praefectus legionis.*"

Layla was about to ask what that meant, when the answer popped into her head. "You were an equestrian legionary commander?"

Servius nodded. "I was part of the army for twelve years, before Emperor Trajan rewarded me for saving the life of a son of a close friend on the battlefield. I was given the opportunity to become a guard here, at one of several residences that the emperors used. This one is in northern Italy. It's officially a home belonging to one of the senators, but it's used by the emperor as a getaway."

"It's stunning."

"It's a sad, lonely place. Mostly slaves and soldiers who have been rewarded with an easy life staff it. We're rarely bothered by anyone, and the family who lived here—a mother, two daughters, and three sons—were all nice enough."

"For slave owners."

Servius nodded. "It was the way of the times. As far as slave owners went, these were kind and allowed their slaves a measure of freedom, but slavery isn't something I remember with any fondness. It isn't something I've ever been proud to say was a part of the world I lived in."

The pair began walking around the gardens, and Layla looked at the statues depicting various Roman gods and goddesses in various states of undress, in amongst colorful flowers and a stream that appeared to run the length of the estate.

"So, when did you get the scroll?"

"I was given it by the emperor as a gift. I kept it for ten years, until raiders came to the estate. They came at night, killing most of the guards, murdering the mother and sons, before hunting for the daughters and anyone remaining in the property. I fought several of them and was badly wounded. It was dumb luck I placed a bloody hand on the scroll, and the rest is history."

"You drove back the raiders?"

"I killed them all. I was confused; my emotions got the better of me and the demon was released. It was only for a matter of minutes, but it was long enough to kill every single person in this estate. Including anyone who wasn't a raider."

The image in front of them changed, became nighttime in an instant. Bodies littered the ground, and the screams could be heard inside the estate, before a creature that had once been Servius burst through the wall, grabbing hold of the nearest raider and tearing him in half. The slaughter of the remaining six men outside the palace was quick and brutal, drenching Servius in blood before he turned back into his human form.

"I fled after this, ran to the hills and didn't come back. Gyda helped me realize what I was, and I spent the next few hundred years living as a nomad, moving from place to place, never staying long. I saw a lot of the world that way, but didn't really have much else. In the end I was killed by a man who wanted to make a name for himself and had heard of my prowess with a sword. The funny thing is, I don't even remember his name. I don't think it really matters, if I'm honest."

"No one who's had these scrolls seems to have lived a particularly happy life."

"The scroll is a great burden, if you allow it to be. I let what I did this night define who I was for centuries after. Gyda took her own life so as not to allow the demon to take hers because no one told her how the scrolls truly operate, and by the time she'd learned it, it was too late. She continues to tell people that killing themselves is the only option. She's wrong there. I was wrong to flee too.

"And Rosa . . . she is the only one of us who truly embraced what it meant to have this power. She used it to try to make the world better, even if I don't always agree with her methods."

"What if I accept it and I become a killer like my father?"

"I can understand your hesitance. But killing to preserve your own life, or to protect those you love, isn't the same as killing for pleasure. It's simple really; you don't become him. I know Rosa told you something similar."

Layla laughed, although there was little humor in it, as the scenery around her began to fade. "It's not that easy."

"It really is," Rosa said from beside her. "Hello, Servius."

The legionnaire bowed his head. "Rosa. I see you've taken to invading my time too."

"We can't have another you or Gyda," Rosa said softly. "And there are things about the demon I haven't told her. That no one has told her. She needs to know. She can only fight this creature with information."

Servius nodded. "The demon will show you things, things of a future you'll want no part of. He'll say that's what will happen if you accept him. He tried with me after I ran from here. He tried with Rosa, and Gyda too. Gyda let him take control because she had no idea what she was doing. I allowed it to happen because of fear and rage. Don't go down those paths. Don't make the same mistakes we made."

"He showed me killing people I loved," Rosa said. "Told me that once I'd accepted him and the spirits, he'd bide his time until I needed to use his power so badly that I'd release him. He told me over and over again until I almost believed him. But I fought through it; I decided that there was nothing he could do to those I loved that any one of my enemies couldn't do if I refused to accept the demon and spirits. Somehow I managed to accept him, although I kept him chained in my mind."

"So, he's going to show me a possible future? Can't I just ignore it all?" Layla turned away from the pair. It was too much to take, too much to absorb all at once. It was beginning to sound like no matter what she did, she was screwed.

Rosa and Servius shared a glance. "Yes, but it's not just something you can ignore," Rosa eventually said. "Everything he shows you will *feel* real. It's how he works. He will make you believe that you don't have a good option. We can tell you right now that you can fight it, but it won't feel like you can when you're in the middle of it all."

Rosa's voice became distant, and when Layla turned to look at them both, she discovered they were no longer there.

Instead of the palace there was nothing, just an empty darkness all around her.

"Is it finally my turn?" a voice asked from the blackness.

"You're the demon?"

"My name is Terhal." Two points of fire ignited in the distance as the darkness surrounding Layla dissipated, revealing the glade she'd ridden around with Rosa. The points of fire were inside the large cage, where the demon remained shrouded in darkness.

Layla sucked down the fear she instinctively felt. "Does that eye trick impress anyone?"

The globes of fire vanished, and the demon grabbed hold of the bars, placing his face against them. His skin was taut over his skull. A ridge sat around the circumference of the top of his head, pulsing a bright orange color, making it look as though he was wearing a crown of fire. His eyes were large; the orange and red flame where the eyeball should have been seemed to spill out across the skin around the socket. He had no nose, just a hole where darkness sat, and there was no skin around his mouth, exposing bone and dozens of small, shark-like teeth.

His ears were large and pointy, and when he opened his skinless mouth, a black tongue flicked across his teeth.

On his chin sat two tendrils, each a foot in length. They were a silver color, and like the ridge on his skull, they pulsed on occasion with red and orange.

"What you were expecting?" Something moved inside the cage and wings protruded through the bars on either side. They were black and torn in places, and looked like they belonged to a bat.

"I can't fly in here," Terhal told Layla. "I can't fly in your realm. I'm not whole in your realm. I remember flying, I remember soaring high above the mountains and forests while I hunted."

Layla did a quick measurement and realized the wings must have been a dozen feet in length, and the demon himself nearly six feet tall. A tail swished out of the cage on one side; spikes protruded from the tip, each one several inches in length, giving it the appearance of a morning star.

Layla wasn't going to allow Terhal to know that she was frightened. "How did you end up in there?" She kept her tone casual, as if it was the most normal question in the world.

"The dwarves dragged me from my realm and imprisoned me in a scroll. They called me a demon; and then they made this cage my new home. Demon. It's a strange word, but I like it."

"You're going to try to make me release you, so you can take control of my body and cause havoc."

"I wasn't planning on it right at this moment. Although I guess that is my end goal. I want to feast on those little humans that are so abundant here. Gyda let me out to feed, and I killed so many people. Servius too. Rosa never did. She was always too detached, too controlled. Shame."

Layla's confidence grew, her fear fading away into the background. "Do we need to do this with the darkness rolling around?"

The demon sighed and clicked his fingers, bathing the area in light, and showing Layla exactly who she was talking to.

Even though Layla had managed to figure out what Terhal looked like in the darkness, she wasn't quite prepared for the hulking beast that stood before her. Terhal had the body shape of someone who bench-pressed buses, and hands that were tipped with jet-black claws that retracted and extended as she watched.

"I haven't been in the light for a while now. No one else ever asked to see me this way. You know being in the light won't save you. Won't help you. I will be free, and you will scream while I devour your friends."

Anger replaced the fear. Who did this demon think he was to threaten her friends? To threaten her? She'd seen monsters before. Monsters in the flesh. She'd escaped Elias, and the ogre, and she'd dealt with her father's crimes. She could deal with this too. "So, I keep you in there and you drive me insane, allowing you to break free? Okay, so I'll let you out."

"But then the second you tap into the power I possess, that makes it easier for me to take control too. You can't win."

"You make it sound like I shouldn't try."

"Oh, no, please try. I do so love it when they try."

"I don't get it. Are you meant to scare me? I understand that if you're released, you'll cause devastation, and I understand that you're a monster, but you're also in a cage. Whether I accept you or not, you're still in a cage, a cage I need to keep control of."

Terhal snarled. "Don't play with me, girl."

Layla stared at the cage for several seconds before laughing. "Girl? You think that's an insult? This girl isn't someone who will let you walk over them."

Terhal screamed in rage, changing the world around them, showing dead bodies piled high. Dozens and dozens of dead.

"Is this what I'm meant to do? You think nightmares are the best way to get to me?" Layla took a step forward, using the anger to force her forward. "I dreamed of nothing but death and murder and pain for years after my father was arrested. I dreamed of hurting people I love, of enjoying their suffering. I've seen the crime-scene photos of my father's murders; I've seen the journals he kept. I know what he did, and how he did it. There is *nothing* you can show me that will do more harm to me than he already did."

Layla turned and walked away.

"You'll be back tomorrow," Terhal snarled.

"Maybe. I'll see how I feel."

The bodies vanished, replaced with a scene of a car crashed head first into a tree. Layla's mother had been thrown from the car and lay dying on the ground.

"How about this?"

Layla took a sharp breath. Her legs felt weak and she thought they would give way at any moment, but she still turned back toward the demon. "Is this really how you want to play this game?" Anger leaked from every word. If they'd both been in the real world, she'd have beaten Terhal within an inch of his life and regretted nothing.

The car vanished, replaced with a demonic-looking Layla standing over a prone and bleeding Chloe, who was pleading with her friend to let her live. The demon-Layla, her claw-like hands drenched with blood, looked over at her and began to laugh, the sound making Layla nauseous. She took a step toward the scene and it vanished, replaced once again with the glade.

"This is what happens when I take control. Either you accept me or you don't, but you can't stop this from being your future. And this *will* happen if you accept me. I guarantee it." The demon didn't sound smug about it, just matter of fact.

Tears fell down Layla's cheeks as everything she'd seen suddenly felt as real as if it was happening to her right then. The sounds, the smells, the horrific brutality on display. Everything. She knew somewhere inside her that what Rosa had told her was true, that none of this was real, but it *felt* so real that she could think of nothing else but the horror before her. Her confidence had been misplaced. She thought she could be stronger than whatever the demon showed her. She had been terribly wrong. Layla wiped the tears away with the back of her hand.

"See you tomorrow," Terhal said.

Layla woke with a start, the image of her pleading friend still fresh in her mind. She lay there for a long time, not wanting to get out of bed for fear that she was still dreaming, still in a world created by the demon. Eventually the sun broke through the curtains, and only then did she feel at ease. How could she let out a demon that would kill her friends? But then how could she keep him caged, if he would eventually take control anyway? She'd been right: she really was screwed.

17

Layla eventually risked leaving the bed, and took a long, hot shower, getting dressed in the clean clothes that Chloe had brought her on her last visit. It had been two days since she'd seen her friend, and she wanted to be able to talk to her. It took her several seconds to remember that she'd never retrieved her phone from whoever had taken it off her, which angered her more than she'd expected. Her phone had contained photos that she had probably lost forever. She hoped they'd uploaded to the cloud since her last check a week ago.

The clean clothes were only a small piece of kindness from Chloe, but they made Layla feel a billion times happier about having to be in hospital.

She was sitting in a chair by the window reading, when the door opened and Chloe walked in, carrying another bag. She placed the carrier bag on the table.

"Some more clothes, a mobile, a charger, some chocolate, and your purse. I went to your place and grabbed a few things. Tommy was over there keeping an eye on it. I wouldn't want to be Elias if he tries that avenue."

"You know Tommy?" Layla asked as she dove into the bag for her phone, as if she'd been starving at sea for a month and it was her first meal.

Chloe paused. "Not well. Hey, we need to get you out of here."

Layla sensed that there was more to it than Chloe was willing to divulge. "Doc Grayson gets to decide when that happens."

"I'm sure it'll be soon. It's not like Elias can hide forever. Sooner or later, Tommy and his people will find him, and then you can go home. Back to normality."

Layla opened her mouth to say something, but instead moved her hand toward the nearby table. The metal legs turned to liquid and the table crashed to the floor. "Not sure normality is ever coming back to my life."

Chloe stared at Layla, before looking over at the fallen table. She looked back at Layla and opened her mouth to say something, when the door opened and Harry walked in. He carried a card, some balloons, and a big box of chocolates. He stood in front of where the table used to be, a confused expression on his face, before tentatively placing his gifts at the foot of the bed.

"What happened?" he asked, sounding both confused and concerned.

"No idea," Chloe said before Layla could speak. "Bit weird, though."

"That looks like liquid metal. I'm not really sure that's meant to happen. In fact, I'm positive that metal turning to liquid isn't considered a manufacturer's fault." He looked between Chloe and Layla. "Either of you plan on explaining what this is?"

"You never seen a puddle of metal before?" Chloe asked.

"I'm pretty certain not like this, no."

Layla wondered why it was that Chloe didn't find the fact that she'd essentially melted a table to be all that odd. She wondered if she were just putting on a front to look less concerned than she was inside, but Layla wasn't certain that was true. She got the impression that Chloe knew more than she was willing to say.

"That balloon for me?" Layla asked Harry, hoping to get his attention away from the table.

He looked over at her, as if remembering she was in the room, and smiled. "Yes. Balloons and chocolates are well known for their healing properties."

"Really?"

Harry shrugged. "I have no idea. The last person I saw in hospital was my aunt, and we just brought her about fifty kilos of grapes. I didn't think you'd like that. You do like chocolate though, hence"—he brandished the box of chocolates—"the largest box I could find." He placed the chocolates back on the bed. "More importantly, how are you?"

"I've been better."

"Nice cage on the window."

Layla followed Harry's gaze. "Yeah, they're worried about people getting into the room."

"They think these people are going to climb up several dozen feet to get to you?"

"They killed a lot of people to get to me last time, who knows what they'll do next."

"It took me two days to get through security to see you. They wanted to run background checks on me. The news is plastered with information about what happened at the train depot. Have the police spoken to you about it?"

"Some special-investigator people have been here, yeah," Layla told him. "I just want to go home and shower in my own bathroom and eat my own food, but then I remember all of those people and . . ." She closed her eyes and took a deep breath.

"Sorry, I didn't mean to upset you," Harry told her. "I'm just worried about you."

Layla smiled. "Thanks, Harry. I'm fine. Tired, but fine."

"Tired?" Chloe asked. "Not sleeping well?"

Layla shook her head. "Bad dreams."

"That's to be expected," Harry said, and paused for a second. "Sorry, you probably already know that. I'm not really much help here, am I? I don't really know what to say. I want to make it better but can't."

Layla placed her hand on top of Harry's. "It's fine, just you being here is enough." She looked at Chloe. "Both of you."

"Have you eaten?" Harry asked. "There's a fish-and-chip shop just around the corner. I can see if I can smuggle some up here."

Layla's stomach grumbled. "Apparently the answer is yes. I'd love a pie and chips. Steak and kidney, please."

"Cod and chips," Chloe said.

Harry promised he'd be back soon and left Chloe and Layla alone.

"I can manipulate metal," Layla said.

"I saw."

"I bonded with some spirits in a scroll. They call me an umbra. I'm essentially a superhero now. I'm going to get a cape and start fighting crime."

"You appear to be taking it in good humor."

Layla stared at her friend. "You're not surprised. You're not concerned or freaking out that I just melted a damn table."

"Technically, you didn't melt it."

"Don't start using semantics on me. Why aren't you more . . . you know . . . weirded out?"

"Weirded? I don't think that's a word."

Layla's eyes narrowed in irritation. "Chloe Range, don't change the subject."

"I've had some experience with weird shit. My mum was a witch. Not a wiccan, a full-on witch with powers and everything. She knew how to curse people and do all kinds of crazy stuff. So I'm okay with what you're doing, because you're my friend and I want to be there for you. But also because I've seen the weirdness already."

Layla wasn't certain what to say to that. She still thought that Chloe was hiding something, but she couldn't figure out what it might be. "Thanks for being honest."

Layla noticed the slightest wince, as if those words had hurt Chloe, but the smile never left Chloe's face. "My mum was insane, and probably evil. So, yeah, that was my childhood. So, back to you. You're taking all of this okay?"

"I'm not sure how I'm taking it. I've spent the last few nights talking to spirits who live in my head. And last night I had a lovely chat with a demon. A demon who showed me a vision of your death at my hands."

Chloe sighed. "I'm not going to die, and you're *certainly* not going to kill me."

"Everyone says I have to accept the demon. Or I'll go insane. But how can I accept it if it's just going to do evil things anyway? Whether I accept it or not, it's never going to go away. I get to spend the rest of my extended life with a demon in my head. That was never part of my life plan, Chloe. Demonic entities were not meant to be living in my goddamn subconscious." She shouted the last few words, allowing the frustration to get the better of her for the first time since she'd been taken to the hospital.

When Chloe didn't say anything, Layla continued, "I heal bullet wounds in days now. Days. I can manipulate metal, and apparently, when this is all done, I'll be stronger, faster, have better senses. I'll be on the big screen soon alongside Spider-Man. The Incredible Terrified Woman."

Chloe hugged her friend. "I'm sorry."

"You didn't do this to me, I did. And one of the spirits killed something while she was in control of me. Two somethings, in fact. Blood elves, she called them."

Chloe's expression changed to one of shock and fear. "Blood elf? Are you sure?"

Layla nodded tentatively. "Yes. Blood elf. Creepy, purple humanoids. They seemed to enjoy the idea of hurting me. I had to seriously hurt one to get out of my cell. When I bonded with the spirits, one of them had to take control of me, and she killed two of them."

"Did you tell Diana or Tommy this?"

Layla shook her head. "I didn't think they'd believe me at first, and I figured they had everything they needed. Blood elves. I've never seen anything like them. Gyda—the spirit in my head—she hates them, though, says they destroyed her home. She's from a place called . . ."

"Nidavellir," Chloe finished.

"That's right. Is that something your mom told you about?"

Pure fear had taken over Chloe, and she looked back at the door. "Stay here. You need to tell Diana everything about the blood elves. I need to go make a call. I'll be back later—just please tell her everything."

Layla nodded, confused about why her friend was now terrified, but she wasn't given a chance to ask as Chloe fled the room, just as Harry was entering with the chips.

The smell of pie and chips was usually enough to get Layla's mouth watering, but she ignored it, more concerned about her friend.

Harry placed the chips on the remains of the table and glanced over at the door. "She was in a hurry."

"Yes, and I don't know why, but something strange is happening."

Diana entered the room a moment later, a similar expression of concern on her face. "Harry, can you give Layla and me a few minutes? You can take your chips to the room down the corridor."

Harry looked to Layla for confirmation.

"It's okay. You can come back in a minute," Layla assured him.

Diana waited to be alone with Layla before speaking. "Blood elves too?"

Layla nodded. "I'm sorry I didn't tell you sooner. I didn't know how to. It felt weird just telling Chloe about the ogre. There was so much happening—I wasn't sure who'd believe me. Chloe trusts you and Tommy, so I guess that's enough for me." She didn't want to ask what Chloe was hiding from her; she didn't want to force Diana to lie and thus end up resenting her for it.

"It's okay. After what you went through, I wouldn't trust anyone either. I just need to make sure that Tommy gets the information. How many elves and ogres?"

"One ogre. His name was Brako. I only saw a few elves, so I have no idea how many remain."

"Brako?" Diana's question was filled with the hope that she'd heard wrong.

"Who is he?"

Diana sighed. "He's an exceptionally dangerous individual, and someone we really don't want to meet again."

"Again? You've met him before?"

Diana's nod was small. "We crossed paths a few years ago. Both of us escaped that meeting with our lives, but both of us were hurt. Ogres are incredibly strong and fast. And on top of that, they like causing mayhem."

"He's the one who killed my friends at the depot. He reveled in it."

"He's vicious, even for an ogre. There aren't many of his kind left, so it's probably for the best that it stays that way."

"And the blood elves?"

"They're a long story, for another time. I need to go speak to Tommy, and if I start telling you about the elves, I'll be here all day. Just know that they're incredibly dangerous. Even more so than the ogre, I think. They're not as strong, or fast, but they fight in groups, like rats. Where there's one, there's usually a dozen more waiting to stab you in the back."

"One of the spirits inside of me killed two of them."

"They are monsters, and with or without the spirits, you had no choice. Doesn't mean you're becoming a killer, but it might not be the last time you're put in a situation where you have to fight for your life."

"I might have to kill again?" Images of Chloe cowering before a demonic Layla flashed into her head.

"Maybe. But let's try not to let that happen. Unfortunately, that's the world we live in. Too many things want us dead to think that we won't have to step over that line. Just take care of how easily you cross it, because doing it for the wrong reasons sometimes leaves you on a side you can't return from."

"The spirits said something similar."

"Smart spirits." Diana turned and walked back to the door. "I need to call Tommy. I'll be right back."

Layla nodded and looked out of the open window.

Have you decided to accept me yet?

The voice sent a shiver up Layla's back, but she refused to look back at the demon. "You told me if I accepted you, I'd murder my best friend."

And if you don't, you'll murder a lot more people. Not a choice I'd want to make.

"Do you get off on causing misery?"

Yes. Humanity has so much optimism. Did you know that? I get that there are wars and strife and bullshit even demons couldn't think of coming up with, but under it all, you're an endlessly optimistic species. I like to poke that optimism with a big sharp stick. I like to make it bleed a little, to pick at it until it's an open wound. He paused. *I'm sorry, I lost my train of thought for a second. Oh, yes . . . essentially, I like to ensure that whatever optimism you people have is crushed under my boot. It's fun.*

"I won't let you win."

The demon laughed. *My dear, I've already won. You're just too stubborn to see it.*

Everything in front of Layla's eyes burst into flame as the screams of people reached her ears. It was only there for a second, but a second was all it took for her to scamper back from the window.

You'll be mine. That woman can't help you. And your friend, Chloe, she can't help you either. And if you think those spirits can help you, then you're just deluding yourself.

Layla turned around to face the demon, who was leaning up against the bathroom doorway, its arms crossed over its chest. The demon's appearance was the same as before, except it was now considerably more female than it had been when she'd seen it in the cage. The demon wore a black suit, which did little to diminish its fearsome appearance.

"You're a woman now?"

"I can change as I feel the need. Our sexes are fluid; we change with a mood, or just because we can. It's weird that so many of you here are so rigid. Besides, I look damn good in this suit no matter my sex."

"I wasn't criticizing," Layla snapped defensively.

The demon laughed. "I don't care. I give exactly zero shits about the thought process of a human."

"Umbra."

"Umbra? You've accepted that, have you?"

"If you're not here to show me anything else horrific, you can just go."

Terhal shrugged. "You can't make me. Not until you're strong enough. Until then, your mind is my playground."

"So, you're going to try to kill me?"

"Oh, my word, no. If you die, I get to go back into storage for the next however long. No, I don't want you dead. A dead you is a bored me. Can't have that."

Layla climbed onto the bed and lay down. "One day we'll be on an equal footing, and then we'll see who wins."

Terhal's laughter reverberated through Layla's skull. "Oh, I'm going to enjoy this." She walked over to Layla, her face was only a few inches from her. "I can smell the fear on you."

"That's my deodorant. It smells of flowers, apparently."

Terhal's expression hardened. "Don't mock me, girl. I don't appreciate it."

Layla held Terhal's stare. "Leave. Now." To her surprise the demon vanished, leaving her alone in her own mind.

"Nicely done," Rosa said from the foot of the bed.

"Do I have to always have one of you out here?" Layla asked.

"You need to pick one of us to be your main guide through your powers. You need to learn how to use them properly, and not just to melt the legs of a table. You can't do this alone. The better the control you have over the power you wield, the better your chance of being able to stop the demon from entering your waking moments until you decide whether or not you can accept us."

Layla sat up. "Whoever I choose, I can still talk to the others, though, right? This isn't forever?"

"Nope. Just while you learn."

"Then I choose you. You're the only one who accepted the demon and spirits and didn't go insane, or allow the demon to murder everyone you love. Gyda's kill-yourself platform isn't really for me."

"You're okay with having an assassin as your guide?"

"Your memories are already bleeding into mine. I can't stop that. I can't stop your abilities from becoming second nature to me. So, I may as well embrace it."

Rosa nodded an agreement. "None of the spirits can take control of you now; none of them can make you do anything you don't want to. Our training starts when you next sleep. Until then, I'll let you relax. Trust me, you're going to want to eat and make sure your strength is as high as it can be. Training will be taxing on your mind and body."

"Something is going on here. With Chloe, and Tommy and Diana. There's something they're not telling me. I'm not sure if it's about my powers, or if it's because they think they can use me to get to my father, but something is weird. My phone doesn't connect to the Internet at all, and the hospital Wi-Fi doesn't work. I need to find out what's happening. I need some answers, and I don't think they're going to give them to me."

"You think they're hiding something from you for malicious reasons?"

"I don't know. Elias mentioned the LOA. You ever heard of them?"

"Avalon? Sure. They essentially rule the world from the shadows."

"I need to know more. I need to know what I'm dealing with. I want to look into Tommy's security firm too. I can't do that from here."

"You don't trust them?"

Layla shook her head. "No, it's not that. I trust that they're not trying to hurt me, and that they *really* want to find and stop Elias. I'm all for that. But there's a lot they're not telling me, and I get the feeling it's stuff I need to know. I need to get out of here. I need to go back to my place and use my computer."

"Elias could be there."

"No. He doesn't know where I live—he admitted as much to me. It's why he came for me at my work. I'll be safe there."

"There's more. You can't keep it from me, Layla."

Layla paused. She wasn't sure if she'd ever get used to having the spirits know everything she knew. "My father's contact details. The details of the agent in charge of the case. They're meant to be classified, but I have them all written down. If Elias does find out where I live, and he finds those, he'll know where my father is, and he'll know who put him there. That's a dangerous amount of information that needs to be destroyed. I can't tell Tommy and Diana because they might want to use that info to talk to my father too. And maybe they've already convinced Chloe that it's the best course of action. She might think she's trying to protect me."

"So, we're going to break out?" There was no part of Rosa's tone that suggested she disagreed with Layla.

Layla grabbed her trainers, which Chloe had brought for her, and put them on. "That's the plan, yes. But I need to do it quietly, and I need to be back here by morning. Can the training wait until tomorrow?"

"You want to come back here?"

"If Tommy and Diana aren't as trustworthy as they seem, they're only going to come after me. Staying off-grid is something I've managed to do for a long time, but I'm pretty certain they find people who don't want to be found."

Layla walked over to the window and removed the metal cage from it, taking metal from the window beside it and using it to create a ladder. "It doesn't reach the bottom. I need more metal."

"When you get to the bottom, use some metal to anchor yourself, and then turn the rest into the remainder of the ladder."

Layla looked over at Rosa. "This isn't an overly sensible thing to do, is it?"

"Sometimes sensible and right aren't the same thing. You need proof you're working with the good guys now. Let's go get some."

Layla climbed out of the window and began to descend the ladder. She touched the ground a few minutes later and dissolved the metal ladder before running off into the night. It was a few miles from the hospital to her home and she wanted to get there as soon as possible. It was time for her to start discovering facts for herself.

18

It didn't take Layla long to get home, although by the time she'd gotten there, she'd realized she didn't have her keys. She sighed.

"Move metal, remember?" Rosa said from beside her.

Layla felt incredibly stupid for a few seconds. "I didn't think of that."

"It's been a long few days. I wouldn't worry about it."

Layla reached the rear door of her building and found it to be unlocked. She pushed it open and almost crept through the hallway to her apartment. She didn't really want to melt the lock, mostly because she didn't want to have to pay to get it fixed. But she guessed when this was all over she'd have to move. Again. The landlord could get the lock fixed out of her deposit.

She placed her finger against the dead bolt and pushed slightly, feeling the hard metal give way as it turned to liquid and spilled out down the doorframe. She took hold of the door handle and it too turned to liquid. She gave the door a small push and it swung open.

"Any chance you can check ahead to make sure no one is in there?" Layla asked Rosa.

"We're spirits—we only see what you see. We can't go exploring for you."

"Well, balls," Layla said, and stepped into the dark apartment. She walked the length of the hallway inside, moving slowly and checking each room to ensure she was alone.

When she'd completed the task, she decided not to bother switching on the lights, just in case someone was watching from outside. Instead, she went to her bedroom and fished out a torch from a bedside-table drawer.

Layla went back into the living room and pulled the red and white rug off the floor, exposing a safe. She tapped the six-digit code into the keypad and pulled open the door. She placed the torch on the sofa behind her, ensuring that the light remained on her at all times, and removed the shoebox from the safe. She placed it to one side and closed the door.

"I want to use the computer first. I'm not sure I'll be in the right frame of mind to think much once I've opened this up." Layla spoke mostly to herself, and wondered if Rosa would think she was crazy for doing such a thing. But something inside told her that, no, Rosa wouldn't think that. She had an unpleasant past all of her own.

Layla switched on the desktop and waited for Windows to load, which, despite the feeble power of the machine, only took a few seconds. A heartbeat later and she'd opened the Internet and typed in "Enhanced Security," the name of Tommy's company.

It brought up a website with lots of nice pictures of the main headquarters and several quotes from happy customers. Everything about it appeared to be legit. There were no pictures of staff members, and the names of everyone bar Tommy were missing, but Layla imagined that was a security precaution.

She left the page and began going through Google to check for any reports on them, but found little apart from the occasional website forum where someone recommended them to someone else. There was nothing to suggest that it was anything more than a normal, human organization.

She added "Avalon" to the search, and after digging further and further into the results, she began to see the sort of things she was looking for. The first page was another forum, by the name of "Fangs and Claws." After reading the first dozen posts, which extolled the virtues of Tommy and his team, there were several which badmouthed Avalon. Three separate posts called it a police state, with one suggesting that trusting them was the same as nominating yourself for execution.

She stayed in the forum and searched for "Law of Avalon", and got dozens of hits. Several of them said how everyone posting here would be caught and arrested if they were anti-Avalon, and a few sounded like conspiracy theorists. She'd seen some of them after her father's arrest suggesting the reason he was out of the public eye was because he was a CIA wet-work assassin.

Layla rolled her eyes at several of the posts, and found a members-only section that she couldn't access. She tried to create an account, but it kept saying that she was not old enough to view these details.

"People don't trust Avalon," Rosa said. "That's why they've put a block on it. Change your birth year to 476."

Layla did as requested, and it allowed her to create an account. "What happened in 476?"

"The Roman Empire died. A lot of people who distrust Avalon use that date as the day Avalon failed to stop something they desperately didn't want to happen. It's the proof that Avalon isn't all powerful."

"Is this all stuff I'll eventually learn as your memories and mine blend?"

"Probably, but do you really want to wait that long?"

Layla shook her head and opened the first members-only forum post, and her eyes widened in shock. "This says that a decade ago Tommy and a Nate Garrett saved a bunch of werewolves from being murdered.

They helped people, saved lives, and ensured that those responsible were brought to justice." Layla turned to Rosa. "Werewolves too?"

"Of course. There are many, many things in this world that aren't human. Werewolves aren't that hard to believe, are they? And that's your proof that Tommy is one of the good guys."

"Because he saved werewolves?"

"No. Nate Garrett, although I knew him as Nathaniel. If he's friends with Tommy, if he worked with him, then Tommy can be trusted. Nathaniel is a good man."

"So, Tommy and Diana are the good guys?" Layla asked. "Doesn't explain why Chloe is hiding something from me."

"Maybe I can explain that?" a voice said from the front door.

Layla shot to her feet, ready to fight, as Tommy walked around the corner and into the front room.

"Not here to fight," Tommy said softly. "Just talk. Diana figured out you'd absconded. I thought it was time you learned the truth about a lot of things. You can't trust me to be honest, if I can't trust you with that honesty."

Layla relaxed and Tommy switched on the lights. "It's okay, I've got half a dozen agents watching this place."

"How'd you find me?"

"I'm a werewolf. I'd show you, but these jeans and t-shirt are nice and I don't want to ruin them. You'll just have to take my word for it." He turned his hand over as his nails grew several inches. "That's about as much as I can do without going all wolf. Who were you talking to?"

"One of the spirits. Her name is Rosa."

"Hi, Rosa," he said, without a hint of mockery. "You mentioned Nate's name. He's a friend of mine. My best friend, actually. That incident you read about where we saved those werewolves, he also saved my life and the life of my daughter Kase."

Layla recognized the name Kase from somewhere, but couldn't quite put her finger on it. She motioned for Tommy to sit, and he sat down on the sofa, while Layla took the armchair. "You said you'd tell me the truth. All of it?"

Tommy nodded. "We've kept you in the dark because we were worried how you'd react. You have a lot going on right now, and we didn't want to add to that."

"You were worried I'd let the demon out?"

"A little. Chloe told us you had that under control. And I trust her."

"Why?"

"She works for me."

Layla felt like she'd been slapped. "Works for you? She owns a coffee shop."

"No. Well, actually, yes, but not in the way you think. Three years ago, she left the world of Avalon to get away from that life. I asked her to move to Ocean Village, and then I asked her to keep an eye on you."

Layla felt like she couldn't breathe. "Keep an eye on me?"

"You want the facts, or do you want to be angry?"

"Let him talk," Rosa said softly.

Layla motioned for him to continue.

"Chloe is a highly trained employee of mine. Her job was to keep an eye on you because we know who your father is. And more importantly, we know *what* your father is.

"Your father is an umbra, Layla. He found a scroll way before you were born, and decided to use it to help others. Over time that turned into him killing lots of people because, as you may have noticed, he's insane. But you are the only documented birth to an umbra. Ever. We had no idea what that power would do, so we kept an eye on you and your mother. Your mother knew for the most part. When she brought you to England, she went to my wife, Olivia, and explained everything, and Olivia told her we'd watch over you for as long as it was needed.

"But then your mother died, and now we had a grief-stricken daughter who may or may not have incredible power buried inside her head. As it turned out, you didn't, not until a few days ago, but we didn't know that at the time. Also, we knew that Nergal was looking for your father."

"Why?" Layla interrupted.

"Your father's power allows him to find anyone, anywhere, in any realm. He just needs to think of that person, or have something belonging to them, and he can find them. It's how he tracked his victims. He'd find evidence at a crime scene and track it right to whoever it belonged. More often than not, it was the criminal responsible. Nergal wants that power so that he can track other umbra like your father. He wants to create an army."

Layla couldn't believe what she was hearing. Not only did Chloe lie to her all these years, but her mother had practically arranged it, and her father wasn't a human. If her father was an umbra, and she was an umbra, maybe she was becoming her father in more ways than she'd ever imagined. Maybe that was how it started with him, and how it would start with her. She'd lose control and hurt people she loved.

"Anyway, back to Chloe. She was just meant to watch and report. That's it. But she grew to like you. And you formed a deep friendship. The only problem was, she was lying to you. She asked me a dozen times if she could tell you the truth, but we weren't sure what you'd do if you learned it. So she got deeper and deeper into her new life, and all it took was Elias to come along for her to be put in an awful place."

"What awful place?"

"She's an umbra. Like you. Like your father. She wanted to be the one to talk to you about her power, about your power, about how to control it. About the demon. But we said no. We weren't convinced that having someone so close to you reveal her true self would pay off. We thought it might trigger the demon."

"Why tell me this now?"

"Because we can't have you running off to look for information, and we can't have you thinking we're keeping things from you. This won't work that way."

"Chloe has lied to me all these years? Pretending to be my friend?" A memory clicked. "She told me about Kase. They're friends."

"No. She doesn't pretend. She doesn't really have it in her. And yes, they are friends. Have been for a long time."

"I trusted her," Layla shouted. "She knows how many people have lied to me my whole life. She knows that everyone I trust lies. They take that trust and twist it for their own purpose, and she's done the exact same thing."

"If you really think that, you're wrong. She worked for me to help me keep you safe. To help me keep others safe from you. Because when you're not sure if the person with no training and a psychotic father is a monster themselves, you tend to want to find out."

Anger bubbled up inside of Layla and she wanted to lash out, to hit something. To hurt someone. "All these years, I've been terrified of hurting someone, of becoming my father, and you all knew that I might. And you didn't tell me?"

"We had no idea, Layla. That's why we had Chloe keep an eye on you. Your mother told us that you had some issues with your anger. That you were capable of hurting people. She was worried you'd inherited it from your father."

The anger vanished, replaced with a feeling like she'd been punched in the gut. "My mom told you about those thoughts?"

Tommy nodded. "You beat a kid into semi-consciousness. You bet your mum told us. She said you were a good kid, but that your father had instilled some . . . lessons in you as a child. Fighting, weapon use, explosives. Quite the childhood. He turned a child into a weapon, and he did it without his wife having a say in the matter. He was a bad guy, your old man."

"Chloe should have told me. She should have been honest with me. How can I trust her now?"

"You should trust her because it's Chloe. No matter what she did or didn't do, she's still Chloe. She knows I'm telling you this, by the way. She's not happy about it, but she knows. She wanted to be the one to tell you."

"Anything else?" Layla's voice was cold and hard. She wanted to talk to Chloe, to find out how her friend could lie to her face over and over again. They might have only been friends a few years, but Layla didn't have many friends and anyone she let in, even slightly, was someone she believed was worthy of her trust. To discover that she was wrong hurt more than she'd imagined.

"Lots of things. We went back to the underground compound you were kept at, but if anyone had been there, they're long gone now. We found a few bodies, though. We ID'd them as some of the people who worked at the depot. I'm sorry."

Layla had hoped some of them would still be alive.

Tommy waited for a few seconds before continuing. "I want to keep you alive, Layla. I'm going to be as open as I can about everything, but you don't have to like me. You just have to realize I'm not the bad guy."

"I thought I did. I thought I trusted Chloe, but she betrayed me."

"You have a black and white view of the world. She didn't betray you. Yes, she lied, but she did it to protect you, she did it because it's her job. And she's exceptionally good at her job. But she's not much of a liar when it comes to her feelings. She can't hide those. She's your friend because she wants to be. No one ordered it; no one said it would be a good idea if you became besties. She's your friend because she cares about you deeply. If you can't see that, then I'm sorry."

Layla thought about Tommy's words for several seconds. She would need to talk to Chloe. "So what happens now?"

"I can't force you to come with me."

"I think you probably could," Layla argued.

Tommy stood and nodded. "Yes, I could. I could force you in a hundred different ways. But I won't. I'm not that person. You want to know how to control the spirits in a place of safety? Come with me. You want to know how to control the anger inside you, so you don't have those thoughts of hurting people? I can help with that too."

"How?"

"I'm a werewolf, Layla. Deep inside my soul is a monster the likes of which makes your father look like Foghorn Leghorn. The beast that lives there wants out. Always. It wants to hurt and feed and kill. And it is a constant battle not to let it. I'm hundreds of years old, and it's still hard work. My daughter Kase is your age, and she let it out once. Almost lost control and killed people. That voice you hear that tells you how much you like fighting, I have one like it, except mine tells me to bathe in the blood of everyone I know.

"We all have our monsters, Layla. But you're not one. You've lived with that voice your whole life, probably think it's part of your father's gifts he passed on to you. It's not. It's just something you need to learn to ignore. You're so terrified of becoming your father, you don't realize you're nothing like him."

"Have you ever met my father?"

"No. I know people who have, though. I've read about his crimes; I've seen what he's done. Trust me, you're not your father."

"I'm an umbra just like him."

"You think that means you're going to become him, that this was how he started?"

Tommy's words were almost exactly what Layla had just thought, and for a moment she wondered if he could read minds too. She smiled, but only for a second.

"I just said what you'd been thinking, right?" Tommy asked.

Layla stared at him for several seconds before nodding.

"That's not how it works. You don't inherit evil. My father was a drunk who liked to beat me for having the audacity to breathe. Some people are assholes, doesn't mean you're anything like them. I'm not my father. I'm nothing like him. And you're nothing like yours. You need to learn that. This world will crush you if you think you're a monster when you're not. There are enough actual monsters out there already."

Tommy crossed the floor and picked up the box next to the safe. "Can I?"

Layla nodded, hesitantly.

Tommy lifted the lid off the box, exposing several thousand pounds' worth of notes, three passports under various names, along with birth certificates and other documents, and a small yellow journal. He opened it and showed it to Layla. "This is the number your father is at, along with the address of the prison, yes?"

Layla nodded.

"Tabitha was in charge of him. She made sure that no one knew the location who didn't need to know." Tommy closed the book. "Do you know it by heart?"

Another nod.

He held out the journal to Layla, who took it, staring at it as if it might be poisonous. "Good. Destroy it. No one but you needs to know how to contact him. I certainly don't."

Tommy looked back in the box. "This is a gun, Layla. A Glock."

"My mother got it after we moved here. Cost her a lot."

Tommy ejected the magazine and found it empty, but discovered a box of bullets. He opened it and immediately closed it again. "Silver-tipped. These will kill most things in our world."

"I don't want them."

Tommy placed them on the sofa. "We'll dispose of them, if you like. The money is yours to do with as you please. The IDs . . . well, I hope you don't need them. What are you afraid of, Layla? This isn't just because you think you'll become your father, so what else is it?"

Layla took a deep breath. "I'm alone, Tommy. My father is gone, my mother is dead. I don't let myself get close to people because . . ."

"What if they go too?" Tommy finished for her.

Layla nodded. "It's easier to not make attachments. But . . . the last few years, I've wanted to try. I want to live a normal life, where I can have friends and love and enjoy normal everyday activities. Where I don't have to worry that the person being confrontational over something stupid will end up dead because I lose control.

"And every time I think I'm okay, those little voices come back and tell me that I should hurt someone, or I get into a fight and I enjoy it. I liked hurting those neighbors of mine who attacked me. I liked hurting Rob when he grabbed me. I'm not afraid I'm becoming my father, I'm afraid I'll be worse. What if that's what the demon inside of me does? What if it turns me into an even worse monster?"

Tommy looked up and saw tears roll down Layla's cheeks. He walked over and hugged her. "Demons, beasts, monsters . . . nothing that can't be tamed, or killed. We'll tame your demon, Layla. We'll make sure of it. You just need to fight, and never stop."

Layla nodded, as somewhere in her mind Terhal laughed as if the idea of fighting her was the funniest thing in the world.

19

Elias had spent several hours trying to figure out a way to find out exactly which hospital Layla had been taken to. Eventually, he'd resorted to calling the hospitals pretending to be a concerned relative, but no one told him anything. It was infuriating.

Fortunately, Shane and Reyes had better luck locating Layla's home address. Unfortunately, it was swamped with people Elias didn't really want to deal with.

"Thomas Carpenter is there," Reyes told him.

Elias rubbed his eyes with the heels of his palms. "Damn it. That man is beginning to become an irritant. No matter. It's unlikely Layla would go back there, which means they're keeping her holed up somewhere secure."

"Well, I have much better news." Shane opened a notepad and began reading through it as he spoke. "We tracked two of her friends. The first is Chloe, who works at a coffee shop in Ocean Village. She seems to own it, although I couldn't find her there. I spoke to the woman behind the counter—a pretty blonde I would love to see again in a more *personal* way—who explained that Chloe owned the place. She was out visiting a friend. I then found another of Layla's friends,

Harry, who lives with several others in a house across town. I talked to one of them, and they explained that he was going to the hospital to see a friend."

"Can we grab either of them?"

"Not Harry. Some of Tommy's people were watching the place as I left. They didn't follow me, but I'm sure they notified Tommy I'd been there. Chloe is a better bet, though." Shane passed Elias the notepad with the address of the coffee shop on it.

"Why?" Dara asked. "Why is she the better bet?"

"More chances to grab her, and I didn't see any of Tommy's people watching the shop."

"So, Layla's probably at a hospital?" Dara said. "There are, what, four in Southampton?"

"And a few not too far from here as well."

"Get me an address," Elias told Shane and Reyes. "Good work. Dara, you're with me, we're going to go pay Chloe a visit. Get some of the blood elves to accompany us. She's going to tell us where Layla is, and then she's going to help us get Layla to agree to our terms."

Elias and Dara gathered the blood elves and drove into Southampton in the Range Rover, parking it in one of the many car parks that sat around Ocean Village.

"I'm going in alone," Elias said, and turned to Dara. "You know what to do."

He exited the car and walked along the marina toward the coffee shop. He continued to look out for Tommy or any of his people, but saw no one watching him, or following. He wondered why Tommy would put people on Harry, but not on Chloe. There had to be a reason. Over the last few years, he'd grown to almost admire Tommy, a man with a singular vision to find Elias and those who worked with him. Tommy had been close on several occasions, had even managed to capture several blood elves who hadn't escaped in time and had executed them in an unexpectedly ruthless manner.

Nergal had been less than impressed with Tommy's actions and had wanted to send a death squad after the man, but Elias had managed to talk him out of it. If Tommy was killed, people who Elias didn't want to deal with would become involved. Tommy was a known entity, but some of his friends were the kinds of people you ran from and never stopped. Nergal might be incredibly powerful and dangerous, but even he would have trouble against some of those Tommy considered friends. It was best to just let Tommy think he was getting close before the end goal was snatched away from him.

Keeping a dog on a leash was easier than getting it back on once you'd let it have free rein. Elias smiled at the metaphor; he thought it summed up Tommy well.

He reached the door to the coffee shop and pushed it open. The aroma of freshly ground coffee assaulted his senses. He didn't dislike coffee, in fact he loved it, but the way it had permeated so many people's lives made him feel as if it was more and more something people bought because they were supposed to, not because they actually enjoyed the taste. Over the years it had become cheap and easy to buy, and not the luxurious commodity it should be.

He walked past several patrons—all on their phones, or in one case, a young woman reading a book—and took a seat at the far corner of the shop. It allowed him a full view of the place and he could see all of the comings and goings of the staff and visitors.

There were eleven people in the shop, and a further two behind the counter. A third member of staff was busy wiping down tables and exchanging pleasantries with some of the customers. The customers themselves didn't concern Elias. All but two were in their twenties or thirties, and those two were well over fifty. They sat beside each other on one of the three chocolate-colored couches, though they didn't talk, apparently completely at ease with the idea of silence. Elias presumed they'd been together a long time and were simply comfortable in each other's presence. He wondered for a second if he'd ever get that, but quickly pushed it aside.

The nine others were made up of four men and five women, three of whom sat around one table. They were wearing designer clothing, carrying designer handbags, and occasionally flashing their expensive, and probably new, phones.

A man and woman, probably a couple from the way they were occasionally touching hands on the table, sat opposite one another by the window.

The remaining customers were either alone, or might as well have been for all the attention they were giving their friends or partners.

Elias looked over at the two baristas, who were busy talking to each other. He didn't care what about; he had no interest in eavesdropping. He got up from his seat and walked over to the counter, where one of the two, a young blonde who Elias was sure was the same one Shane had discussed, walked over to him with a smile.

"Can I help you?" she asked, the happiness in her smile traveling into her words, something Elias hadn't been expecting.

"Hi. Can I have a latte, and do you happen to know if Chloe is about?"

The girl's smile faltered just a little bit, but not enough for Elias to be concerned. "She should be in today; she's been away for a few days. Are you friends?"

Elias passed her a five-pound note, and returned the woman's smile. "We have a mutual friend, the one in the hospital. I saw Chloe at the General yesterday, and she told me to come see her here."

"Oh, isn't it horrible? I heard about Layla. She's such a lovely person, and it's so sad what happened to all of those people. I'm so sorry. I'm sure the doctors and nurses at the General will do everything they can to help her, though."

Elias nodded, while inside he knew he had the information he wanted. He'd contact Shane and Reyes and tell them to get over to the

General. He'd guessed it was this one because it was the largest hospital in the city. "It's a sad thing. I'm hoping Layla will get better soon. She's a fighter."

The woman passed the change to Elias. "She really is. I took a few classes with her, and she's tough."

"Classes?"

"The MMA stuff that she goes to with Chloe."

"Ah, right, sorry, I wondered what you were talking about." He chuckled. It was forced, but he'd had enough practice over the years to make it sound almost genuine.

The shop door opened, making a small chime that Elias hadn't noticed when he'd first come in. He turned and saw a young woman take a step into the shop and freeze as she laid eyes on him. The smile on her face melted. Elias wondered how this person knew him.

She walked over to Elias and nodded to the woman who had served him.

"A friend of Layla's," the barista said.

"Thanks, Sam," Chloe said, with every appearance of happiness. "Hello, Elias."

"Do you have a few minutes?" Elias asked. "It's about Layla."

"I know." She glanced around her at the other patrons. "Let's go out the back, we won't be disturbed there."

"Glad to hear it. Lead the way."

Chloe turned to Sam. "Can you deal with everything here? We'll only be a few minutes."

Sam nodded, and Chloe walked off, pushing open a door at the far end of the coffee shop and walking down a small corridor. Elias followed close behind, until they'd left the shop and walked out onto a footpath behind the building. The path was next to the water, where several boats moved gently on the waves. A wooden bench overlooked the serenity of the area, and across the marina was a construction site. There would be no one around to see what happened next.

Chloe stopped walking when she reached the black railing that separated the footpath from the water below. She turned around to face Elias.

"So, how long have you worked for Tommy?" Elias asked. "I only mention it because he put a security detail on your friend Harry, and I know for a fact there's one at the General Hospital. That is where Layla is, right?"

Chloe said nothing.

"Anyway," Elias continued, "I wondered why Tommy hadn't put anyone to keep an eye on you, but after the way you behaved in the shop, I'm guessing they think you don't need protecting. Their mistake. Also, you knew who I was, and you shouldn't have. Not unless someone showed you a picture."

"What do you think is going to happen here, Elias?" Chloe asked. "You're going to kill me?"

"Actually, no. You're going to come with me, and together we're going to convince Layla to help me. Or I'll start skinning you in front of her. That should get her attention. Does she know you work for Tommy? I imagine not. Which does leave one question: were you sent here to keep an eye on her because of who her father is? Or is this all a happy coincidence?"

"Are you going to try to kidnap me, or talk to me until I fall into a coma?"

Elias removed his hat and placed it on the nearby bench. "Don't want to get it dirty."

He turned and rushed toward Chloe, channeling his power into speed and strength. He threw a punch at Chloe, who dodged aside, striking out with one of her own. Elias easily avoided the blow and moved back a few paces. She was faster than he'd anticipated, and if she was working with Tommy, it was unlikely that she was human.

He darted back toward her, feinting with a right hand, and then kicking out with his left leg. She blocked both blows, but Elias stepped in and punched her in the kidney, making her gasp in pain. He grabbed the back of her head and drove his knee into her stomach, once, twice, and a third time, before letting go of her and kicking her in the chest, sending her sprawling on the concrete path.

"Not as good as you think you are," Elias said, walking toward her.

The second he was within reach, Chloe grabbed hold of his legs, lifted him up off the ground, and dumped him on the floor, bouncing the back of Elias's head off the concrete.

She grabbed his arm and locked the elbow, wrenching back on it, trying to break the joint. Elias rolled toward Chloe, and punched her in the face with his free hand, but Chloe didn't release the hold until a second punch. She head-butted Elias on the nose and kicked him away, rolling over and getting back to her feet. Blood streamed from her broken nose, and a cut on her lip caused her to spit blood onto the pavement.

Elias cradled his arm. It hurt like hell, and he hadn't expected Chloe to be so proficient at defending herself. He used some of his power to heal his wounds and was back to full health a few seconds later. He knew he didn't have enough reserves of power to continue that course of action, though. He needed to end this.

"I expected more of you," Chloe told him. "Elias Wells was a name people told me in whispers. You scared people. Humans, I'll grant you, but still, I expected better."

"Not up to my full strength, I'm afraid. Instead, I brought help."

Chloe glanced behind her, before looking back at Elias. "Three blood elves and, I assume, Dara. All for little old me? I'm flattered."

Elias watched Dara and the elves continue their steady walk toward Chloe. There was no point in hurrying it, it wasn't like she could escape anywhere. "Just make this easier on yourself. You might actually survive the experience."

Chloe laughed. "That's your sell? I *might* survive?"

"Might is better than won't. Which is what will happen if we have to take you by force."

"Please, Elias. Come take me by force."

She turned toward the nearest blood elf, who'd started to run toward her, and raised one hand. A blast of yellow power left her palm, slamming into the blood elf and throwing it back against the wall.

The remaining blood elves continued toward Chloe, their curved swords out, as they screamed a battle cry.

Chloe turned back to Elias and aimed a blast at him too, but he dodged aside, rolling across the ground as the blast removed a portion of the railing beside him.

The blood elves were on Chloe a second later, although both were soon blasted back as more power left Chloe's hands. She turned to face Elias again and began walking toward him.

"Not human after all," Elias said, waiting for his chance. He needed Chloe to be closer, and there was no more doubt in his mind that he needed to put every ounce of power he had into his attack. He'd be nearly drained of his power, but he had to risk it.

"Umbra," Chloe told him, and raised her hand—palm out—toward Elias. "Good-bye."

The railing beside Chloe leaped free, smashing into her, and knocking her into the wall of the coffee shop.

Dara released her grip on the railing, but only after wrapping her hands in steel. "Always did need me to save you," she told Elias.

Elias walked over to Chloe as she got back to her feet and punched her in the stomach hard enough to lift her off the ground. Another punch to the jaw spun her around, and she dropped to her knees.

"We could have done this the easy way," he told her. He hadn't used all of his power in the blow—he didn't want her dead—but he'd used enough to subdue her.

At least he thought he had, right up until the moment that Chloe began laughing. "My power, Elias, is to absorb and redirect kinetic energy." She leapt up faster than he could react, and blasted him in the chest, sending him into, and over, the bench.

Dara hit Chloe in the side of the jaw, knocking her aside, but Chloe spun away and blasted her with more kinetic energy. The steel around Dara's hands formed a shield in front of her, blocking the power. A second later the same steel struck out, changed into a battering ram, hitting Chloe in the chest, throwing her to the floor.

"You can absorb it, but the blow still hurts," Dara said. "Interesting. I'm going to enjoy finding out the limitations of your powers."

"Alchemist, yes?" Chloe asked as she stood, rubbing her shoulder. "And a redcap. Interesting group you've got here."

Dara walked over to the railing, placing her hand on it. It snaked up, lashing out at Chloe, who tried to dodge aside as it coiled around her, a metal python capturing its prey.

Elias was back on his feet walking toward the pair when Dara changed the steel into a sword, drawing a dagger from the sheath on her hip. "It's silver," she told Chloe. "It'll kill even you. If we can't take you alive, I'd rather not take you at all."

Chloe had been forced to her knees, unable to move, barely able to breathe. "You're welcome to try."

Dara took a step forward and the whole thing turned to shit.

20

Elias saw Chloe's face change as the demon inside of her emerged. Her face mostly stayed the same, but orange and red power glowed under her skin, which began to crack, although there was no blood to be seen. Her eyes changed shape, narrowing, as the white sclera turned blood red. Chloe's hands became claw-like, the fingernails growing as if unsheathing talons.

It all happened in the blink of an eye, but before Elias could yell a warning, power exploded out of Chloe. Pieces of metal, torn from the railings that had held her in place, pinged around the footpath like shrapnel. One of them struck Elias in the stomach, just below the ribs. He dropped to his knees as his power began healing him.

Dara was thrown back ten feet, impacting with the same piece of wall that Chloe had hit only moments earlier.

The first of the three blood elves reached Demon-Chloe as she stepped out of the remains of the railing. She hit the elf in the chest with a blast of power, sending it flying into the railing and then into the cold water with a splash.

The second elf swung the blade at her head, but she ducked and punched it in the stomach. It lurched forward, and Demon-Chloe snapped its neck, dropping the body to the floor with nonchalance.

The third elf screamed as she blasted its face, tearing away the flesh only a second before she ran its sword through its skull.

Elias had healed by the time the last elf died, and he charged at her, knocking her aside before she could use her energy blasts. He pummeled her about the head and back, trying to put as much strength into each blow as possible. Demon-Chloe attempted to fend them off, eventually grabbing his arm. Her other hand shot out, blasting him in the chest and sending him flying back over the railing and into the side of the hull of one of the boats in the marina.

Before he hit the water, Elias managed to grab hold of the boat's railing and pull himself up onto the deck. Pain wracked his body, and he turned back to Chloe, only to be hit by a second blast that propelled him into the side of the cabin.

Elias dropped to his knees, blood flowing from a dozen wounds. He'd used a lot of power, but he hadn't expected Chloe not to be human. In hindsight, he should have brought the ogre.

He looked out over the water, where Dara had engaged Demon-Chloe in combat, using the sword and dagger to try to get inside her defense. Dara cut across Demon-Chloe's arm, causing her to scream and dart away, putting distance between the two of them.

Dara didn't give an inch, using her alchemy to change the sword to a whip, lashing it against Demon-Chloe's other arm and forcing it to wrap around her limb. Dara stepped toward her and swiped the dagger up toward her face, but her opponent was fast and moved aside, trying to use her blasts to knock Dara back.

Dara dropped to the floor, and the concrete exploded around Demon-Chloe, knocking her back, but the whip still wrapped around her arm tugged her back toward Dara and the waiting dagger.

Demon-Chloe grabbed hold of Dara's wrist as the metal whip snaked up around her neck and began to choke her.

Dara avoided another blast of energy and kept the pressure on, tightening the metal around Demon-Chloe's neck. Elias had managed to drag himself back to his feet and watched with glee as a thin trickle of red dripped down her neck.

Dara took a step toward Demon-Chloe and easily avoided a weak punch, kicking her in the chest and sending her to the floor. Demon-Chloe's hands clawed at the whip as it tightened, a futile attempt to stop the inevitable. She swung another punch toward Dara, who avoided it again and laughed at the weakness of her enemy. Elias couldn't hear what Dara said, but she raised the dagger to plunge down into Demon-Chloe.

But before she could hit the target, Demon-Chloe grabbed hold of Dara's arm, twisted the dagger around, and drove it up into Dara's chest. Elias could see the look of shock on Dara's face as it cut into her, and the world slowed for him. He jumped over the side of the boat and began swimming to the nearest pontoon. Dragging himself out of the water, he ran as quickly as he could toward Dara, who had dropped to her knees, the dagger in her heart.

By this time, Chloe had disappeared, presumably so she could run off to report to Tommy. Getting Layla would be a lot more complicated now. But that could wait; Dara's injury was of more immediate concern.

He hurried to her side, but Dara was already gone. The dagger had punctured her heart and killed her almost instantly. He picked up her body and carried her back to the car. He didn't notice anyone watching until a man came up to him while he was trying to put Dara in the rear seat of the Range Rover.

"I think she needs an ambulance," the man said.

Elias exploded with rage, grabbing hold of the man and repeatedly smashing his head into the corner of the open car door until the metal was slick with blood. He dropped the dead man onto the ground and stomped on his head over and over, until the rage was spent. Only then did he climb into the front seat and set off, driving over the corpse he'd just created.

He didn't look at the back seat during the drive toward the abandoned farm that he'd had his people go to after they'd left the compound. Once there, Elias stopped the car and carried Dara's body into the main building. The farmhouse was two stories high and contained over a dozen rooms, not to mention the stables and pens.

Elias ignored the stares from the blood elves standing guard around the property as he took Dara through the farmhouse to the living room.

Shane and Reyes were both in the room when Elias walked in carrying their dead comrade. Neither of them said anything; they just stood and stared at Dara.

Elias laid the body on the nearest sofa and, his hands still covered in blood, walked over to the sink and started washing them. Only when he was done, and his hands were clean and dry, did he speak. "We need to bury her."

"What happened?" Shane asked.

"Chloe is an umbra. We were unprepared. She was more formidable than I'd anticipated, and we paid for that mistake. It won't happen again. Layla is at the General Hospital. No doubt in a secure ward. We're going to need more blood elves; Chloe killed three of them. I'll talk to Nergal. In the meantime, I want you both there watching the hospital. They'll either try to move Layla to safety, or they'll shore up the security. Either way, find out, and get back to me."

"Are we to engage?" Reyes asked.

"No. But take note of where Chloe is and where she goes. I need to feed—I haven't done it in so long that I'm getting weak; at full strength I might have been able to kill her. I need to go back to my home to do it, though, so it'll have to wait for a few days. In the meantime, bring me someone from outside. Someone who won't be missed in a hurry.

178

Do you happen to have anyone in the compound you've taken for yourself, Shane?"

Shane's grin would have normally made Elias feel dirty, but right now he needed sustenance more than he needed to worry about Shane's recreational activities.

"I picked one up the other night. I don't think she's even made the news yet. I can give her to you, if you like. She's barely hurt."

Elias nodded reluctantly. "You have your jobs. Go do them."

Reyes paused. "Sorry about Dara."

Elias nodded absentmindedly. "I'm going to hurt her killer. I'm going to prolong her agony until I feel the debt has been settled."

When Elias was alone, he opened the laptop and contacted Nergal, who appeared on screen a moment later. Elias gave his report, leaving nothing out. Nergal sat in his office without comment. Eventually Elias finished and sat back, waiting for Nergal's reply, waiting for his boss to tell him that Dara's death was his fault and he was clearly incompetent.

"I'm sorry for Dara's passing," Nergal said. "She was good at her job."

Elias nodded.

"And for the loss of three blood elves. They are not an unlimited resource, Elias. Please be more careful with them."

Elias nodded again.

"I will send you another six. That'll put your total at twenty?"

Another nod.

"I'm also going to ask an associate of mine to join you. Her name is Masako. She's a jikininki. She knows Thomas Carpenter quite well and should be an asset for you should an attack on him become necessary. She will answer to you and only you, but warn your people to stay away from her. The human-flesh-eating aspect of her kind extends to anything humanoid. She won't differentiate between her need and your team."

Elias made a mental note to keep her separate from the others. Jikininki were humans who had died and come back. They fed on human flesh to keep themselves alive, but unlike mindless zombies, they kept all of their mental faculties. They were also incredibly strong and hard to kill. Having one nearby wasn't something Elias was happy about, but she would be of great benefit if Tommy and his people ever needed to be stopped. "Thank you, Lord Nergal."

"Find this Layla woman before she becomes too much trouble and I'm forced to interject myself. And, Elias, do not let your need for vengeance cloud your judgment. Killing the person responsible for Dara's death is important, and it sends a message to those who would oppose us, but Layla is the target. Do not forget that. We need her father's help.

"As for Thomas Carpenter, I do so wish I could just kill him and be done with it, but let's not bait that particular jackal until necessary. As much as I'm sure Masako would be more than capable of destroying the man, I'd rather not have to unless we have no other options. Try to avoid the man, which I understand is like trying to avoid a cold, but do so anyway. His people are afforded no such protection. Kill as many as you need to."

Elias bowed his head in thanks.

"You'll need to go home soon, Elias."

The change of topic almost caught Elias off guard. "Yes. I'm taking measures to ensure my power is topped up and will be adding another victim to the hat, but it won't be long before I'll have to empty it. I'll need to feed properly. The small amount of power I gain from each person added to the hat is nothing compared to the power I gain from feeding properly. Once Layla is in our grasp, I will go back to my home and feed. I will be away for a few days until my power fully recharges."

"You have already put it off too many times. See that you fulfil your end of the bargain. A redcap who forgets what he gave up to become one is of no use to anyone."

"I always remember, my lord." Elias was unlikely to forget what he had to give up for the chance to gain the power in his possession. It was a decision he'd made quickly, despite the heavy consequences. And a decision he would continue to accept without pause until the day he died.

Nergal ended the call as Shane entered the room. "I've put your meal in your room."

Elias stood. "You'll take no one else while we're here. There's too much at stake now. When we're back home, you can do as you wish."

Shane looked somewhat crestfallen, which made a part of Elias feel ill. "Fine. But when we're home, I'll need to go play."

Elias shrugged. He wouldn't be there, so he didn't care. He'd never liked Shane's need to indulge his less palatable passions, and the bodies he'd left behind at several locations had caused unnecessary complications on more than one occasion, but he was good at his job, so Elias allowed it. Everyone had a vice; it just so happened that Shane's was murdering people for fun.

Elias walked off toward his room, still thinking about Shane. He could understand killing out of necessity, or because it was his job, or even for revenge, but doing it for sadistic pleasure wasn't in his make-up. He paused outside of his room. Killing for food was important too. He sighed. It was one of the less pleasant aspects of who he was, but like everything else in his life since he'd become a redcap, he accepted it without complaint. He pushed open the door.

21

When Layla woke back in her hospital bed the following day, she found Rosa by the window, ready to continue her lessons. Rosa had been teaching her all through her sleep too; apparently it was easier to learn control when asleep. The fact that the demon occasionally interjected didn't make it a fun experience.

Layla had woken with an aching body and an exhausted mind, due to the stress the training had on her. She took a deep breath. Learning was important, even if it brought pain. Besides, that pain was only for a short time, and although a short time is subjective when in pain, she could push through it. Once she'd learned how to use her abilities to a half-decent degree, she would be in a better position to become more powerful, which would mean she would find some of the mental conditioning and concentration much easier.

Layla certainly hoped so anyway. She had spent most of the morning practicing turning the coffee-table legs into various shapes and forms as quickly as possible, before moving on to more taxing lessons.

After putting the table back together, Layla was given the task of changing several coins on the table in front of her into origami-type models. She'd been doing it for the last ten minutes—this one was a swan, although the bronze-colored two-pence pieces didn't exactly look as swan-like as Layla would have liked. But she hadn't found any silver coins when she'd looked in the drawer beside the bed, just the half-dozen twos.

"Do you feel better now that you know the truth?" Rosa asked.

"I feel better about Tommy. And Diana. And I'm angry with Chloe. And I know I shouldn't be. I know that being angry with her is pointless, that she is my friend and she only wants what's best for me. But she lied, and I can't get past that. Tommy and Diana weren't a part of my life for the last two years. I know it sounds crazy, I just . . ."

"The lies from her hurt because you expected more."

Layla nodded.

"Have you thought more about accepting the spirits and demon?"

"Is Terhal really a demon? You know, a full-on biblical demonic entity? A denizen of hell itself?"

"No, as much as he —although I know Terhal shows as a female to you now, so maybe 'she' is more appropriate—might like you to think that, she's not really a demon. I'm not sure biblical demons actually exist in any form. Her species is called a drenik. I learned that when she let it slip. She doesn't like to talk about herself much; she prefers to talk about what she's going to do to ruin your life."

"And she's only evil? There's no good there?"

"I don't know originally, but I do know that after being forced out of her realm and trapped in a scroll, she isn't keen on helping people. She likes to hurt them. Whether that's a by-product of what happened to her, or if her species are all like that, or whether she's just a psychopath, I don't know. I know two things about her for certain: she cannot lie outright, and she will hurt people you love given a chance."

"You know, I'd like to be able to say that this is all my father's fault. That everything awful that has happened to me has something to do with him. But Tommy's right, his evil isn't an inheritance. I can't blame him for everything, no matter how much I want to."

"You want to talk about him?"

Layla was about to say no, then she paused. "I loved him. That's why it hurt so much, that's why it still hurts now. He betrayed my mom and me so he could go off and kill people. He enjoyed it. He kept a journal on each murder and handed them all over to the FBI when they came to our house. He kept hundreds of these journals in a lockup. My mother and I were questioned, and I didn't quite understand what was happening. He never said sorry. He never told us *why* he did it. Not once."

"You're still afraid you'll become him?"

Layla nodded. "Terrified. I know Tommy told me it doesn't work like that, but a few hours of being told I'm not a psychopath doesn't really compete with a decade of thinking I am.

"And then there's Terhal. I want to punch his face in. I want to show him the anger inside of me, but then he shows me all of those things and it's like I'm incapable of fighting back. I'm tougher than that, damn it. But he just makes me feel scared and alone, and . . . and like I felt the night the FBI or LOA or whoever busted into our home at three in the morning, and I hid under the bed because I thought the bad people my father told me about had come to get us. Terhal makes me feel like I'm that fourteen-year-old girl again, who had been taught to do all of these insane things to defend herself, but just ran and hid when push came to shove."

"You were fourteen."

"Yes, I know. And it's the same feeling I had when Blake raised his hand to me. I froze. But then the last few times, when those thoughts bubbled out, I hurt people. And I liked it. I liked showing those bullies and thugs that they can't scare me, that I'm stronger than them." She rubbed her face with her palms and sighed. "My brain feels muddled."

The door flung open, and Chloe and Diana came in.

"What's going on?" Layla asked, when she saw the look of concern on both women's faces.

"We're leaving the hospital," Chloe told her.

"And we're going where exactly?" Layla asked, feeling the anger in her voice.

"I know you think I lied to you."

"Think?" Layla interrupted. "You lied to me."

Chloe nodded. "We need to get somewhere safe. Please."

The group left the room and met Harry as they walked along the corridor.

"Hey, gang," Harry said. He glanced between each of the three faces in front of him. "What happened?"

"Shit," Chloe whispered. "Well, you're here now, and frankly, if you don't come with us, they're going to come after you, so you might as well be in on the chat."

Harry looked confused. "Who is them, and what are you talking about?"

"Turns out Chloe isn't the person we thought she was," Layla said.

"I'll take Harry to the lift," Diana said. "Make this quick."

Chloe stopped and turned toward Layla. "Yes, I've been lying to you. I've known Tommy since I was twelve. His daughter Kase and I went to the same school. A few years ago, I went through a really hard time—my mother murdered my father and almost got me killed in the process. I wanted away from the life that I was getting sucked into, and so I moved to Southampton and was going to get my head straight. Tommy asked me if I'd look after you instead. He asked me to keep an eye on what you do, just be friendly and nice.

"I figured out where you went to the gym and what martial arts classes you took, and I joined them. I set up a coffee shop as a cover, which I didn't exactly expect to become a hit, but you started going there and I went from being nice and keeping an eye on you to actually liking you.

"We grew close, and I now consider you one of my best friends. But for the entire time I've known you, yes, I've also worked for Tommy.

I'm twenty years old and I'm not human. I'm an umbra, like you. I've been one for three years. Unfortunately, I ended up befriending you."

"Unfortunately?" Layla shouted.

Chloe immediately realized her mistake. "No, not like that, no, shit. No, Layla."

It was too late. Layla saw red, and everything she'd been thinking about since Tommy had told her the truth the night before spilled out in one rush of anger. "Screw you, Chloe. Screw you and your damn lies. You fed me bullshit for the last two years. You say you're my friend, but friends don't lie to one another, friends don't hide who they really are, or spy on their friends. Friends don't let each other go through everything I'm going through right now and not say anything. You know how I feel about being lied to, about being let down by people I trust, and you just carried on like it was fine.

"Tommy told me about you last night in an effort to make me trust you all. And it's made me realize that you are an umbra, Chloe. Instead of being here helping me go through all of this, you've been off doing who knows what. I'm not sure a friend would lie so convincingly for so long, or that they'd let someone go through all of this alone, when they could have helped."

Chloe took a step toward Layla, her hands out. "Please."

"If you touch me, I'll break your arm," Layla said, her voice almost a snarl, the words out before she could stop herself.

Chloe stopped and took a step back. "I want to keep you safe." Her voice was low, barely above a whisper. "I don't want you to get hurt. And more than anything in the world, I wanted to tell you who and what I was. You have no idea, Layla."

"You lied to me for two years, Chloe. Telling me you wanted to be there for me but couldn't be because you had to talk to the person you're really working for isn't much of an excuse in my book. You fabricated our entire friendship because it was your job."

The pair walked away in silence, finding Harry next to the set of lifts. "Diana went on ahead, told me to wait here for you both."

Harry looked between Layla and Chloe, clearly noticing that something was amiss. "So, why am I here?"

"Elias and his people will try to get to Layla by going through us," Chloe said. "We have people watching your home right now, but they could still try. They tried to kill me this morning."

"Are you . . ." Layla started, and then stopped. The concern in her voice for Chloe made her angry again. She didn't want to feel concern, or sympathy, or anything else, she just wanted to be furious and aim that rage and anger at the person who had lied to her.

"I'm fine," Chloe said, glancing at Layla, before looking down at the floor between them. "I killed three of the blood elves and one of the women—Dara, she was an alchemist."

The lift opened and the three of them got in, and Harry pressed the button for the ground floor.

"You're talking like you're all playing some really heavy Dungeons & Dragons," Harry said. "Alchemists, umbra, blood elves? Anyone want to bring me up to speed?"

"Monsters are real," Chloe said. "Every mythology you've ever heard of, every pantheon you can think of, they're all real. Some are the same person in different guises, but the myths are real. They're not gods or goddesses, but they are creatures with incredible powers. Sorcerers, witches, umbras, ogres, you name it, it's probably real. And many of them just live normal lives, so you'd never know they were there, but some . . . well, some like to let the humans know they exist. They think humans should be on their knees praying to them as they believe they deserve. Those are the ones who hunt, hurt, and kill without remorse.

"Elias Wells is one such person. He's a redcap; a nasty little man who feeds on the souls and blood of his victims, and it makes him terribly powerful. Probably not so powerful now that he got hurt, but still problematic."

"Ghosts?" Harry asked.

"Real. Also, a little weird."

"Werewolves?"

"What do you think Tommy is? He's several centuries old and one of the most powerful werewolves in the world."

"Dragons?"

"A few years ago, in London, there was a report of an accident on the Millennium Bridge? Remember it?"

"They said it was an accident with a boat hitting it. A few people online say that they have footage of a creature landing on it, but I've seen that footage, it's totally CGI bullshit. Same with the video of a supposed dragon flying around the city."

"Dragon landed on it, and not a good landing. The dragon flying through the city is true too. Her name was Tiamat. She was not happy and she wanted to tear the city apart, until friends of mine killed her. Even so, dozens died, dozens more injured. Lots of things to cover up, video removed from anyone who uploaded it, that sort of thing. They made it look like anyone hurt or killed was in an accident or a victim of crime."

"Who could cover all of that up?" Harry asked.

"Conversation for later. Right now, Elias knows where you are, Layla. He's on his way here, and he will kill innocent people to get to you. We need to move you."

"To where?" Layla asked.

"Winchester," Chloe said. "We have some friends who work there, and you'll be safe. Elias wants you, but he'll think twice before attacking somewhere where there are a lot more people around you who can fight back."

Layla wanted to say no. She wanted to tell Chloe exactly where she could put her protection, but she wasn't an idiot, and her ability to stay away from Elias without Chloe was almost zero. She didn't trust Chloe, not after her revelation, but she believed that she didn't want to hurt her, or see harm come to her. Everything else could be dealt with when she wasn't being hunted.

Layla looked between Harry and Chloe. "Harry comes too."

"Yes," Chloe said. "Don't argue, Harry. You come, or I knock you out and you come. Either way, it's too dangerous for you to stay here."

Harry sighed. "Fine. I need to stop for some clothes and my laptop."

"Everything you need will be brought there once we're at the destination."

Harry turned to Layla. "I know you're angry, but I really don't want to be caught up in whatever this guy has going. And if keeping you safe means I have to be whisked away, then so be it. When do we go?"

"Now."

22

The group made their way down to a black Range Rover, where Diana was waiting.

"You all took your time."

"I don't think we'll be escaping from a lot in that," Harry said.

"Engine has been modified," Diana assured him, patting the car's side panel with affection. "This thing will do just fine."

Layla paused at the open door. "Wait, it's just dawned on me that if you knew about my father and you know who I am, you also know that my name isn't Layla Starsmore."

Chloe nodded.

"Wait, you're not Layla Starsmore?" Harry asked from inside the car. "Who are you then?"

Layla climbed in and buckled up. "My last name is Cassidy. I changed it to hide from people like Elias Wells, and people who would use me to get to him."

"Chloe, you drive, I'll take shotgun."

Layla wasn't sure if Diana had offered Chloe the chance to drive to give her some time apart, but she was grateful. The car journey was going to be uncomfortable enough just having to be in close proximity to one another; sitting in the same row would have made it almost unbearable.

Chloe drove the car out of the hospital car park and through the Southampton streets, as Layla looked out of the tinted window beside her. It didn't feel like everything had been normal only a few days ago; it felt like weeks, like her whole life had turned into craziness once again and had been that way for as long as she could remember. She was exhausted, but she knew it wasn't over yet.

Eventually she managed to drift off to sleep, and thankfully her dreams didn't include anything to do with spirits, murderers, or drenik.

She woke with a jolt as the car slammed on its brakes, and she was momentarily disoriented. "What happened?" she asked, fearing that they'd had an accident of some kind.

"We're being followed," Chloe told everyone. "Ever since the General. We're on the A31 heading into the New Forest, but I don't think we're going to be able to stay here for much longer."

"I thought we were going to Winchester?" Harry asked. "That's in the other direction."

Layla looked out of the window and noticed that the signs gave the distances to cities in the opposite direction to Winchester.

"Yeah, well, plans change," Diana explained. "We've changed direction to try to lose the tail, but there's no guarantee it'll work. This car is made to go off-road, so hopefully we can lose them on some of the dirt roads further ahead. It means a bumpy ride. We're going to meet up with some friends."

"I've contacted Kase and told her to meet us," Chloe explained. "We'll be there soon. I imagine she took the helicopter to get there, so we'll have a means of escape that doesn't involve being on the ground."

"Hopefully she has an army with her," Harry said.

"If Kase is there, we won't need an army," Diana explained.

A few seconds later, the Range Rover lurched to the side as the car following them sped up and tapped the right side, just above the back-right wheel.

"Shit," Chloe snapped. "Any chance you can help us here?"

Layla looked through the rear window, trying to pinpoint the car behind them. "I'm not sure I can use my power while holding on for dear life back here."

"She was talking to me," Diana said, her voice a deep rumble. "How far from the meeting point are we?"

"A few miles. The turn-off is in about six hundred yards."

"Get the car off the road and then stop. You'll have to get out and run the rest of the way. Let me see how they like my surprise."

Layla watched with a mixture of anticipation and fear as the car slowed and made a sharp left turn down a road that was barely more than dirt and trees. There wasn't even a sign to say it was possible to make the turn.

The Range Rover flew down the dirt path. Chloe's driving was confident and assured, although Layla wondered if that's how she felt inside. Layla certainly didn't feel either of those things.

The car behind them struck their rear bumper, forcing Chloe to struggle for control of the car, which narrowly avoided the trees pressing on either side of them. In a battle between oak trees and car at seventy miles per hour, there will only be one winner, and it won't be anyone inside the car.

Chloe turned the wheel sharply, taking the car out of the trees, and pulling the hand brake skidded the two-ton vehicle into the car park, ignoring the parking bays and signs to drive carefully. "Everyone out, we're going through the woods."

Layla and Harry jumped out and leaped over a small wooden fence. Chloe was next, just as a BMW X5 smashed into the passenger door of the Range Rover. The force flipped the Range Rover onto its side as

Layla tried to use her power to lessen the impact, but the car was too big and moving too quickly for her power to grab hold of it.

Diana hadn't gotten out of the car. "Diana!" Layla shouted.

"She's fine," Chloe assured her, as the windscreen exploded, fragments of glass bouncing across the car park.

The passenger door was torn free, and Layla gasped as what used to be Diana emerged with a low growl. Diana had the appearance of a monstrous grizzly bear, but with human proportions. It was as if someone had mixed a human with a bear, leaving a terrifying beast in its wake.

"Werebear," Chloe told her. "That's her beast form. We need to leave. She'll be fine." Several blood elves left the BMW as a second vehicle entered the clearing.

"Run," Chloe snapped. "There's a clearing a mile in that direction. Get to it. I'll catch you up."

Layla and Harry didn't need telling again, and they fled through the woods as the sound of gunfire echoed around them.

After a few hundred feet, Layla risked a glance behind her. Neither Chloe nor Diana were there. She heard the growl of a predator, though, and saw several blood elves giving chase. She turned and ran again until her lungs were burning and her legs felt as if they had nothing left to give, but she continued on unabated. She wasn't going back to Elias. Not now. Not ever.

A short time later Harry fell to the ground, rolling down a nearby hill. Layla stopped and ran down after him, trying not to trip, and managed to reach the bottom without incident. Harry was on his feet, a knife imbedded in the back of his thigh.

"This hurts," he said through gritted teeth. "Probably not going to be doing a lot more running."

Layla stood beside her friend and glanced up the hill, and saw five blood elves watching them and laughing. "Get your belt off. Wrap it around the top of the thigh to stop the bleeding."

"What are you going to do?" he asked, wincing as he removed his belt.

"Come on, you bastards," Layla said, and cracked her knuckles. "Let's see what you can do up close."

Layla smiled as the urge to fight filled her. She wasn't going to allow herself to be taken. Not again. They would have to kill her first.

"Move back to the trees," she said to Harry, and she heard him groan in pain as he did as she asked. She followed him, never taking her eyes off the enemies in front of her, and hoped the number of trees around them would make it harder for the elves to fight effectively as a team.

Four of the elves didn't appear to be all that concerned as they jumped down the hill with abandon, drawing swords and knives.

"You come with us," one of the elves said, "and we'll kill him quick."

"Or you don't," a second said, "and we eat him in front of you."

"That's a brilliant offer," Layla said. "But I'm going to have to go with the third option of you all pissing off."

The first elf swung a metal pole toward Layla. She raised her hand, and the elf's movement stopped. A flick of her fingers and the bar melted, the liquid dropping to the grass before hardening again over the elf's feet. A second later the metal changed again, this time to long spikes that skewered the elf to the ground, causing it to scream in pain.

The other elves paused, but Layla wasn't going to give them an inch. She rushed toward the nearest one, taking control of the sword it wielded and pushing it away with everything she had. The elf hadn't let go in time and sailed back into a nearby tree.

The remaining elves all dropped their metal weapons.

"That's not going to help."

The third and fourth elves tried to attack at the same time, but Layla blocked their blows, grabbed the third elf by the wrist, breaking it, then pushed the creature into the path of the fourth. The fourth elf shoved its comrade aside, but that moment's distraction allowed Layla

---

to connect with a kick to the side of its head. Both elves hit the ground hard, the third crying out again because of its broken wrist.

Before either of them could move, Layla was on them, raining down punches on the third elf, eventually knocking it out. She stood as the fourth elf got back to its feet and kicked out its knee, putting as much force into the blow as possible, and heard a satisfying pop as it dislocated. She didn't need to worry about hurting these creatures; she only needed to worry about Harry and her surviving.

Despite the pain, the blood elf shot up from a kneeling position, grabbed hold of Layla, and took her off her feet. The air rushed out of her body as she slammed into the ground, the blood elf using its leverage to throw punch after punch. It was stronger than a human, and Layla gritted her teeth and bore the pain as she blocked the blows.

Finally, she managed to grab hold of the blood elf's arm, locking her own arms around it. The joint broke a few seconds later. Bone protruded from the elbow and thick black blood began to pour over Layla, who shoved the elf off her and rolled aside. She turned the metal in the weapons around her into a fist-sized battering ram and smashed it into the side of the elf's head as fast as she could. The elf was immediately knocked out cold.

Layla stepped back, breathing hard. She looked up at the fifth and final blood elf. "Come on then."

She manipulated the metal fist, melting it down to liquid before forcing it to cover her fists and arms as armor. She flexed her fingers; it felt like she was wearing comfortable gloves. Layla could feel the metal, feel the impurities and the tiny flaws in her newly acquired armor. She couldn't do anything about them, but she knew they were there. She'd figure out how to deal with that later.

The elf was soon joined by half a dozen more. They laughed, but their laughter was cut abruptly short when a howl echoed through the woods. A second later, another howl sounded, closer this time. The elves appeared to be as nervous as Layla felt.

A third howl, and the elves took a collective step back. Something had them scared. "What scares monsters?" Layla asked, although she wasn't expecting the answer to be so immediate.

A blast of ice tore into one of the elves, throwing it back against the hill, pinning it in place. It struggled to free itself as its comrades looked on in fear. It managed to get an arm free just as something jumped out of the tree, landing beside the elf, driving a sword into its skull.

"That's a fox," Harry said. "A fox just killed an elf. Not a sentence I thought I'd ever say."

The fox stood on its back legs. It was three and a half feet tall, and was a humanoid version of a fox. It wore black leather armor and carried a two-foot broadsword, both of which must have been specially made for it.

"Hello, you bastards," the fox said to the remaining elves. It had a vaguely posh English accent.

Harry and Layla shared a look.

"You should probably run now," the fox continued.

The elves grinned and stepped toward the fox, but their confidence was short-lived as something much bigger sprinted out of the trees, its movements almost a blur as it barreled into the group of elves, grabbing hold of one by the front of its skull and driving it head first into the nearest tree.

The creature paused, allowing Layla to get a proper view of the werewolf who stood there. There was no way it could have been anything else—it looked exactly how Layla imagined a werewolf to look. Six feet tall and covered in dark gray fur, its maw opened, showing the razor-sharp teeth inside. It sprung forward, grabbing hold of a second elf in its mouth, and tore its arm off with a free hand. The werewolf tossed the limb aside as a black substance pulsed from the stump.

The fight was bloody and quick, with the fox and werewolf killing all five of the elves in only a few seconds. They fought as if they'd been a unit for a long time, each of them covering the other's back while they worked their way through the group.

When it was over, the remains of the elves lay littered across the leaf-strewn ground. The fox turned to Harry and Layla, its fur matted with elven blood. "My name is Remy Roux. Come with me if you want to live."

The werewolf glanced down at Remy and laughed, the noise almost more alarming than the howls it had made earlier.

"Remy," it chastised, the voice not as deep as Layla had been expecting.

"Always wanted to say that," Remy said with something approaching a smile, although he showed far too many sharp teeth for Layla to find comfortable.

"My name is Kasey, but you can call me Kase," the werewolf said. She took a step forward and held out one massive, blood-drenched paw. She paused. "Shit, sorry."

"Tommy's daughter," Layla said. "He told me about you."

A second later Kasey was no longer a werewolf, and in her stead was an incredibly attractive woman, although her light brown skin was covered in blood.

"You're really naked," Harry pointed out.

"Umm . . ." Remy began. "You get used to it. Werewolves and their ilk don't really have body issues. Naked is just a fact of life with them, it's not like they can wear clothes while they're in their beast or animal forms."

Kasey glanced down at herself and shrugged.

"You're a talking fox," Layla pointed out.

Remy froze, glancing at his hands for the first time. "Holy shit, am I? Oh, not again. I'm a damn fox, Kase. Did you know that?"

"He knows," Kasey said drolly. "He's also a giant pain in the ass." She sniffed the air, and turned as a naked Diana appeared at the top of the hill, with Chloe beside her. Kasey's smile grew as she saw them. "I assume all of this is your fault."

Diana shrugged.

Layla poked Harry in the side of the head. He was staring. "You've seen breasts before, Harry."

"Yes, and yet this is the single most terrifying and wondrous thing I've ever witnessed."

"We need to leave," Remy said to the pair. "As long as you're okay and don't need a moment, or a cigarette or something."

Harry shook his head. "I don't think I can walk, though. Stab wound."

"Diana was a literal goddess," Remy explained. "I get the staring. Doesn't mean you should to do it, unless you like being punched in the face."

Harry winced as Diana walked over to examine the wound, which caused his expression to alternate from painful to embarrassed, as Diana removed his jeans to take a look.

"The wound is not deep, Harry, and I see no serious bleeding. But walking on it could tear it. I shall carry you."

Harry was about to protest when Diana picked him up in both arms, his jeans falling to the floor. Layla covered her mouth and tried not to laugh.

"Wait a second. Diana, as in the Roman goddess?" Layla asked. Even though she'd heard that the gods and goddesses of mythology were real, she hadn't expected to be standing in the presence of one of them. Nor for them to be friendly and easy to talk to. And especially not for one who was still naked to be carrying an exceptionally uncomfortable Harry through some woods.

Remy nodded. "Not all of them are as pleasant as she is, let me assure you of that." He paused. "Sorry, I know he's hurt. But damn, Harry, that's gotta be killing you."

"I'm fine," Harry called out in a tone that suggested he would rather not be in his current situation while everyone else was watching.

Diana smiled. "You have nothing to be ashamed of, Harry. You have a fine body. It's manly."

Layla didn't even chuckle once, although she clamped both hands over her mouth to stop it. Kasey and Chloe also had to physically stop themselves from laughing. Remy, on the other hand, just laughed. Loudly.

The group walked a little way to a clearing, where a powerful black helicopter—the type Layla had once seen in a film about the US military—sat. Diana and Kasey grabbed some clothes from inside and quickly dressed in dark blue combat fatigues. The pilot, a man who nodded hello to Layla but otherwise kept quiet, started the engine once they were all inside and strapped in.

"So, now we go to Winchester, yes?" Layla asked.

"That's the plan," Diana said. "It's time you learned more about the world you now live in. We're going to meet with one of the directors of the Law of Avalon."

"I read a bunch of stuff about them not being trusted," Layla said.

"You can trust this one," Kasey told her.

"Why this one?" Layla asked.

"She's my mum."

23

The helicopter landed behind a massive thirty-story building constructed predominantly of glass and steel. The edges of the building were curved slightly, giving it the appearance of twisting as it rose up into the sky. Behind the helipad was a large section that had been turned into an assault course. Several buildings of varying sizes dotted the dozens of acres of land. Armed men and women patrolled the ground, each of them dressed in dark blue military fatigues identical to the ones Diana and Chloe had found in the helicopter.

Layla counted four towers around the rear of the property, each one fifty feet high, and from her vantage point she could see armed soldiers in them.

"Sniper nests," Kasey told her. "This place was attacked a few years ago by a monster. Nearly killed my dad and me. My mum runs it and wanted to make sure it would be a lot harder for anyone to get into. There are about a dozen of those towers around the property, a guard station to get into the property, and twenty-foot rune-scribed walls. We're safe here."

"Rune-scribed?"

"Ah, sorry, I forget you haven't been around our world for long. They're words of literal power. Like on the scroll you found. Anyone tries to force their way through those walls, they're going to get a nasty surprise. Mostly of the explosive, permanent kind."

"You know Chloe."

The change of topic visibly surprised Kasey, but she nodded that she did. "We've been friends for years. I get that you're probably angry with her for lying to you."

"She fabricated her entire life to get close to me. She's a stranger to me."

"Bullshit," Diana said, turning around. She'd set off in front, leaving Kasey and Layla to talk, but apparently had heard enough. "She loves you like a sister. Same as Kase here. Her job was to keep you safe, a job she didn't manage to fulfil, and she's devastated by it. She might not have told you the truth, but she doesn't have it in her to fabricate a whole personality. What you saw is her. The past doesn't matter one jot. Only the person you are."

Diana turned and set off once again toward the main building.

Layla wasn't sure what to think anymore. So much had happened that she felt as if a tidal wave had picked her up and carried her along, giving her no say in her destination. It wasn't a nice feeling.

"How do you know my father is an umbra?" Layla asked as they reached the rear entrance to the building.

"My dad told me," Kasey told her. "He'll explain a lot, I'm sure. He's good at it. Have you met Thomas Carpenter? Tommy?"

Layla nodded. "He seemed nice."

"He's awesome. A bit overprotective of his one and only daughter, but he's getting better."

"Overprotective?"

"I'm twenty years old and I've been able to use my powers since I was fifteen. It took Dad a while to get the idea that I'm capable of taking care of myself. And boys, it took him a while longer to get used to those."

"He doesn't like you seeing people?"

Kasey laughed. "No, nothing like that. My dad had a family once, centuries ago, and he was forced to leave them. So when I came along, he found it hard not to think I'd leave, or he would. Like I said, he's better now. He lets me out after dark and everything."

It took a few seconds, and Kasey's grin, for Layla to realize that she was joking.

The three of them entered a glass lift, and Kasey pressed the button for the top floor. Layla felt nervous as she watched the ground move further and further away.

"You not a fan of heights?" Kasey asked her.

"I'm okay with them, just glass lifts are a bit weird."

"You get used to it. Or you go crazy and refuse to step foot in the building. Probably one or the other."

"Not as bad as Nate," Diana said. "Took him centuries to get over his fear of heights. He's still not thrilled about them."

"Nate?" Layla asked.

Diana smiled, and Layla knew she felt genuine warmth for the man. "Friend of ours. Nathan Garrett. He's not here at the moment. In fact, I'm not sure where he is or what he's doing. Probably getting in trouble. It's what he excels at. If you stay around long enough, you'll meet him, though."

"If?"

"You're not a prisoner, Layla," Kasey pointed out. "You're free to go, we'd just rather you didn't. Keeping you safe is easier if we know where you are."

Layla sighed.

Kasey placed a hand on her shoulder. "I know it's hard."

"Do you?" Layla asked. "My whole life has been turned upside down. People who were friends have lied to me, people want to kidnap me, others would probably rather I was dead. I've seen people murdered, I've seen monsters and things I'd have been quite happy to have never witnessed in my whole life. Do you have any idea how all of that feels?" She breathed out and immediately regretted the tone she'd used. "I'm sorry. I didn't mean—"

Kasey shook her head. "It's fine. I was born into this life. Everything here is something I grew up knowing existed. I know it's a lot to take in; I still find things hard to take in. Gods, goddesses, monsters, it's a huge amount to get your head around. And you have spirits in yours vying for attention. I get that. I understand that accepting all of this must feel terrifying, but we're trying to help. I promise you that."

The lift stopped and the doors parted into an empty hallway. Kasey opened a door and led Layla into a second hallway that had several doors along each side with large windows showing the meeting rooms beyond.

At the end of the hallway was an intersection. Layla looked left and right, but saw nothing other than more doors leading to what were probably more meeting rooms. Directly in front of her was a door with a golden sign adorning it, which said "Director" in big, black letters.

Kasey knocked and pushed the door open, holding it so that Diana and Layla could go in first.

Layla followed Diana in, looking around the room as she walked. It was large, with a wall of glass opposite her. A desk sat over to one side, behind which sat a young woman with brown skin and dark red hair. Next to her stood Tommy, who smiled and walked over to Kasey, hugging her tightly.

"How'd it go?" he asked.

"Blood elves," Kasey told him. "A fair few of them. I didn't think they were able to come through to our realm."

"Apparently Nergal and his people have managed to keep all kinds of secrets from us," the woman behind the desk said as she got to her feet and walked over to Layla. "My name is Olivia Green. I'm the director of the LOA."

Layla's expression remained blank. "The same people who arrested my father? The ones who weren't exactly forthcoming about who you actually are?"

"I'm sorry about that. If I'd been in charge of your father's case, you would have known all about us." She motioned for Layla to take a seat in one of the two large brown leather chairs in front of the desk.

Layla did as she was requested, hoping she might actually get the answers she wanted, rather than having to ask even more questions.

"I'll see you later, Layla," Kasey called out. "My parents will walk you through everything."

Layla turned back to Diana and Kasey. "Thank you. Both of you."

Diana walked over and grasped Layla by the shoulder. "You're safe here, Layla. Nothing is going to happen to you."

Layla's small nod was to ensure that the uncertainties inside her mind didn't spill out of her. The last thing she wanted was to make things worse by allowing her emotions to overwhelm her.

24

When Layla was alone with Olivia and Tommy, Olivia returned to her seat opposite Layla, and Tommy took the one beside her.

"Do you want me to go?" Tommy asked. "If you'd be more comfortable just with Olivia, I'm okay with that."

"I'm fine," Layla promised him. "I just want to know what's happening and why I feel like Alice in Wonderland right now."

"The LOA stands for Law of Avalon. We . . ." Olivia paused. "Let's start at the beginning. With Avalon's creation. With Merlin."

"Merlin?" Layla asked. "*The* Merlin? Knights of the Round Table, King Arthur? That Merlin?"

Olivia nodded. "The mythology and reality are usually quite different. Merlin is . . . hard work. Many believe he took his authority too far, but many others feel that he hasn't gone far enough. He's a divisive figure."

"And he's your boss?"

"No. Merlin created Avalon, although he had help from many other people from mythology. The Greeks were the first to join, then the Romans, Egyptians, and so on and so forth. These days, most of the people from tales of myth either work for Avalon in some form or another or are dead. Few fall outside of those brackets."

"So where does Avalon come from? What does it do? Who do you work for? How does it impact what's happening to me?"

Olivia grinned. "Okay, each of those in turn. Avalon was created thousands of years ago after the Titan War between the Titans and the Olympian gods. Merlin, Zeus, and several others decided that it could never happen again. Merlin somehow managed to create it so that Avalon was in control of everything and changes were done through voting in a council.

"Over the years more pantheons came to work with Avalon, folding their power into Avalon's. Things worked well until Merlin was forced to leave his position as head of Avalon, and it was passed over to Elaine Garlot. Although with Arthur wanting to take the reins back, things have become much more complicated than they've ever been before."

"King Arthur?"

"Yep, the one and the same. He's a *really* long story, but the short of it is: he was attacked and cursed to stay in a coma for a thousand years. Now he's awake and wanting to resume where he left off. Most are happy about it, but some are fighting him. People don't like change, even ones who live for millennia.

"Getting back to your questions. I work for Elaine. Only Elaine. I was the director of the south of England, and now I'm sort of still doing that job, which is why I have this office, but I unofficially give information to Elaine. There's been too much uncertainty since Arthur returned. People are scared and concerned, and I want to make sure we're doing things right. But none of that has anything to do with why you're here."

"So Avalon is like a large security force?"

"Not exactly. Avalon rules everything. The humans in charge of countries know we exist, and we mostly allow them to do as they please, so long as it doesn't interfere with our plans and lives. Avalon is the real power behind the world and everyone in it. The LOA is the law-enforcement side: we monitor, investigate, and deal with crimes against humans committed by Avalon members, or crimes against Avalon members. We're a little like Interpol or the FBI in terms of power within Avalon."

"My father worked for Avalon?"

"No, but he was a special case. Umbra have been kept hidden from the majority of people for a long time, only recently coming to light. Your father's abilities were kept largely secret, until three years ago, when umbras came to the forefront of Avalon's investigations. Essentially, we discovered that there were a lot of umbras running around, and we had never heard of them. We didn't even know if umbras could pass their powers on to their children, which is one reason why Tommy had Chloe keep an eye on you. Most powers for nonhumans don't start until they've reached their teens, and with your mother dead, we needed to make sure you weren't about to turn into a bomb or something.

"Turns out, they can't, but you still became an umbra anyway. Not even Elaine knew that umbras existed until Chloe became one. I assure you, the fact that Tabitha and the LOA office she works for kept umbras a secret did not go down well. Your father is one of three umbras currently under lock and key. There are approximately five thousand in this world right now. And that's just a best-case guess."

"And, Tommy, you work for Avalon too?"

"I used to work for the SOA," Tommy said. "They're the . . ."

"Shield of Avalon," Layla interrupted. "Sorry, the spirits' memories bleed over into mine. The SOA is essentially Avalon's MI5 and MI6 combined into one, yes?"

Tommy nodded. "I left a long time ago. Like I told you before, I run my own firm now. I'm completely separate, but obviously still have friends in Avalon."

"Why'd you leave?"

"Things weren't going in a way I was happy with. I wanted distance from the organization and the people who were trying to grab powe" for themselves. Avalon is like any large-scale organization: people—be they human or werewolf—still allow power to corrupt them. I decided to get out before I needed to deal with those who were attempting to use that power to further their own aims."

"So, what you're saying is that people are assholes everywhere, no matter what their species is."

Tommy laughed. "That's essentially it, yes."

"So, if you don't work for Avalon, why are you here? Why have Chloe—specifically her, instead of someone from Avalon—watch me?"

Tommy shared a look with Olivia that Layla couldn't quite read, but it didn't appear to be a good one. "I'm here because we don't trust certain people in Avalon to deal with this situation. Chloe was given the job because *I* trust her. Olivia is here to give support. Officially, Avalon knows nothing about you, your abilities, or what's happened."

"Which means what?"

"It means you don't exist on their radar, and I'd like to keep it that way. There aren't many people who know that you exist, let alone that you're the child of an umbra."

"You said before that being an umbra child means nothing. I inherited nothing from my father's power."

"Doesn't mean someone out there won't try to find that out for themselves. Some people will think you're lying, or we're covering it up. Or they'll want your power to help them do something crazy. I imagine if your father wasn't on lockdown somewhere, more people would be trying to find out the truth about him too. His power is something many groups would like to get their hands on."

"You told me my father could find anyone anywhere on earth. Do you want to use him to do that?"

"What makes you ask that?" Olivia asked.

"I just want to know. I don't want to be here, helping you, and then when it's over with Elias, you end up wanting me to do the same thing he did. You saved my life, so I owe you one, but I want to be upfront about everything."

Tommy shook his head. "Look, I told you I'd be honest with you. Your father's power could help us track people; it could help us find bad people."

"That's if he even decided to help. I told Elias the same thing. He might say no. He doesn't really care about me. Only himself. Elias told me that it isn't true. That my father loves me."

Olivia removed a USB stick from her desk drawer and passed it over to Layla. "This contains transcripts from every conversation the LOA have had with your father. I contacted Tabitha and told her about you, and she made sure we had them. She told me to send you her love. She said you were a good kid."

"I liked her," Layla said, taking hold of the USB drive. It felt much heavier in her hand than it had any physical right to.

"You can use my laptop to read what's on there. Your father is not a good man, but he really did think he was doing the right thing. Read what's on there if you want to know what he really thinks of you. Or don't. It's your choice."

"But if I can get him to help, he could save lives."

"Yes," Tommy said. "That's the plan, anyway."

Layla placed the drive in her pocket. "I can't be distracted right now. There's too much at stake. I'll read it all later, but when this is over, and if I can convince him to help, I will." She breathed out slowly, feeling as if she'd just made a monumental decision. "One condition: he can't be allowed out of that jail. Not now, not ever."

"Your father hunted down twenty-seven serial killers during his time," Tommy said. "That's twenty-seven that no one knew existed. Between them, they killed over seventy people in a decade. Your father stopped that, but there's no way we're going to allow him to continue killing people. He's not going anywhere."

"I've been thinking, did the demon . . . sorry, the drenik, tell him to do it? Did my father allow the drenik to control him?"

"Not according to what Tabitha transcribed," Olivia said. "Your father did it because he says it needed doing. No other reason. Your father is . . ."

"My father is the Punisher," Layla interrupted. "And however cool that character is in fiction, in real life it's pretty damn horrific."

"I was going to say that he's without remorse for those he's killed. He thinks of them as cockroaches beneath his feet. He says they deserved it, each and every one of them. I'm not sure if the drenik inside the scroll broke his mind or not, but ninety-nine percent of the time, he's completely ordinary. Then you ask him about a set of crimes, or a killer, and something inside of him changes."

A horrible thought dawned on Layla. "His power to track people, can he see the lives of the people he tracks?"

"To a limited degree. He can see the action that gave him the evidence. So if he finds a footprint at a murder, he can tell whom that footprint belongs to, but also see them commit the crime."

"So my father could be watching my life. He only has to think my name and . . ."

There was an uncomfortable silence in the room, and Layla instantly felt sick.

"Yes," Olivia said eventually, her voice soft and understanding. "I'm sorry."

Layla walked over to a window and pushed it open a few inches, feeling the powerful breeze this high above the ground.

"You okay?" Tommy asked.

Layla nodded. "That's why Nergal wants him. He could use my father's power to find people who agree with him, who would join him. He's going to use my father to help him create an army, isn't he?"

"We think that's the plan, yes," Olivia said. "Nergal has a large compound in America, and inside he forces humans to take the spirit scrolls so that he can see what powers they get. If they're not useful to him, or they don't deal well with the power given to them, they're killed and the scroll is given to someone else. An endless cycle of pain and death. Nergal would like to find those umbras who already have powers, who already deal with their spirits and power on a daily basis. He wants people with exceptional abilities to join his cause."

"And what *cause* is that?"

"He's working with an organization that wants to bring down Avalon and place themselves as the rulers of all things."

"But you implied that Avalon is partially corrupt."

"And it is," Tommy said. "But these people want to out us all to the world and ensure that humanity spends the rest of its time on earth bowing down to Nergal and his allies as slaves. Nearly six billion slaves for people who think nothing of ending life, human or otherwise."

"Your people killed blood elves, isn't that the same?"

"There's a difference between killing people who are inherently evil, people who torture and kill and enjoy it, and killing people because it's a Tuesday and they're in your way. If your father had stuck to murdering psychopaths, I don't think we'd be having this conversation about him, but he didn't. He decided to kill criminals who stole or who sold drugs; he decided who should live or die. We kill to protect, or for self-defense; none of us would ever dream of going out and murdering people because we felt like it. Nergal and his people have no such compunction."

Layla was taken aback by Tommy's hard tone; she hadn't expected it, and could tell that as far as he was concerned, those who murdered indiscriminately were as low as you could get.

"Nergal has tried to find your father for several years," Olivia told her. "But your father is in a secure location that's not directly acknowledged by Avalon. In fact, I don't think any Avalon employees, except for the two we're aware of, know his whereabouts. At least I hope not."

"You really don't trust your own people?"

"I spent several years hunting down people who claimed to be working with us when they started to try to murder my friends. So, no, I don't trust anyone I haven't known for a long time. Tommy only gets a pass because he's my husband, and he's too busy to take the time to try to bring down Avalon."

"She has a point," Tommy agreed, a smile spreading across his face.

"So, I'm staying here?"

Olivia shook her head. "Too many people might see you. We're moving you to a secure location on the other side of Winchester. Tommy will be staying with you, along with several of his people. People he trusts."

"I can never go back, can I?"

"To your old life?" Tommy asked. "No. I'm sorry. You can still live your life, though. Once this is over, there's no forcing you to join Avalon, or work with me, but the days of living in ignorant bliss are over."

"Elias will still find me. He seems to be good at it."

"He might, but we'll be waiting. He's a dangerous person, as are those he works with."

Layla thought about the dead blood elves back in the woods, and she realized for the first time that when she had fought them, she hadn't worried about losing control. She hadn't been shaky or had any voices telling her to hurt them. She'd felt good after, but never out of control. Maybe she was finally coming to grips with whatever had been telling her to hurt people; maybe the fact that she was fighting monsters meant she no longer had to worry about going too far when fighting them.

"They can't have a lot of blood elves left," Layla said eventually.

"We have no idea," Tommy admitted. "The blood elves aren't meant to be able to come to this realm. So that's another mystery we need to look into."

"At some point they're going to use their ogre again. If it was ever released in a populated area . . ." Memories of her friends flickered to the front of her mind.

"I'm sorry about what happened to you and everyone at the depot," Olivia said. "We'll deal with the ogre. It's why you're being moved to somewhere more secure."

"And less populated?"

Olivia nodded. "Winchester is not a massive city, but even one innocent person dying because of Elias and his people is one person too many."

"Elias killed my ex-boyfriend." Layla explained about what Elias had told her: that he'd murdered her ex and his new girlfriend, before killing her ex's friend and framing him.

Olivia jotted it all down in a notebook. "I'll look into it. Elias has been a problem for a great many years."

"He said he killed his parents."

"He's a redcap," Tommy said.

"He told me that, too. I don't understand what that has to do with his parents, though."

"Redcaps are born human, and at some point they make a deal with another redcap. I don't know how it first happened, or who was created first, but it's a chicken-and-egg situation we don't need to think about too much. Anyway, basically someone makes a deal with a redcap that they'll join their kind. The redcap performs a blood-magic ritual around the human recruit's home, and the recruit has to go in and murder everyone inside. Once the ritual is complete, the newly born redcap is able to absorb the souls of its victims into its hat. It does it by soaking up all of the blood from the victims—essentially a sort of vampire. The blood sustains it and is absorbed into the body over time, allowing it to maintain increased strength, speed, and the like.

"After it's gotten its fill of souls, it goes back to its home to perform another ritual, which will allow it to feed on all the souls it's collected. It has to be done once every five years. Without fail. The longer it's left, the weaker the redcap gets."

"So that hat is soaked in blood?"

"The redcap is able to create some sort of small realm inside the hat where the souls and blood go. There's no blood inside the hat. They can only open the realm to feed once back at their home. It means that over the years they get weaker and weaker, and then in the next second, incredibly powerful. They can feed a small amount outside of their home, but it's just to tide them over. Unfortunately, trying to capture one after they've fed properly is incredibly hard work."

"Where is Elias's home? Can't you just find it and burn it down?"

"Elias was born in England. We know that much. We don't know where or exactly when, though. We also don't know where his family home is; it's information that any redcap will go to great lengths to keep secret. Destroying the home would be difficult—the spells around it are set up so that it can't be destroyed. Even the smallest piece of land left would allow him to recharge. But stopping him from recharging in the first place would mean he'd just wither away and eventually die. Obviously that's a lot more complicated than it sounds."

"He said he was a big fan of my father. He admired him."

"Your father's crimes were big news in the human world when he first committed the murders, although Tabitha saw to it that most of the details were kept from human eyes. His fame only increased three years ago when it was leaked what he was: a human who became an umbra accused of killing lots of humans. It was big news. Murdering humans isn't exactly encouraged, and the fact that he'd killed so many and wasn't executed for it intrigued people. Some people don't see what he did as being wrong. Some probably want to do something similar."

A phone on Olivia's desk went off and she answered it, spoke for a few seconds with whoever was on the other end, then replaced the receiver and sighed. "We're ready to go. You'll be safe with Tommy and his people. And I'll keep an eye on things from here. I'm sorry I can't be more involved, but I'll do what I can."

"Thank you," Layla said, and got to her feet. "It's all so confusing, but I think things are beginning to make sense."

Tommy got up. "I'll see you outside, front parking lot." He left the office, leaving Layla and Olivia alone.

"He's upset that you're angry with Chloe. He didn't put her there to hurt you."

"I know. I just don't like being lied to. And I don't like feeling as if our friendship was all a plan from the beginning. My father lied to me for a long time, and while I'm not equating her with a serial killer, it still hurts all the same."

Olivia walked around the desk. "Give her a chance. I know it hurts. A few years ago Tommy and Kasey were kidnapped by a monster. A creature of immense power, who wanted to use their torment to hurt me. Up until that moment, I'd been working with a friend of Tommy's under the assumption he had been ex-Avalon. After they were taken, he told me the truth about who he was, and what he used to do for a living. I was horrified, hurt, and angry that anyone had kept such things from me."

"What was he?"

"An assassin for Avalon. He worked for Merlin, did bad things to bad people, but that didn't make it better. If anything, it made it worse. It felt like the friendship we'd formed was based on a lie."

"What did you do?"

"Honestly, I sucked it up and got on with it. I needed to get Tommy and Kasey back, and that was more important than my ego. Also, he was able to do some questionable things to some awful people to get answers about where they were being kept. I couldn't really hold who he was against him, when he was helping me get my family back.

"It's not exactly the same situation as you're in, but I get it. Chloe isn't the kind of person to fake a personality to get close to someone. She made friends with you because she cares about you. Simple as that. I doubt she lied about her family or her past. She's not much of an undercover operative. That was never why she was put there."

"Why was she put there? Why her, I mean?"

"Her mother was responsible for sending her and my daughter to a nightmare world. One where the blood elves number in the hundreds of thousands. Chloe got sick, almost died, and had to be given a spirit scroll to heal.

"Turns out Chloe's mum had also sent her ex-husband—Chloe's father—to the same world. He died trying to get his daughter home to this realm. Chloe's mother was arrested, and currently resides in a deep, dark hole. Chloe lost control of her power, almost hurt a bunch of people, and decided that she wanted time away. We granted it. While here, we asked her to watch over you. It wasn't only about wanting to see if you'd develop powers like your father. We were worried about you."

"Why?"

"Your mother's death. We weren't sure it was an accident. Still aren't, to be honest. We knew that Nergal would have preferred to get hold of her rather than you, but obviously she died before that could happen."

"You think my mother was murdered?"

"The investigation never uncovered conclusive evidence proving murder. When all of this is done, I'll be happy to find the file for you. You can look for yourself."

"Thank you." Layla's mind reeled from the possibility that her mother hadn't actually died by accident, that someone had intentionally caused her death. "All this death because my father caught the attention of Nergal."

"Yes. I'm hoping we can turn things around, go on the offensive. Because having the specter of Nergal and his people somewhere out there waiting for us to make a mistake . . . frankly, it's exhausting. And we only get to make one mistake."

Layla glanced out of the window at the fields behind the building. She wondered if Elias and his people were already out there, waiting for the moment they could spring their next trap. She wanted to do something, wanted to go on the offensive, to bring the fight to them.

But first she needed to know where they were, and that meant sitting tight and waiting for them to come to her.

"What if we made it look like we were making a mistake?" Layla asked.

Olivia smirked. "What do you have in mind?"

"I want to bring them to me. I want to end this."

"I think we need to have a chat with the rest of the team before we decide anything, but you're thinking a lot more like someone who's done this for a while than I expected."

"The spirits. They've been through things like this, and their calmness about the whole situation helps me to be calm too. I think parts of their personalities are going to start blending into my own. I'm not sure when that starts to happen, though. Besides, there's no point in denying what's happening, even if I don't necessarily accept the spirits and drenik at the moment."

"That's something you'll need to do. Sooner rather than later."

"I know. Right now, Elias is higher on my list of concerns. But if he thinks I'm going to go quietly into the night to become a bargaining chip, he's mistaken."

25

Two Mercedes G-Class SUV's were parked outside of the building. The first contained Chloe, Diana, Remy, and two other people, while the second held Kasey, Harry, and Tommy, plus a spot for Layla, who was glad for the chance to ride shotgun.

"These things are beasts," Tommy said with a smile. "You ready to get going?"

Layla nodded. "Let's go see the new surroundings."

Tommy started the ignition and beeped the horn, signaling the first car to start moving. "You're safe in here. The bulletproof glass is tinted from the outside. The tech we have at Avalon is a few generations ahead of what humans have. So be prepared for possible surprises along the way."

Layla switched on the air conditioning and adjusted one of the vents. "That okay?"

"It's all good with me, Layla. We want you to be comfortable, even in this thing. We might be at the new compound a few weeks. Depends on how desperate Elias becomes. Oh, we got you some of your university work. And an extension. Sounds like you're doing some interesting stuff."

"I think so. Not everyone agrees."

"It's boring," Harry called from the rear passenger seats with a slight laugh.

"Ignore him, he's just upset because he couldn't understand half of the big words I used."

"Not half," Harry argued. "About a fifth."

Tommy laughed. "We have some video games, board games, and the like at the property. Just in case the chemical components of metals begin to overwhelm you. Not Monopoly or Risk, though. We want you to relax, not kill one another."

"Do my parents know about this?" Harry asked. "I haven't spoken to them."

"We've contacted them and said you'll phone soon. We told them that you were helping with some odd marine life we've found washed up on the shores of Iceland. Apparently we *had* to have your help. Your parents sounded exceptionally proud."

"Thanks, Tommy," Harry said.

"No problem. Once this is all over, I'll show you the remains of a kraken. I'm sure you'll enjoy it."

"As in the legendary creature of the sea?" Harry asked, sounding like Christmas had started early this year.

"Yep. They're not from this realm, but they do exist. I get the feeling you're going to see a lot of things you didn't think existed before a few days ago."

"Magic and monsters," Harry said. "My Dungeons & Dragons-playing fifteen-year-old self would be having the time of his life. If people weren't trying to kill him."

"Fifteen? You play D&D every other weekend," Layla pointed out.

"Yeah, but we drink whiskey while we do it. That makes it incredibly manly."

"Really?"

"No. Just means games last longer when someone throws the dice with a bit too much force."

"I've never played D&D," Kasey said. "Maybe we can get a game going at the property. Facing off against magic-wielding monsters sounds a lot more fun when you're not getting your hair singed."

"You've fought magic monsters?" Harry asked, clearly awestruck.

"Sorcerers, sure. They're not exactly a barrel of laughs."

"I'll tell Nate you said that," Tommy said with a laugh.

"Kase mentioned him before. He's a friend of yours, yes?" Layla asked. "Will he be at the property?"

"He's not around at the moment. He's . . . Actually, who knows? He vanishes every now and then to deal with whatever is currently trying to kill him. He's a good friend to have. And he's a sorcerer, a fairly powerful one too. Nergal likes him about as much as he likes me."

"You've met Nergal?"

"Once. A few years ago. I think being blasted back fifty feet through a concrete wall means I lost that fight. He's feared for a reason."

"And we're going up against him?" Harry asked, his awe replaced by fear.

"I *really* hope not. He's never come to England before, and I can't see why he'd start now. No, you're safe from him."

Layla remained silent for the rest of the journey, opting to look out of the window at the passing countryside. Eventually the car went down a dirt track, which after about a half mile revealed a massive complex ahead.

Tommy slowed the car and pulled in through the front gates, which were manned by several armed security guards. There were no twenty-foot-high walls, just a small wooden fence that encircled the property.

The car drove along the curved path up toward the stately home that sat at the apex. The house appeared to be several centuries old, and Layla stopped bothering to count the windows when she hit thirty. And that wasn't even half of it. The building had two floors and ramparts on the roof where more armed guards patrolled. Yet more guards walked around the estate, across perfectly maintained lawns, and beside beautiful, ornate statues and colorful flowers. A large statue of a fish sat in the center of the lawn, water flowing out of its mouth and into the fountain below.

"What is this place?"

"It doesn't exist," Tommy told Layla. "Officially this is a pig farm."

"I don't think you want to keep pigs in there," Harry said.

Tommy stopped the Mercedes behind the first car and got out, motioning for Layla to do the same.

The rest of the group were gathered at the bottom of a set of a dozen steps leading up to the double front doors, which were currently open. Two guards, a man and a woman, stood in front of them, like a heavily armed version of the staff from *Downton Abbey*.

"If the people in *Downton Abbey* all had machine guns, I'd have watched it," Harry said.

"Because that's what it was missing? Heavily armed soldiers?"

"*Downton Abbey* needed more Jason Statham."

Layla stared at Harry in disbelief.

"Everything needs more Jason Statham," Harry said by way of explanation.

"Everything?"

"Sure, why not? You're telling me that show wouldn't have been more entertaining if he'd kicked a few heads in?"

Layla considered it. "Fair point." She turned to Tommy. "So, this is my new home?"

"Everyone's new home for a while. Until we find and stop Elias and his people, anyway. There are thirty-seven of my people here, divided between four shifts, with two overlapping at any one time. That's not including us. We are literally in the safest place I can imagine that isn't on the moon."

"Can you get us to the moon?" Layla asked.

"No," Tommy said with a slight smile.

Layla followed Tommy into the house, admiring the beautiful decor and furniture. Colorful rugs lay on dark wooden floors, and paintings of landscapes adorned the white and blue wallpapered walls. Electric lights that had been made to appear like gas lamps sat beside them. A grand staircase led up and around to the floor above.

"How many rooms are in here?"

"A hundred and something or other," Tommy said. "I never bothered to count. There are several in the basement. This place used to belong to a member of Avalon who really thought he could become a king. It was confiscated from him after his death and kept as a sort of hidey-hole, should we ever need one. Only three people in Avalon know it exists: Olivia, Elaine, and Lucie, the latter of whom is currently in charge of the SOA."

"You trust all of them?"

"With my life. And with the lives of everyone here. If I didn't trust them, we'd be somewhere in the middle of nowhere in a foreign country."

A young man walked toward the group. He appeared to be slightly older than Layla, although considering Tommy was several centuries old and appeared to be no more than mid-thirties, the newcomer could have been any age. He had long dark hair that fell over his shoulders, the beginnings of a beard, and piercing blue eyes. His skin was pale, and he had several burn marks on one of his forearms.

"My name's Jared," he told Layla, his words wrapped in an Irish accent. He offered her his hand, which she took. "I'm sorry about what happened to you. This is all a lot to take in. Being an umbra takes some getting used to."

"You could say that," Layla agreed. "You went through something similar?"

He nodded. "It was a few years back now, but when I found the spirit scroll, it wasn't exactly a good time. We'll talk some more once you're settled."

"I'd like that," Layla told him.

"Everything arranged here, Jared?" Tommy asked, breaking whatever moment had existed between Layla and Jared.

"Yes, boss. If Elias or his people turn up, they're gonna find themselves in a bit of bother."

Tommy turned to face the rest of the group. "Remy, can you show Harry and Layla to their rooms, please?"

"You want me to carry their bags too?" he asked.

"I think walking with them is probably enough," Tommy replied. "But I guess if you want a tip, you'll have to carry the bags as well."

Remy coughed into his hand. "Screw you," he said between coughs. "Sorry, it's a terrible affliction."

The sides of Tommy's mouth creased upward. "Once you're settled, I'd like to see you all in the drawing room. Let's say in an hour." He pointed to the left. "It's through that door."

"Just say in there," Remy said snidely as he walked past. "Drawing room." He tutted.

"Your father was a rich lord," Tommy said, as Remy began to ascend the stairs.

"Yeah, but I like giving you shit. It gives me a sense of well-being."

Kasey and Diana turned away from the group and chuckled, while Layla and Harry followed Remy up the staircase to the next floor.

It didn't take long for Remy to show them to their rooms. They were right opposite each other, halfway down a huge hallway that ran off toward the right of the building. Layla had counted four doors before reaching the one to her room, and there were another four further down the hallway.

"Eight rooms on this side, and eight on that side," Layla said. "This really was built for a king."

"Someone who thought they would be. It didn't end well for him. That's the thing about the world you've found yourself in. You're going to meet a lot of people with delusions of grandeur. And a lot more people who might not be so deluded in a lot of ways, but still have enough power to snuff us all out and barely break a sweat. There's always someone else who needs stopping, someone else who's allowed their power to go to their head. It's never ending, and in many ways exhausting, but stopping them is better than letting them continue unabated."

Remy opened Layla's bedroom door. "I'll leave you to get used to your new surroundings." He walked over and opened Harry's door too. "My advice: make a cup of tea or coffee, get it down, and get back downstairs. I get the feeling Tommy has a lot on his mind."

Layla entered the room and sat down on the king-size bed, wondering who would have picked the *Star Wars* quilt cover and pillowcase. She flipped both of them over to check if the pattern was on both sides, and was just grateful that Jar Jar Binks wasn't on it. He'd ruined enough things without ruining sleep too.

A green suitcase sat on the bed in which she found several changes of clothing and more hygiene products than any one person could possibly require. She needed a shower and would be grateful to have a clean pair of pajamas on at the end of the day.

The room was spacious and decorated in a similar manner to the rest of the building. There was an old wooden chest of drawers, on top of which sat a forty-inch television. A leather armchair sat in one corner of the room, next to the large window that overlooked the rear gardens.

Layla pulled up the window and stared at the incredible feat of gardening below her. Colorful flowers dominated the landscape, with apple and plum trees to one side, away from the flowers. At the rear of the property was a hedge maze. It reminded her of *The Shining*, and she had no intention of going anywhere near that maze. Or walking around the halls alone after dark.

On the opposite side of the room sat another chest of drawers made of the same dark brown wood as the first. A small fridge sat beside it, and she opened it revealing a pint of milk and several chocolate bars. She removed one, a Double Decker, and unwrapped it, taking a bite, before putting the kettle on. The coffee and tea was beside the kettle, along with two light blue mugs of completely different sizes. She picked the considerably larger one and poured herself some coffee, forgoing the milk, and walked over to the armchair to sit and drink in peace.

Layla looked out of the window as a peregrine falcon hovered briefly and then dive-bombed to the ground at incredible speed. She watched in awe as it vanished behind a hedge, before reappearing with something in its claws. She loved birds of prey—going to a falconry show with her parents was one of the few good memories that contained her father. She'd simply refused to let his presence in her memory spoil what had been a magical time for her.

The falcon vanished from view as it continued toward the forest at the rear of the property. She hoped that wasn't meant to be a metaphor for her future.

She remained there for a few more minutes, finishing her coffee, then closed the window and made her way back downstairs to the drawing room. She got the feeling it would be better to hear whatever Tommy needed to say sooner rather than later.

26

"This does not appear to be going as smoothly as you suggested it would." Nergal's words stung Elias as if he'd been slapped. A cold anger settled inside of him.

"The blood elves—" Elias started.

"I did not expect the blood elves to be waylaid by a young woman who has had her powers for mere days," Nergal interrupted.

Elias was beginning to regret ever using the computer to talk to Nergal. At least with a handset you could pretend you had lost reception. It was harder to do those things when the other person was watching you.

"Thomas Carpenter and his people were waiting for us," Elias explained. "Diana was there."

Nergal smiled. "Ah, Diana. She always was able to put her nose in places it wasn't wanted. Fine, we're no longer dealing with one scared woman; we're dealing with a formidable opponent. I suggest you think of a way to get access to Layla without having to fight your way through however many people Thomas Carpenter has decided to guard her with. Do we even know where she is?"

"No."

"So, we're back to square one. I'm beginning to think that this woman is more trouble than she's worth. The person in charge of getting her mother screwed up, and the mother died before she could be extracted. I assume you know what happened to the person I'd placed in charge of the mission."

Considering Elias had been part of that mission, he knew only too well. "You had her expelled for gross incompetence."

"She's still in the realm I sent her to, dealing with hundreds of thousands of blood elves. Would you like to help her?"

Elias shook his head; he had a hard enough time dealing with only a handful of the vicious little bastards. He was never sure of how far their loyalty went, or how long it would be until they decided to become their own masters.

"No, Lord Nergal. We will find and capture the woman."

"Reinforcements will be with you soon enough. I can't restock your blood-elf count beyond those who are coming with Masako. She should be there soon. Please heed my warning about her: she does not play well with others." Nergal paused for a second, before sighing. "It may become prudent to remove Thomas Carpenter and his friends from the equation. There are others who would be upset with that decision, but it's looking more and more like that is the best course of action. Do you have a plan for getting close to Layla?"

"Her friend Chloe killed Dara. I'm going to kill her for it."

"That's not answering my question. Kill who you need, but do you have a plan?"

"Yes."

"Keep me informed." Nergal ended the call, leaving Elias staring at a blank screen.

"Boss still not happy?" Shane asked as he entered the room and grabbed a can of Coke from the fridge.

"I believe he's running out of patience with our inability to capture Layla."

"We weren't to know that the cavalry would arrive," Shane said defensively. "We followed in the truck and engaged as needed. The blood elves wanted vengeance, though. They went after Chloe to kill her."

"She will be mine to take," Elias said, with just a touch of threat in his voice.

"I don't really care who kills her, Elias. I'm just saying the blood elves risked their lives to go after her. They didn't care about the cavalry, or about Diana. A lot of them were killed because of it."

"We need to find Layla and end this. Nergal's patience is barely capable of dealing with small set-backs."

"So, what do we do?" Reyes asked.

She'd been in the far corner of the room, reading. Elias was happy to see that his last 'talk' with her had seemed to give her the impression he was not to be messed with. After Elias had throttled her, she'd avoided being alone with him for too long. Elias hoped the fact that she'd felt comfortable enough to be in a room with him meant she still knew her place. He didn't want to have to speak to her again about her behavior.

"Do we have anyone who works for Avalon that might know where Thomas and his boy scouts have taken her?" Shane asked.

"You have me," a woman said as she entered the room. The newcomer was Japanese, no more than five foot two, slim, and looked to be no older than mid-twenties. Her black hair was in a topknot, with loose strands falling over her ears. Darkness encircled her eyes and her pupils were blood red. She wore a simple white dress that ended just above her knees and black trainers. "I worked with Thomas Carpenter many years ago. He . . . saved me, as it were. I know where he takes people he's trying to keep safe."

"And you are?" Reyes asked.

"Masako," she said softly. "I am here to make sure you succeed."

"Nergal sent us someone who knows Thomas Carpenter?" Shane asked.

"He felt I might be of service."

Elias's eyes narrowed. "You want to explain why you didn't let us know you'd arrived?"

She smiled, showing completely normal-looking white teeth. "I like surprises."

"So, you're a jikininki," Reyes said, finally putting her book down and standing. "I've never met one of your kind before."

Masako's smile didn't falter as she looked over at Reyes. "Lucky you."

"Where is Thomas Carpenter?" Elias asked, not wanting the conversation to go too far off track.

"A mansion not too far from Winchester. He took me there when we first met. 1977, I believe it was. My kind don't age. Our deaths see to that."

"How old are you?" Shane asked.

"Sixty-seven. I was twenty-five when I died, which was when I became a jikininki. As much as I'm sure you have questions about my life and my kind, I would advise you to drop the subject now. It tends to . . . upset me."

The amount of venom put into the word "upset" made Elias agree that right now there were better things to be discussed. "I'm going to need the exact address."

"Of course. I shall find it on a map for you. In the meantime, I'd like to take my bag to a room. The blood elves who came with me are waiting for your orders by the lift."

"Shane, take Masako to one of the rooms here. Pick a nice one."

Shane nodded, looked over at Masako, and gave her his most charming smile. "This way."

"You should know something, Shane," Masako said as she walked toward him. "I'm aware of your past and your abilities. Do not attempt to make me one of your victims. You won't like where that takes you."

Shane's smile was replaced with a nervous expression, but he soon regained his composure, and the smile along with it. "Not a problem, never dreamed of it."

"We both know that's a lie," Masako told him, but followed him out of the room anyway.

"She's delightful," Reyes said to Elias when they were alone.

"She's going to help us find Layla. Her personality matters little in that endeavor. If it did, you wouldn't still be here."

"Ouch, boss," Reyes said, with humor in her eyes. "I'm damn sad about that."

"Reyes, leave me be."

Reyes giggled and picked up her book. "If she knows where Carpenter is, this might all be over soon. You can go back to working for Nergal in his compound until we're needed again, and then we run off and do this all over again with whoever Layla's daddy manages to find. You think this is worth it?"

"Nergal does."

"Not what I asked, boss."

"Is it worth finding umbra who would join us? Is it worth finding sorcerers, trolls, and anyone else who would aid us in the plan to control Avalon? Yes, obviously it is."

"You really are a believer, aren't you?"

Elias felt the pressure of his anger building inside. "Don't mock me, Reyes. It won't go well for you."

"Wouldn't dream of it. I was actually being sincere. I've met people who say they believe in what Nergal and his companions want to create, but few truly believe. Most just want to ride the coattails until they can have the cast-off power and glory."

"I don't care about either of those things. The ritual to make me a redcap gave me power, but Nergal gave me *purpose*. His dream, his plan, and the plan of those he works with *is* my dream. *Is* my plan. I am with him until the end."

"How noble."

"Not really, Reyes. Just loyalty and trust. They're all that really matters in our world. Power is fleeting, and there's always someone who wants to claim it for their own, who wants to fight you for a taste of what you have, but loyalty and trust are commodities that are more important in the long term. Without either of them, Nergal's plan would be a pipe dream."

"I agree with you, boss. I just want to make sure that we find this girl and get out of here before whatever anger you're bottling up boils over."

"I *will* kill Chloe for what she did."

"What if I told you I had a better idea of how to deal with Chloe?"

Elias crossed his arms over his chest. "Please, do go on."

27

It turned out that all Tommy wanted was to tell everyone the rules of the house. They essentially boiled down to no going out after dark, and not walking around the grounds alone. Layla understood why Tommy felt the need to tell everyone, but she really just wanted to feel like she had more control over her life, not less.

She left the room wondering whether Elias and his people were already on their way to find her.

"You need to take your mind off it," Jared told her as she walked out of the front door and sighed.

She turned to him—he was sitting on the top step of the stairs leading to the drive.

"Do you happen to have a large bottle of vodka on you?"

He patted himself down. "I left it in my other jacket pocket. Sorry."

She sat opposite him. "So, how long have you been an umbra?"

"A few years now."

"And you accepted your drenik and spirits?"

"Well, I'm not a drooling wreck, nor am I trying to kill you with a spoon, so I'm going to say yes. I accepted them all. You having trouble with that?"

"The drenik showed me visions of me killing people. I can't say it was the most fun I've ever had." She considered explaining how she'd fought for so long to ignore those little voices in her head that told her to hurt someone, and that she got enjoyment out of fighting. Out of winning. But she didn't because she'd just met Jared, and also because she liked him and didn't want him to sprint off the second she admitted it.

"They like to do that. The problem is, you can't just say you accept; you have to actually mean it deep down inside your core. Anything else just doesn't work. You need to accept the drenik and all of its insanity. It's a hard thing to do. Took me a while to get used to the idea of having a dangerous being trapped in my head."

"So much has changed in such a short period of time."

"We live in a weird world, Layla. But it takes a bit longer than a few days to get used to it all. Even now there are things I've never seen before. Magic that can create storms, or people who can turn into incredible beasts; it's exhausting trying to remember it all."

"So, what can you do?"

Jared held his hand out in front of him and his fingers began to glow orange as he created a small sphere in his palm. When the glowing stopped, the sphere was about the size of a marble and shimmered a mixture of gold and red.

"I am . . . the Incredible Marble Boy!" he said dramatically.

"Seriously?"

"No, not seriously." He tossed the marble to the bottom of the stairs and watched it roll toward the grass. He waved his hand and it stopped. "Ready?"

Layla nodded, interested in what would happen next.

Jared clicked his fingers and the marble exploded, shooting fire up a few feet into the air and leaving a small crater in its wake.

"Holy shit," Layla said. "The Incredible Marble Boy can blow stuff up."

"I create spheres of energy. I can control them to some degree and explode them when I want to. I've been practicing increasing the spheres' distance, but they just dissipate if they lose their connection to me."

"Isn't the power linked to some deep-seated emotional connection? You love marbles?"

Jared laughed. "Yes, actually. Marbles were a pretty big part of my childhood, so you're right. As strange as that might seem."

Layla stared at Jared for several seconds, wondering if he was mocking her. "I don't think it's strange. Okay, I do, but that's a pretty cool power."

Jared shrugged. "It isn't the most convenient power in a fight, but I've been working on that. The blasts don't hurt me, so that's nice. I hear you can manipulate metal. Like Magneto."

"Ian McKellen or Michael Fassbender Magneto?"

"Does it matter?"

Layla thought about it. "No, probably not. Is there a female Magneto?"

"Polaris," Kasey said from behind Layla. "Or Toph Beifong."

"Both badasses," Layla said. "I can live with that."

"Someone created a small explosion at the front of the house," Kasey said with a smirk. "My dad is pretty close to mobilizing the guard at this point, please don't give him any more reasons to be stressed."

"Sorry," Jared and Layla said in unison.

"You need the practice, Layla," Kasey told her. "If I was you, I'd go change into something a bit more appropriate and hit the practice area out back. Chloe said she'll stay away from it while you're there."

"I never asked her to do that," Layla said, sensing the slight anger in Kasey's tone.

"I know. That's just the kind of person she is. She puts other people first, always has done."

"I'll get changed then," Layla said, and she thanked Jared before running into the house, back to her room. She burst through the door, slamming it closed, and then realized how stupid that was and sank onto the bed. "Why can't things just be easy?" she screamed.

"Because it's life," Rosa said from the chair beside her. "You need to practice. You need to train. It won't be long before you'll need to decide whether or not to accept us."

"I could tell you that I would, but I'm not sure I mean it. I don't know how to get past that hump, how to just mean it."

"It's different for everyone. Part of you right now is angry and scared, and full of this rage at everything that's happened. You need to let it out. You need to deal with it."

"By punching something? Because I've been trying to stop myself from doing that for my entire life."

Rosa shrugged. "It helped me, might not work for you. Or it might, I don't know."

Layla got up and opened her bag, removing some gym shorts and a vest. "I need to get out and exercise. I'll feel better after that."

A half hour later, after she'd run some laps, she knew she'd been right. Her mind felt clearer, like she'd be able to deal with all of the stresses and trials that she'd faced and would continue to face.

She stopped by a large oak tree and took a swig of water from the bottle she'd taken with her. She was a few hundred meters from the rear of the house, and she looked around, waving at several guards, who returned her wave.

You're going to get all of these fine people killed, Terhal said, stepping out from behind the tree. She wore an expensive black suit and high heels as if going to some sort of board meeting instead of torturing Layla.

"Piss off. I'm not in the mood."

"Not in the mood!" she said, her voice reverberating around Layla's skull. "Well, let's see if we can change that."

The scene in front of Layla melted away, to be replaced with fire and the bodies of those who had promised to protect her. Tommy was sitting against a tree, his chin touching his blood-drenched chest and his arms limp by his side. A dozen arrows protruded from his torso. Kasey was close by, three more arrows in her head.

Layla began walking back toward the house, seeing more and more death around her. The mansion was on fire, the flames leaping from the destroyed windows, part of the roof already caved in. Screams of pain and suffering floated toward her, and she tripped and fell onto the grass, where Harry's body greeted her. Half of his face had been torn off and there was a hole where his heart used to be, as if someone had just punched their way through his ribcage.

"What is this?" Layla demanded to know.

"This is you. This is all you. You are going to be responsible for everyone here dying horribly."

"No." She simply refused to believe that as she staggered back to her feet.

"No?" Terhal asked with a laugh. "You think you have a choice here?"

"You're lying."

Terhal couldn't have looked smugger if she'd tried. "I can't lie. If you accept the spirits and me, this is your future." She took a deep breath. "Inhale the burning-flesh smell, there's nothing quite like it."

Layla turned and ran toward the house, just as another Layla walked out of the rear doors, flames licking at her feet. The second Layla held the scruff of Chloe's collar in one hand, dragging Chloe behind her.

Layla froze as the other Layla stopped only a foot in front of her and dropped Chloe's bloody and battered body to the ground. "She deserved it," the second Layla said, her voice full of darkness.

"I would never do this."

The second Layla laughed. "You will torture and maim and kill, and you'll do it all because you let the demon inside."

"Drenik," Layla corrected.

"Semantics. This is your destiny if you accept Terhal. The murder of your friends and loved ones. You'll make our father look like a saint in comparison. You'll watch the world burn at your feet and you'll love every second." Just then the door opened and Jared walked out, tossing several marbles back into the house, which exploded. "You'll corrupt or kill. That's all you can do."

"I won't," Layla told her. "That's not who I am."

The second Layla laughed. She spun a complete three-sixty, raising her arms as she did. "All of this is what you are. You just don't know it yet. You think you're safe from Terhal's influence, you think you can beat her if you accept her. The second you get a taste of true power, you become everything you always said you hate. It's intoxicating."

"I don't think so," said a familiar male voice from inside the burning house. How Layla could hear it over the sound of the building breaking up, she didn't know, but it was as clear as if he was standing beside her.

The second Layla turned back to the house and hissed as Dr. Grayson walked out of the flames. Layla remembered him from her time in the hospital, when she'd found him to be a pleasant and kind man. Clearly he was yet another way for Terhal to play with her mind. Grayson stopped next to Jared and tapped the boy on the head, making him vanish from view.

"Let's not make this any more complicated than it needs to be," Grayson said.

"You are not welcome here," the second Layla hissed.

"Show your true form, or I will force you to show it." Grayson's words were said calmly, but with an iron certainty that he would follow through with that threat.

The second Layla melted away, replaced with Terhal. "This is still your future."

"It doesn't have to be," Grayson told her.

"How are you here?" Layla asked.

"It's a long story. I haven't had to do this in a really long time. Telepathy isn't my favorite ability. But everyone saw you scream and drop to your knees, and whenever anyone got close, any metal near you went crazy and tried to attack them. I thought it best I step in."

Layla was horrified that she might have hurt people without meaning to. There was no enjoyment or rush of adrenaline at the thought of fighting, just a deep horror that she hadn't been in control.

"She is mine," Terhal snapped. "She is mine to twist and corrupt as I need."

"She can't lie," Layla said. "This could be my future."

"Yes, that's true," Grayson admitted. "It could also be a dream or a nightmare, or you could come down with a fungus infection that turns you into a zombie. Lots of things *could* happen. Doesn't mean any of them *will*."

"This is her future," Terhal screamed, her impatience showing. "You can't rescue her. She's not your damsel in distress to swoop in and help."

"You're right, I can't," Grayson said, his eyes never leaving Layla's. "I can't stop this. I can't rescue you. You need to do that yourself. Layla, this is your mind, not hers. This is your power, not hers. The drenik was put in the scroll to be the source of power, and that is it. It was meant to be like a well with a bucket. The drenik is the deep well full of water, and the spirits help you create a bucket. Over time you get a bigger and bigger bucket, until you can take as much water as you can stand. The more water you take, the harder it is for the drenik to stop or corrupt you."

"I want her to go away," Layla said, and looked over at Terhal. "Leave me be. Now."

"You're not powerful . . ." She paused.

"Just piss off!" Layla screamed, causing Terhal to roar in pain as the fire and death began to vanish, replaced with nothing. With pure calmness.

Layla stayed silent for several seconds, allowing herself a moment to breathe steadily. "So, if I accept Terhal, she could still corrupt me?"

"Yes. That's true. You could become a great and powerful force of evil. Just as I or Kasey or even Tommy could. I once succumbed to that temptation, and it took me a long time to return from the darkness that consumed me."

"What did you do?"

"I destroyed those who stood against me. I burned anyone who dared try to stop me. I allowed something evil to create more evil. I wasn't strong enough to stop it."

"And what if I'm not strong enough?"

"I don't know, Layla. I wish I did. But I can't say what kind of person you'll be with the power at your disposal until you've accepted it. I do know that even without accepting the drenik and spirits, you're more powerful than many umbras I've met."

"With great power, etc., etc."

"Ah, yes, Uncle Ben. Tommy has quoted it several times over the years. In case you don't understand yet, Tommy is a massive geek. He could also bench-press a truck, but still . . . massive geek."

Layla laughed. "So, what happens now?"

"When you're ready, we leave this part of your mind. I take you to your room and you get some rest. No one will think less of you for what you're going through. Everyone understands. Any embarrassment you will feel is unnecessary."

"How do you know I'll feel embarrassed?"

"You freaked out in front of everyone and scared people half to death. You'll be embarrassed because anyone would be."

Layla smiled. "You're the wise old guy, aren't you?"

"Old, yes. Wise, not so much. Are you ready to go back? Just relax, and I'll take us there."

"Just one more question. What are you?"

Grayson smiled. "That is a story for another time. What I am is not something I share lightly, even with my closest friends. Maybe one day you'll find out."

Layla smiled. "Everyone has their secrets."

She closed her eyes and a few seconds later opened them to find Chloe beside her, a look of abject fear on her face.

"Is she okay?" Chloe almost shouted at Grayson as he got to his feet.

"Yes," Layla told her. "I'm fine. I'm just . . . I'm . . ."

Chloe hugged her tight. "I'm so sorry for everything, Layla."

Layla hugged her back. "Me too. I don't know if I can just forget, but I'm going to try."

Chloe helped Layla to her feet. "Thank you."

"You're my best friend. Doesn't matter how or why it came about, you're still my best friend. You can't fake that." She took a step and stumbled, holding her hands out to stop herself, but she never touched the ground. The water pipes from deep underground stuck up through the soil at just the right angle to support her.

"Did I do that?" she asked, as the pipes pushed her upright, before vanishing back into the dirt.

She stared at everyone in front of her: at Tommy, Diana, and Harry, who had a big grin on his face.

"It appears you're a lot more powerful than we'd anticipated," Tommy told her. "And that you've ruined my lawn."

Layla looked around at the holes on the lawn in the vicinity of where she'd been standing. Layla had dragged the metal out of the earth. Several rifles and revolvers littered the ground nearby, torn from their owners' hands as she'd manipulated the magnetic field around her.

"I'm sorry," she whispered to Tommy as he stood before her.

"New house rule," Tommy whispered back. "Never say sorry for being awesome. And judging from all this, you're the definition of the word."

240

She'd used her power without even meaning to. Terhal had forced her to believe she was living in a nightmare, and her mind reacted accordingly, protecting her from harm. The Terhal situation would need to be resolved, and soon. She would need to find a way to accept the drenik for what she was. But for now, and for the first time since her abduction and the murder of her friends and co-workers, Layla felt accepted.

28

The next few days of Layla's stay at the mansion were relatively quiet. She spent her mornings training with Diana, and after the first day, Harry decided to join in, determined to pull his weight. After twenty minutes of Diana's training, they were both drenched in sweat.

"This is torture," Harry said, after doing another sprint with weights around his ankles and wrists. "She is a master of breaking people."

Layla was on all fours, sucking in oxygen. "I don't think she likes us."

"I don't think she likes herself, if this is how she exercises."

"I like myself just fine, thanks," Diana said with a smile. "I just like torturing you both. It's so much fun."

"She's a cruel mistress," Remy said with a chuckle after running over to the group. "So, are you done breaking them? Because I'm pretty sure it's Chloe's turn to break Layla."

Diana's smile intensified. "I guess we can continue this later."

"Yay," Harry said, with about as much enthusiasm as he could muster. "I'm so happy."

The pair of them managed to make it back to the mansion, where Layla spotted Chloe sitting on a nearby bench. "Maybe I should have a shower first?"

Remy shrugged. "Doesn't really matter to me, you all smell awful either way."

Layla stopped. "We smell awful *after* the shower?"

"You use scented soaps and body wash. My nose is about a hundred times more sensitive than yours. You all lather yourselves in those scents, and it smells ridiculously strong. I've gotten used to it because it's either that or I go insane, but sweaty or not doesn't really make much of a difference to me. Your underlying scent is always there."

"I'm going to try to forget you said anything about my scent."

"Good luck with that," Remy said with a smile, and he walked away.

"So, how are you feeling?" Harry asked as the pair walked toward Chloe. "It's been a few days now. Your powers improving?"

"I'm getting a better handle on them, and I'm beginning to think I might actually be able to do this. And Terhal hasn't bothered me since Grayson intervened."

"That was crazy. Like, badass crazy. I've never seen anything like that. It hurt to look at Grayson when he walked over to you. It was as if power was literally coming off him in waves. After it was over, I asked him if he was an angel."

"An angel?"

"Hey, a few weeks ago I'd have said there's no chance, but after seeing monsters and magic and all this insanity, why not an angel?"

"What did he say?"

"He laughed as if it was the funniest thing he'd ever heard. Eventually, when I felt as stupid as possible, he said no. Apparently he's not an angel."

"I don't think he wants people to know what he is. It seemed like it was a big deal to keep to himself. Maybe one day he'll tell us."

"I kind of want to know, just so I can say I know. Does that make sense? I don't like mysteries."

Layla chuckled. "Yeah, I pretty much figured that out, considering you Google every film we watch for spoilers before watching it."

Harry smiled. "I like to know where things are going."

"This must be hell for you."

"I can keep myself busy, so it's fine. Besides, this whole world is something I'd never have imagined. It's pretty crazy."

"Tell me about it." Layla stopped in front of Chloe. "Reporting for duty."

Chloe stared at Harry. "You here for moral support?"

"No, I'm here because I want to hide from Diana. I think she might kill me." He glanced over to where Diana was currently bench-pressing several hundred kilos as if it were nothing. "I'm going to go eat."

Chloe waited for him to walk away before she said, "You've been doing well with your training." She placed a pin on the wooden bench between the two of them. "I want you to push this pin through the bench, but without making a hole bigger than the pin."

Layla stared at the pin. It was a regular pin used by tailors. It was two inches in length, and there was nothing special about it. Layla wondered what this would teach her.

"Control," Chloe said, as if reading her mind. "This lesson is about control."

"Control," Layla reiterated. "Sure, why not." She raised a hand toward the pin, which raised itself off the bench, the sharp point just touching the bleached wood. Layla closed her eyes and concentrated.

"Open your eyes."

Layla did so, and the pin fell back onto the bench. "You made me drop it."

"Yes. Because when you're in a fight, you don't have time to close your eyes and concentrate. You need to be able to control your power without stopping and thinking about it." She removed her iPhone from her pocket, opened an app, and music began to play.

"I never took you for a disco fan."

"This will hopefully help you learn control while you're being bombarded with information." She turned the music up and motioned for Layla to get on with it.

Layla managed to grab the pin without any problems, but the second she got it upright and ready to move, the music managed to distract her and she had to start all over. And if it wasn't the music, it was Chloe, who either hummed along or made funny faces.

After what felt like the hundredth attempt, Layla managed to get the pin into position and began pushing it into the wood, but stopped when Chloe shrieked.

"Seriously?" Layla asked.

"Never said training was easy," Chloe pointed out, pausing the music. "I know what it's like to let the drenik take control. Mine did. And it took a lot of people to stop it. I allowed my emotions to get the better of me, and"—she clicked her fingers—"that's all it took."

"And now?"

"Now I can use the power of my drenik to great effect. I can even allow the drenik to take control for a short time, boosting its own power. We have managed to come to an agreement. It might not work for everyone, but it does for me."

"How did you get past the drenik wanting to kill you and everyone you love?"

"I made him respect me. I made him understand me. I beat him before it could beat me. I made it submit to my will. Maybe it was easier for me because he was allowed out before I'd managed to assert my control over it and wasn't as strong afterwards, or maybe he's just not as big an asshole as Terhal. No real way to know. It's your mind, Layla. You're in control, not Terhal. You just need to realize that and things will be easier." She pointed at the pin and restarted the music. "Again."

Layla exhaled in one long, exaggerated motion, before going back to the pin.

"You need some help?" Rosa asked from beside her.

If I talk out loud, I'm going to look like an insane person, Layla said inside her head.

"You can use us to block out the world around you. It's all about moving your own consciousness slightly, so you're still aware of your surroundings but also oblivious to them. You need to concentrate on the pin and feel your mind drifting off toward one of your spirits."

That sounds ridiculous.

"You're essentially using magic to try to push a pin through a bench. You really want to tell me what sounds stupid?"

Point taken, Layla conceded.

"Just relax and feel your mind slipping, feel it shifting slightly."

Layla jolted. "I felt it," she said aloud.

"Felt what?" Chloe asked.

"Umm . . . Rosa, my spirit, told me to shift my consciousness. I felt it."

"Ah, you're finally using your spirits to learn on a regular basis. That's a large portion of how we learn. It's also why you gain so much power once you're bonded fully with them. Try again."

Layla nodded, now enthusiastic to try. She concentrated on the pin and did as Rosa had instructed, and began to move her consciousness to think of Rosa. The pin began to spin, slowly at first, but it soon gathered speed, moving faster and faster until it was a blur of motion. Layla pushed a fraction harder and the pin shot out of the bottom of the wooden bench, imbedding itself in the concrete slab beneath it.

Chloe switched off the music, and Layla stopped concentrating. She looked under the bench at the concrete, which had a neat hole where the pin had burrowed in. Chloe reached down and picked up the third of the pin still showing, pulling it out of the concrete. It looked pristine. She touched the point to her finger and it bled.

"You sharpened it," Chloe said, sticking her finger in her mouth. "Also, ouch."

"Yeah . . . not really sure about that one."

"I'm impressed. Honestly. I half expected you to shoot the pin out the side of the bench and into the wall behind us. This is some serious progress, Layla. You should be proud."

"This will help with keeping Terhal at bay until I can accept them all?"

"I hope so."

"Because I want to accept them. But then Terhal makes me think that accepting her really will bring about some sort of apocalypse, and I just can't."

"I know it's difficult. Jared had trouble too. You keep up your training, though, and I'm certain you'll be able to keep Terhal in check."

Layla didn't feel so sure, but it was nice to feel like she was getting somewhere. "You know, we haven't really spoken about everything since Grayson had to help me the other day. We've been so busy practicing all of this that we've barely had time to talk properly."

"I know, it's all a bit crazy at the moment."

"I don't want it to feel awkward between us. I get why you did what you did, I really do."

She was about to say more when Kasey came over.

"Sorry to interrupt, but my dad wants to see Chloe."

Layla cursed Kasey's bad timing, but Chloe assured her they'd talk once she was back, and she went off with Kasey, leaving Layla alone.

"Long day?" Harry asked as he sat down beside her.

"Something like that, yes. I can't believe it wasn't that long ago I was just thinking about finishing up at uni and trying to find a job.

Now I'm fighting monsters and learning how to deal with spirits that live in my head."

"When you put it like that, it just sounds weird."

Layla spent a few hours with Harry. They hadn't really had the time to chat since coming to the mansion, at least not beyond both being driven to an early grave by Diana.

"You think you can control this Terhal?" Harry asked.

"So far, I've been trying to, yes. If I can keep my emotions under control, she has less chance of doing anything to hurt me. Or anyone else for that matter. It can't go on indefinitely, though. I need to figure out a way to accept her without thinking she's going to use me to destroy everyone."

Layla and Harry got up and walked into the mansion, where they met Tommy, who was walking back to his office with a large plate of food.

"All of this still weird?" Tommy asked after Harry had left.

"Getting less and less so every day."

"Yeah, I understand. Lots to take on board. I'm not sorry I had Chloe lie to you about what she was and who she was. She needed to be safe too, and there are people out there who would use people like Chloe to get to me. She's been through a lot of training in the last three years, and more intensively than most people her age. Hell, even the LOA don't accept recruits under thirty."

Layla understood that. She hoped she could put everything behind her and move forward with her friendships. "It looks like you're building an army."

"I know, that's why we've been careful with our numbers and who we accept. Anyway, that's not why you're here. I wanted you to know we did a full sweep of the compound they kept you in. I was going to tell you earlier, but it's been one thing after another since Elias arrived. We found a lot of traces of them, but don't know where they've gone."

"They would have had a back-up plan. Elias wanted to get me on a plane to America."

"Yes, Nergal is there. Where, we don't know, but I'm sure he'd take great delight in having you help him. The ogre went too. We found his cage. Wherever they are, the ogre will need to be kept secure, otherwise it'll just do what it wants, and usually that's destroying things.

"Also, we looked into your ex-boyfriend's murder, along with that of his new partner. You were right: Elias framed another man for those crimes. A man he also killed. Unfortunately, that went to the human police, and Olivia tells me that reopening the investigation as an Avalon case will cause no end of trouble. Turns out Robert, the man Elias framed, was a nasty little toad at the best of times, and had managed to walk away from two serious assaults in the last few years. It's not ideal, but he's going to have to stay the killer."

"I don't understand Avalon politics. Human crimes are dealt with by humans. But this isn't a human crime."

"That's true, but in this case we had no idea it wasn't a human crime until you told us. By that time the police were actively investigating. Avalon involving themselves at that stage just to change the killer from one piece of crap to another isn't something they'd bother doing. If Rob had been a saint, or at least a good person, they might have, but he was a nasty little man, so Avalon doesn't care. It's not exactly ideal, but we will get Elias, I promise you that."

"He doesn't strike me as an easy person to get."

"No, he's a slippery little devil. Been after him for a while now, and his boss Nergal since what happened in London three years ago."

"The dragon landing on the Millennium Bridge? Chloe told us."

"Yes, well, Nergal was involved in the whole mess. Had been for centuries leading up to it. No one even knew he existed, and that's the way he likes it. So the fact that we found him and went after him is something that he finds most vexing. We have no idea where he actually is, and America is a big place, but we'll find him. Eventually. Hopefully before whatever insanity he calls a plan comes to fruition. But one step at a time, and Elias comes first."

"When you go after him, I want in."

Tommy paused, before taking a deep breath and letting it out slowly. "That's a bad idea. You haven't even accepted your spirits yet. You could go off and hurt people. You could go off and hurt yourself."

"I need to look him in the eyes and tell him he will never hurt anyone I care about ever again."

"You'll get your chance, but leave the actual capture to us. We've been at this a long time and we know what we're doing."

The two chatted for a while longer, although they stayed away from conversations about powers and monsters, sticking to more pleasant topics.

Suddenly, Grayson burst through the front door, half carrying a heavily bleeding Jared, with Kasey following.

"What happened?" Tommy asked, dropping his plate of food on the floor and helping Grayson carry Jared into the medical room.

"Where are Chloe and the others?" Kasey asked.

"In a minute, Kasey," Doc Grayson told her, moving Jared onto a bed before beginning an examination.

"What happened?" Kasey asked, aware that Tommy had just asked the same thing, but needing answers.

Grayson cut through Jared's bloody shirt, revealing a dozen puncture wounds. "He's been badly cut," he said. "Silver blade, judging from the burns around the wound."

"What happened?" Kasey demanded again, shouting.

"Leave if you can't keep your cool," Tommy told her. "We have more important things to do."

"I asked Grayson a question," Kasey snapped. "I want to know what happened."

"Leave. Now." Tommy's words were spoken with complete authority and were to be obeyed without question. Kasey stared at her dad in disbelief, before turning and storming from the room.

"They found us," Jared managed to say. "They found us."

"Goddamn it," Tommy snapped.

"Don't you bloody well start," Grayson told him, his voice cold.

"I don't know how. We were on the motorway, when we got shunted, spun around. Kate was driving. She . . ."

"Where's Kate?"

"Dead."

There was a moment of silence in the room at the news that one of their own had died. Layla hadn't spoken to Kate much, but the short, blonde woman had always appeared to be happy and easy to talk to.

"Where's Chloe?" Layla asked, her voice breaking.

"They took her. I'm so sorry, Layla. They took her."

Elias had Chloe. Elias and his people had taken her friend. Elias and his people would hurt her, would do awful things to her. Anger built up inside of Layla the likes of which she'd never felt before; a fire of pure unadulterated rage. But when she spoke, her voice was calm and betrayed no hint of the emotion she was feeling. "Then we'd bloody well better get her back."

"We will," Tommy assured her.

"Why were you all out of the mansion?"

"We needed supplies," Jared said, before screaming in pain as Grayson began to cauterize the wounds in an effort to stop the effects of the silver poisoning.

Tommy helped hold Jared down. "Silver kills most things," he said. "Many die because they can't stop bleeding. We need to stop it."

"Can I help?"

"No," Grayson said. His tone wasn't unkind or sharp, but it was all business. "I need to save this young man's life."

Layla left the medical room. "We'll find her," she told a pacing Kasey.

"I know, and thanks." Kasey hugged Layla, and Layla was grateful for the companionship.

Tommy emerged a few minutes later and told anyone in the vicinity to leave, and that he would sort out going after Elias once he knew Jared's condition.

"We're going now," Layla said.

"You're not ready, Layla. You'll get yourself killed."

"A monster has my friend. I need to go find her."

"Not today you don't. Just go find something to keep yourself occupied. Chloe will be fine."

Layla wanted to believe him, but couldn't. She ran upstairs to her room, stepped inside, and closed the door. "Rosa."

"What's up?" Rosa asked as she appeared.

"How do I accept you? All of you?"

"You tell us, and if it's true in your subconscious, we'll permanently bond with you."

"Fine, I accept you all. Including the drenik." Nothing happened.

"You have to mean it, Layla," Rosa explained, her voice soft. "You don't."

"I do," Layla shouted. "I mean it. I accept you all."

"Layla."

"I just want this done," she shouted, releasing her frustration. "My father trained me my whole life to fight. And then when he was gone, I continued to train, but the first time I was in a situation where I could fight, I froze. Blake raised his hand, and I froze. And that's something that even after all these months still gets to me. And now he's dead. Then I fought a bunch of blood elves and there was no freezing, just me being lost in the moment of the fight. And it felt good.

"But when I think I'm done hesitating and worrying, Terhal makes me watch as I murder everyone, and I'm back to being that scared girl who hid under the bed when the LOA came to arrest my father. And now my best friend has been kidnapped by a group of crazed psychos, and I can't do a damn thing. I want to help here; I don't want to sit around like a damsel in bloody distress while everyone else does the work. They're protecting me, and I'm done with it. I *need* to help. I need to save my friend."

"All you can do is keep practicing, and hopefully you really will accept all of us one day soon."

Layla flung herself onto the bed, before sitting up. "This sucks. This both sucks and blows."

"Hello, Layla. Miss me?" Terhal said from the corner of the room.

"I'd hoped you'd gone," she said, getting up from the bed.

"I can't leave, Layla. I'm part of you. That . . . man, Grayson, just postponed the inevitable." She came and stood in front of Layla. "You will be mine. One way or the other."

Layla walked toward her and took a swing, her fist going through Terhal, making Layla pitch forward and land on her knees as the drenik laughed.

"Interesting choice of attack," Terhal said. "Here's mine."

The room burst into flame. The paint on the walls bubbled under the intense heat, and the bed exploded into an inferno. Layla scrambled back against the door, trying to avoid the flames as Terhal continued to laugh.

Fire licked at Layla's feet and she pulled them up toward her, hugging her knees against her chest.

"Scared, Layla? Scared of dying, or burning alive?"

The fire disappeared, showing Layla that nothing had happened. "I'm getting stronger, little one. And soon your spirits will no longer be able to stop me from consuming your mind. I'm looking forward to it." And she vanished.

Layla sat there for several seconds, allowing the fear to drip away, before she got up and went to the bathroom to splash water on her face. She'd spent the last few days working with Diana and Chloe to increase her power, while trying to master Terhal's influence over her mind. Considering she hadn't seen Terhal since Grayson helped banish her, Layla had thought she'd been winning. But it seemed the more confident she got, the more powerful Terhal was. She was becoming more and more dangerous.

She'd deal with that later, but first, Chloe. Because she was going to go after her whether Tommy liked it or not.

29

"They killed one of Tommy's people," Masako said, her voice full of anger. "I told you all not to do anything stupid. Killing his people is classified as stupid."

Masako and Elias were alone in one of the many rooms in the farmhouse. She'd stormed in there the second Shane and Reyes had returned with a semi-conscious Chloe.

"It was a risk worth taking," Elias said. "It's better to have grabbed one of his people than storm the mansion. This way we have leverage."

"Leverage? Or is this just about getting revenge on Chloe for killing Dara?"

Elias fought back the rage that exploded inside of him. "I am a professional. I don't allow my personal feelings to get in the way of a job. I'd really like to skin the little bitch alive, but right now she's useful." He got up from behind the desk he'd been sitting at and walked around it toward Masako.

"If this all goes to hell, Nergal will hear of it. That means my neck too, and I'd rather not make an enemy of the man unless forced."

"It will be fine. I'm going to go speak to Chloe right now and ensure that she knows how to behave."

"Do not kill her."

"Wouldn't dream of it."

Elias left the room and walked to the far end of the farmhouse, where two blood elves stood guard outside of a white door.

"Unlock it," he told one of them, who did as commanded.

There was a shriek from inside the room as the door was pushed open and Elias stepped into the doorway. He liked the little whimpering noises the inhabitants made whenever he arrived.

"How often are you given food and bathroom breaks?" Elias asked the fifteen men and women inside.

No one answered.

"I asked you all a question."

"Every six hours," one of the captives said. Elias had made sure the windows were boarded up and there were no lights inside the room, so it was hard to say who had spoken.

Elias turned to the blood elves. "Give them free rein of the bathroom opposite this one. They may go between the two as they wish." He turned back to the group. "Take this act of kindness for granted, and you'll be killed."

More whimpering. He looked back at the blood elves. "Grab two of them and come with me. I don't care who."

The elves entered the room and dragged two people from it, as the remaining captives cried out in horror. Elias waited outside in the hallway for the two captives to be brought to him. He didn't know their names, nor did he even care to know. It was information he didn't need. As far as he was concerned, they were a man and woman. The man was older, probably mid-forties, and the woman early twenties.

"One of you elves stay here, the other comes with me. Remember what I said about the bathroom. I'm not a monster."

The blood elf that remained behind nodded. The second elf followed Elias, occasionally pushing the two captives to keep them walking.

At the opposite end of the farmhouse, where four more blood elves stood guard, Elias opened a second white door, although this one was considerably more faded in color. Chloe sat inside, chained to the wall by thick manacles. She got to her feet and glared a look of pure hatred at Elias.

The room was sparsely decorated and consisted of one single bed with a dark blue quilt and several pillows, a small sink, and a toilet. Elias hadn't wanted to risk Chloe being moved when she needed to use the loo.

"Bring them in," Elias said, stepping into the room. "Hello, Chloe. I'm sure you think you can escape from here at any time."

Chloe's lip was bleeding and there was some swelling around one eye. Elias smiled; Reyes had told him that Chloe had been forcibly subdued.

Chloe remained silent.

Elias wasn't deterred. "You probably think that you can run around here and build up enough power to force yourself free. I'm here to show you otherwise."

"Who are they?" Chloe asked.

Elias turned back to the two captives. "Oh, how rude of me. Please introduce yourselves to Chloe."

"Jack Simmons," the man said.

Elias pointed at the woman and motioned for her to speak.

"Star Davis."

"Jack and Star," Elias said with a smile. "Aren't they lovely? Nice, wholesome people. Salt of the earth, you might say. Tell Chloe something about yourselves. Jack, do you have any family?"

"Wife and son," Jack said. "I miss them."

"Ah, how sad. Star, you?"

"No, I'm single. I don't have any kids. I live with my parents, until I can afford my own place."

"Just starting out in the world and this happens to you." Elias looked over at Chloe. "It's just so sad, isn't it?"

"If I try to escape, you're going to hurt them. Is that it?" Chloe asked, her voice hard and angry.

"Not quite." Elias nodded to the blood elves, and the five of them grabbed the two humans, forcing them to kneel. "You see, every time you displease me, I'm going to kill one of these captives."

"Don't you dare," Chloe said.

Elias ignored her and drew his stiletto blade from the sheath on his back. He leaned over Jack, placing the tip of the blade against his jugular.

"Please don't," Jack begged.

"I hate begging, Jack. Hate it." Elias pushed the blade up into Jack's throat as Chloe and Star screamed at him to stop. He never took his eyes off Chloe as he pushed the blade further and further in, until Jack shuddered and died.

Elias withdrew the blade and pushed Jack's body onto the wooden floor, his blood seeping between the floorboards. He looked at Star and smiled. "Do you understand the kind of man I am, Chloe?"

"Yes, yes, please stop," Chloe pleaded.

"His death is on your head. You murdered Dara, and now you know what punishments will be given to you if you ever cross me while you're here." He pointed the blade at Star. "Take her back to the others. If Chloe does something wrong, we'll kill her first."

The blood elves dragged Star out of the room.

"You're going to die for this," Chloe said.

Elias laughed. "We all die at some point, but I'm willing to bet you'll go first."

One of the elves went to move Jack's body, but Elias stopped him. "Leave it for a day. I want Chloe to think long and hard about her decision and the consequences it brought. Let her see what happens to those who cross me."

He left the room to find Masako standing in the doorway. "Was that necessary?" she asked.

"Are you squeamish? You eat people."

"Using up leverage just to make a point doesn't make me squeamish. It's just not a good idea to piss off someone you're trying to get to behave. That kind of thing makes rebellious thoughts. You know the first chance she gets she'll try to kill you."

"Then we'll kill more of the captives. Eventually her need to kill me will be overridden by the number of dead in the room with her."

"Do you actually have a plan beyond torturing her?"

Elias grinned. "Of course."

They entered the main room of the house, and Elias picked up a mobile phone from the large table in the middle of the room. "This is Chloe's. We found it on her and it's been ringing every hour on the hour. Tommy's the one calling."

"You're making him wait?"

"Of course. The angrier he is, the better for me."

The phone rang again.

"Right on cue," Elias said with a chuckle, before answering it. "Hello, Tommy."

"Elias," Tommy said, his voice deep and full of anger.

"Ah, so good to hear your voice. Don't bother trying to trace the call. You'd only be insulting my intelligence by thinking that I would be stupid enough not to counteract it."

"What do you want, Elias?"

"Layla. That's it. You give me Layla, and I give you Chloe. She's mostly unharmed, although I don't think she'll stay that way forever if she keeps that mouth of hers going."

"Not a chance. I'm not going to give you Layla."

Elias put the phone on loudspeaker and sat down on a nearby chair, placing his feet up on the table. He removed his fedora and placed it on the table beside him. "You're going to bring me Layla because you think you'll have a chance to save her before she vanishes into the wilderness. If you don't, Chloe will die. She'll die hard, Tommy, and I know you don't want that."

"If you really think I'm just going to let you take anyone else, you're even more deluded than I expected. I'm going to find you, and I'm going to kill you."

"Are you even going to ask Layla what she wants to do? Does she want me to murder her friend?"

"I'll do it," Layla shouted from somewhere in the same room, her voice slightly muffled as if someone were trying to get her away from the phone.

Elias smiled. He guessed Tommy would be considering the use of speaker phone on his end to be a mistake right about now.

"No," Tommy snapped. "No."

"Yes, I'll do it," Layla shouted again, sounding as if she was being hurried from the room. "I'll come to you, Elias. You let Chloe go first, and I'm all yours."

"Not how it works, I'm afraid, Tommy. You're going to go with Layla to an address I give you. While you're there, and once we're free and clear, Chloe will be released. I don't actually trust any of you not to screw me over, so we do it my way or I send pieces of Chloe to you over the next few days. What's first, a finger or a foot? It'll be a fun guessing game for the whole family."

"Where do you want the meet to take place?" Tommy asked.

Elias smiled at the defeated tone in Tommy's voice, and gave him the address to a building site where work had stopped some months previously. Elias knew the area, and knew that there were multiple routes in and out, but the mass of flat land meant that he could see if Tommy decided to play games and send people after him.

"I don't want a were to bring Layla."

"That's not going to happen," Diana said. "You'll get who we send."

"I don't trust weres, and I certainly don't trust any of you not to try to kill me. Do you have someone older, weaker?"

There was a pause of several seconds. "Grayson," Tommy said. "He's a doctor here. He's not a were."

"What is he?" Elias asked.

"Human," Tommy said. "He's a human doctor."

"Dragging humans into this, tsk-tsk," Elias said with a slight chuckle. He had to admit he was quite enjoying himself.

"You dragged him into it when you murdered Layla's ex-boyfriend and his new girlfriend, and then blamed another human. Grayson is just a human doctor involved in something he wants no part of, but who also wants to make sure no one gets killed."

"People still might if you screw with me on this. You have six hours, and if you're not there . . . well, you probably don't want to know what happens after that. I have your address, so I could always send you pieces of Chloe in the post." He read the address of the mansion just in case Tommy didn't believe him.

"How'd you get those details?"

"Hello, Thomas," Masako said. "Remember me?"

"How could I forget?" Tommy almost snarled, his displeasure at hearing from Masako evident from his tone. "I always like to remember the monsters I meet, especially the ones who don't look like monsters until it's too late."

"Let's not have any more death today. I want this to be done with as little bloodshed as possible, but there are others here who do not share my restrained view. They would rather storm the castle, so to speak. Handing Layla over in return for Chloe is the only sensible decision you have left. Please don't force our hand. I would hate to have to turn Chloe into my next meal."

"You don't touch her, Masako," Diana said, her voice a low rumble of threat.

"If you're all done puffing out your chests, can we get on with this?" Tommy asked. "Six hours, Elias. We'll be there."

Elias ended the call without another word and turned to Masako. "You and Tommy don't get on?"

"We've had run-ins in the past. He takes action against those who have hurt people he sees as part of his pack. You know he's going to come after you when you don't hand over this woman?"

"Of course. But we'll be long gone by then. Do you know this Grayson?"

Masako shook her head. "Never heard of him. I can contact a few people in Avalon and check him out, but Tommy's certainly desperate enough to use humans in place of any other species."

"Check anyway. You're coming with me to get Layla."

"Where are you going to put Layla when you have her? I thought you'd be taking her back to America?"

Part of him wanted to tell her that he wanted to kill Chloe before going anywhere, and that he wanted a chance to feed before going back, but being honest wasn't going to get him anything but arguments. "I need her to get in contact with her dad first. I need evidence that she can do so. Taking her to Nergal without it would result in his displeasure. Besides, I want to use Chloe to get Layla's cooperation, and that's easier to do here than it is thirty-five thousand feet in the air.

"As for where we're putting her, there's a wooden cabin out back. I've had the blood elves gut the place and change the locks to a thick plastic. There's no metal there; even the mattress on the bed we left her has no metal springs. She can't use anything as a weapon."

"Security feed?"

"The cameras and their components contain no metal. They weren't easy to come by, but they'll work."

"So, we can keep her contained."

"For as long as we need to, yes." Elias stood. "I'm a professional, Masako." He picked up his fedora. After all the trouble he'd gone through to get Layla, it was finally coming to an end.

30

The building site was cold and damp, and as Layla arrived in the BMW X5, she began to wonder if they couldn't have picked somewhere more public. The emptiness that surrounded them as they drove onto the site did little to make Layla thrilled about her current circumstances.

"It'll be okay," Grayson said after stopping the car and switching off the engine.

"I know. I'm just preparing myself to be back in Elias's grubby little hands. It's a lot to take in."

Grayson placed a comforting hand on her shoulder. "Tommy won't let anything happen to you."

"You know he's not going to let Chloe go, right?"

Grayson nodded. "Of course. Elias has no intention of doing it. We're not stupid. But because we know that, it means we can prepare for it. How are the visions from your drenik?"

"Still there, getting stronger. Terhal isn't exactly fun at the moment; in fact, I don't know if she was ever fun. She seems to enjoy hurting me, though, so maybe that's a drenik's idea of a good time."

"I don't know many umbra, as you're much rarer than your current circumstances would suggest, but I don't think anyone has ever enjoyed their drenik's company. Certainly not to begin with. Chloe and Jared didn't."

A black Range Rover pulled onto the site and parked a hundred feet in front of the BMW.

"Let's get this done," Layla said, and opened the door, stepping out into the increasingly bad weather.

Elias and an unknown woman got out of the Range Rover and started walking toward Layla, who followed suit, with Grayson beside her. Layla reached out and grabbed Grayson's hand, squeezing it slightly, and she noticed that Grayson squeezed back.

"Good to see you, Layla," Elias said. "This is Masako."

Layla stared at the Japanese woman. "Another umbra?"

"I'm jikininki," she told her. Masako's voice was soft and almost song-like.

"Flesh eater," Grayson whispered. "Bad news."

"I have excellent hearing, doctor," Masako said. "I assumed a human doctor wouldn't know much about my kind."

"I've learned a lot from reading Tommy's books. Lots of species, so little time to read about them all."

"I'm glad to have been on the list you had time for." Masako turned to Layla. "I recommend you join us in the car."

Elias hadn't stopped staring at Layla from the second they'd arrived, and it was beginning to make her feel even more uncomfortable than she already felt. "You appear to have grown in the short time we've been apart. The spirits in your body make you both stronger and weaker at the same time. It's quite interesting."

Layla took a deep breath to steady her voice, letting it out slowly before speaking. She wanted to punch Elias, to hurt him just like he'd hurt so many, but she had to remain calm. "Be interested somewhere else. It's cold and raining, and I'd like to see Chloe."

"I explained she wasn't with us when we spoke on the phone."

"I know. Take me to her."

"You wish to be a prisoner so much?"

"Don't taunt her," Grayson snapped.

Elias walked over to the doctor and punched him in the stomach. Grayson dropped to his knees.

"Humans should know their place. Yours is to be silent until allowed to speak."

"Leave him alone," Layla shouted, drawing Elias's attention.

"I was merely showing him his place. Get in the car. Now."

Grayson looked up at Layla and nodded that he was okay.

"He's lucky I'm not going to kill him, the worthless bag of flesh that he is."

Layla walked with Elias and Masako back to the Range Rover and got into the front passenger seat, as Masako slid into the one behind her.

Elias climbed into the driver's seat, started the engine, and said, "Try anything and Chloe will die."

Grayson finally got back on his feet and steadied himself against the BMW, while Layla wondered how hard it had been for him to not fight back. She hoped he was okay.

The Range Rover pulled away and drove out of the building site, down winding roads for about a mile, until they came to a layby, where Elias pulled over and switched off the engine. "Get out."

Confused and concerned, Layla did as she was asked. It was either that or risk Chloe, and she wouldn't do that. Instead, she exited the car and stood beside the door, as Elias walked around.

"Arms in the air. I'm going to search you for bugs."

Again, Layla complied, and Elias performed a professional search, never lingering or taking liberties. When he was done, he stepped back. "Do you have any electronic devices on you?"

"No, I left my phone with Tommy."

"Shoes off too."

Layla sighed and removed her trainers, passing them to Elias, who searched each one before giving them back. "You can't be too careful," he told her once the search was completed, and he motioned for her to return to the car.

"You should have let me do that," Masako told Elias when he was back behind the wheel.

"No offense, but when I do something myself, I know it'll be done right."

Masako laughed, the sound almost like a lullaby. "Control freak."

Elias said nothing more as he maneuvered the car back onto the road. For the next hour, they drove through villages and along dual carriageways, across tiny dirt roads, and through a stream. Clearly Elias didn't want anyone following.

Layla sat in silence, watching the scenery fly by as she tried to figure out where they might be heading. It was obvious to her that Elias didn't care if she knew where she was; otherwise she'd have a bag over her head. Eventually, they arrived at a large farm in the middle of nowhere, and after parking the car outside of the main house, Layla was ordered to get out.

She did as she was told, waiting by the car while Elias came to her. "We're going through the house. If you behave, you get to see Chloe once you're in your cage. If you don't, you get to hear Chloe scream instead. Are we clear?"

Layla held Elias's stare and nodded. She wasn't going to be intimidated by him or his people, and she certainly wasn't about to show him any of the fear she felt.

Satisfied with the answer, Elias led Layla around the farmhouse to a small wooden cabin behind it. It was really just a large room, but as she stood before it, she saw the heavy-duty plastic door lock that would ensure she stayed inside.

Elias removed the thick wooden pin from the lock and pulled back on the handle, drawing the lock out of the door frame. He opened it and motioned for Layla to step inside.

The cabin consisted of a small bed with a table to one side made of a light wood. A window overlooking the fields behind the property gave the room a meager amount of light. A sink sat under the window and there was a small bathroom in an enclosed space that reminded Layla of being in a caravan.

A camera sat against the ceiling in one corner of the room, watching everything she did.

"There are speakers in the ceiling. They're hidden, so don't try to search for them. If at any point we see you messing around with either the camera or the speakers, we kill Chloe."

"I do anything to piss you off, and you kill Chloe. I get it. I assume you want me to contact my dad now?"

"Later. First we're going to make sure we weren't followed. This evening, I'll bring you a phone, and you'll use it to contact your father's prison."

"An Avalon-controlled prison. That's why you can't do it yourself, isn't it? You don't know who is on your side and who isn't."

"Smart girl. Now stay smart and don't give us a reason to hurt anyone else."

"Don't call me a smart girl. My name is Layla. I'm not a puppy."

Elias grinned. "Okay. I'll leave you to become accustomed to your new surroundings. Food and fresh water will be brought to you in an hour. I wouldn't drink from the water in the sink; I can't vouch for its drinkability. If you pull the same trick you did back at the cell, I'll pull all your fingernails out . . . You don't need those to help us."

Layla looked over at the sink and remembered the last time she'd been Elias's prisoner and what she'd done to the blood elf to escape.

"There's nothing there to help you escape this time."

Elias left her alone, locking the door behind him, and Layla sat on the hard mattress, wondering exactly how long it would take Tommy and his people to find her. He had sworn that they would, she just didn't know how. She stared out of the window as the smell of burning filled her nostrils.

"Why fire?" she asked Terhal, who was leaning up against the door.

"I like fire. I like that crackle as something burns. It's cathartic."

Layla turned around and stared at the drenik. Terhal had changed back into male form, and wore a pair of black jeans and a white t-shirt. "I thought you preferred the female form?"

"I do, I just got bored looking like a woman. I figured I'd change to male for a while."

"You're not actually a demon. You know that, right?"

"I like to live up to the image you people imposed on me all those years ago. So, are you ready to have your mind broken?"

"I thought we went through this. I'm not going to let you out."

"Fight him," Rosa said, appearing in front of Layla. Unlike her normal appearance, Rosa was translucent.

"Her power is waning while mine increases." Terhal clicked his fingers and Rosa screamed, vanishing from view. "See how pitiful the spirits are? Once your mind is broken, your body will be mine. I will be free. Or you could just accept me."

The bodies of her friends appeared piled up in a corner of the cabin, forcing Layla to look down at her feet.

"But we know how that works out, don't we?"

"Leave, Terhal," Layla said, fully aware that her voice held no authority, and hating herself for it.

Terhal laughed as the door opened and Masako entered carrying a plate of sandwiches and a pitcher of water. She placed the items on the nearby table and stared at Layla with unknown intent. "Just do as they ask and no harm will befall you."

Layla couldn't help but laugh. "You don't believe that. And where's Chloe?"

"You will see her soon enough. Elias and his people are concerned about both of your abilities. I do not believe anyone here wants Elias to play the ogre hand again. You saw what that creature did last time."

"Yes, I was there. Thank you for the food and water."

"So you understand that until there are certain guarantees about your behavior, you'll both be kept apart. I'm sure Elias will bring Chloe with him when he asks you to contact your father. Is there anything else you need?"

"Some books to read. I have enough problems with my mind without going crazy through boredom too."

Masako nodded. "Do not make me regret my charity."

The second she was gone Terhal reappeared. "Now, back to our alone time." He walked over and crouched in front of Layla. "Let's see what happens to your friends one more time."

Terhal showed Layla horrific acts of barbarity being perpetrated on those she loved. People she cared for were murdered and tortured in front of her, and while a part of her knew it wasn't real, her mind still reacted as if it were. At the end, when Terhal was finally done, he left her alone.

She opened her eyes. She was lying on the wooden floor, her sweat-drenched clothing clinging to her. Terhal's visions were becoming ever more real, and even when she closed her eyes she couldn't see anything but the evil visions.

There was a knock and the cabin door opened. Elias stood there, looking down at Layla. "The demon is beginning to take control."

"Where is Chloe?"

"I brought her." Elias stepped back outside, and Layla dragged herself to her feet, staggering toward the door. Just outside, bathed by a spotlight, was a kneeling Chloe. Her lip was bloody and her clothes dirty, but otherwise she appeared to be okay. Reyes stood beside her, holding a length of rope that had been wrapped around Chloe's neck.

"Chloe!" Layla called out. She took a step forward, but Elias stood in front of her, barring her way.

"First we get what *we* want."

"Chloe!" Layla shouted again, ignoring Elias.

"I'm okay, Layla," Chloe called back. "Tired, and I really need a vodka. These guys don't really know how to have a good time."

Layla glared at Elias.

"I can't say I care much for dirty looks, Ms. Cassidy. I just want you to see your friend, because in the morning you're going to contact the prison and you're going to get your father to help us. And if you don't, we're going to start hurting Chloe. Or maybe we'll hurt the survivors from the depot. We've got a few of them here—I'm sure you'll be happy to see them."

"I can't be the only one who can help you," Layla said softly.

"Take Chloe back to her room," Elias commanded. "Allow me to be honest with you, Layla. No one knows where your father is. He's in a prison somewhere in North America under Avalon control. There are no human prisoners there, and none of the prisoners have a name; they are merely a number. Not even the agent who took him there knows the number assigned to your father.

"Only four people have ever known how to contact that prison. The agent in charge is one, and their boss, the director of the east coast LOA office, makes two. Frankly, going after either of them is opening a can of worms we can do without. Your mother was another, but she died before we managed to get hold of her. And the last is you. I know you know the prison's phone number because I've seen the list of contact names for your father. It's the only thing we could find with his name on it that pointed us toward you and your mother.

"So, yes, you are the only person who has these details. You think you don't know where his prison is because you don't want to know, but the reality is, even if you did want to know, they wouldn't tell you. But considering how much your father loves you, I'm sure he'll be only too eager to help."

"Why are you so sure of it?"

"I've read the transcripts of his interviews with Tabitha—we have people who work in the same LOA office as her, and they kindly passed along anything we needed. He talks about you with great affection. And I think someone threatening his little girl is going to get him motivated to help pretty quickly. And just to give you a little incentive—" He kicked Layla in the chest, knocking her to the floor. The air rushed out of her and pain coursed through her torso.

"I hope you enjoy the fun we have planned. Let's see if you're more susceptible after a night of no sleep. Enjoy the current UK top forty chart." He closed the door as music began blaring into the cabin, forcing Layla to clamp her hands over her ears to stop it from reverberating in her head, but it did little good.

Terhal sat beside Layla on the floor and tutted. "I guess now's as good a time as any to finally break you." And the world around Layla turned to blood, fire, and pain. She succumbed to the darkness that encircled her.

31

Hours passed, with Terhal inflicting every kind of painful torture on Layla's friends. At some point during her time there, Terhal returned to her female form, wearing the exact same outfit as before, and continued to barrage Layla's mind with insanity.

Layla lay motionless on the floor, the images too much for her to deal with all at once.

"You broken yet?" Terhal asked with a laugh.

Layla concentrated on her breathing. "Why are you like this?"

"Why? Because I want to be. Because I don't want to be here. I never asked to be torn from my home and placed in a scroll. I never asked to have my soul bounce from human to human. And I didn't ask to sit in someone's head, never quite able to be free. This is my prison, and you ask *why*? Whatever I may have been back in my world, I was free. I hunted, I fed, and I enjoyed my life. So now, with your mind as my new life, I will hunt and feed here instead. And you are my prey."

Layla pushed herself up to a kneeling position and coughed. She looked around at three cages that had appeared close by, each containing one of the spirits. Gyda's expression was one of terror, while both Rosa and Servius just looked angry.

"They didn't hurt you," Layla said, pointing to the cages. "They were as innocent as you were."

"They hate and fear me. They always have and they always will." Terhal walked over to the cage with Gyda in it and snarled at her. "You especially. I did awful things when I took over your body. Do you remember them?"

"You murdered my friends."

"And the same could be said for Servius. Lots of people he cared for died too. I have that effect on people. I wonder who I might kill when I take you, Layla. I mean, your parents are dead, so maybe Harry. He likes you—maybe I could show him a good time."

Layla didn't bother telling her to leave Harry alone; it would have done no good. Terhal was going to spout whatever evil she wanted, and Layla had no choice but to listen.

Terhal continued to walk past the cages until she reached Rosa. "You were special, Rosa. You accepted me so quickly, within a few hours. But then you always liked the darkness, didn't you? Always saw a lot of yourself in me. You fight so hard to conceal it, but we both knows it's there."

Rosa opened her mouth to shout, but no sound came out.

"Yeah, sorry about that; I had to turn down the volume. Frankly, your voice bores me, and I could do without having to listen to you try to rouse Layla to fight back. She can't fight back, or she won't. Either way means I win."

"This isn't a game," Layla said. "It never was."

"Of course it's a game, Layla," Terhal snapped. "And I win. Or would you rather this?" She waved her hands and the loud pop music streamed into the world around Layla, causing the ground beneath her to shake. She slammed her hands over her ears, but as quickly as it started, the music stopped. "I think this way is more civilized. I like being able to talk to you, Layla. I like seeing the hope drain from you."

Layla sat up and sighed. "I'm done with this, Terhal. I'm done with you, and with Elias, and frankly with anyone else who wants to try to control me. I'm done." She got to her feet. "You can't kill me, and you certainly can't break me, no matter how much you like to believe you can. This is *my* mind, not yours. I wonder what your life was like before you were forced to come here. The others showed me, but you haven't. You've just threatened and twisted my mind. I wonder what you're afraid of."

"Nothing," Terhal snapped.

"Show me then." The world around Layla twisted and changed, the fire and death replaced with rolling valleys and green grass. She stood and felt the grass between her bare toes.

Birds flew high above and close by a ten-foot waterfall fed into a stream that opened up into a large river further along.

"This is where you lived?"

"No!" Terhal screamed. "You can't do this. You can't see this."

"Why?"

"I'm in control here. You don't have the power to stop me."

Layla looked over at Terhal, who was on her knees, screaming at the world around her. "This is where you lived? It's beautiful."

Layla walked off toward the stream and saw brightly colored frogs sitting in the mud of the bank. A low growl broke the peace, and a large cat-like animal with six legs bounded down the bank toward a larger animal that looked like a deer crossed with a unicorn. The six-legged creature was obviously the predator, a fact that was reinforced when the prey turned and jumped over the stream, running off.

"A deericorn," Layla said to herself. "I really wish people were here to hear me be clever."

"They're called dromath," Terhal said.

The brown and white dromath skidded to a halt and then turned toward the predator, spearing it in the side with its sharp horn.

"Nothing here is helpless," Terhal said. "Everything is prey, but everything is dangerous too."

The predator swiped with one paw, slicing through the side of the other animal's neck, but the dromath was not only larger, it was also faster, and the fight was soon over as the dromath's horn pierced the underside of the predator's throat, killing it.

"The cat-like creature is called a tyori. They're vicious but stupid creatures."

The dromath, instead of fleeing, lapped up the blood of its defeated opponent.

"Like I said, everything is dangerous."

"And you were the apex predator?"

Something that looked a lot like Terhal sprinted from the nearby long grass, colliding with the dromath and knocking it to the floor. It grabbed hold of the horn and yanked it back, ripping it out of the creature's head and casting it aside, before it set about feasting.

"We were the top of the food chain. Beings who could hunt and kill with a strength and speed that few others matched. Each of us had the ability to transform ourselves depending on our surroundings and needs. It took a few days of being cocooned, but once we emerged, we could grow limbs, wings, and night vision; whatever we needed to survive. We were as close to gods as this land got."

Layla looked over at Terhal and discovered that her frightening appearance from before had changed. She still had the ridge around her skull, but there was now skin around her mouth. "And then you were taken."

"We were physical in this world, but in your world we lost that ability; we became spirit-like, bonded to a scroll for all eternity. Those of you who created these scrolls thought nothing of what they did—they just wanted to create power, and damn the consequences."

"I'm sorry about what happened to you. Did you live in families or alone?"

"Are you asking if I had a family? The answer is no. We were solitary creatures for the most part, only coming together to mate and be on our way. I do not wish to see this anymore."

"Why?"

"I do not wish to be reminded of what was."

"Is that why you torture me? Because of your anger at missing this place?"

"I torture you because I cannot torture those responsible for my current circumstances. I torture you because it is survival of the fittest, and you have not proven yourself to be anything close to it. And I torture you because if I'm going to have your hate and disdain, I might as well do something to earn it."

"Why would you have my hate or disdain?"

"I've seen other people when they've taken a spirit scroll. I've seen the way they speak about the drenik, the fear and loathing they have for them. It does not make me want to help you. And no, not all of the drenik in scrolls are like me; some are kind and sweet, some want to bond with the human to create something better. I've listened to my hosts speak to many umbra over the years—the drenik are not a one-size-fits-all kind of species. Just like humanity."

"Why not work with me?"

"Because you won't let me out. You'll keep me in here until you die, and then I get to wait another hundred years or longer until I can go through this whole thing again. The spirits in here hate me, do you know that?"

"Have you ever given them a reason not to? Gyda feared you, and then you murdered her people."

"It was my first time out. I reacted like a cornered animal would have, and then I realized the more I deliver the evil they expect of me, the harder it is for the human to take control. I get to live outside of this facade so long as I behave in a way that you people would consider evil."

"Doesn't sound like much of a life."

"Rosa was the only one who understood me even slightly, and even she was scared of what I could do if I were ever allowed to take control. Rosa kept me locked down unless it was an emergency, and beyond that, I just sat in my cage and waited."

"You're saying that those who took the scroll were wrong about you, that you're not a cruel, vindictive monster?"

"I'm drenik. We believe that the strongest survive and the weakest are there to serve us, or be our next meal. Gyda was weak. Rosa was not, but by then she'd heard from Gyda and Servius and distrusted me."

"Why are you telling me this?"

"Because you are not afraid of me. You challenged me and brought me here; I've never had a host able to do that. Rosa sat and spoke to me, but it was more about learning than actual bonding with her. As if she wanted to get to know me just enough so that she could accept me, but never enough to actually go beyond that. She didn't want to understand me, or where I was from. Gyda and Servius had already imparted their stories to her by then."

"You murdered people when you took Servius."

"His emotions were a mess, and they translated to me. Fear, hate, rage, and the need to destroy those who dared to oppose him. He didn't have a chance to tell me to stop; he just let me out to do whatever I needed to. I can't tell friend from enemy. For my kind, everyone's a potential enemy. Even when mating, you get in, get out, and don't wait around for them to decide whether you're a nuisance or danger."

Terhal walked toward several large stones in the center of a fire pit. "This was my camp while I was here. I was about to move to the east. The winters are bad here, and evolving just to survive it is a monumental effort. I preferred the jungles of the east, anyway. But I'm never coming back here now. This is all I have left. Memories and dreams. I hate you, Layla. I hate you and your kind; humanity is a curse that was inflicted on my people when the dwarves dragged us from our realm and put us into those scrolls. When they turned us into weapons. I can't think of anything else other than to hate you for what happened to me."

There were no words that could make it better, so Layla just stood silently, watching Terhal.

"I might not be able to break you, but I can never trust you, I can never stop trying to fight. It's not in my nature. Sooner or later, humanity will betray me. It seems to be all you know how to do. Betray, conquer, and destroy."

"That's all you've gotten from your life? All you've seen are those things?"

Terhal thought for a second. "No, I've seen kindness and I've seen mercy, but none of those things have been directed at me, so why should I care? I told you, my kind doesn't care about anything but surviving. Mercy is a weakness, and kindness is more than likely to get you killed. Drenik have to be strong, have to be ready to fight at a moment's notice. The only drenik I ever respected were those that bettered me in combat. All others were to be held in contempt."

"I'm sorry that's all you've known."

"I don't want friendship, Layla. I don't need it, and I'm happier without it, but I need my host to be strong. So far, only Rosa has come close, and she was still afraid of me."

"I'm afraid of what you can do. Of what you could do if you ever managed to take control of my mind."

"We are not naturally good or evil, Layla. We are drenik. The only way to survive is to be the best, to be the strongest for the battles that come. There is glory in the hunt and the fight. It's something we revel in. But we are not a cruel or sadistic species. Not naturally. But your kind, you label me with words like evil and monster, and none of those are true. Why shouldn't I become the thing you people think I am? Why shouldn't I torment and break those too weak to ever be my equal? If I am your better, why should I allow you to control me?

"I've saved lives that needed saving; pregnant animals, animals that would draw danger. Even other drenik on the rare occasions we needed to work together. This world was harsh, but it always seemed fair. And most importantly, it was *my* world."

"You say you respect the host only for its strength, and that I don't appear to be strong enough for your respect. But Chloe's drenik was easy to bond with, according to her. She said she beat it before it beat her. She made it submit to her will."

Terhal laughed. "You're not strong enough to make me."

Layla punched Terhal in the face with everything she had, knocking the demon to the ground. "You want me to show you I'm worthy of your respect through survival of the fittest. I'm betting I can beat you."

Terhal's eyes flared with anger. "Is this really how you want to do this? Trial by combat?"

"I brought you here, so I don't think your control over my mind is as great as you think it is. What's wrong, Terhal? Can't fight without tricks?"

Terhal got back to her feet. "You will regret that." She darted forward and threw a right hand that Layla blocked, pushing the arm away and kicking out Terhal's knee. The drenik quickly rolled away, putting distance between the two of them.

"Where are all the burning fires and dead friends, Terhal? Did you use up your good stuff a little bit too early?"

Terhal screamed in rage, charging forward, moving much faster than Layla had anticipated. She grabbed hold of Layla around the waist and took her off her feet, planting her on the dirt. She tried to get enough leverage to throw a powerful punch, but Layla kept hold of the drenik, never allowing her to gain any sort of advantage.

Terhal soon changed tactic and struck Layla in the kidney, which caused her to gasp in pain. It gave the drenik the opportunity to put her hands around Layla's throat, squeezing as hard as she could.

Layla fought against the grip, but it was too strong. She punched Terhal in the face, but the drenik just smiled, even as blood dripped from the cut on her lip.

"I wonder, if you die here, can I just take control forever?" Terhal asked with a bloody grin. "You're lying in the dirt beneath me. It's where your kind belong."

Layla wasn't about to die in her own mind, and reached up above her head, taking hold of whatever was there and smashing it into the side of Terhal's skull. The drenik was knocked aside, and Layla coughed and spluttered as she rolled onto all fours.

She looked at the fist-sized rock in her hand, which was smattered with Terhal's red blood, and got to her feet. "You know something, Terhal? All my life I've had this little voice in my head that says I should hurt people. That says fighting is good, and that I'm good at it. It always wants me to go a step further than I know I should. And I've fought against that voice for years. Every now and again it creeps through, and you are just like that voice."

Terhal was up on her knees, blood pouring from an open wound on her scalp. "You can't beat me, girl. I am better than you."

Layla walked over to Terhal, holding the rock so tightly in her hand that her knuckles were white. "You need to accept me as your host. You need to accept me so that I can accept you and don't have to worry about you trying to murder my friends."

Terhal laughed.

Layla smashed the rock into her face, knocking her to the ground. "The thing is, Terhal, this is *my* mind. That means *my* rules. You're just a parasite living here."

"How dare you!" Terhal began, before Layla hit her with the rock again.

"I can lose control here. I can beat you like a goddamn drum all over this place if I choose." Terhal tried to get up, and Layla hit her again. "I don't think I can kill you. I think no matter what I do, you'll always be here. You've been wronged for centuries, and I'm giving you a chance to do something better. You want survival of the fittest, then help me become the best damn umbra who ever lived."

Terhal giggled and spat blood onto the floor. "This is my world."

Layla dropped the rock. "No. It really isn't. You see, Chloe told me something that didn't quite sink in at the time."

Terhal spat more blood onto the ground. "And what's that?"

"This is my mind."

Terhal screamed in agony as Layla took hold of the iron compounds in Terhal's blood and began the process of dragging it out of her, lifting her off the ground at the same time.

"I know we're only in my mind, but I can make this feel real for you, Terhal. My power here is unlimited. With enough strength and practice, I'll be able to do this, be able to manipulate the metal deposits inside a person."

"Stop it!" Terhal screamed.

Layla released her grip and Terhal fell to the floor. For the first time, Layla saw fear in her eyes.

"Don't make me hurt you again. You've been hurt enough over your life. Work with me, fear me, love me, I don't care. But if you ever threaten those I love again, I will bring you back here and see how long it takes you to put yourself back together. I don't want to cage you, Terhal." Metal tore out of the rock around where Terhal sat, forming a cage over her.

"Enough," Terhal said. "I have one request."

"Name it."

"Can I stay here? I know it's not real, but I'd like to live here, not in some cage somewhere. None of the others did this. None of them fought me. I didn't know you could."

"Me neither. And yes, you can stay here."

A second later, Gyda, Servius, and Rosa appeared beside Layla.

"You can't just let her free like this," Gyda shouted. "She'll take control."

Terhal shook her head as she remained on the ground. "Still afraid. Still learned nothing."

"I didn't call you here for opinions," Layla said. She walked over and stood in front of Gyda. "I understand your fear and reluctance to allow Terhal any sort of freedom. I would rather work with you all than be afraid of any of you. I accept you, Gyda."

Gyda nodded once and vanished.

"Servius," Layla said moving in front of him. "You are a great warrior and a man I'm sure I can learn much from. I accept you."

Servius winked and he too vanished.

Layla turned to Rosa. "I understand you most of all, I think. I'm not a killer, but I know parts of the life you led, and why you decided to become one. It was the best option in a trove of bad options. Since all of this happened, you're the one person I've grown closest to, and I accept you."

"About bloody time too." Rosa hugged Layla, before vanishing.

Layla turned to Terhal and walked toward her, crouching within arm's reach. She wanted to show Terhal she wasn't afraid, that no matter the drenik's power in her mind, she, Layla, was the only thing that mattered. "If you ever misplace my trust, I'll take all of this from you and place you in a small cage underground, in a place where only my fears live. You think I'm bad, wait until you meet my father."

Terhal nodded.

Layla reached out and placed a hand on either side of Terhal's head. She moved forward and kissed the drenik's forehead. "I accept you, Terhal. I accept you for who you are and what you're capable of."

Terhal exhaled slightly, a look of shock on her face as she vanished. All four spirits had merged with Layla, their memories and personalities pushing their way into her own as the surroundings melted back into the cabin.

Layla found herself on her knees on the wooden floor, the loud music blaring all around her. She was drenched in sweat and could taste blood. She placed her forehead on the floor and allowed the spirits to fully merge with her. The sensation was something she wasn't sure she could manage if she was upright.

When it was done, she got to her feet and tried to block out the music, while inside her all she could feel was power. Pure, dangerous power. Layla looked around; she couldn't flee right now, and she couldn't fight without getting Chloe killed. While the music boomed around her, she could barely think. She wanted to send a message to Elias that she wouldn't be broken, that he couldn't do anything to beat her.

Layla looked up at the camera and smiled. And then she started to dance, allowing the rhythm of the music to aid her in her rebellion.

32

Elias had been on a call to Nergal, updating him on exactly what had happened and how they'd managed to catch Layla, when he heard a stifled laugh from a nearby room.

He ignored it and continued talking. "We'll be ready to go within the day, although I'd appreciate it if I could go back to my home and recharge. I'm sure that once on a jet, there would be nowhere for her to go."

"Do you have a plan to stop her from using her abilities? Thirty thousand feet is a high place to be if she decides to take the jet apart."

"Once we're certain she'll help us, we're going to tranquillize her. We just need her to make the initial contact."

"What convinces you she won't try to stall or get out of her agreement?"

"We used her friend as a way to gain her cooperation."

"Will you be bringing this girl with you?"

"No need. Once we have contact with her father, we can use Layla as leverage to get her father to help, but Layla's role will be over. We just need her to get through to her father so we can pinpoint his location. It might take several attempts to do this, but we knew that might be the case. She'll convince him to help us, and we'll have his location in a few days, max."

Nergal smiled. "Excellent. Please feel free to take some time to recharge. The next phase of our plan will require a lot of traveling, and I'd hate to not have you at full capacity."

Nergal ended the call, and Elias went to the room where the rest of the team were looking at one of the screens showing Layla.

"What's going on?" he asked.

"I think you should see this," Shane told him, and he moved aside to give Elias a better view of the screen.

Elias watched for several seconds as Layla danced around the room, seemingly oblivious to the torment the loud music was meant to be causing her.

"What is she doing?"

"She's dancing," Masako said.

Anger began to flood through Elias. "Turn the music up."

"This is as loud as it goes," Reyes told him.

Elias watched as Layla stopped dancing and stood on the bed, looking directly at the camera. She mouthed something.

"What is she saying?" Shane asked. "'Can you . . .' I can't make out the rest."

"'Can you put some Prince on?'" Masako translated. "She's making requests. Looks like your prison is actually a club."

Elias thought he saw a slight smirk on Masako's otherwise emotionless face, but when he turned to confirm it, her expression of neutrality had returned.

"So, Layla thinks this is all a big joke?" Elias snapped, his voice rising with every word. "She thinks this is a damn game? I'll show her a game. Shane, take Chloe back to our guest. Show her what happens to people who play games with us."

"You want me to kill her?"

Elias shook his head. "Just make her watch while you make an example of her. Screw it, I'll come with you—it looks like Layla could use a talking to at the same time. You wearing anything metal?"

Shane emptied his pockets of his phone and wallet, dumping them both on a nearby table.

The pair of them went to Chloe's cell and unlocked the door. Chloe sat on the bed in the corner, a model prisoner. Jack's body had been removed. The manacles were no longer needed; Chloe wouldn't escape with innocent people's lives at stake.

"You're coming with us," Elias told her. "Apparently your friend still thinks this is playtime."

Chloe got up and walked over. "I wonder, why didn't you just use your power on me, Shane?" she asked as she walked through the house to the outside. "This would all have been much easier if you could have just made me go with you."

There was silence for several seconds, before Chloe chuckled and shook her head. "I get it: your power doesn't work on other umbra. That has to be really embarrassing."

Shane ignored her, giving Chloe a hard shove to get walking. They reached the rear door, and Chloe opened it, stepping through without holding it open for anyone else. "I know if my power didn't work on a whole group of people, I'd be pretty embarrassed."

Shane balled his hands into fists, and Elias placed a hand on the younger man's shoulder. "She'll get what's coming to her," he told him. "Be patient."

Shane nodded once and continued on without comment, stopping outside of Layla's small prison cottage, the music inside barely audible to the three of them.

Elias opened the door, feeling thankful that neither Reyes nor Masako had turned the music down, and found Layla standing in the center of the cabin.

Anger bubbled up inside him. "You don't seem to be grasping the seriousness of the situation."

"I think you're a pathetic idiot who believes he has something he doesn't," Layla told him.

"We brought Chloe for you to talk to," Elias told her, stepping aside as Chloe was shoved into the cabin.

"You okay?" Layla asked her.

"Peachy."

Elias nodded to Shane, who punched Chloe in the stomach. She stepped back, but didn't fall to her knees like he'd intended. "Again."

The second blow was harder and caused Chloe to exhale all at once as she dropped to all fours, coughing and spluttering.

"Do you understand what your role is here?" Elias asked Layla, whose expression had darkened. He wondered if he'd finally get her full cooperation, or if he'd have to get Shane to break some of Chloe's fingers.

"My role is to give you everything you want, everything you need, and everything you deserve. The drenik inside of me took over for a while there, but I have it back under control. Please stop hurting my friend."

Elias nodded toward Shane, who took Chloe by the arm and dragged her out of the cabin.

"Thank you. If you get me a phone, I'll contact the prison. I know it'll be early there, but I'm sure I can get hold of someone. I want to try."

Elias wasn't convinced and wondered exactly what the plan was, but even if Layla did manage to escape, where would she go? There were miles of nothing all around them, and it wouldn't take long for the blood elves or the ogre to track her down. Besides, she wasn't about to put Chloe at risk, and Elias only needed a reason to finally kill her and gain vengeance for Dara. He glanced out of the open door at Chloe and clenched his fists. He could feel his blood boil inside, feel the need to give Chloe everything she deserved, to kill her slowly and painfully. But he pushed it aside. He could not allow those baser instincts to drive him forward.

"Stay here," he told Layla, closing and locking the door. He turned to Shane. "You keep *her* occupied. I don't want Chloe and Layla to communicate. At all. Understand?"

Shane nodded. "Won't be a problem."

Elias left them alone and went back into the house, grabbing a phone from his bedroom. He'd just stepped back into the hallway when there was an explosion downstairs, followed by shouting, as all hell broke loose.

33

Layla had waited until Elias had closed the door and walked away before setting her plan in motion. Originally, she'd hoped that Elias would have just sent Reyes or some other crony to come and quiet her, but then she realized that if she'd used that moment to escape, she'd have no idea where Chloe actually was, and by the time she got to her, it might already be too late.

But they'd brought Chloe to her. Okay, it had been to use as a punch bag so that Layla behaved, but still, Chloe was right outside the door with Shane. If Layla could only get the door open, she'd have a good shot at stopping Shane and keeping Chloe safe. It had made her furious that Chloe had been hit, that she'd been attacked and humiliated. Layla wasn't going to do anything in Chloe's name; she was going to help Chloe get free so that she could do it in her own name.

"You bonded with us all, now what?" Rosa asked after appearing on the bed. "You don't have long."

"There are no lights in this cabin, no electric cables either, but there are speakers in the ceiling. They contain metal. I can feel it." She concentrated and began to pull small wires out of the ceiling, snaking them down toward her, then wrapping them around her hands and wrists.

She didn't care about the camera because by the time she was done, it would be too late for anyone watching to do anything. She hoped.

"There's not a lot of metal there," Rosa told her.

"It'll be enough," Layla explained as the end of one of the wires snapped around her wrist, while the others hung down, like a dozen thin whips. She flicked them toward the door, hardening the metal in them as they punched through the wood. A flick of her hand, and the thin metal wire tore the door in half, allowing her to step outside, where she found a terrified Shane standing behind Chloe.

"You take her," Shane said. "Just don't kill me. I'm not a fighter, I'm just here to help out."

"Are you okay?" Layla asked Chloe, ignoring Shane. "Stupid question, I know."

"I'm fine," Chloe told her. "A little bruised, but my powers are healing me quickly enough. What do you plan on doing with the dipshit behind me?"

"He's all yours."

From a kneeling position, Chloe spun up and toward Shane, planting an uppercut just under his chin that lifted him from his feet and dumped him on the ground.

Chloe bounced up and down on the spot for a few seconds, before stopping and walking over to Shane. She picked him up and threw him against the cabin wall, causing a cracking sound as his ribs broke from the impact.

Chloe didn't even pause and sprinted flat-out toward Shane, driving her knee into his face as he tried to get back to his feet. She rained down punch after punch onto his face, and Layla had to look away as the sound of fists breaking bone became too much.

"Chloe," Layla almost whispered, "I think he's done." She risked a look back at her friend, who was covered in Shane's blood.

Chloe got to her feet and staggered a little, before kneeling beside Shane and placing a hand on the side of his head, moving it so he could look at her through his one good eye. "Can you hear me in there?" she asked Shane, who could only murmur a response. "Right now, I could kill you. And there's every chance that one day I will, but I'm not going to do that today. There's going to be enough killing soon, and Tommy is going to want someone to talk to about Nergal and Elias. I'm volunteering you." She punched him in the face with enough power to knock him out, and he went still.

Layla took a step toward Shane, paused as she saw him breathe, and went to Chloe. "Are you okay?"

Chloe let herself be helped up, using Layla as support. "Exhausted," she said. "Just exhausted. And really sore. I may have pulled a few things fighting him."

An explosion tore through the night, followed by shouts that drifted all around them. Several armed men and women ran to the rear of the building, close to Layla and Chloe, followed by Remy screaming obscenities at the top of his voice.

"Hey," he said, stopping beside Layla. "You two okay?"

Layla nodded as Diana ran down from the hill, a broadsword in one hand. She stopped beside the group and took Chloe from Layla.

"She needs rest," Layla said.

"I'll take her to the cars out front. Come join us when you're done." With Chloe in her arms, Diana ran off without another word.

"And the sack of shit on the floor?" Remy asked, pointing at Shane. "Is he a pin cushion, or is he there for a more helpful reason?"

"He needs to be questioned."

Remy stared at the wires hanging from Layla's hands, as more shouts and the sounds of fighting left the farmhouse. "You going to join in?"

"There are people here from the train depot. Elias had them captured."

Remy shouted at one of the nearby armed men, who nodded and was soon carrying Shane away, although he was considerably less careful about it than Diana had been about Chloe.

Remy drew his broadsword and smiled. "Let's go find your friends, and give some people a really bad day."

Layla followed him into the farmhouse expecting to find chaos and insanity all around her, but whatever action there was had been quick. Three dead blood elves lay by the front door, as Tommy organized a search of the property.

"How are you?" he asked Layla. "I'm sorry it took so long to get here. We had to make sure we weren't going to cause your death by triggering an alarm or trap."

"I'm fine," she told him. "You tracked me?"

"Well, Grayson did, but he's back at the mansion now. Any idea where Elias is?"

Layla shook her head and explained about the train-depot captives.

Tommy sniffed the air. "There's a bunch of scents coming from upstairs. Remy, you go with Layla and find these people."

Remy nodded.

"What about Reyes and the Japanese ghost lady?" Layla asked.

"Masako? No sign of either. I'm thinking they rabbited the second we came through the doors. This place is huge, so it'll take a while to search."

"And did you find the ogre?"

"Not yet, but it's an ogre, how hard can it be to find? Go look for these people. When you're done, Jared's in the building across the yard; it's the one with a thatched roof. Don't push yourself too hard."

"She's fine, Dad. Stop fussing," Kasey said as she exited a nearby room.

She walked over to Layla and hugged her. "Glad you're okay," she whispered. "I'll come upstairs with you and help you search."

The three of them reached the landing, and while Remy walked away toward one side of the huge building, grabbing a few agents on the way, Layla and Kasey took the other.

They both stayed silent as they looked through the many rooms, most devoid of anything larger than rats and mice.

It wasn't until they turned the corner that they heard muffled screams. They ran toward the end of the hallway, the noise growing by the second. Kasey had already changed into her werewolf form the second she ploughed into the door, tearing it apart.

Layla stepped inside and saw the bodies on the floor, four blood elves standing above them, while more captives cowered in the corner.

Layla recognized several of the people as those she'd worked with. But the second she saw Star's horror-filled gaze from where she huddled in the corner with two more of her old co-workers, Layla lost control.

She reached out with her power, grabbing hold of any metal in the floorboards, and dozens of small nails and screws slammed into two of the blood elves at high speed, ripping through them like paper. A quick punch with a metal-wrapped fist to both of them, and they were down on the floor a moment later.

Kasey had thrown one of her two blood elves through the barricaded windows, while she snapped the neck of the second.

The screams and cries grew louder as Kasey—all fangs, claws, and blood-splattered fur—turned to speak to the captives.

"Get some help up here," Layla told Kasey, who nodded and ran off.

"You're okay," Layla said soothingly, but no one was listening. They'd all been through so much, and her appearance had only made them even more terrified. She waited until several agents arrived, and left them to deal with the survivors. She hoped they would all recover, but was saddened and angered by what they'd gone through.

Layla walked away, leaving the farmhouse as Shane was led into the back of a BMW X5. His face was no longer a bloody mess, but he still looked like he'd remember what Chloe did for a long time. Layla couldn't say she was upset about that.

She crossed the courtyard and found the front door to the smaller building open. She stepped inside, blinking a few times into the darkness beyond. "Jared, you in here?"

The building was two stories high, but about a fifth of the size of the main farmhouse, and from the outside Layla had guessed it was probably about the size of a two-bedroom cottage.

She entered what at one time had probably been the front room to the property, but which now sat disused. It had clearly been used as a rubbish dump and was full of bits of trash and old pieces of rusting machinery that had long since outlived their usefulness.

Layla navigated her way through the throng of junk and reached the staircase, which was beside an open door. She poked her head through and found a kitchen that she wouldn't have eaten in if it was the last place on earth. Old food, dead rats, and the smell of mold and rot made her gag, and she quickly walked up the stairs to the floor above, taking them two at a time in case the smell somehow prevented her from escaping.

"Jared, you up here?" Layla called out.

"Back here," Jared shouted from the room at the far end of the hallway.

There were only three rooms upstairs: a bathroom and two bedrooms, but the door to the second bedroom was considerably further away from the other two and required stepping over some floorboards that had probably seen better days.

The wooden floor creaked as Layla placed a foot on it and, for a second, she thought that she would go straight through to the other side. She launched herself over the floorboards, hoping that whatever she landed on would be slightly less wobbly. Thankfully, it was and she maintained her footing.

She reached the bedroom door and stepped inside. Jared was on his knees, Elias behind him, a blade to the younger man's throat.

"Layla," Elias said. "It's a shame . . ."

He never got to finish the sentence as Layla's rage flooded through her. She controlled the metal in the blade, detaching it from the hilt, before throwing it to one side and into the far wall. Elias pushed Jared aside and stepped toward Layla, blocking her punch and kick, before delivering one of his own to her chest, sending her spiraling to the ground.

Layla scrambled back to her feet as Elias kicked Jared in the face, busting his nose. He picked Jared up and threw him at Layla, who couldn't move in time to stop the collision, sending them both crashing to the floor. The air was knocked out of her and she struggled for breath.

"You should have worked with me," Elias said. "Now I'm going to kill you."

Wiring leaped from the ceiling, wrapping itself around Elias and keeping him in place while Layla got back to her feet. She'd twisted her ankle in the fall, but it wasn't bad enough that she was unable to fight. And she doubted Elias was just going to lie down and accept defeat.

Elias gave a roar of anger and used his brute strength to tear the wiring apart, throwing it aside as he ran toward Layla, who couldn't move fast enough. He grabbed hold of her and drove her back out of the doorway, landing on the floorboards in the hall, which finally gave way.

The pair crashed through the floor, landing in the kitchen with a loud bang. Layla had managed to twist out of Elias's grasp at the last possible second, so instead of having his whole weight fall on her, it landed only on her legs. It hurt like hell, but she punched Elias in the face as she scrambled out from under him and dragged herself upright.

Elias was back on his feet in a second, grabbing hold of Layla and throwing her to the side. Layla slammed into the rusty freezer and hit the ground once again, scaring off a large rat in the process.

She rolled to the side and used her power to throw the freezer at Elias, who caught it mid-flight, but that only allowed Layla to turn the knives and forks in the drawer next to the sink into a dozen small missiles.

Elias kept the freezer in front of him, blocking the incoming weaponry, and then flung the freezer aside as voices came through from the front door. "We're not done," he said to Layla, before running toward the sink and launching himself up and through the window behind it.

Layla got back on her feet, watching as Elias sprinted faster than any man could possibly move. She stayed there until he reached the tree line and vanished from view.

Layla placed her hands on the metal sink and screamed in rage and frustration, tearing it free from the base and throwing it through the remains of the window, along with most of the other metal in her vicinity. It included an old stove, which made a large hole in the side of the building.

"He escaped," she said to Diana, as she entered the room. "I couldn't stop him."

Diana nodded and looked out of the rear of the property in the direction Elias had run. "Reyes is gone too. And Masako."

"Tommy told me."

"The ogre still hasn't been found, although we've stopped these particular blood elves from ever being a problem again." She placed a hand on Layla's shoulder. "Don't be hard on yourself."

"I thought accepting the spirits and drenik would make me powerful enough to stop him."

"It takes time. You don't become all-powerful in a few hours. I'm amazed you managed to throw a stove through a wall. That takes some power."

"How many from the depot survived?"

"Twelve. You managed to stop them before they'd killed too many. Most of them are physically okay. Emotionally . . . well, that's another matter, isn't it? We'll make sure they get everything they need, though."

Layla nodded. That would have to be enough. Even if nothing would ever be enough to wipe this experience from their memories.

Shouting reached Layla's ears. "What's happening?"

Diana shrugged just as Jared dropped through the hole in the ceiling. "I'm beginning to get fed up of being a punch bag for these people."

"You'll get your chance," Diana assured him.

Remy ran through the building into the kitchen. "We have an ogre problem. Might be an idea if you all help out."

Layla sighed. An ogre problem. It never rains but it pours.

34

Layla rushed out of the building to find Brako fighting off the majority of Tommy's agents. There was a roar and a huge werewolf leaped from the roof of the farmhouse onto the back of the ogre's head, tearing chunks of flesh from the giant monster. It lasted only a few seconds, until the ogre managed to get hold of the werewolf and throw it across the farmyard as if it was nothing more than a tennis ball. The werewolf hit the ground hard, bouncing several times before coming to a stop.

Diana and Remy sprang into action, both of them closing the distance to the ogre in seconds, with Diana removing her clothing and turning into her werebear form almost in one smooth motion.

Once changed, Diana was still several feet shorter than the ogre, but she was fast and strong and managed to block or avoid most of the ogre's attacks. All the while, Remy darted around it, making cuts on its legs and feet, trying to get the ogre off balance.

Brako kicked out at Remy and managed to catch him on his tail, sending him sprawling into the dirt. Layla ran over to check on him, but found that he was okay, if slightly dazed.

"How do we fight an ogre?" she asked.

"With style," a werewolf Kasey said. She opened her maw and ice exploded from it, smashing into the ogre's legs, freezing it in place.

Brako swatted one more agent, sending her flying, before trying to free himself from the ice prison.

By the time Kasey had made it to the ogre, he had managed to shatter the ice, throwing a punch at the werewolf that she only just managed to block, although it still sent her to the dirt alongside Remy.

Layla didn't want anyone else to be hurt. She reached out with her power, feeling the metal all around her in the house and car. She wondered if she could throw a car, but the BMW only budged an inch. Instead, she concentrated on the car door, which tore free and flew at Brako, smashing into the side of his head with such force that the door almost disintegrated.

Blood poured from the ogre's broken jaw, drenching his chest within seconds. He rounded on Layla and screamed something, but she couldn't figure out what.

"You're done hurting people," Layla said, flinging a second door at him. It smashed into his stomach and knocked him back several feet, allowing Diana to dive at his head, sinking her massive teeth into his skull.

Within moments, Tommy had joined in the fight, and for a second it looked like they would win, but the ogre flailed at them and managed to knock them both aside.

Murderous rage consumed the ogre's eyes, and Layla wasn't certain that they could beat the creature, who refused to fall. Refused to die, despite horrific wounds.

There was a shimmer behind the ogre that caught Layla's attention. The ogre saw it too and swiped the air beside him, but the shimmer was already moving again. And as quickly as it started, it stopped.

In an instant Masako sat atop the ogre's head. She said something that Layla didn't understand, then the pretty woman morphed into a monster. Her jaw dropped low, like a snake, revealing rows of

Steve McHugh

razor-sharp teeth. Her fingers elongated, forming talons, which she drove into Brako's skull, tearing it open. She jammed her face into the open wound and began to feast noisily.

Layla froze, partly fascinated, partly sickened by what was happening before her. Masako was quickly drenched in blood, riding the dead ogre to the ground, most of its brain now inside her stomach. She sat on the ogre's neck for several seconds, before licking the blood from her fingers in a way that reminded Layla of a cat cleaning itself.

"What the hell was that?" Layla asked no one in particular.

"That was me saving all of you," Masako said, her hands and face returning to normal. "Anyone want to get me some wet wipes?"

"I don't understand. You work for Elias. Well, Nergal."

"I do. I have for many years. But I'm also not blind to what is happening here. Elias has lost control. I'm a professional, not an idiot."

Tommy had changed into his human form and walked over to Layla. "Everyone okay?"

"My pride is pretty banged up," Remy said, and kicked Brako in the side of the head. "Oh, and I'm going to need some bleach to get the image of Masako tearing into the ogre's brain like it was a chicken wing out of my head."

"Ogre brains taste funny," Masako said.

"I'm gonna go lay down, maybe vomit a little," Remy said casually. "Might regret ever meeting any of you. I haven't decided yet."

He walked off toward the BMW, which was still in one piece close to the farm entrance. Layla wished she could go with him.

"I should arrest you," Tommy told Masako.

"Why? For saving your life? Is that an arrestable offense? Do you even have the power to arrest me?"

Tommy shrugged, and Layla got the impression it didn't matter one way or the other. "Why are you here?" Tommy asked. "And don't give me that ogre bullshit."

"Elias has allowed this matter to become personal. I believe that is a mistake. Kidnapping Chloe was stupid, as was keeping an ogre and having it murder a bunch of people at a train depot. Nergal is fine with these matters, but I am not. I work for Nergal because he offers me certain things."

"Hands up if you think it's brains," Kasey said.

A human-looking Diana put her hand up.

"You people sicken me," Remy shouted as he continued on toward the car.

"My arrangement with Nergal is at an end. I have no interest in watching him murder innocent people, and I have no interest in watching him try to take over Avalon. Avalon would be best outside of the hands of someone like him or his associates. I'm here because I'm done, and I needed to help you live so that you didn't run after me once this was over."

"You think because you killed an ogre that we're going to just let you go?" Kasey asked. "I'm not sure that's how it works. You have killed people for Nergal."

"Yes, many. But they were all bad people. How many have you killed? Tommy? Diana? What about your friend Nate? How many deaths have you all been responsible for? I'd put my money on it being more than a few."

"That doesn't mean you're a good guy," Jared said.

"First of all, I apologize for the attack on your transport. It was not my idea to kill Tommy's employees. I know one died. Shane was responsible. I assume you have him in custody."

"What do you want, Masako?" Tommy asked, finally losing patience.

"I want to interrogate Shane. I'll get the answers you need, and then you let me go."

"What answers do we need?"

"Where Elias has gone, for a start. You don't think this is over, do you?"

No one said anything.

"He's gone back to his home," Layla said. "He needs to recharge."

Masako nodded. "And once he's done, he's coming after you. A fully charged redcap. He'll be more than enough trouble for your people, Tommy. You can get to him before he gets to all of you. I advise you to let me help."

"Nergal will come after you."

"Nergal is my problem. I need to do this. Do not mistake this for a change of heart. I was being paid to do a job, and now I don't want to do it anymore, but I'm also not willing to let Layla talk to her father. For several reasons."

"Name one," Layla snapped.

"Your father killed a friend of mine. If Nergal uses him to find the other umbra in the world, a lot more friends of mine could die. Or be folded into Nergal's plan. Neither of those things appeals to me."

"I say let her help," Kasey said. "But if she tries to screw us over, we kill her."

Masako smiled. "Sweet that you think you can."

"You want to do the conversation here?" Tommy asked.

"Back at your mansion. You can cuff me or whatever else you want to do, but you're going to need to plan what you do next and see to your wounded. I doubt you want to do any of that here."

"If you screw around with us . . ." Tommy said.

"You'll hunt me down. Yes, it's all exceptionally scary. Yet I find myself not caring, *Thomas*. You don't scare me."

Tommy whispered something in Masako's ear that Layla didn't hear, but whatever it was it caused the jikininki's expression to change into complete and total fear.

Tommy stepped away. "Deal?"

Masako nodded once, her eyes never leaving Tommy's face. "I swear I have no intention of crossing you, Tommy."

"We'll discuss things further back at the mansion," Tommy said, turning to the rest of the agents working around him. "I want this place searched for any information about where Reyes and Elias might have gone. I want them found."

"So, we're running away?" Layla asked. "We beat them, and now we're running?"

"We're not running," Tommy said. "We're getting the injured back to the mansion so we can hopefully figure out where Elias might have gone."

"And you think Shane knows?"

Masako nodded. "He's been with Elias for a few years. I'm guessing he knows."

"And how are you going to extract that information from him?"

"Well, I could ask nicely. Or I could threaten to take his flesh."

"You're going to eat him?"

"We'll see. I'd rather not. But one dead body is as good as the next when it comes to nourishment."

She walked away, leaving Layla in the middle of the yard, radiating anger. She wasn't even sure who the anger was aimed at, she was just angry. "No," she shouted. "No, we're not just going to walk away and let him regroup. He doesn't deserve to do that."

People turned to look at her, but she didn't care, she needed to vent the rage inside. "He doesn't get to go back to his home and try to come after me *again*. How many times are too many? How many times before we actually act, not react? We need to find Elias. And we need to do it now."

She spun on her heel and walked over to the car where Shane had been put, pulling open the door and forcing him out.

"Hi, beautiful."

"Shut up, Shane. Where is Elias?"

"Who?" Shane asked with a smirk.

"Layla, don't do this here," Tommy called out as he walked toward her, with Diana and Kasey in tow.

"Where is Elias?" Layla asked, ignoring Tommy. She didn't care what other people thought, she just wanted answers.

"I think I hit my head, so I don't know," Shane said, that same smirk on his face. A smirk that Layla wanted gone.

His metal handcuffs began to tighten, digging into the skin around his wrists.

"What the hell?" he shouted. "Stop it."

"How strong are you, Shane?" Layla asked. "Strong enough to heal missing hands?"

Shane shouted as the cuffs bit deep into the flesh, drawing blood that quickly began to flow in a steady stream.

"Where is Elias?" Layla asked.

"You're not a torturer, Layla. You don't do this," Shane said, a pleading tone to his voice.

"Today I do, today I allowed my spirits to bond with me. Today I watched as you beat my friend. I think this is fair game."

Shane cried out in pain.

Kasey grabbed hold of Layla and tried to move her away from Shane, away from the source of her anger and rage, but she'd anchored herself to the ground using the metal in the earth around her to keep her in place.

"I don't want to be moved," Layla said. "I want to know where Elias is."

Kasey got in front of Layla and forced the young woman to look at her. "I know he hurt Chloe, and I know you've gone through a lot, but this isn't you. You're not a torturer. That's a line you can't come back from once you've crossed it. We will get answers from this piece of crap, but not like this. You need to rest before we go after Elias. We're going to find him and burn his house down with him inside. But we can't do it with you, Chloe, and Jared all hurt. Elias with full power is as strong as that ogre. We need to be just as strong."

Layla stopped using her power and dropped to her knees. "I just want this done."

Kasey placed an arm around Layla and sat beside her. "Me too. And it will be. We're going to get healthy, get prepared, and find Elias. And then we're going to take his head. And after that, it's Nergal's turn."

Layla nodded as Tommy got Shane back into the car and dealt with the bleeding. He was an umbra so it wouldn't take long to heal, but no one wanted blood all over the car.

"I'm impressed," Masako said. "Didn't think any of you had that sort of thing in you."

Layla looked over at her. "I think you should find those answers quickly. Before Elias realizes what you've done and tells Nergal."

Masako pursed her lips. "That is probably a good idea."

She walked off, and after a few minutes Layla got into the back of another car belonging to Tommy's people. Soon, the motion of the car caused her to fall asleep. It was the first time in days that her dreams were hers and hers alone.

35

For the next few days, Layla became increasingly anxious about finding Elias and putting a stop to his plans. Shane had been of little help, and he either didn't know where Elias was, or was capable of withstanding whatever Masako did to him down in the basement.

Chloe had healed within a few hours of arriving back at the mansion, and Jared had been fine before they'd even gotten back. In fact, he'd spent most of his time in the gym since returning, and hadn't wanted to talk to anyone.

Everyone was on edge, and Layla wondered if Tommy and his people knew more than they were letting on. Eventually the frustration became too much for her and, knowing that Tommy was in a meeting with Diana and Remy in his office, she knocked on the door and entered.

"Layla, I assume you need something," Tommy said, with no hint of annoyance at having his meeting interrupted.

"Most people don't knock before they march into an office," Remy said. "That's like *really* British of you. You know, like *super*-British."

"I want to know what's happening," Layla said, ignoring Remy. "It's been three days, we're all healed, and I want to go after Elias."

Tommy pushed his hands through his hair. "Me too. But it appears that there have been some developments, and now going after Elias is more complicated than first expected."

"I don't understand. What complications?"

"Avalon complications," Diana said. "When we returned here, we updated those we trust in Avalon and explained what had happened. We hoped with a positive ID of Elias's whereabouts that they might swoop in and grab him before he attacks again or Nergal manages to get him out of the country. That doesn't look like it's happening."

"My wife, Olivia, called," Tommy said. "She's been informed that Elias is off-limits. Apparently he's too big a fish for my wife to go after. Which is odd considering she's probably one of the three most powerful people in the LOA. Officially, she can't touch him without taking flak."

"And Olivia is okay with this?"

Tommy shook his head. "Not even slightly. That's why she told me about it. Avalon's power structure is a mess right now. So many people all trying to grasp whatever bits of power they can, while people like Nergal and his comrades prowl around waiting for weakness."

"Mum wants you to get to him first?" Kasey asked as she entered the room to Tommy's obvious irritation. "What? I assumed this was a free-for-all meeting."

Chloe and Jared entered behind Kasey, with Harry in tow.

"We don't know where Elias is," Tommy continued, as if he hadn't been interrupted. "But then no one else seems to either. And if they do, they're not sharing that information. But it won't be long before Nergal contacts his allies in Avalon and either has Elias removed from circulation and brought back to him, or removed on a more permanent basis. We need to find Elias before anyone else. The one good thing is that redcaps do not tell people where their original home is. We'd hoped that Shane might be able to tell us, but he doesn't know."

"So, torturing him was for nothing?" Layla said with a touch of anger in her voice.

"Torture doesn't work on everyone, and it certainly wasn't going to work on Shane. Masako just spoke to him and got nowhere. She's a scary lady."

"We have another good thing," Harry said. "Elias wants Chloe dead."

"Seriously?" Chloe asked. "That's a good thing?"

"Sure," Harry said without an ounce of irony. "He seems like the kind of person who doesn't let things go easily. I've been reading up about him, and frankly he's insane, but he also lives by his own moral code. And you killed someone he cares about. He won't quit until he's dead, or Chloe is."

"You want to use me as bait?"

Harry shook his head. "How did you get that from what I said? Seriously, you need to go on holiday or something. You've been around crazy people too long."

"Today, Harry," Tommy said.

"My point is, Elias isn't just going to pick up sticks and leave, not while Chloe is still alive, and not while Layla is still free. He's been hired to do a job, and he'll complete it or die trying."

"And you know this how?" Diana asked.

Harry brandished a USB drive. "I downloaded everything you have on him and went through it. It's not like I had anything else to do, so I figured why not. Anyway, his past crimes show that he doesn't like to leave things unfinished. He once hung around in a country for a month after the job was done, simply to remove someone who had been a witness. He risked his life to do it. He's not going anywhere."

"Okay, so that's sort of good news," Jared said. "But where is he?"

Harry raised his hand.

"You don't need to do that," Tommy explained.

"Oh, okay, great. I know where he is. Or at least, I know where he might be."

"Might be?" Jared asked.

"It's better than no bloody clue," Chloe said.

"Fair point," Jared conceded. "Where do you think he is?"

"Can you all come with me into the second dining room? It would be easier to show you."

Everyone left, with Layla, Jared, and Chloe the last out of Tommy's office.

"There's a second dining room?" Layla asked.

"I know, right?" Jared said. "There's like five reception rooms, and I don't think anyone has ever used one of them."

They followed the rest of the group through the house, saying hello to several agents on the way. Layla noticed that everyone looked busy; if nothing else, Tommy made sure that people always had work to do. Except for her. No, she had been left to her own devices. She wasn't sure if that was his way of allowing her time to deal with everything, or if he wasn't sure how to act with her. Either way she appreciated it, but now she wanted to feel like she was contributing, and not just in a "brought all of this to their attention" kind of way. Right now, she felt like a bit of a third wheel.

They reached the second dining room, which, as it turned out, was identical to the first—a room Layla had been in exactly once, and that was because she'd got lost.

A long table sat in the middle of the room, with a dozen chairs around it. They were made of a dark wood that matched the two cabinets and three chests of drawers that stood around the edge of the room.

A projection screen had been assembled at one end, and a laptop was at the far side of the table, six or seven feet away from the screen.

"Did you do this?" Tommy asked Harry, sounding impressed.

"I've been bored. I'm not exactly good at hunting monsters or demons, and while I can fight pretty well, fighting ogres is a bit out of my weight class. So I did this."

"You set up a movie theater?" Remy asked. "Needs some beanbag chairs, along with the smell of cannabis and lost hope, but it's almost there."

"It's not a movie theater," Harry said. "Okay, it is a little bit, but that's not why you're here. Look."

He clicked a few things on the laptop, while Layla grabbed a chair and moved it slightly so that Remy beside her could see. He thanked her with a thumbs-up. Layla smiled, and when she turned back to the screen, there was a picture of Elias.

"Okay, this is Elias. I know you all know that, but here he is anyway. Now, I've read everything you have on this guy."

"You said earlier, but really, everything?" Tommy asked.

"I'm a quick reader and I absorb information like a sponge. I don't need a superpower, Tommy. I already have one."

Tommy laughed. "Okay, sorry. Please go on."

"Right, well, he's British. Born and bred here. The first known record of his involvement with Avalon is 1841." Harry clicked on a link and brought up a piece of paper with barely legible handwriting on it. A wax ring seal was on the top right-hand corner.

"That's an Avalon seal," Diana said. "I don't know who, though."

"Yeah, it's too degraded," Harry said. "I couldn't get a good look at it. But the document says that Elias Wells was put to work within Avalon. It's basically a contract of employment."

"You can read that?" Jared asked.

"My mother is a doctor," Harry told him. "This is pretty neat in the scheme of things. Anyway, there's no signature, but this is pretty good evidence that a man named Elias Wells was given work in Dorset."

"Why Dorset?" Tommy asked. "What's there?"

"I went through a dozen more Avalon personnel records and checked their first postings."

"You did what?" Diana asked. "How did you get clearance?"

"You gave me a laptop with no passwords or encryption. I just opened the software."

Tommy glanced over at Diana.

"Okay, moving on," she said swiftly. "What did you find?"

"Each person was given their first postings in their country of birth. Without exception, they were sent to the place they knew best. Not necessarily the city they were born in, but that first assignment made sure they were sent somewhere they knew. And all of the assignments were the same: they were told to just keep an eye out, to deal with an Avalon office in the area and do what they were told."

"There's an Avalon office in Dorset?" Kasey asked.

"Not anymore there isn't," Diana said. "Hasn't been for . . ."

"Since 1850," Harry finished for her. "When the people there were killed by an ogre." The screen was replaced with a picture of Brako.

"Elias set it up?" Layla asked.

"Either that or he made a pact with the ogre. I did wonder how they managed to get the creature across the world without anyone noticing. Answer: they didn't. Ogres don't fly or travel outside of their home. Ever. I researched them too, just to be sure. An ogre's territory is for life. And that territory is big enough to encompass Dorset, Hampshire, and a little of Wiltshire. There are no exceptions to the size of a territory. So, Brako— that was his name, by the way, for those who didn't know—he never left the UK. He was always here, always waiting."

"So, Elias had an Avalon office wiped out?" Diana asked.

"My guess is yes. He vanished soon after, and didn't reappear for another hundred years, working for Nergal."

"So, Elias was born in Dorset, that's what you're saying?" Chloe said.

"Yep."

"Dorset is a big place," Kasey said. "We'd never find him in time."

Harry raised his hand again, immediately putting it down when he caught himself doing it. "Like I said earlier, I may have found him."

"How?" Tommy asked.

"Redcaps murder their families. Anyone in the family home on the night they take the ritual is killed. Now, Avalon doesn't care about human murders for the most part, so none of you would ever have seen this, but I checked out all local murders at the time. It was hard work, but I found something."

A picture of a manor house alongside a painting of a man and woman arrived on the screen. "This is Elias's mum and dad. I checked murders from the early eighteen hundreds, and from the notes you made when you interviewed Layla about what had happened to her, I found that Elias mentioned he'd murdered his parents."

"Yes, he did say that." Layla said. "I'd almost forgotten."

"Well, at the time double murders of middle-aged people weren't exactly common in the area. There was more crime, and certainly more murders, but double murders of wealthy landowners were always going to get someone's attention. And they did. A local wrote about the crime and passed the information on to whoever investigated. Over the years the information was logged into the bowels of whatever government building it now sits in, but there's been a big leap in putting these old documents online for people to read. And people love a good murder mystery, so these went online about two years ago. There are whole websites dedicated to murders in various time periods.

"On the fourteenth of May, 1839, Mr. and Mrs. Wells were murdered in their homes. Their throats were slit and each was stabbed exactly twelve times in the chest. There's not a lot more to go on, but three months later the deeds of the house were passed on to one Elias Wells."

"Where's the house?" Tommy asked, eagerness in his voice.

Another picture arrived on screen. "This is Google Earth. This is Elias's manor house. It's not too far from Dorchester. The site is well maintained, and yet no one is ever spotted going in or out. I called the local newspaper and spoke to a helpful woman about it; it's known as the murder house, even after all these years. She said that it was apparently sold to a business a decade ago, but no one has ever come to work on it. They think it's being kept while the land's price increases."

"It looks in good keeping."

"Yeah, that's the thing about the curse on a redcap: it means they age slowly. The property they do the ritual in also ages slowly. The grass almost never grows, there's no dust or cobwebs. The reporter said that there's a rumor in town that it's cursed, as no birds fly over it."

"You could have just told us this to begin with," Diana said.

"Always show your work. No one would believe me if I just put that picture up and said it's where Elias was. You'd have wanted proof. Now you have it."

"I could kiss you," Remy said. "I won't, but the feeling is there."

People filed out of the room in quick succession, leaving Layla behind. "You did good, Harry. Thank you."

"I like it here. I like the people; I like feeling like I'm helping. I might ask if I can stay on. I think I can make a difference."

"I think you're right." Layla walked around the table and hugged her friend. "I'm glad you're here. I'm glad you're not hurt, and I'm really glad you're my friend. Thank you. For everything."

Harry winked. "Go help them kick the shit out of Elias. He deserves it. Then you can buy me a bottle of wine as thanks. Expensive red wine."

"Deal." Layla ran off, almost bumping into Tommy, which was useful because that was who she was looking for.

"I want to go with you," she told him.

"I figured you might. You shouldn't. You're not a member of the team, but you've proved yourself over and over, so I'm willing to change my own rules. When this is done, would you consider working for me?"

"I don't know. Ask me when it's over."

Tommy nodded that he understood. "Harry has a job here if he wants it, by the way. Human or not, his brain scares me."

"It scares everyone, but he'll like that."

"I'll talk to him. Let's not start celebrating until Elias is done. One way or another."

Layla nodded and ran off to get ready. This was going to be the last time she had to deal with Elias Wells. Like Tommy had said, one way or another.

36

It had taken several hours for an injured Elias to reach his home, even with Reyes's help. They'd wanted to make sure they weren't being followed, and so switched cars three times and drove through Wiltshire to get to Elias's manor.

After that, an exhausted Elias just wanted to complete the ritual, and imbue himself with all of the power from the spirits he'd taken over the last few years. He'd stashed his hat at the manor a few days earlier, just in case plans went awry and Tommy's people found it. The sight of it on the dining-room table had made his heart soar.

The ritual was complicated and took a day to complete, something he hadn't the time to do while dealing with Layla and Chloe; rushing such an important thing was unwise. But now they were no longer in his custody, he wanted to get the ritual done as soon as possible. Retiring to his bedroom, he drew the necessary glyphs on the walls and floor, taking his time to get them correct, as he muttered the incantation over and over. During that time the ritual was in effect, he was completely helpless as the spirits he'd taken flooded his body. Once it was done, Elias slept for nearly twenty hours, and woke feeling refreshed and ready to fight an army.

Now that he was back to full strength, Elias was stronger, faster, and considerably more resistant to harm than he had been before. He pulled at his fingers, making each of them crack in turn.

Reyes politely coughed from Elias's bedroom door. "Nergal wants you."

"Excellent." Elias followed his companion to the drawing room, to find Nergal's face on the laptop screen.

"Elias, I assume you're feeling well."

"Better than I have in a long time."

"You have failed me, Elias. Masako is in enemy hands, as is Shane. I have my own spies within Avalon; they are saying that Tommy will not allow Avalon access to them. Unfortunately, his wife is doing a good job of ensuring that doesn't change."

"You want me to go after Olivia Carpenter?"

"No, I'm just telling you exactly where you stand right now. As of this moment, you no longer work for me. You've failed to bring me the girl Layla, and frankly I believe that it would be easier for me to find another way to get to her father, or indeed spend time and effort in creating someone who has the same power. You've failed to do anything but fail. You even got Dara killed. You were a great asset to my team for a long time, Elias, but that time has come to an end."

Rage bubbled up inside of Elias as he watched Nergal's lips move.

"So, for those reasons, I think I need to cut you loose. If you manage to get out of the mess you've made, feel free to come back and beg for your job, but otherwise you're either going to be dead or arrested. And if you get arrested, well, we'll just have to make sure you keep quiet. I'm sorry it's come to this."

"You think I'd rat you out? You think that after all these decades of doing your shitty dirty work that I'd rat you out like some common punk thug? How dare you question me, Nergal, how dare you imply that I would be anything but loyal to you and the cause? You want to disavow me, fine, do it, but I'm not getting captured, and I'm sure as hell not getting arrested.

"Here's what I'm going to do. I'm going to kill Layla and Chloe and the rest of those assholes who just don't know when to quit. And when they're all dead, I'm coming for you. I'm going to tear you apart, Nergal. You think you can threaten and betray me like this? You think I'm going to rat you out? I'm going to take your secrets to the grave, but you're going there first."

Nergal's eyes narrowed. "You would do well not to threaten me, Elias."

"Shove it firmly up your arse, or ass depending on which word you prefer. You're thousands of miles away, hiding in a bunker so that people like Tommy don't find you. You're a coward, and frankly I'm not sure if you're still capable of being in control. Maybe I should go to your bosses and let them know how you've failed. Perhaps that would be a better use of my time."

"Reyes, kill Elias."

"No, I don't think I will. I'm not a big fan of Elias, I think he's a pompous dick, but you just cast him away after a hundred years of service. I think he—I think anyone—deserves better than that. So I'm with him to the end. And if he decides to go after you, then I'll rethink my position, but right now he's the one I'm loyal to."

"I will have your eyes torn out," Nergal shouted at the screen.

"How?" she asked. "Unless you have the power to come through the screen like that girl out of *The Ring*? Can you do that? Can you crawl out of a laptop screen? No? Well, blow me, then." She turned and marched out of the room.

"If you survive the onslaught, I will hunt you down, Elias. I will carve my name into your soul."

"You've been watching too many eighties action films if you think that's an effective threat. I'll be seeing you real soon, Nergal. Probably down the barrel of a high-powered rifle." Elias switched the laptop off and stared at the black screen. He grabbed the computer and smashed it over and over again onto the table, showering the whole area in pieces of glass and electronics.

"So, I assume you have a plan?" Reyes asked from the doorway.

"Thank you for staying with me."

"Don't tell me it means something to you. You paid me, not Nergal. I'm part of your team until the end, so let's get this done. I'm not planning on dying here, Elias. Don't think you've earned that level of loyalty."

"Even so, thank you. We have a lot to do to prepare for the inevitable attack."

"How do you know they'll even come here? No one knows you have this place; no one even knows it exists. So how do you go about getting Tommy and his people to come for you?"

"Leave an anonymous tip. Tell them that someone matching my description is here. Or just tell them that I'm actually here. I don't really care. This place should suffice to keep us safe when they come."

"So, it's just the two of us against an army?"

"No. I have some plans for them when they get here. You'll find everything you need in the basement. The door to it is in the kitchen. I'm going to get the backup we'll need."

"Backup?"

"Trust me."

Elias left the house and walked through the field behind it until he reached a large pile of stones that had probably been there for a thousand years. The pile was twenty feet high and sat at the bottom of a steep hill. He had no idea who'd put it there. But that didn't matter. All that mattered was what was underneath. He walked around to the side of the pile where there was a large gap between the stone and the hill. He stepped into the mouth of the cave, peering deeper into the darkness inside.

"It's me," he shouted, taking a step into the huge cave.

"It has been a long time," something called from the depths, the voice reverberating off the walls.

"I know, but I need you. They killed Brako."

There was a low rumble from down in the darkness. "He was always too keen to fight. Always too inexperienced to follow through."

"Will you help me?"

The laughter that followed sent a shiver up Elias's back. It was a laughter filled with evil intent. "Will I get to kill people from Avalon?"

"Yes." It was a slight lie, but one that he told easily. These people might not work for Avalon, but they were allied with his enemies inside the organization. They were all the same thing as far as he was concerned. "As many as you can."

The laughter sounded again. "Things have changed since you last came for me, Elias. My appetites have grown."

"Feast. Feast on your enemies and grow stronger for it."

"I will help you, Elias. But I hope you're prepared for what will happen. Innocent lives might be lost."

"No life is innocent."

"How true. I will prepare. We will be ready."

"Thank you." Elias left the cave and paused as he realized that the creature in the cave had said *we*. There should only be the one female down there. Which left an excellent question: just how many creatures of pure evil was he about to unleash on an unsuspecting countryside? Elias shrugged. It didn't matter. All that mattered was that he won. And he'd just made sure that he would.

He looked over past the dozen different rocky formations that littered his property toward the trees a few hundred feet away that signaled the end of his land. The birds diverted so as not to fly over it. The dark magic he'd used here had seeped into the land, tainting everything. The animals knew. They always knew. And soon enough, Tommy and his people would know too. Elias smiled. It was going to be a good day.

37

Six armored BMWs arrived outside of the mansion early in the morning, the noise of them waking Layla up. She quickly showered and got dressed, then ran downstairs, to be greeted by Tommy, who passed her some black body armor that covered most of her torso, along with pads for her elbows and knees.

They would be leaving Masako at the mansion, with several agents to keep an eye on her. Tommy was certain that, even if she did escape, she wouldn't hurt any of his people. Layla didn't believe it for a second, but as Tommy knew her better, she deferred to him.

"Not a request," he told her, and she didn't argue, instead walking off to get changed. Today would be the day her life became free of Elias. She would make sure of that. But Elias would be ready, she was sure of that too.

"It's possible that these people will have guns," Remy told Layla as she entered the living room after getting ready. Also in the room were Jared and Chloe, and all of them wore the same armor that she had been handed. "This armor is rune scribed. It'll stop a few bullets and make sure that magic doesn't tear you apart. We have a dwarf on staff who makes them."

"You have a dwarf?"

"Yeah, a dwarf. As in Norse dwarf. They're alchemists. It's a long story, I'll explain later. Anyway, he makes these things."

"They're life-savers," Jared said. "Literally, in my case."

"You got a minute?" Chloe asked. Layla nodded and the pair left the room, walking to the kitchen. "I just want to say that I know you said you were going to try to forget about what happened, but if anything goes south today, I want you to know that I never meant to hurt you."

Layla grabbed her friend and hugged her. "Let's just move forward. And nothing is going south, Chloe. We're going to get Elias and drag his sorry, no-good, murdering ass back here."

An hour later, Layla was in one of the armored vehicles with several of Tommy's people. They were all silent as they contemplated what would happen next.

The tension and anticipation was almost too much to bear, and Layla wondered how people did this on a regular basis. The idea of driving toward what was sure to be a battleground wasn't something she'd ever thought she'd entertain.

After driving into a section of woods bordering Elias's property, the BMWs all stopped. Everyone got out, and Tommy beckoned them over.

"Right, this isn't going to be a walk in the park. Elias is going to fight, as is Reyes, but they don't have anyone else. Look out for traps and mines, and stay away from open spaces. We're going to split into three groups, and each will take one side. Chloe, Layla, Remy, you're with Kase and me. We're going the shortest distance from trees to buildings. There are a few small rock formations that should give us cover if we need it, but don't go crazy.

"From what we can ascertain the house has two floors, but there's also a basement, so when you get in make sure you take the time to do a room by room search. Try to leave the basement for last; I don't want anyone getting trapped down there."

"Any info on fighting a fully powered redcap?" Chloe asked. "I fought him when he was seriously underpowered last time."

"Yeah, he'll be much stronger, faster, more able to heal. My advice is don't get anywhere near him, at least not alone. He'll be as strong and fast as I am. If he engages any of you, run. Trying to be a hero will get you dead."

He took a moment to look at each and every person there. "Take it slow and steady. There's no rush. These assholes aren't going anywhere. You've all got five minutes to get into position, then we go together."

The three groups moved off toward their assigned areas, while Tommy took a moment to talk to everyone who remained. "We're going to move up toward the rocks over there. Layla, you're going to have to get Elias's attention. I need him focused on us, not on those people about to rush the house. There's no way both of them can focus on all three groups."

Layla nodded and the group set off toward the side of the manor house, pausing momentarily at the edge of the tree line, before sprinting across the grass toward the first rock formation. They jutted up from the ground every few dozen feet, but that still left several feet of exposed ground to cover. Layla knew that if Elias or Reyes were using any kind of rifle, it wouldn't be a difficult shot for someone to make.

After making it to the sixth rock formation, Layla motioned for everyone to wait, and stepped out from behind it. It was maybe five hundred feet to the house, and she wanted to know if Elias was watching. But when nothing happened, she motioned for everyone to keep going, and they ran toward more rock formations.

"This is easier than I'd expected," Remy said. "I like it easy." He paused. "Don't you say a word, Kase."

Kase smiled and mimed her lips being zipped shut.

Layla looked over at the second group, who were running toward the rear of the manor, while Chloe looked toward the first, who were going toward the front.

An explosion made the ground shake, and everyone dropped to the ground.

"The front assault group is scattering for cover," Chloe said. "Mines. They're going to have to go through slowly, leaving them sitting ducks. We need to get Elias's attention."

Tommy removed his buzzing phone from his pocket. "Not a good time, Harry."

Harry said something that stopped Tommy from ending the call, instead putting him on speaker, before turning the volume down as low as possible to still be able to hear what Harry had to say.

"Right, I've just spoken to Grayson about the ogre," Harry said. "Brako wasn't the ogre who destroyed the Dorset LOA office. He wasn't old enough. He's an adolescent."

The group shared an expression of horror. "You mean there's another one around here?"

"They live for a few hundred years, so yes. And it'll be old. And really big."

"Thanks for the info," Tommy said and hung up. "Right, change of plan."

"I'm going to get rid of the mines," Layla said. "I can do it from a distance."

Tommy nodded, although he did so reluctantly. "Kase, can you get the front squad to pull back to here? Remy, I need you to get everyone in the rear squad prepared for a really big—"

Tommy never finished his sentence, as the ground shook, and for a moment Layla thought that it was another mine, but this time it was accompanied by an almighty roar as part of a rock formation exploded, followed quickly by a second, showering the squad behind the manor with rock and dirt, leaving only huge holes in the ground.

"It's a cave system," Layla whispered.

An ogre pulled itself out of the first hole and batted away the closest agent, who flew a few dozen feet toward a second ogre, which was emerging from where the next explosion had occurred. That one was smaller than the first, about the same size as Brako, but it still took hold of the dazed agent and tore him in half, tossing each part aside as if they were waste paper.

"We've got a female adult and a male adolescent ogre to deal with," Tommy shouted. He roared and changed into his werewolf beast form mid-stride, before sprinting over to help the remaining members of the team. Kase did the same and ran to help those behind the minefield, waving them over to the trees. They would need everyone they could find to destroy the two ogres.

"Go, Remy, we'll be fine," Chloe told him, and he was off toward the ogres like a shot, dodging the pieces of rock that the smaller of the two threw at him.

"Can they beat them?" Layla asked.

The first and biggest ogre wore some sort of metal armor that covered a large part of her arms and torso. She was easily twenty feet high; her companion was maybe half that. Her skin was black and red, as if a burn had been allowed to fester.

"We need to go," Chloe snapped. "They'll be fine, but we won't be if we stay here."

Layla nodded and they ran together toward the mines, keeping just inside the trees in case someone took a shot from the house. When they were close enough, Layla concentrated and reached out with her power to sense the mines.

"There are six," she said, scanning the entire front of the house. "I can feel them in the ground."

"Can you disarm them?" Chloe asked.

Layla used her power to take hold of the mines, but she had no idea whether or not doing anything to them would cause them to explode. "I can pinpoint where the mines are while people run over, but doing more than that without knowledge of mines is going to cause a mess.

I've got hold of each of them though, just in case any detonate, but if you want your people here, you'd best hurry."

"You ready?" Chloe asked.

Layla made sure she had hold of the mines and nodded. She told Chloe the exact locations of the mines. Having to concentrate on six different parts of the front of the house at once was hard work, but she gritted her teeth and focused until all of Tommy's people were beside them.

"What do we do with the mines?" Chloe asked after telling all but two of the agents to go help Tommy and the rest of the group. "That side door to the house is barred. Any chance you could do something about that?"

Layla pulled at the mines, taking them out of the ground, but keeping the triggers firmly in place. She moved them slowly toward the barred door, making sure the top of each mine faced the door. "Everyone should take a step back."

She waited for everyone to move, before doing the same and releasing the triggers. The mines tore through the wood and most of the wall surrounding the door in an instant, making enough noise to shake the ground.

"They know where we're coming in," Tim, one of the two agents, said. He was just over six feet tall and had the large build of a boxer.

The second agent was a woman by the name of Jane, who was shorter than Layla, but had eyes that darted around constantly, as if she was always expecting something to jump out. Layla hadn't spent much time with either of them, but she knew them well enough to say hi.

Jane sniffed the air. "I can't smell anything inside. Too much smoke."

The four of them made their way toward the hole in the side of the house, and once the agents were certain the room beyond was clear, they went in, with Chloe and Layla following behind.

The house itself was barren, with no pictures or furniture anywhere to be seen. The pair moved through the room and out of the open door into a second, larger room that mimicked the first in terms of its appearance.

As they left the second room and entered a hallway, the sounds of battle outside became louder. Roars of murderous intent were punctuated by cries and shouts from those fighting back.

With Chloe leading the way, the four of them remained low and moved slowly through the building. Chloe paused at the end of the hallway and looked around the doorway. She motioned for Layla and the two agents to stay still and crept into the room. And the door slammed shut.

Layla and the agents rushed to the door and tried to open it, but it was locked. Layla used her power to try to move the lock, but she couldn't get a grip on it and it took her a few seconds to realize the door lock wasn't real. There were metal tubes that ran from the door into the wall, keeping it in place. She changed the direction of her power and pushed with everything she had. The door was ripped from its housing and flung into the room at high speed, breaking apart as it hit the far wall.

Before Layla could enter the room, a smoke canister exploded a few feet in front of the trio. Several shots were fired, striking Tim and Jane. They dropped to the ground. Layla wasn't sure whether they were alive or dead.

Reyes was inside the room, standing close to the window. She smiled as the smoke cleared and aimed a semi-automatic rifle at Layla's head.

Layla saw that both Tim and Jane had bullet holes in their heads. They had both been dead before they hit the ground.

"Can't have anyone getting in the way."

"You didn't need to kill anyone."

Reyes shrugged. "You might want to get used to people you love dying. There's going to be a lot of it going on outside." She smiled.

"Where is Chloe?"

"Wait and see," Reyes said with a chuckle. "You'll see her before she dies." She glanced out of the window. "The fight isn't going well for your people. You've hurt the younger ogre, but the mother is tougher, bigger, and stronger. You know what it's like to be stronger than the men around you, don't you? I wonder if you're strong enough to save them all from being torn apart."

"I have no idea what you're blathering on about. But you're going to tell me what I need to know, or I'm going to make you tell me."

Reyes laughed. "You're not a killer. Not even much of a fighter. You know *how* to fight in your head, but you don't have the motivation to *really* fight, to keep going until one of you is dead. You'll learn over time, I'm sure."

"You're not going to shoot me."

"You're right, I'm not. But the second I feel your power starting to influence anything metal, I pull the trigger and one round goes through your head."

The fighting continued to rage outside, and Layla wanted to go help, to make sure that her friends were safe. She wanted to fight Reyes. To hurt her. But Chloe was missing, and finding her was Layla's first priority.

"Where is Chloe?" she asked again.

"I told you to have some patience."

After a few seconds, a part of the floor silently moved aside, revealing a path down under the house, lit by small torches placed on the ceiling.

"You first," Reyes said, waving the muzzle of the rifle toward the hole.

Layla tentatively stepped forward and began to descend the path, eventually finding herself in a tunnel wide enough for two to walk side by side and just under seven feet high.

"Keep walking," Reyes said from behind Layla.

Layla did as Reyes commanded, until she came to two different tunnels ahead.

"Left," Reyes snapped.

Layla continued and after a hundred feet began to hear voices somewhere ahead. Another hundred feet and it began to sound more like one person shouting at someone who didn't speak. The closer Layla got to the voice, the more she knew it was Elias, and she hoped that Chloe was okay. A burning anger began to bubble up inside of her at the thought of Chloe being hurt.

Calm yourself, Rosa said inside her head. *Losing control of your emotions means losing control of Terhal. Despite your victory over her, a loss of control over your emotions will still allow her to be free. And now is not the time to release her.*

Layla pushed the anger aside and continued toward the voice, eventually walking into a large chamber. It was a few dozen feet high and wide enough to park several cars with ease. There were several beds against one wall and a stove against the far wall, next to a small fridge. But all of that paled in comparison to the cage that was close to the chamber's entrance. A cage with a semi-conscious Chloe inside.

"What did you do to her?" Layla demanded, running to the cage, trying to get her friend's attention.

"Tranquillizer," Elias told her. He sat in the center of the chamber, next to a small fire. "I needed to split you up. Can't have two umbra running around fighting us. Frankly, I wish I'd thought of it when we had her in the farmhouse. I guess my anger at her existence overrode common sense." He motioned to a chair opposite him. "Please, sit."

Layla did as Elias asked, not wanting to fight until she knew that she had a better chance of winning than she had at that moment.

"I'm going to kill Chloe," Elias said. "She took Dara, and that needs to be paid back. But you needn't die with her. I was going to kill you, but I've changed my mind. You're going to be what stops Nergal from killing me. You're going to be my insurance policy. If you come quietly, if you come with me to Nergal, I'll see that those friends of yours who are still alive aren't hunted down and slaughtered for their defiance."

Layla glanced between Reyes and Elias. "I'm not going to help you after you kill Chloe. That's never going to happen."

Elias hurled a glass at the wall beside Chloe's cage. "Look, you little shit, you either work with me or die."

"Then I die. But at least I die knowing I didn't help you do a damn thing." Layla took a deep breath and felt a calmness flow through her body. She should have been scared. Terrified. But for some reason, she felt quite peaceful.

"Then everyone you know will die," Reyes said with a smirk.

"We'll die fighting then."

Reyes stepped up to Layla and raised the butt of her rifle, ready to strike.

Layla put up a hand as if to stop the blow, but instead manipulated the metal of the rifle and forced it to fire. The bullet roared inside the chamber, and Reyes screamed as the blast damaged her ears. Layla was on her feet in an instant, taking hold of the rifle and pushing Reyes back toward the cage, before striking her in the face with the weapon, knocking her to the ground.

Layla spun toward Elias, aiming the rifle at him, ready to pull the trigger, but hoping it wouldn't come to that. "Surrender," she said.

"Shoot me," he told her.

She paused.

"You can't shoot me, can you? You're not a killer. Not like those people you call friends. They're trained to kill. You? You're a university student and the daughter of a mass murderer. Even if you could find it in yourself to pull that trigger, you don't actually want to."

"On your knees, hands on your head."

Elias laughed. "Pull the trigger."

Layla's finger quivered above the trigger. She'd practiced using firearms while staying at the mansion, and her father had trained her in their use when she was a child, but she'd never thought she'd actually have to use one against someone.

There was a noise behind Layla, and for a moment it sounded like Reyes was getting back to her feet. She moved so that she could keep both Elias and Reyes in her line of sight, but quickly discovered that it was Chloe, removing the keys from Reyes's jeans and unlocking the cage.

The large metal lock fell to the floor and Chloe pushed open the cage door, stepping over Reyes, who was beginning to stir. She walked over to Layla and placed a hand on the barrel. "No one is expecting you to shoot anyone," she told Layla. "It's fine."

Layla allowed Chloe to take the rifle from her, which Chloe quickly aimed at Elias and shot him twice in the chest. Elias collapsed to the ground, just before Reyes dove into Chloe, tackling her and knocking the rifle aside.

Before Layla could intervene, Elias was back on his feet. "Guess it takes a bit more than being shot to kill me."

Reyes leaped back toward Elias with impossible agility.

"She's an umbra too," Chloe said.

"We don't all get flashy powers," Reyes snapped.

Chloe reached over and took Layla's hand, squeezing it slightly.

"Ah, how sweet, the last moments of friendship," Reyes said.

Chloe released Layla's hand and blasted energy at the rock above the heads of Reyes and Elias. "Run!"

Layla didn't need telling twice, and the pair of them sprinted past the collapsing roof and into the tunnel as Elias's screams of anger echoed around them.

38

"Are they dead?" Layla asked after she and Chloe had been running down the tunnel for a few minutes.

"No idea. Don't care."

Layla was surprised that she also didn't have a problem with it. She did not care if Elias was dead or alive. She felt like she should be ashamed of even thinking it, but Elias had murdered or tried to destroy everything and everyone she loved. The state of his health was not something she gave a crap about.

A huge explosion sounded behind them, spurring them on further into the snaking tunnel, until they found themselves in a cavernous chamber, several times larger than the one they'd been in. There were lamps on the wall, the electric cables joined to a generator in the corner.

"What is this place?" Chloe asked, looking around.

Layla took a step and the smell of meat struck her, but it was mixed with something else, something she couldn't quite remember. A few seconds later the memory of being outside of the ogre's cell hit her like a truck.

"We need to leave. Now," she said, slightly panicked by this realization.

"Where are we?" Chloe asked.

"You're in an ogre's lair," Elias said as he ran around the corner of the tunnel. His face was covered in blood, which had also drenched his normally white shirt. "The ogres aren't here right now, but I think I could cripple you both and let you wait for them to come have their fun. They'll probably be exhausted from killing your friends, so it might take you a few days to finally die."

"I assume it's just you now?" Chloe asked.

"Reyes died in the collapse. It's not something I'll waste tears over, but it is an annoyance. She could have cheered me on while I killed you both."

Chloe cracked her fingers. "We're not going to die in here. But you might."

Elias laughed. "Come try."

Chloe rushed toward Elias, with Layla just behind, and threw a punch, which Elias avoided, landing one of his own to Chloe's ribs. He turned and kicked Layla in the stomach, knocking her to the ground, before punching Chloe in the side of the face, sending her to the dirt.

"You're just not good enough. I wonder how much killing Reyes took out of you. Can you still use your power?"

Chloe swiped her leg out toward Elias's, forcing him to step back into Layla's path. Layla shot up from the ground, launching herself at Elias, grabbing hold of his arm, and getting her legs around his neck, dragging Elias to the ground in a flying armbar. She locked his arm in place and wrenched it back, breaking the limb but Elias refused to drop. He used his good arm to lift Layla and smashed her down on the floor.

Darkness swarmed Layla's vision as her head struck the ground. Elias picked her up to do it again when Chloe tackled him, taking him down. Layla fell onto her back, the air knocked out of her, and rolled onto her front, forcing herself back to a standing position as Elias beat on Chloe.

Layla ran back into the fray, and avoiding a kick from Elias, planted one of her own into his stomach, just as Chloe spun around and kicked him in the side of the head.

Elias rolled with the blow, kicking out and catching Chloe in the chest with his foot. He avoided a second strike from Layla, grabbed hold of her arm, and threw her over his head into a nearby boulder.

Layla hit the floor and spat blood onto the ground, before quickly rolling to the side to avoid Elias's stomp to the face. She rolled again and again, as Elias continued his barrage, trying to land a kick. He was only stopped when Chloe kicked him in the back, sending him sprawling.

Elias was fast and strong, and was soon back on his feet, staring at the two women before him. "Come on then," he said with a smile.

Chloe and Layla traded kicks and punches with Elias, each trying to find a weakness in their opponent. Most of the blows were blocked or avoided, but occasionally one of Elias's would get through, leaving the other woman to fight him alone for a few seconds, which was long enough for his strength and speed to give him an advantage.

After a minute of fighting, the punches and kicks had taken their toll on all three combatants.

"That strength and speed of yours is waning," Chloe told Elias. "You can't keep this up forever—you're using too much of the power you've just given yourself by coming to this place."

"You can't talk. You used a lot of your energy blowing a hole in the roof. If you hadn't, this wouldn't be a hand-to-hand fight. Besides, I have enough power to kill both of you." Elias darted toward Chloe, before changing direction at the last second and snapping a vicious back-handed punch toward Layla.

Layla deflected it, but the force of the blow pushed her back, allowing Elias to strike out with a foot to her knee. She landed on her back and avoided the stomp, as Chloe kicked him in the stomach, forcing him to put distance between them.

"You know, Layla, I didn't mean to kill your mum. Nergal wanted her alive, and it just went south. Total accident on my part. But your death isn't going to be as quick as hers, I promise you that."

Layla got back to her feet. She knew that once the adrenaline wore off she'd ache and probably not be able to move much, but that was then, and right now she needed to stop Elias. She needed to beat him. Not for her, not for Chloe, but for everyone whose life he'd stolen, for the people at the train depot, for Blake and Bianca. She allowed the rage and pain of the last few weeks to fill her.

Chloe ran toward Elias, who blocked her punch, but she ducked under his arm, twisting as she moved until her elbow connected with his nose. She spun back to face him, punching him in the kidney as she went. Elias grabbed her by the throat, picking her off the ground, and Chloe reared back, kicking him between the legs with everything she had.

Elias tossed Chloe aside with fury, screaming in pain as he staggered back toward the edge of the chamber. Chloe struck a rock formation and tumbled over it, crashing into the wall with a fearsome impact.

Layla felt that last drop of rage fall inside. It overflowed, spilling forth in a guttural roar. She charged toward Elias, leaping up and driving her knee into his chest, slamming him against the wall once more. All of her need to hold back, to never quite let go, was forgotten in an instant.

She punched his chest over and over again, pushing him down to his knees. She continued as she moved up his body to his face, until he was on his back on the ground. Layla straddled his chest, using her knees to pin his arms as she unloaded a barrage of blows to his head. Elias's face was torn apart, his nose flattened, and his lips ripped open from the force of the blows. One eye was swollen shut and the other had turned a blood red, but Layla refused to stop, refused to allow Elias even a chance of getting back to his feet.

After what felt like hours, Layla allowed herself to sit back. Her hands hurt, and she knew she'd broken at least one finger.

Elias chuckled, a bubble of blood coming out of his mouth. "Didn't think . . ." He coughed and spat blood, which trickled down his cheek. ". . . you had it in you."

Layla got to her feet and dragged Elias into a sitting position against the wall. She smashed her knee against his face. "You." Smash. "Will." Smash. "Never." Smash. "Hurt." Smash. "Anyone." Smash. "Again." Smash, smash, smash, she continued, until she could no longer tell what Elias had once looked like.

Chloe wrapped her arms around Layla, dragging her away. "Don't. You can't turn back once you've killed. You might need to be that person one day, but you need to be sure."

Still full of rage and hate, Layla wanted nothing more than to take Elias's life. "They say you never forget killing your first person." She walked over to Elias and pulled his head back, exposing his throat. "You don't deserve to always be a part of me. Fortunately, I know that your healing ability is going to let you live through pretty much anything I can do to you, so"—she slammed her forearm into his throat, crushing his windpipe—"heal that, you son of a bitch."

39

In the heat of battle, Layla had taken a gamble that Elias would heal his crushed windpipe. It was a gamble that she was glad had paid off, as she helped Chloe drag a semi-conscious Elias out of the chamber. As they got closer to the cave's exit, the sounds of fighting grew ever stronger. Both were exhausted. Layla knew that Chloe wanted Elias dead, but she was determined to drop him at Tommy's feet. Determined to prove that she was good enough to be a part of his team. What happened to Elias after that, she didn't much care. She didn't want to know.

As they reached the fresh air outside and saw Tommy and his people still fighting the mighty ogre, they dropped Elias and immediately ran toward the fray.

Remy clambered up the back of the ogre's leg, using a dagger to stab into the flesh over and over as he scrambled up. He had to avoid the ogre's massive hands, but when he reached the top of her shoulder, he drove a sword into her, causing the ogre to cry out in pain. She tried to reach round to Remy, but he was already leaping free, landing in mud close by.

Several of Tommy's agents were badly injured and more than one lay on the ground, unmoving. Layla ran over to Jared, who was dragging another agent to safety—a woman who Layla had seen around the mansion several times.

"She crushed her leg," Jared said as he propped her against a tree.

"We can't win," the agent said.

"We have to," Layla told her, and glanced at Jared. "Are you okay?" He nodded.

"Good. Keep her company."

"What are you going to do?" Jared asked her.

"What I need to do." She ran back toward the ogre and saw Chloe blast it in the face, but the force was weak because of the tranquillizers still in her system, and she narrowly avoided the ogre kicking out at her.

Diana, covered in matted, bloody fur, ran from the tree line and launched herself up at the ogre, clawing away at the monster's stomach in an effort to disembowel her. Ice from Kasey's mouth slammed into the ogre, freezing one of her arms in place, while Tommy ran at her legs, smashing into one of them like a freight train.

As the ogre fell, she grabbed hold of Diana, wrenching her free and throwing her aside. Diana hit the ground and tumbled several dozen feet before slamming into a pile of rocks.

The ogre fell onto her back with an almighty cacophony of noise. The ground beneath Layla's feet trembled at the impact, but Tommy barely paused; he ran toward the ogre's head, snarling and slashing at her throat. She swatted him away, broke the ice that had held one arm in place, and threw a huge chunk at Kasey, who dodged aside just in time.

Layla looked over at Chloe, who was on her knees, and caught a glimpse of Elias as he started to move away toward the woods. In an instant, Layla reached out with her power, ripping free the sword that Remy had sunk into the ogre's shoulder, causing her to scream in pain. The sword flew toward Elias quicker than he could anticipate, impaled him in the chest, and flung him back toward the cave, pinning him to the rock.

Chloe turned around and walked over to him. "You dead yet?" she asked.

Elias mumbled something unintelligible, and Chloe placed a finger against his forehead and used her power to blast a hole in his head. Elias's body slumped.

Layla turned back to the ogre, who was trying to avoid the blasts of ice coming from Kasey's mouth. Tommy was back on his feet, as were Remy and Diana, but she swiped at anyone who got too close.

Layla walked toward her, ignoring Chloe's calls to stay back. She pushed out her power, wrapping it around the metal armor that covered the creature's torso, and with a twist of her hand replaced the dented armor with a hundred spikes that punctured her chest and stomach.

The ogre screamed in pain, dropping to her knees, blood pouring from dozens of wounds. Layla moved her hand again, and the metal fell from the ogre, cascading like liquid over her body, mixing with her blood as it soaked the ground.

Kasey sprayed ice across the monster's hands, keeping her in place, while Diana and Tommy raced toward her, each simultaneously striking her on both sides of the head. The ogre jerked and tried to get back to her feet, but a dozen small marbles of flame landed just in front of her face, exploding upward.

Layla turned to watch Jared stalk toward her. "She's dead because of you," he shouted, the rage coming off him in waves. He reached the ogre's head and created a palm-sized sphere in his hand, tossing it into her open, bloody mouth, and immediately exploding it.

The ogre's face tore apart from the force, shattering most of the bones and ripping flesh like paper. She still tried to get back to her feet, but Jared ran under her, creating a second sphere and shoving it up into one of the gaping holes in her chest made by Layla's spikes. The force of the subsequent explosion threw several of the attackers back, but it almost ripped the ogre in half. She was dead before Layla managed to get back to her feet. Covered in blood, Jared walked off without saying a word.

The ogres and Elias were dead, but as Layla looked around at the dead and injured, she wondered what it had cost.

"We lost good people here today," Tommy said as he walked over to her. "Are you all okay?"

Layla nodded, and Chloe gave the thumbs-up.

"Jared . . ." Layla began.

"The woman the ogre killed was his friend and one of my employees. A good person, one of many we lost today. Thank you both for your help." He walked over to Elias's body and kicked it. "Just making sure."

"Is it finally done?" Layla asked, slightly surprised at the tension in her own voice.

"No," Diana said. She'd changed back into a human, but was still covered in blood and dirt. "Not while Nergal lives. Not while his allies make plans against us, but for today it is over. You can rest."

Layla remained seated next to Chloe. Remy walked over and sat with them, and Kasey soon after. "I did not enjoy that," Remy said.

"Liar. You enjoyed it a little," Kasey contradicted.

"I got bounced across the ground like a pinball. Not a lot of enjoyment there. Glad to see no one else had to die, though. How many did we lose?"

"Five," Kasey said. "Four more will need serious attention."

"Speaking of which," Remy said, pointing across the field as Grayson walked toward them, accompanied by half a dozen others with medical equipment.

"You took your time," Kasey shouted with a smile.

"I'm sorry I couldn't help," Grayson said. "My being here would have made things worse, and I needed to ensure we had a big enough medical team to tend to the wounded. I'd hoped you'd have been able to make it back to the mansion for treatment, but Tommy told me about the ogres and I got here as soon as possible. Do any of you need help?"

Everyone shook their head. "Go help those who need it," Remy said.

Grayson hurried off, and Layla and the others were soon ushered back to the cars, where they found Diana.

"Where's my dad?" Kasey asked.

"He's helping the wounded," Diana told her. "He won't leave until it's done, you know that. You all did good today."

"Thanks," Remy said. "But I always do good."

"I wasn't talking to you."

"Well, fine then. Shove that up your arse."

Diana smiled and shook her head in disbelief, while Remy opened the car door and vanished inside.

Chloe and Layla were next in, but Diana stopped Layla. "Seriously, good job. That can't have been easy."

Layla looked at Diana, who had put on some clean clothes, and hugged her. "Is it always like this?"

Diana smoothed Layla's hair in a soothing fashion. "Not always."

Layla nodded as exhaustion began to take hold. Diana helped her into the car, before leaving to continue cleaning up.

It's been a tough day, Rosa said in Layla's head.

Layla could do nothing but nod.

Rest, Layla. Sleep, and when you wake up, maybe things will be clearer.

"Do you really believe that? I could have killed Elias and the ogre today. I wanted to."

It doesn't matter. All that matters is that you and yours are safe. All that matters is that you continue to get stronger and stay safe. You have learned so much, so quickly, but there's a long way to go. If you're willing to take that road.

Layla nodded again. "Yes. I want to help people. I don't want Nergal or his people to ever hurt anyone again."

Rosa's image vanished from Layla's mind, replaced with Terhal.

You did well. Better than I'd expected. You are a strange one to me, Layla Cassidy. You are not what I expected.

"The feeling is mutual, Terhal."

The drenik laughed. It was a peculiar sound, almost songlike, but with a tinge of menace about it. Layla did not trust Terhal—she did not trust anything that had spent so long trying to break her—but she got the feeling that Terhal didn't trust her, either. She hoped their truce would last, but she wasn't convinced. All she knew was that her acceptance of Terhal and the other spirits had given her immense power. Power she would put to good use. Power she wouldn't let corrupt her.

She lay down on the car seat and closed her eyes, intending only to rest for a moment, but when she opened them again the car was moving, and the motion caused her to fall back to sleep.

40

When the group returned to the mansion, they found that Masako had fled the area, but not before she'd torn out Shane's heart and eaten a part of it. She had written *goodbye* in his blood, and left. Tommy had been right; she hadn't hurt a single person who worked for him.

Two weeks later, and after no more craziness, Layla found herself in the mansion study going through her university work. She'd put it off as long as she could. She knew it needed to be finished, but she'd found the practical applications of her power a lot more interesting and fun than reading about things in books.

Fifteen days after Elias had died, most of Tommy's staff had moved out of the mansion, leaving only a skeleton crew behind. Tommy had explained that the building was to be used for another purpose and his people wouldn't need to be a part of it. There was a lot of sadness among those who worked for him. They'd lost friends and comrades in their fight against Elias, but all of them appeared to be glad that they'd helped stop him.

Layla needed to talk to Tommy about what would happen next. The thought worried her, but she knew he'd be leaving soon too. She couldn't put it off.

So, after staring at the same page in the book for the better part of a half hour, she went in search of Thomas Carpenter.

She bumped into Jared and Grayson as they moved medical supplies out of the mansion.

"Any idea where Tommy is?" she asked.

"His office," Jared said, putting the box of supplies on the floor. "You planning on sticking around?"

"Maybe," she said with a smile. "Depends if I'm wanted."

"Oh, you're wanted," he said, and then realized what he'd said as Remy walked past.

"Smooth, my good man. Real smooth," Remy said with a chuckle.

"That's not what I meant," Jared said quickly. "Well, it is, but it's . . ." He stopped. "I'm going to shut up now."

"Wisest thing you've ever done," Remy called from outside.

"I'd like you to stay, and I'm sure lots of others would too," Jared managed to say eventually, blushing slightly.

Layla smiled. "Thanks. I'd like to stay. I'd like to help."

Jared nodded several times before stopping again. "Look, I'm not good at this. I'm sort of bad at it."

"Are you trying to ask her out?" Remy asked from the door.

"Well, you're not making it easy," Jared snapped.

"Actually, this is the most fun I've had in a week. Please continue." Remy crossed his arms and leaned against the door frame.

"He's an asshole," Jared said.

"I'm no expert, but is discussing assholes usually considered a first-date flirtation?" Remy said with a massive smile.

Jared quickly turned toward Remy. "That's . . . You're a degenerate. You know that, right?"

"Yep. Good at it too."

"Layla, would you like to go out with me on a date or something?" Remy clapped.

"You're quite cruel, Remy," Diana said as she walked down the stairs.

"Oh, I'm only mocking."

"I'd love to," Layla said. "But without everyone around us."

Jared smiled. "Oh, yeah, that's not going to be a problem because I'm going to kill Remy."

"Eight lives left, baby," Remy said.

"I'm going to kill him eight times, apparently."

Remy walked over to Layla and took her hand in his paw, planting a kiss on it. "It was a pleasure. I hope you stay around. It's nice to have beautiful and pleasant women to talk to."

"You know I'm here, right?" Diana said.

"A beautiful, pleasant woman who won't tear my head clean off."

Diana chuckled. "Nice catch. If you're looking for Tommy, he's in his office. And if you decide to stay, it would be my pleasure to help train you."

"Run," Remy whispered.

"I'm going to find my bow and arrows and hunt you for sport, Remy Roux."

"Fox hunting is illegal in the UK," he said smugly. "It's barbaric."

"I never said I was going to kill you. Just maim. Maybe a little off the tail."

Remy sighed. "And the fun sponge has arrived."

"What did you call me?" Diana asked, as Remy winked at Layla and walked out of the front door.

"Remy is . . . unique," Jared said.

"He is that."

Jared pulled out a piece of paper and wrote his phone number on it, passing it to Layla. "Not sure if you have it, but when you're ready, give me a call."

Layla nodded and watched as Jared picked the box back up and walked out of the mansion.

"He's cute," Kasey said from behind Layla.

Layla turned and was immediately embraced in a tight hug.

"It's been a pleasure. I hope you decide to stay."

"I'm trying to find your dad to say that exact same thing."

"He's about. This place is going to be empty soon, and that's a little weird. I hope you're okay after everything you went through. Our world can be a rough one, and you had a harsher introduction to it than most."

"I'm dealing with it. I still have nightmares, but the spirits are helping with those."

"Good. I wouldn't want to see you hurting. Elias is never coming back. Trust me on that one."

Kasey picked up a rucksack and slung it over one shoulder. "Well, I'd better get this stuff in the car. You go find my dad. I'm sure I'll be seeing more of you."

They hugged again, and Layla walked off toward Tommy's office. She had reached the east wing of the mansion when Harry called her.

"Hey," he said after jogging over. "You going to stay then?"

"Does everyone know this?"

"I just figured. I've already asked and they said yes. Whatever money I need to work, they'll provide it. They've also arranged for me to be able to complete my doctorate, and every student loan to be repaid. I'm literally the happiest person on earth right now. It's a weird feeling to have."

"You did a lot of good work here. They're lucky to have you."

"That's what Tommy said. I want to be here for people, Layla. I want to make sure that what happened to you doesn't happen to anyone else. I want to use my powers for good."

"Like Spider-Man?"

"Just like him. Except for the powers and spandex. Other than that, I'm *just* like Spider-Man. An Asian Spider-Man. I'm excited about the marketing possibilities."

"Obviously. And the forthcoming movie."

"Oh, I'm going for a TV show. I feel that would better suit my character." Harry laughed. "It's good talking to you again without all of that mess we just went through." He waved his arms around to signify what *that* was.

"Yeah, it feels like a lifetime ago when we were at that club."

"And now I'm sort of like a secret agent."

"So, you're James Bond and Spider-Man."

"I can be both."

Layla raised an eyebrow in question.

"I *can* be both. Don't crush my dream, Layla Cassidy."

Layla laughed. "I'm going to go talk to Tommy before my super-hero name gets taken."

"Get in there quick, Magneta."

"No."

"The Steel Warrior."

"No. Please stop."

"Titanium Terror."

"I'm begging you here, Harry."

Harry laughed and walked away, leaving a still smiling Layla to knock on Tommy's door. After receiving no answer, she knocked again, before opening it and finding the room empty.

Layla walked into the office. "Great. This is shit."

"You looking for Tommy?" Chloe said, entering the room. She walked over to Layla and hugged her tight.

"I am."

"He's waiting for you in the living room. He asked me to come fetch you. Remy made a joke about dogs and got punched for it."

"Sounds like him."

They set off together without another word. "This place was just beginning to feel like home," Layla said.

"Yeah, I know what you mean. I've always loved it here."

The pair had spoken several times since Elias had been killed, and their friendship was stronger than it had ever been. Layla had been worried that Kasey and Chloe's long-term friendship might mean that she would be frozen—no pun intended—out, but the exact opposite had happened.

They reached the door, and Chloe stopped Layla from opening it. "Are you sure about joining up?"

Layla nodded. "I can't sit on my hands and do nothing. Not after everything I've been through. And not after everything I've learned I can do. It would be . . . unlike me."

Chloe opened the door and stepped inside, with Layla beside her. Tommy sat on a leather armchair in the living room. Sitting around him were Remy, Diana, Jared, Harry, Kasey, and Kasey's mum, Olivia. She got up and hugged Layla and Chloe, who sat down next to Remy, leaving Layla standing.

A man she'd never met before stood beside Tommy. He was about five foot eight, with short dark hair and broad shoulders. He wore a pair of dark blue jeans and a white t-shirt with a picture of the *Ghostbusters* symbol on it. He rubbed his hand over several days' worth of stubble on his jaw and smiled. Layla thought he had a rugged handsomeness to him, and when he smiled his face lit up, but there was something behind his eyes. Part of it was a darkness that made her nervous, but there was also power. A lot of power.

He offered Layla his hand, which she shook. "I don't think we've met," she said.

"My name is Nate Garrett," he told her. "I'm a sorcerer and used to work with Tommy, back when we worked for Avalon."

"You don't anymore."

"No, I'm more freelance these days."

Remy coughed and spluttered, and Nate sighed, but never once glanced his way.

"I have a proposition for you. I want you to work with Tommy and his people."

"I was going to ask to do just that."

"I know; it's been the worst-kept secret since I arrived here yesterday. But I don't mean in general. You see, Nergal and his people are going to try to overthrow Avalon. They're going to try to expose us all to the world. They want to enslave all humans who are capable of helping them achieve their goals of turning this planet into their empire, and slaughter anyone who isn't. Nergal won't stop with Elias's murder. So, I need to ask you to do something."

"What?"

"A few years ago, I promised I'd train Kasey to be a better fighter. I then started training Chloe, and a few months ago several more joined that group, including Jared. I want you and Harry to join too."

"Why?"

"Because I want all of you, in this room, to be a strike force. You're mostly unknown by Avalon, and that's in our favor at the moment. Also with Diana, Remy, and Tommy helping and guiding, you'll be excellent at it, I'm certain."

"A strike force for what?"

"To stop Nergal. To find out who his allies are and stop them too. To find umbra before they do. To stop innocent people dying."

"And how many are in this group?"

"With Jared, Chloe, Harry, Kasey, and yourself? Another four. You will officially be outside of Avalon control. But unofficially, Elaine has given the go-ahead to do this. You are all exceptional people, and with Tommy's backing, I think you can do a lot of good."

"Do we get a code name?" Harry asked.

"Ask Tommy, I'm sure he has a million ideas by now. Most of them will be geeky and probably infringe on a hundred copyrights."

"The U-men," Tommy offered.

"U-men?" Nate asked.

"U-people?"

"That isn't any better." Nate turned back to Layla. "Now, there's one thing you're not going to like about this. We need you to contact your father. He's someone Nergal wants, and we need to remove him as an issue, and he can help us find umbras. He's under LOA control, but according to Tabitha he's said many times over the years that he'll only talk to you. He can help us find Nergal and his people. Can you do that?"

Layla hesitated and then nodded. "He's dangerous."

"So is everyone in this room," Nate told her. "If you accept this, your training begins tomorrow. I'd advise you to keep my participation quiet."

"Why?"

"People in Avalon want me dead. People outside of Avalon want me dead too. Basically a lot of people would really like me dead."

"Or they hate you," Remy said.

"Or that. Thanks, man."

Remy gave the thumbs-up, ignoring Nate's sarcasm.

"So, you in?"

Layla nodded again. "I need to help stop these people."

"That's the plan," Nate said. "Welcome to the team."

Everyone congratulated her before leaving the room, allowing Nate, Tommy, and Layla to be alone.

"You okay?" Nate asked.

"This is a lot to take in."

That's Hellequin, Rosa said inside Layla's head.

"What's a Hellequin?" Layla said aloud, causing Nate to give her a strange look.

"That's me," he said. "Where did you hear that word?"

"My spirit told me. Her name is Rosa Kendall."

Nate smiled. "It's been a while since I heard that name. I didn't realize you had Rosa in your head. She was a good person."

So was Nate, Rosa said.

"She said you were too."

"Don't use the name Hellequin. It's not exactly going to make you popular. Trust Rosa. I worked with her a few times and she's good at her job. Ruthless, but not without compassion. You are fortunate to have such a good spirit."

"So why aren't you officially involved in this little idea?"

"I have other things I need to do. I need to know that when I'm away people are still helping Elaine fight whoever needs to be fought. And Nergal needs to be fought. He's cruel and vicious, and he won't stop until he has what he wants. You need to prepare for that."

"We'll get her ready," Tommy said.

"I'm around for a few months," Nate said. "I'll help where I can. Fortunately, with the spirits in your head, you'll learn a lot quicker than a human could. I hope you don't mind a lack of sleep and having your body ache, because that'll be the next six months of your life."

"Nergal was responsible for my mum's death. Whatever I need to do to help bring him down, no matter how much it hurts, I'll manage," Layla said with a grin.

"This isn't about revenge," Nate said. "This is about protecting people."

"Will Nergal get what's coming to him?"

Nate nodded. "That's the plan." He walked over and offered his hand again. Layla shook it without hesitation.

When Layla glanced at Tommy and saw the smile on his face, she remembered fighting alongside Kasey and Chloe, Remy and Diana. She remembered their fierce protection of one another. She had never had people be like that around her. It was an odd but pleasant thought.

"Welcome to the club," Nate said. "We're going to kick all kinds of ass."

Somewhere inside of Layla the spirits and drenik smiled. Layla smiled too.

"Can't wait."

ACKNOWLEDGMENTS

I always knew I wanted to write a book set in the Hellequin universe, but completely separate from those books. Unfortunately, while I had a main character and general premise, I wasn't certain exactly how it was all going to come together to form a story.

Over time, and with the help of several people, the original story morphed into the one you've just read, or are about to read if you're one of those people who reads the Acknowledgments first.

Layla, along with her cast of friends and enemies, was a character who I found a lot of fun to write, and if you've read the Hellequin Chronicles books, I'm sure you'll have spotted a few characters who will be familiar to you.

But books don't just write themselves; trust me, I've tried letting them and it gets me nowhere, other than the feeling that I should be working, not playing video games. And there are a lot of people who help me work on the story, characters, or just help to polish the book to a standard that I'm happy to have published.

My wife is always the first person I need to thank. Whether she's being a sounding board for story ideas, or trying to keep our children occupied so I can get some work done, nothing would get done without her help. I love her very much, and even if the dedication isn't to her, every book is because of her.

My three beautiful daughters, who inspire me to lock myself away in my office every single day and hope they don't find me. I write because of them, I write for them, and they are the reason I first sat down years ago and decided to give this whole writing lark a proper shot. Can't thank them enough for that.

My friends and family, who are supportive and impatient in equal measure—supportive about my writing, but impatient to read what I'm writing. I thank you all for your kindness.

To Paul Lucas, my agent, and someone I'm proud to call a friend. To have someone as awesome as him in my corner is more than I could ever have hoped for.

To D.B. Reynolds and Michelle Muto. Two incredible writers and wonderful friends who have helped me become a better writer over the years. There aren't enough ways to say thank you.

To Jenni Gaynor, my editor, and the person who makes me a better author, thank you for all of your hard work and patience.

A big thank you to my publisher and everyone there who works so tirelessly to help put this book together. A special shout-out to Alex Carr, who helped me tweak this book from its original idea, making it much better in the process.

To the Fleet Performance team, yes, you got a dedication, but I just wanted to say it was a pleasure to have worked with you all for so many years before leaving to write full-time. Kev Burman, Mark Dolan, Toby Wilkes, Andy Brown, Ash Newman, Steve Petzer, Ziggy Greenwood, and so many others who came and went over the years, and who all showed support and friendship when I was first starting out, and after becoming published for the first time. You're a great bunch of people, and I wish you all the best.

And in a similar vein, thank you to Mark Duell and Torsten Richter, who couldn't be two more different managers if they tried.

And to everyone reading this, thank you for picking up the book. Whether this is your first time reading my work, or you've read everything I've ever published, I thank you for your time and money, and hope you enjoyed reading something I enjoyed writing.

Layla's story will continue in Book 2
of the Avalon Chronicles, due later in 2018.

In the meantime, Steve McHugh's
Crimes Against Magic—also set in the same
universe as *A Glimmer of Hope*—is available
now from 47North.

ABOUT THE AUTHOR

Photo © 2013 Sally Beard

Steve McHugh is the author of the popular Hellequin Chronicles. He lives in Southampton, on the south coast of England, with his wife and three young daughters. When not writing or spending time with his kids, he enjoys watching movies, reading books and comics, and playing video games.